To my family, related or of the heart

They say we stand on the shoulders of the generations that came before us. Years ago, my uncle Lloyd Rodwin told a story about his trip to Poland in the late 1970s. It wasn't much of a story, but from its dry bones this novel was born. As head of the Department of Urban Studies and Planning at MIT, he had been invited to speak at Warsaw University. Afterward he was offered a car and driver, a protocol of the Communist era when the government exercised control over the whereabouts of foreign visitors. He asked the driver to take him to Łomże, my grandfather's birthplace, which he assumed was some backwater town. When they arrived at a small city with a cathedral, he realized he didn't know of a single landmark by which he might recognize his father's world. Over a lifetime, my grandfather had never described his hometown and my uncle had never asked. At a loss for what to do, he took a quick tour of the cathedral and the city and returned to Warsaw. The story, scarcely an anecdote, suggested to me something so uniquely part of the American experience, the loss of one's family history once the journey to the New World has been made. I wondered, what if a gatekeeper had remained in the Old World to tell the tale. And so began *A Day of Small Beginnings*.

A Day *of* Small Beginnings

A Day *of* Small Beginnings

A Novel

LISA PEARL ROSENBAUM

Little, Brown and Company
New York   Boston   London

Little, Brown and Company
Hachette Book Group USA
1271 Avenue of the Americas, New York, NY 10020
Visit our Web site at www.HachetteBookGroupUSA.com

First Edition: November 2006

The characters and events in this book are fictitious. Any similarity to real persons, living or dead, is coincidental and not intended by the author.

Excerpt from the poem "Separation" by Juliusz Słowacki. English translation copyright © 1995 by Walter Whipple. Used by permission. Quote from Rabbi Bunam from Pzhysha from *Tales of the Hasidim.* Copyright © 1948, 1972 by Martin Buber. Schocken Books, Random House and Company. Excerpt from the poem by Adam Asnyk from *Poles and Jews: A Failed Brotherhood* by Magdalena Opalski and Israel Bartel. Copyright ©1992 by the Trustees of Brandeis University. Reprinted by permission of the University Press of New England, Hanover, NH. *A History of the Jewish People* by Max Margolis and Alexander Marx. Copyright 1927 by The Jewish Publication Society of America.

Library of Congress Cataloging-in-Publication Data

Rosenbaum, Lisa Pearl.
   A day of small beginnings : a novel / Lisa Pearl Rosenbaum. — 1st ed.
      p.   cm.
   ISBN-10: 0-316-01451-6
   ISBN-13: 978-0-316-01451-9
   1. Jewish families — Fiction.   2. Spirits — Fiction.   3. Poland — Fiction.   I. Title.
PS3618.O83163D39 2006
813'.6 — dc22   2006002334

10   9   8   7   6   5   4   3   2   1

Q-MART

Text design by Meryl Sussman Levavi
Printed in the United States of America

PART I

ITZIK

שמע קולנו ונשובה

Hear our voices and we will return to you.

WHEN I WENT TO MY REST IN 1905 I WAS EIGHTY-THREE AND
childless, aggravated that life was done with me and that I was done with
life. I turned my face from the Angel of Death and recited the Psalm of
David: *What do You gain by my blood if I go down to the Pit? Can the dust
praise You?* If God's answer was punishment for my sins or praise for my
good deeds, I cannot say.

Understand, I did not call Itzik Leiber to my grave that spring night
when my return to the living began. The boy had already jumped the wall
of our cemetery, our House of the Living, as we call it. He was down on all
fours, like an animal, looking for a place to hide. What's this? I thought.

Sleep, Freidl, sleep, I told myself. An old woman like you is entitled.
What did I need with trouble? I was a year in the grave. My stone was
newly laid, still unsettled in the earth. I had no visitors. In death, as in life,
people kept their distance. In our town, a childless woman's place was on
the outside.

And yet, from the hundreds of gravestones that could have hidden him
that night, Itzik Leiber chose mine. His knees, his toes dug into the earth
above me. His fingers scraped at the bird with open wings engraved on the
dome of my stone. He panted and he pushed against the indentations of
my inscription like an insistent child at an empty breast. *Freidl Alterman,
Dutiful Wife,* it read there, as if this explained the marriage.

Itzik Leiber's small, skinny body smelled of fear's sweat and the stale-
ness of hunger. But through his fingers his soul called out to me. Plain as a
potato, his soul.

From the outside, he didn't look like much either. A poor boy, maybe a
year past his *Bar Mitzvah*. He had a head the shape of an egg, the wide end
on top. And kinky brown hair, twisted up like a nest. His cap was so frayed
the color couldn't be described. But under the brim, the boy had a pair of
eyes that could have made a younger woman blush — big, sad ovals, and
eyelashes like feathers.

I remembered him, of course. In a town like ours no one was a complete stranger. Itzik the Faithless One, they called him. Faithless? I can tell you Itzik wasn't faithless that night, not when he whispered against my gravestone, his voice thin as a thread, "Help me! Please, God, help me!"

God should answer him, I thought. A child's tears reach the heavens. *Listen to the boy and leave me to my rest,* I prayed. But God had other ideas. Rest would not return to me. Itzik wrapped his arms around my stone, his body curled there like a helpless newborn. How could I ignore him? I wanted to cradle the petrified child, to make him safe.

In life I liked to say, God will provide. But who could imagine He would wait until after I was gone to the dead to provide me with a child? Such a joker is God.

A night wind gathered like a flock of birds around our cemetery wall and swept through the thick confusion of graves. The soft soil began to pound above me with the heavy tread of men. They were so near I could feel their boots making waves in the earth. What had he done, this Itzik of mine, to incite the Poles to come out so late at night?

Raising myself, I saw torches in their hands, murder on their faces. The faint whiff of alcohol floated over our neighbors like a demon. You never know what a Pole will do. One minute he's ready to kill you, the next he's offering to sell you apples, smiling, ingratiating, like nothing's happened. There were as many Poles in our town as there were Jews. But we never counted them among us, and they never counted us among them.

Itzik whimpered. He gripped my stone with a frenzied, furious fear. His eyes rolled toward heaven. *Make them go away,* he prayed. In the moonlight, his breath formed sharp white puffs that disappeared in the shadows of the gravestones.

I prayed too. *God help him,* I said. *Give the boy's poor soul a chance to cook, to become a man.*

What else could I do for him? I knew I was no *dybbuk* that could invade the world of the living. I had made my journey to *Gehenna* already and eaten salt as punishment for my pride. About this, all I can say is that at least for me it was short, not like for the worst sinners, who stay in that place eleven months, God forbid. After my time there, I returned to Zokof's cemetery to sleep with my earthly body and to wait for Judgment Day.

Itzik pulled at my gravestone so hard it fell over at his feet and broke in two. Who could have imagined that a boy's clumsiness would stir me so?

My soul tugged and beat at me. *Gevalt,* how it struggled to tear itself from death's sleep. Such a sensation — frightening and wonderful — the feel of it pushing upward, freeing itself from the bony cavity once softly bound by my breasts.

I asked God, Is this life or am I again in Gehenna? I never heard of such a state as I was in. But fear was not in me. When my soul was finally released from my resting place, I hung like a candle-lit wedding canopy over Itzik's unsuspecting head. In my white linen shroud, my feet bound with ribbons, I felt lovely as a bride and as proud and exhausted as a mother who had just given birth.

A tree near Moishe Sagansky's grave gave a snap. So new was I to being among the living again, I could not be certain who did this, me or God. The Poles stopped to listen; then one of them looked in my direction and began to holler, "A Jew spirit's out!" They took off. Just like that. Such a blessing that the Poles of Zokof were scared of dead Jews. If only they were so scared of live Jews, maybe we'd have had less trouble with them.

My Itzik, terrified boy, lay stiffly on the ground until silence returned. He crawled to Ruchelle Cohen's tall stone, and without so much as a glance at the carved floral candelabras engraved there, he swiped a pebble that had been placed on top by one of her children. With the loving care of a son, he laid it on top of my fallen stone, respecting my memory. Regret at my childlessness passed through me again. When Itzik rose, unsteady as a toddler, I could not help being moved by him. He held out his arms and unrolled his clenched fists. Grass fell from his fingers.

I shook with pain and thanks to God for this boy, delivered late, but maybe not too late. A child, at last. Oh, the joy I felt! My heart! He had gathered grass for me. I swept close around him, ready to receive his prayer for the redemption of my soul. I waited for the words: *May her soul sprout from this place as grass sprouts from the earth.* I waited, pregnant with expectation.

What came instead was a sharp, thin cry, quickly stifled, and the insult of his foot kicking apart the little mound of blades he'd dropped on my grave.

2

Sweep the house, people say, and you find everything.
When the Angel of Death came for me I was a widow already. My husband, Berel, was four years under his stone on the men's side of our cemetery. The attendant from the Burial Society took the feather from my nostrils and said I breathed no more. "God has taken our Freidl, smoothly as a hair removed from milk," he said. My neighbors opened my windows and covered the mirrors so that no ghosts would be captured. They came to ask my pardon for shunning me, a barren woman. They recited the psalm, *He shall cover you with His feathers and you shall find shelter under His wings.* But they did not find the secret I had kept inside my house all those years.

I was not barren. All my life it was plain to me that my womb could have held a score of babies. My breasts could have suckled children and delighted an attentive husband. But from the day we stood under the wedding canopy, my husband, Berel, could not perform his marital duty.

Her conjugal rights a husband shall not diminish, God commands married couples. Sabbath evenings, those first weeks, we went to our bed with pure thoughts, knowing it was a holy thing to make a child. But Berel's seed came too fast, or not at all. In the beginning I thought it was my books that drove away his desire. A woman should not be more learned than her husband, my mother always said. I put my books out of sight and discussed with him only household matters. This changed nothing between us. I watched for signs that he wanted someone else. But my husband did not look at women, plain or beautiful. After not even a year, he stopped with me entirely.

I admit the sin was mine, lying for a husband who had defied God's commandment to be fruitful and multiply. The Talmud teaches that our abstinence was like shedding blood, taking life. I should have brought my case before the elders of our community and pleaded to end the marriage. I could have argued it was *his* share to love his wife at least as much as himself, to honor her more than himself. But if I had brought about the end of the marriage, what a scandal for us both.

Instead, I hid his shame. At first I hid it out of pity, though, God forgive me, in time my pity turned to disgust. Later, I hid it because I realized I didn't mind so much, being childless. I could study in peace, like my father. I prayed to follow in the tradition of Edel, the Baal Shem Tov's daughter, a woman of such valor and intellect that all who met her said the Divine Presence shone on her face. To me, it was an impossible combination that Edel was also a mother, who raised the brilliant Feyge, mother of the Storyteller, Nachman of Bratslav. I thought I was a woman who would only lose herself in mothering and come to resent her children. Not for me, to let my books gather dust in the corner while I slave to feed twelve children, like Ruchelle Cohen, all worn out at fifty.

Twenty years into the marriage, when it was too late to make a change, I realized I had not only disobeyed His commandment to be fruitful and multiply, but also turned my back on my own nature by not becoming a mother. There was part of me that would never grow because of this. What was the purpose of all my study if it did not reach a new life I had tended? Whose mind would I shape, like my father had done for me? Whose hands would take up the penknife and the board, my secret pleasure, and glorify our God with intricate *oissherenishen* — my paper cutouts?

A woman has no right to be so bitter about her husband. She is his helper in life, his footstool in heaven. That is God's will. But for the rest of my life hot, painful anger at my childlessness stirred me up inside. Not a day went by that I did not taste the sin in this and serve it to my husband like a poisoned meal. Eventually, it killed the marriage.

At his funeral, I was a dutiful wife. I hired the mourners to tear their hair and wail for him. But I stood silently at his grave, the anger reawakened by the finality of my loss.

At the moment of my death, regret rose again like a demon, and I refused to be still. When the mourners placed my body in the ground, seven blades of grass beneath it, and proclaimed over me, *Blessed art Thou, the True Judge,* I argued with God for more time to redeem myself. *Let me teach someone what it is to love You. Let me pass just that much on,* I begged Him.

God's answer, I believe, came to me on that cold spring night, one year later. *Itzik.*

Of him, I knew certain things. I knew they said Itzik's mother was a pious woman, a woman who gave money to Rebbe Fliderbaum for the *yeshiva*. This she did even after her husband, Mordechai the Ragman, left her for who knows where. Five young children Sarah Leiber had to feed, poor soul. People said the Leibers would have starved if Itzik hadn't left school and gone to work at Avrum Kollek's mill.

Everyone agreed it was all for the best that Mordechai the Ragman had abandoned his family. The man had dressed like a Hassid, but he'd been no blessing for a husband. What kind of Hassid, what kind of person, boasts in *shul* that he'd stamped his muddy boots on his wife's wedding dress just to show her what's what? Their neighbor Rivka Fromin said Mordechai called the poor woman a crazy cow in front of her children. Such a father must have made Itzik feel like an orphan even before the man left home.

After, when his father was gone and Rebbe Fliderbaum came by to offer the family help, Itzik threw the rabbi out of his mother's house. Called him a thief. "Prayers don't feed my family," he'd said.

So people called him Itzik the Faithless One. Faithless? Anyone could see the boy was just angry at his father. Anger like this is passed down, generation to generation. Mordechai the Ragman had been angry like that at *his* father, Yankl the Porter, maybe even became a Hassid to spite him.

But even from so bad a match as Sarah and Mordechai Leiber, good children are born. I followed Itzik when he left my grave.

3

WHEN THE POLES WERE GONE, ITZIK WENT LIKE A THIEF TO the center of our cemetery, where all the paths connected like spokes in a wheel. Every few steps he stopped and listened.

For myself, what a blessing, what a joy, to float in the air with no effort at all. I settled like a scarf around the inside of his shirt collar — such a filthy thing. I flew over him, around him, wherever I wanted to go. True, my vision was double or triple, and the colors were not right. There were too many shadows, and things didn't look so clear. But at least bad eyesight wasn't going to kill me.

As for Itzik, he had no idea I was swooping like a crazy woman around him. Maybe if he had seen me he would not have looked so grim when he pulled the cap over those eyes of his and headed down the main stone path, past the monuments and mausoleums of the generations. We reached the stones of the Kohanes and the small marker of our oldest resident, Israel, buried in 1568. I stopped, out of habit, to pay my respects.

We passed the burial house at the entrance. Exalted, I flew outside the iron gates. I turned for a last look at our town's House of the Living and got a shock such as I never had in life.

The walls around our sacred grounds had risen into a dome of crisscrossed gray hewn blocks. He, God of My Destiny, Creator of All Boundaries, had locked me out of my resting place, my Eden. The words of the Book of Lamentations, alive in my memory as they had been in my father's study, came to me: *He has blocked my ways with cut stones. He has made my paths a maze.*

Almighty God, I prayed. *What have I done? The boy came to me. Did You want me to refuse him? Show me an opening. Show me how I am to regain my place among the dead. I beg you, do not condemn me to roam the earth forever.* But He gave me no sign, just Itzik.

The boy crept into the shadows of the birch trees that lined the road back to town. Several times he stumbled in the rutted dirt. He made little grunting noises like a frightened pup, and looked over his shoulder constantly. I watched him, not knowing what to do, until I realized God had tied our fate.

I quieted myself as best I could. What did I have to fear? I was already dead. I told myself it was God's will that I listen, that I understand what He expected of me, what He wanted me to do for Itzik. The boy had reached the outskirts of town. I flew to him. Pay attention, Freidl, I told myself. He is in danger.

From the stables, Itzik wound his way in the direction of the main square. He kept away from the open sewer on the one side of that muddy street and stayed close to the houses. Houses? Rats shouldn't have to live in such places. Decayed wooden hovels, halfway to falling down, shutters broken with Jewish poverty and gashed by Yudel the Teacher's hammer. Six days a week Yudel would bang at those shutters until the mothers gave up their reluctant boys for a day of study at his miserable *cheder*.

Passing Chaim the Baker's shop, Itzik ran his fingers along the ledge on the half door where Chaim stacked bread for sale during the day.

A dog barked. Itzik jumped for the shadows of Velvl the Water Carrier's lopsided shed, its roof nearly collapsed. I hoped maybe he'd stop there at Velvl's. Velvl was as pious and wise as he was poor. But Itzik circled back to the main square under the shadows of the walls. He tripped on a stone doorstep and cried out in pain when it split open his right boot. I could see the bare toes. The night air had gotten cold, and he shivered. *Please, God,* he whispered.

Please, God, I prayed also.

A few doors off the main square, he stopped in front of the two-story brick house of his employer, Avrum the Flour Merchant. Now, Avrum Kollek was one of the richest men in town, but he was the kind of man who acted from the heart only when it concerned his immediate family, a man who gave to charity because it is written that he had to, who made a big show when he gave the shul a new prayer book. Not a bad man, understand. But not a man to count on.

Itzik hesitated on the stairs. I could see he had his concerns about Avrum too. But he lifted his head, took a short breath, and stepped up to the doorway. For a long time he knocked softly on the thick wooden door, as if he knew Avrum wouldn't welcome the sight of him. Receiving no answer, he knocked louder.

"Who's there?" Avrum called.

"Itzik Leiber," the boy answered, digging his fingers into the palms of his hands.

Avrum opened the door and stuck out his bushy head. "What's going on?"

"Please, let me in," Itzik whispered.

A goose honked somewhere behind the house. It startled them both. Avrum patted his *yarmulke,* a habit that gave him time to compose himself. "What do you want from me at this hour?" He tugged at the great leather truss with the brass clasps that his wife, Gitl, may she rest in peace, said he always wore. "The ache from the truss lets him ignore the sorrows of others," Gitl always said. "I've got pains of my own," he would tell the beggars.

"It was an accident, Avrum Kollek," Itzik began. "It was the Pole who sells you wheat, Jan with the broken teeth, the one who laughs."

I came close as a breath between them. An accident with Jan Nowak was no small thing. The peasant was a born troublemaker, but no one could cross him. His father, Karol, was famous in our parts. He claimed he'd seen the Virgin Mary over the Tatra Mountains, and his people believed him. Why not? Every town needs a hero. Of course, if I drank as much as Karol Nowak, I'd have seen Moses crossing the Vistula.

Avrum looked like a horse that had been reined in hard. His eyes went a bit wild too, as if he was about to rear. "Come inside." He checked the street over Itzik's shoulder and pulled the boy across the threshold.

Itzik stood in the corner of the salon, his cap in hand. When Avrum lit a kerosene lamp, Itzik barely moved. He sneaked looks from the sides of his eyes at the patterned carpet and the framed photographs on the fleur-de-lis wallpaper that was once Gitl's pride.

"Shuli, come quick!" Avrum called.

Itzik's eyes shot back down to the floor.

Avrum's daughter came out from behind the double doors on the other side of the room. Her blue shawl was wrapped tight around her shoulders, from cold or modesty I couldn't tell. In the year since I'd been gone, she'd become a woman, a beauty with pink cheeks and her mother's thick dark hair.

God forgive me, but I'd wished a pox on Avrum Kollek many times because of this girl. Imagine, he sold vodka to peasants so he could buy her fancy dresses. When people told him to stop, that he was endangering the whole community with such dealings, he threw up his hands. As if it had nothing to do with him when those same peasants got drunk and beat up

Jews. But to see Avrum now with his daughter, I understood him better. The man was still amazed he'd produced such a lovely child. It blinded him to the dangers.

"Close all the curtains and light the lamps, my *shayna maidel,*" Avrum said, with a tenderness I'd never heard in his voice before.

Shuli did as she was told, but not before her eyes stole wistfully over Itzik. She reminded me of how, as a girl, I'd looked at my beloved Aaron Birnbaum. Better she shouldn't look, I thought. Longing for a boy who was out of the question as a marriage match could only bring bitterness between a father and his daughter. My love for Aaron had cost me the faith that my father was my truest ally. He knew Aaron Birnbaum had won me with his tunes and his kind, intelligent face. But he chose Berel, a man who, as he put it, had only a taste for Torah but a butcher's steady income. My father said it was his duty to make me a good match, not a happy one, especially in perilous times. In my father and Avrum Kollek's eyes, Aaron and Itzik might as well have been Poles.

Shuli loosened her shawl, let it slip just enough to show a little more of her nightdress. It was a bold move, in front of her father, but a brave one. Sometimes the heart does what it must. I wondered if Itzik had it in him to grasp what had just been offered. But he was staring at his image in the mirrored doors of the enormous mahogany wardrobe, as if he'd never seen himself before. Something about the way the boy stood, with his shoulders hunched inward, made me think that even if he was here on less serious business, this girl would be wasting her time on him. He didn't know about women yet. Maybe he never would. It was that raw, potato soul of his. Or maybe Yudel the Teacher had done his work on him in cheder, telling the boys if they looked too much at women, they'd hang by their eyebrows in the fires of Gehenna.

Shuli paled at Itzik's inattentiveness, and I felt the familiar nick of heart sadness. She offered him a last look, but receiving no encouragement, she just wilted, poor girl, closed her shawl back around her body, and sank into the upholstered green chair by a small table.

"*Nu?*" Avrum said.

Itzik stared at the floor.

"Well?" Avrum repeated more loudly. He was so impatient with the boy, he didn't see Itzik's anger. But even through the veil of my blurred vision,

I could see that anger was something this boy knew well, an old companion who gave him strength and comfort, whose smell was as familiar as his father, Mordechai the Ragman.

Itzik looked up at Avrum. "I stopped him," he said slowly, defiantly.

"Stopped who?"

"Jan Nowak." He twisted his cap uncomfortably. "It was an accident. The grass was wet. He slipped. The horse pulled the wagon."

"Grass? What are you talking about?" Avrum clapped his hand on Itzik's shoulder. "You're talking like a *meshuggener,* boy. What's happened?"

Itzik winced. "Please, Avrum Kollek! I was on the Gradowski road tonight. I had to get wool for my mother, from Kolya Ostrowski's farm." Itzik looked desperate.

Avrum let go of his shoulder. "And?"

"I saw Jan Nowak and his wife in their wagon."

Now Avrum looked completely confused. "You wake me up in the middle of the night to tell me who you saw on the road?" But I could feel his fear. It pulsed from his temples to the back of his neck and down his back.

Itzik had his eyes on the floor. "They were out there on the road, on their way home from Yudel the Teacher's. Tzvi Baer, Chaim Apt, and another one — I didn't see his face in the dark, but he was maybe three or four years. They had Yudel's kerosene lantern. It was hitting the ground. They couldn't carry it without bending their arms, and they were too tired to hold it up."

This was how it was for the boys in our town. The men insisted on the tradition of sending them to cheder when they were three years old, but what a pitiful thing to see these little ones, barely awake on their baby legs, traipsing home down dark roads at ten at night after a day of sitting on hard benches, reciting Hebrew without understanding, taking blows from Yudel for every mistake they made, suffering his constant spitting. It was a miracle if they learned to love the holy Torah in spite of Yudel.

"You know what Yudel the Teacher does if a boy breaks a lantern," Itzik said. The words ran together, as if he was afraid he'd be cut off.

Avrum sat down heavily in his chair and stared at the boy with growing alarm.

Itzik angrily snapped at imaginary reins in his hands. "It's a beating for sure. But then, Jan Nowak came. He brought his wagon up next to the children. He said, 'Who'd you steal that lantern from, you dogs? Give it here.' The little one whose face I couldn't see, he had the lantern." Itzik looked off, as if remembering. "Then Jan stood up and got him with the tail."

"What tail?"

"The whip." Itzik's head dropped. The room was silent except for a clock ticking on the far wall.

"The little one dropped the lantern," Itzik whispered. "Tzvi tried to get it, but Jan beat him hard. Hard. In the face. All over. Laughing that laugh he has. You know it. Then Jan's wife started screaming, 'Make them hop. Make them dance.' Jan hollered, 'Hop, you devils, hop!' He made those circles on the ground with his whip. When they tried to get out, he lashed them, hard. There was blood pouring from their faces. The horse was jumping around too, from the sound of the whip and the children." Itzik's jaw quivered.

"I ran to the wagon. I tried to grab his arm to stop him from hitting. I yelled to the kids, 'Go home.' Jan said, 'Who's jabbering like a Jew?' He grabbed the lantern, but the fire went out. I couldn't see. Jan was whipping and whipping at me in the dark, but he missed me. I grabbed his wrist to stop him from using the whip. Then his horse bolted, and Jan fell from the wagon. I put my arms up to break his fall, but I couldn't. He fell by the wheels. I tried to pull him out in time, but all I got was a handful of grass."

Silence again. Avrum's eyes were bulging. He was figuring what he had to do now. I felt for him. He knew what was what here. "How bad is Jan?" he said slowly, as if speaking to an idiot.

Itzik paused. "He's dead. The wagon's wheel rolled over his head."

Avrum sat in his chair, dumb with shock; then I could see the terror come to his face. "Does anyone know?"

"His wife. She told them. The Poles already came after me."

"Where did they come after you?"

"At the cemetery. I hid there, behind Berel Alterman's wife's grave."

"Did they see you?"

"No, something scared them away."

Some *thing?* Is he not saying or doesn't he know about me? And the grass. Was this what he was still holding at my grave, grass from Jan Nowak? *Ptuh! Ptuh! Ptuh!* No wonder he kicked it away.

Avrum wasn't interested in what scared the Poles away from my grave. "What do you want now from me?"

Itzik didn't answer. The strain of having to ask for anything was all over his face. "My mother, can you make sure nothing happens to her and the children?" He said it so softly, you could barely hear.

"Wait here," Avrum said, and left the room.

Shuli looked at Itzik as though it wouldn't take much for hope to bloom on her face. But he didn't return her gaze.

"You did a brave thing. It's a *mitzvah,* what you did," she said softly.

He just shook his head.

Avrum returned with his coat and a small money bag. "I'm going for the Russian magistrate. Pray that he'll send a detachment of soldiers to keep the peace. God knows what trouble we'll have now with the Poles for hiding behind Russian skirts." He rubbed his forehead worriedly. "I'll get the *droshky.* Take this money," he said. "Give it to your mother. Tell her it's wages." Itzik grabbed the pouch and bolted out the door.

4

Sarah Leiber's home was more shed than house, one of
the worst of its kind on that narrow alleyway of mud and stench. Itzik
opened the door that hung crooked on its hinges and slipped inside without kissing the *mezuzah* on the doorpost as a Jew should. Itzik the Faithless one, I clucked at him, my heart full of new maternal feeling that was
mine to savor only a moment more. His real mother was waiting up past
midnight for her eldest son, the man of her house.

I slid through a crack in the wall behind the noodle board, into a room
that smelled from the rot of wood, cooked cabbage, dust, and too many children living too close together. The sight of her made my feelings for Itzik
seem foolish, a vanity. What was I playing at? To take more from a woman
whose eyes were already hollowed out like two halves of an empty walnut?

Sarah Leiber sat by her fireplace, knitting socks. Her hands were
twisted and swollen from work, the knitting and sewing, washing clothes
for a few zlotys, buying milk in buckets to sell at market. I used to see her,
going out to the goose herds for the feathers or taking the slaughtered
birds to pluck and sell the fill for pillows. This is what the poor soul did to
feed her children.

The musty, unclean smell of her home was stronger than that of the bar-
ley soup simmering in the pot that hung from an iron bar in Sarah's brick
fireplace. On its back ledge, four children lay sleeping, rolled next to each
other like uneven blintzes on a tray, the two longer bodies curled around
the shorter ones in the middle.

"Where have you been?" Sarah's voice was sharp, cutting. "There's
trouble in the town. Men yelling. All night you expect me to sit up wondering if you're dead in the street?"

Fear had transformed her completely from the woman I remembered. It
quickened her speech and focused her normally bewildered expression.
Under the circumstances, maybe she couldn't afford tenderness. All right,
I thought. I'll be the one now to teach Itzik with sugar, not salt.

She looked at him with an anger I would not have expected from her, this woman who all the town thought was docile as a cow. "In a few hours I have to get the milk. What was I going to do without you here to watch the children until the trouble passes? I don't have enough to worry about, Itzik, without this?" She flung her hand in his direction.

I felt the wild beat of Itzik's heart hammering at his shirt. In the dirt between the rough floorboards he tapped nervous circles with the toe of his split-open boot. "I brought you money, Mama," he said. The voice was soft. He pulled his hand slowly from the folds of his jacket and took a few steps to the room's only table. Without looking at the money bag in his palm, he laid it down and pushed it across the rough boards as if he wanted to be rid of it.

She stayed in her chair. "Who gave this to you?" she hissed at him. "What did you do?"

"It's for you, Mama. Avrum Kollek gave it to me. To help you. It's wages. For later, Mama . . ." His voice trailed off as he looked over to the children. For the first time that night, I saw his eyes sparkle with tears.

"Itzik! What are you telling me?" She jumped from her chair and grabbed his arm desperately. "Is it for the military service? Is he paying so he can keep you at the mill?"

Itzik avoided her eyes. "Jan Nowak whipped the cheder boys again tonight, on the Gradowski road. You remember. He goes after the little ones." He checked her face, as if waiting for her to understand. Sarah stared back at him. She dug her fingers into the hair under her scarf, as if she would scream. But no sound came.

"Mama?"

She didn't move.

"I couldn't leave them there like that. One of them was younger than Hindeleh." He paused and looked up at one of the small bodies on the fireplace shelf. Hearing her name, a red-haired little girl's sleepy face rose momentarily from between the warmth of her brothers' bodies. She puckered her lips as she stretched and lay down again, asleep. Itzik whispered to his mother, "I couldn't. I had to stop him."

"*You* had to stop him? Why you? You, with a sick mother and four starving brothers and sisters. You had to be a *macher* — a big shot?" She spat. "Just like your father! What have you done to us? You have killed us."

A furious look passed between the boy and his mother. It must have frightened them both because they turned quickly away. Itzik's face had gone white. His body sagged, as if tottering under the weight of her abuse. What kind of mother blinds herself to her child's suffering, or lunges at him, blaming him without knowing what's happened?

Sarah rubbed her sides angrily. "What now? Has Jan gone to the police? They'll arrest you, if the hoodlums don't get you first. Is that what you came here to tell me?" Her eyes darted around the room, fast as her speech. "Squire Milaszewski will side with them. He needs to fix things with the peasants. It's him that's stirred them up, raising their rents, taking Schmuel Cohen's side about those hides."

Itzik shook his head. "Jan didn't tell anyone what happened, Mama. He's dead."

Sarah looked at her son in horror. "Because of you?"

Itzik nodded.

She tore at her clothes, then clasped her hands in front of her. "Y-you took a life?" she sputtered.

"Someone had to stop him. We're not dogs," Itzik said.

"We're not murderers."

"It was an accident. Avrum Kollek said so." Itzik's voice wavered.

"You took a life."

"He could have killed them, like he almost killed me. Remember, Mama?"

Sarah turned her head away, refusing to lift the blame from his shoulders. The little ones on the fireplace ledge began to roll out of their sleep. One by one they rubbed their eyes and let out muted cries like kittens pulled from the tit. With their hands propped under their chins they stared with wide eyes at their mother and brother, and called out to them. "Quiet," Sarah warned. "And if anyone ever asks, you didn't see your brother here tonight. You were asleep. Understand?" The frightened children nodded solemnly.

"It was an accident," Itzik said to them all, but he seemed less certain this time. The silence between mother and son became terrible. Itzik's chest had contracted as if she'd punched him.

I could take no more. *It was an accident,* I pleaded with her. *Look at your son!* But she didn't hear me. She was realizing, I could see, that she was going to lose her child. Pitiful, splintering moans rose from her throat. The children looked at her in terror. It went on and on. She was bent double by the time she could make herself stop.

Finally, she tore herself from her misery and said, "You can't stay here and wait for them. What chance has a Jew in such a business?"

The room was so swollen with grief, I couldn't bear to stay still. She couldn't hear me, I knew, so I wrapped my soul around her and hummed one of Aaron Birnbaum's tunes, the sweet one he whistled to me from the street. We called this his "Bird Tune" because it had a little hop. I thought, God willing, the "Bird Tune" would calm her.

Sarah began to rock gently. She loosened her clenched fists. The wild terror subsided from her face, and I relaxed too. She was a woman of faith, after all. That much we had in common. We knew what it was to find solace in devotion to the rituals assigned to us, the *mikva* baths of purification, the lighting of our Sabbath candles, the burning of the piece of dough when baking *challah* bread. We knew that if we breathed holiness into these daily acts we could sense the presence of the Almighty God. Sarah knew God was with her at that moment. So did I.

"What will we do?" she asked Itzik, her voice calmer now.

"I'll go, Mama."

She gave him a nod of resignation. "Take Avrum's money. You'll take the railroad from Radom to Warsaw. Poppa's cousin Mendel the Blacksmith lives near Plac Grzybowski. Ask him to help you get to America. His son, Shima Ganzekovsky, lives there. He goes by the name Simon Ganz. Poppa wrote him a letter." She sighed. "Such a godless place, America, if a Jew doesn't even keep his own name."

Itzik nodded. "But what about you, Mama, and the children? It's not safe for you here either."

"We'll manage." A vein in her neck pulsed like a hummingbird. She turned and for the first time spoke to the boy perched on the fireplace ledge, a ten-year-old, by the looks of him. "Gershom, tomorrow you'll go to Chaim the Baker and tell him you're ready to start as his apprentice."

The boy's face collapsed with disappointment and loss. He sat up and let the single blanket the children shared fall from his shoulders. "What about my studies with Rebbe Fliderbaum, Mama? Don't you still want me to be a scholar?"

When Sarah sighed, I heard the echo of her soul, as if it had been dropped from a great height. "You'll have to take a different path now, Gershom. A baker and his family never go hungry."

Itzik was toeing rapid circles on the floor again. I could feel the shame coursing through him and heat scorching the skin of his potato soul.

"It will be all right," Sarah said to her children, as much as to herself. "God is just. He will not betray us."

"He betrayed me," Itzik whispered hoarsely. "Gershom too."

Sarah spun around. *"Ptuh! Ptuh! Ptuh!"* she spat. "Keep that faithless mouth of yours out of this house, Itzik. You didn't make enough trouble for us tonight? You want to defame the name of God now too?"

"I didn't make the trouble," Itzik muttered, his eyes downcast in submission. "God made trouble. God always makes trouble for us."

"It's your temper that makes trouble for us. Just like your poppa."

Itzik raised his head and looked his mother in the eye. "And then God leaves us," he said evenly. "Just like Poppa."

Sarah raised her arm. Itzik stiffened but did not resist her blow, which knocked him to his knees beside the broken wood bench at the table. "That will teach you to respect God."

Itzik knelt there, head bowed like a Gentile at a roadside shrine. I was afraid what he might become.

"Get up now, Itzik." The anger was gone from Sarah's voice. She lit a naphtha lamp. The smoke-stained globe was patched with paper. Slowly, silently, she began to pack.

There wasn't much to take. A coat, a scarf, an extra shirt and pants, some underclothes, a bit of bread for the journey. Sarah went to the cupboard and took out a bottle of the *kvass* she'd made from beets and sour bread. "Take it," she said, pressing it between the clothes. "Give it to anyone who won't let you pass and there's no other way." What could she know to tell him about the world outside our town? A whole life in one place, that was her story.

Without another word, she swiped Avrum's money off the table and tucked it under the kvass with a little pat. Then she went to the cupboard again and took out a string purse with her mother's gold ring and earrings inside and put that in too.

The children scrambled down from the fireplace. "Chana, give Itzik his soup," Sarah told the twelve-year-old girl. "Dovid, you help."

The little red-haired Hindeleh, maybe four years old, hugged Itzik's leg. "Take this," she said. Such a darling, how she pulled the red ribbon from her hair and offered it to her brother. What else did she have to give him?

A mass of tight red curls now circled her face. Such an angel, how she looked up at him, those light-brown eyes so earnest and wise and adoring, her lips tucked in to hold down the cry that was winding up her throat. "But don't give it to anyone," she said.

"I can't take it, Hindeleh," Itzik told her. "It's your only ribbon."

"Take it," the little one persisted, and draped her offering over her brother's hand. "Where are you going, Itzik?"

"I'm going away."

"When are you coming back?"

A fist banged at the door. The family froze, all eyes on the front of the house. Sarah pushed Itzik to the back window and thrust the sack of clothes at him. He already had one leg outside when they heard the whispered voice of Shuli Kollek calling to be let in. Gershom quickly opened the door.

"They came to my house with torches," she said to Sarah. "Jan Nowak's people. They wanted to know who did it. They knew it was a Jewish boy."

Hindeleh whimpered. Gershom picked her up and rocked her on his hip.

Shuli spoke to Itzik through tears. "I saw how they were. They'll kill you, Itzik. Run. Before they know it's you!" She took a step closer to him. "May God keep you safe and return you here someday." Turning to Sarah, she said, "He saved those children tonight. A blessing on your son Itzik."

Sarah shook her head, perhaps already worrying what was to become of her and her remaining children. Itzik bit his lip and looked painfully beyond her to his brother Gershom.

"Hurry," Shuli cried. "I don't know when my father will get here with the Russian magistrate's detachment."

"They're coming?" Sarah asked hopefully.

"I know they'll come if my father asks. They'll come. We'll be all right here. But, Itzik, you have to go, for now. You'll provoke them."

Itzik nodded, still keeping a formal distance from Shuli.

I should have left them at that moment, gone to Avrum and made sure the detachment was on the way. But I wasn't thinking what could happen. I wanted to see Itzik's farewell to his family, so I chose to believe Shuli knew her father's arrangements with the local Russian authorities.

Sarah avoided Itzik's eyes. "Be careful," she said to her son. "Go where I told you and remember your prayers. Cut your fingernails every week to clean away the evil spirits under the nails."

"Yes, Mama."

The little ones crowded around him, clutching his arms and legs. He didn't resist them, but he didn't say anything to them either. He was too shocked for that, I think. With a last look around the room where he'd been born, Itzik hugged them and pulled away from their midst, waiting for his mother's embrace. It didn't come.

Why she refused him, only Sarah would know. Maybe she couldn't put her anger at Itzik away fast enough; maybe she couldn't face parting with her oldest son. But when Itzik grabbed the sack and jumped through the open window, I knew he would take that unforgiving moment with him for the rest of his life. The bright red of Hindeleh's ribbon in his hand was the last they saw of him.

5

*I*TZIK TOOK THE BACK STREETS, AWAY FROM THE MARKET SQUARE, past the Kestenbergs, the Mandelsteins, the Shlufmans, Goldfarbs, and Flumenbaums, my neighbors who I remembered so well, generations of them in those houses. A few faint kerosene lights from the windows were the last he saw of our town of Zokof, where the Leibers had lived for generations, even before Jan Nowak's people.

For the rest of the night he ran across the rye and wheat fields on that flat plain. When he got far enough from the town, he made his way over to the road. It was easy enough to find it, between the lines of trees. Even in the dark, you could see the silhouettes of the willows and the bent apple branches that always made me sad. Why, I asked my father, should something have to be cut until it looks like a cripple for it to make such sweet-smelling blooms and tasty fruit?

"Freidleh," he said to me, "food is better than beauty."

"Only for the hungry," I said. "Otherwise, is it not as natural for the tree to reach for the heavens as it is for man?"

My father, may his name be for a blessing, made his little grunting sound. But underneath the beard, I knew he was smiling at me.

I floated above Itzik along that road. In the hour before dawn, I watched for trouble from the village walkers. They were on their way to the local farms to trade their grain or leeks or potatoes. When he saw one, Itzik slowed to a walk. He kept his head down. I was sure no one recognized him, bent as they were under the heavy sacks on their shoulders.

A Jew, Nahum the Driver, plodded by, his wagon heavy with hides for Goldfarb's tannery in Zokof. "My horse don't have eyes for humans anymore," Nahum used to say. "Why should he? I don't have money to buy him oats." Nahum didn't raise his eyes for Itzik either, thank God.

At morning light Radom wasn't far off. Itzik fell exhausted onto a patch of dandelions, under a stand of birch trees. *Sh'ma Yisrael. Adonoi eloheinu, Adonoi ehad,* he prayed. He took off his shoes, and careful as can be, he pointed the toes in the direction of the city, so he should know where he was going when he awoke.

What? I thought. *I should sit here and eat cherries?* I had discovered I had strange powers of observation. I could see hundreds of images at once, each stacked on top of the other, but every one clear to my strange new eyes. I saw again the crooked streets and alleys of Zokof. Inside each household, the grandfathers and the grandmothers, the fathers and the mothers, the children and even the great-grandparents were rising from their beds and making their first water of the day in pots and privies. The men laid *tefillin* around their arms and heads and wrapped themselves in prayer shawls. The women woke the children with prayers. I heard their voices drifting from the windows, hundreds of them, old and young, giving thanks for the new day. As the saying goes, one who takes the joy of waking in the morning without giving thanks to God is like a thief.

When I lived, those half-sung prayers were as much a part of me as the skin on my bones. How I missed the voices of our Jews. Even the best death, like mine, is still a lonely thing. Who knew that after, when you can no longer speak, the only sounds your soul can make no one can recognize as you. To the living, you are the stray call of a bird in the trees beyond the town, the lift between two notes, the sharp hiss of sparks from a fire. You are not at all the human who cursed your children one minute, sang their praises the next, and every year, on the Day of Atonement, said *Al Chet* for these sins of cruelty and pride.

Still, I got a shock to hear the first few notes of Aaron Birnbaum's tune. It rose above the din of the Zokofers' prayers like the blowing of the ram's horn on Rosh Hashanah, ushering in the New Year. Even now, a year in my grave, this melody had the power to clutch my heart, to make me remember feelings I thought I'd lost in girlhood.

The truth was, despite my love for Aaron, I'd felt a little ashamed to live in Zokof, where the Hassidim believed in the ecstasy they found in their music as dearly as their Torah study, maybe even more. My family was known, for generations, for its scholarly piety. "The Hassidim have it all turned upside down and inside out," my father lamented. "The music is for the Jew, not the Jew for the music."

But on the morning after Itzik and I left Zokof, I hoped the music of the Hassidim would never end. When Aaron's tune rose like smoke through the chimneys and vanished in the wide Polish sky, I fought the temptation to leave Itzik and fly away with it. It was no triumph to discover Poppa had been wrong, that sometimes a person, his own daughter even, could be for the music and not the other way around.

Itzik awoke with dragonflies winging around his head and a snail creeping into his shoe. He hugged his bundle to his chest like a rag doll and flicked the snail away. As he set out again, he skittered back and forth across the dusty road into the fields to avoid being seen. Every few minutes he looked nervously back at Zokof, as if the town itself would give chase and attack him like a peasant's dog.

When no one appeared to be coming after him, he relaxed. I looked back to Zokof too. Shuli's innocent face floated above it, contorted by a terrible grief. She's lost the boy she loved, I thought. Oh, the pity of a girl in love with Itzik. It was easier for him to hate God than to believe he was entitled to lift his eyes to look at her.

By midmorning, we'd reached the paved streets of Radom. Pots of red and white flowers decorated the high doorsteps of the brick row houses, but I'm sure Itzik didn't notice them. From the way he kept bobbing his head around every corner, checking his direction, I guessed he had never been there before. He hid under the cap he'd pulled over his face and carefully wound his way through the crowded streets, skirting the noisy open stalls in the market square, until he reached the train station.

The stationmaster, a Pole with eyes blue and careless as the sea, looked down with a certain disdainful amusement at the ragged Jewish child digging in his bundle for the fare. Out tumbled the money bag. As Itzik grabbed it up, I could see his confusion at discovering his mother's gift. He hesitated, ground his jaw until the muscles rippled across the sides of his face, and for a moment I thought he might even turn back to Zokof. But slowly, without lifting his head, he muttered to the stationmaster, "A ticket for Warsaw, mister."

The stationmaster turned to the porter squatting on a stool behind him, and said, "What's this, Pawel? Another Yid?"

The porter, all of whose features were squashed against his flat face as if he'd been hit by a skillet, stood up and nodded in Itzik's direction. "They say Warsaw is full of Jewish fleas like that one." The words whistled through the gap in his mouth where his front teeth used to be. "Watch you don't give someone an itch, boy." He lurched over the counter and smacked Itzik's shoulder.

Itzik shrank back. His hand, which had been reaching up to receive the ticket, now hovered in midair, staving off further attack. The gesture provoked the stationmaster and the porter to howls of laughter that shook the walls of the stationhouse.

I watched Itzik's eyes go slack, as if he didn't have anything to say to them because he saw himself as they saw him — inferior, unacceptable. The boy had nothing inside to give him strength. I felt the heat of danger all around. A Jew can't afford to be so starved in his soul. Not when he lives in a country where insults to his character roll off the tongues of strangers every day, cool as idle chatter.

In 1863, when the Poles tried to oust the Russians from our part of the world, my father, may his name be blessed, spoke to some headstrong young Jews who wanted to join the rebellion and show the Poles they were nationalists too. Poppa had tapped his finger on his Talmud and said, "This is where you show what you're made of. Here, in a house of learning. Out there is *narrishkeit,* foolishness. Why should you fight their battles? They don't trust you. 'Christ killers,' 'host poisoners.' This is what they think of you! Just remember this. Poland without Jews is like a barren woman. It produces nothing but sausage." He laughed. But his laughter was as angry as the stationmaster's and the porter's, the sound of two sovereign people resentfully sharing the same sad scrap of land.

The stationmaster flicked Itzik's ticket in front of him. "Get along, boy," he said. "Go to America. Poland is for Poles."

Such a rage and shame came over me, who had promised Itzik's mother that I would protect him. And here I was, as helpless a woman in death as in life, unable to keep this child safe, to nourish him any more than his mother. *Nourish him,* I renewed my vow. As long as Itzik remains with me, I must nourish his soul.

In my fury, I barely noticed that as I flew back and forth across the room, the tickets on the stationmaster's desk began to rustle and flutter. The porter glanced down at them. His laughter slowed like a train coming into the station. I paused, amazed at myself.

In that moment of the stationmaster's uncertainty, Itzik threw the fare on the counter, grabbed the ticket from the man's hand, and ran out of the stationhouse.

Outside, the sun shone on his cold hands. He squeezed the ticket like a good-luck piece and stuffed it in his pack.

I was wild with joy, dancing with it. I'd offered help and he'd taken it. *Itzik,* I called to him. *Now do you hear me? Itzik!* But Itzik heard nothing. He bought a bit of herring from a Jewish woman in the market and asked directions to the shul.

"Have you heard about the trouble in Zokof?" she said.

"What trouble?" He turned his face from her curious gaze.

"Trouble with the Poles. They say there's been lives lost. People made to run away with the shirts on their backs. A pogrom is what I heard. A real pogrom." She was looking side to side, as if she expected Zokof's pogrom to sweep through Radom like a summer hay field fire, as well it might have. It wouldn't have been the first time.

Itzik's body got cold. He shuddered.

Why didn't my soul have the power to show me what had happened last night? *God, give me mastery of what strengths I have left, for the boy's sake,* I prayed. Who had died? Who'd paid the price for all this folly? It was not enough, what God had given me, a snatch of information here, a veiled image there. Not enough.

Itzik took his fish from the woman and hurried from the market square, sweat beads dropping from his brow. He walked faster and faster, until he was running. He didn't stop until, out of breath, he'd reached the brick walls of the shul. Inside, he breathed in the smell of dust and wax and sank into the protective shadows of a large column, well away from the *bimah,* where he might be seen. His whole body was shaking as if with a fever.

Eat a little, I pleaded with him, knowing he'd need all his strength now. Itzik gave no indication that he'd heard me. The fish remained uneaten. I shouted, I flew back and forth in front of him. Nothing. Itzik was deaf to me.

I thought of Zokof. Pogroms were not so much a part of our lives in Congress Poland as they were to the east, in Ukraine and such terrible places as they had in Russia. But we'd had our share of the tremors of fear, the steady beat of whispers behind closed shutters, the quick click of boots assembling. I imagined the terrified Shuli squatting in the cellar, her eyes hot with silent tears, wondering when her father would arrive with the detachment of Russian soldiers to break up the mob. This must have been what I saw in that grieving face, not the loss of Itzik. But where were the Leibers now? I prayed they'd left town, but I couldn't leave Itzik to find them.

An old man, the *shammes* of the shul, shuffled by, doing his job of replacing candles in the wrought-iron lamps. When he murmured a vague greeting to Itzik, the boy hid his face in his bundle and crept out the door. Who could be more wretched, I thought, than a homeless Jewish child who feels like a stranger in the house of his God?

With great sadness, I remembered a question my father, of blessed memory, once asked his students. "Why do children from religious homes sometimes become impious?" When none of them gave him a satisfactory answer, he turned to me with those dark, penetrating eyes that kept most people at a respectful distance. "What proverb is responsive, Freidl?"

"Proverb Twenty-two," I said, from my usual place, beside his shelves of tall books. They had the honor of resting against the driest wall of our house so that they shouldn't touch the dampness we ourselves felt in our beds. To me, these books, our most precious possessions, always looked like a group of *rebbes* leaning comfortably on each other, sharing Talmudic commentaries.

My father's eyes danced with pleasure as he smiled at me. "Recite for us, please."

" 'Instruct a child in the way he should go, and even when he grows old he will not depart from it,' " I'd said, proud of my father's delight in me.

"Exactly right, my Freidleh. If a child has a good upbringing, he will love God. Faith will become a habit with him, and he will not forsake it. But if a parent teaches faith and disrespects God by behaving immorally, the child may become impious. What's more, the child will imitate the parents' acts when he grows up."

He looked at me again. "What a shame she's only a girl," he said, still smiling. "A tea, if you would, Freidleh. I'm a little dry."

At that moment, nothing could have given me more pleasure than the honor of drawing a cup of tea from the samovar for so exalted a rabbi, so righteous and loving a man as my father. And if he was less pleased with me for being a daughter instead of a son, well, this is the way men are, even when they admire a woman's intelligence. What I felt always was his loving guidance. All his life he protected me from the talkers of our town who declared, as if God Himself had revealed it, that I was cursed with a male soul. Years after the marriage, they told each other, "Naturally, she is childless."

I looked at Itzik, sadly making his way back to the train station, and felt crushed for us both. I wanted so much for him to know I was watching over him, that I would teach him in the way he should go.

Seven or eight people stood on the small platform, peering down the tracks for the train to Warsaw. Like a beaten dog, Itzik hung far back from the stationhouse. When the two-o'clock train arrived, he scrambled up the stairs to the almost empty car. I wrapped myself around him and whispered comforting messages about how strong a faith in God would make him, how I would teach him to be the man he should become. But if he heard me, Itzik didn't show it. Through the whole, long trip to Warsaw, over the miles and miles of flat fields, he shook with muffled sobs.

6

At Warsaw Station, Itzik stuck to his train seat as if he hoped the ride would last longer. Who could blame him, poor soul? The boy had arrived alone to a big city with nothing but the name Mendel the Blacksmith, his father's cousin who lived near Plac Grzybowski.

Freidl, I told myself, go find Plac Grzybowski for him. In a few hours it will be dark. The boy needs a roof to sleep under tonight. His eyelids are drooping already. I floated through the roof of the train and left the station through a small window.

Warsaw. Even the name had a magic for me. City of I. L. Peretz, whose books I could only buy in secret from *pakn-tregers,* book peddlers who didn't know or care if Freidl, Rebbe Eliezer's daughter, read *trayf* — non-kosher. If I were a man, they'd have given me trouble. Men are supposed to have eyes only for Torah. But no one expects much from a woman, as long as she acts pious. "It's a shame Freidl's only a girl," Poppa had always said. But to me, a girl who could read stories *and* Torah had all the riches a person needs in life. More than a man.

And now, as I looked around the great city, I realized even Poppa had never been here. I flew like a drunken bird through the teeming streets, into the wide courtyards. Children played tag under lines of laundry that swung like curtains from wall to wall. I smelled the baking breads and cakes, the stink of tar and sewage mixed with lilacs, and the cool breeze coming over the Vistula, bringing a scent of grasses and pine from the forests.

Everywhere I went I heard the voices of the three hundred fifty thousand Jews who lived in that city. Three hundred fifty thousand! From the stone bridge to Praga to the tailor shops on Niska Street, where young men crushed together, hunched over their clattering sewing machines. On Nalewki Street they were selling lace, stockings, fancy goods. At Tłomackie Street, I had to stop, so awed was I by the sight of the Great Synagogue. It was said three thousand could pray there at the same time. Who could even imagine such a thing?

Finding Plac Grzybowski was no trouble. I let myself be carried along the cobbled pavement by the cries of the peddlers. "Hot chickpeas, the best in Poland, right here! Lemons, fresh lemons! Hungarian plums, juicy as they come!" At lantern-lit stalls and on doorsills, merchants with leather pouches slung around their waists made their trades.

The center of Plac Grzybowski was packed with Jews. This one selling furs, that one hats, cloth. Jews selling more Yiddish newspapers than I'd seen in my life. People ran like chickens after feed. Women haggled over shirts and candles, pickles and potato latkes, bread, pickled apples, and cider, each one arguing her price with the fervor of a Talmudic student defending a point of law.

I cannot look at such women without thinking what a mixed blessing was my childlessness. If I'd had more mouths to feed, I also might have had a voice gone hoarse from hollering in the market. The wagging tongues of Zokof said Berel was modern because he earned the living instead of me. They said Berel worked too hard, that I should have helped him more so he could have more time in shul. They supposed I thought myself too good for him.

But if Berel and I had to testify before God, I would have said Berel worked himself into an earlier grave because that was easier than facing the marriage. He wouldn't have argued. His conscience gave him trouble too. Why else did he beg me on his deathbed to transfer half my good deeds to him so he could take credit before God? "Didn't I study Torah for your salvation as well as mine? And if I hadn't left you alone all these years, what good works would you have done?" he said, tormenting me. "You would have been a curse to a husband who made you bear children."

"I made you a home," I said.

"A home for two people who lived alone with each other."

He was right, of course. And now, as I sailed through Warsaw's streets, I prayed that after his death Berel too had found a share of happiness.

At the train station, I looked for Itzik, this boy who had brought me here from the grave, who'd taken me farther in death than I'd ever been in life. This was *naches* like a son gives his mother. Such a pleasure.

He lay crumpled on a bench with his sleeping face resting against the cold wall.

Itzik, I said softly. I circled his ear. *Itzik!* Nothing. Surveying the small body, I cried out, *Master of the Universe, how do I talk to him? Is there a text, a commentary, to guide me? How can I protect Your Itzik, teach him to be a* mensch, *if he can't hear me?*

But God wasn't talking any more than Itzik was listening, so I drifted into the portals of the boy's ear again. *Itzik,* I called, hoping to penetrate his dreams. *Wake up now. Come with me. Wake up.* I might as well have been calling into a hole in the earth. What I would have given at that moment for my elbow, a finger, anything to nudge the boy awake. Instead, from amid all those hundreds of people in the train station, along came Hillel.

I noticed him right away. Who wouldn't, even at my age? He had such a walk, a rolling motion in the hips that sent his shoulders swinging effortlessly. Young manhood's proud elegance, the long dark hair, combed back from his face like a mane, distracted the eye from the worn jacket that tugged at his shoulders and the turned-up toes of his dusty shoes.

Hillel reminded me of Aaron Birnbaum, how he'd have looked in his early twenties. They both had that distinctive, soulful beauty that I had always loved in Jewish men. But something about him disturbed me. His face was clean-shaven as a Pole's.

Freidl, I scolded myself, you're acting like a silly young girl. Go find a proper Jew to show Itzik around, not some young ruffian who thinks looking like a goy is a sign of enlightenment. Oh, I knew plenty about those rascals, the *maskilim,* they called themselves. Enlightened ones, ptuh!

But as luck, or the Almighty, I never knew which, would have it, there were no other Jews around. So I took a closer look at Hillel as he paused to hitch up the lumpy bedroll and guitar slung around his back. The eyes were good. They had depth, warmth, kindness. I decided to give him a try. As the saying goes, better a Jew without a beard than a beard without a Jew. What choice did I have?

He hesitated when he passed Itzik, the way Aaron Birnbaum used to hesitate when he passed my window, humming his tune, his sweet call, with its hop here and there, like a bird's. He would wait for me to sing it back to him. Was that hopping, hoping melody so haunting it could persuade Hillel to stay with Itzik? Or were Aaron and I so captivated by it because it was our forbidden fruit, a prayer sung together by a man and a woman. Who ever heard of such a thing? my father would have said, if he had known.

Now in Warsaw's train station, I sang Aaron's tune into Hillel's ear, hoping it would be enough to make him come to Itzik's aid. My voice sounded so familiar yet so strange to me, disembodied as it was.

Hillel stood perfectly still, then, to my delight and my relief, he looked around for the singer. When he began to sway to the tune's rhythm, I moved from his shoulder to Itzik's, raising my voice around the sleeping boy's face. Hillel looked puzzled, but he followed the sound obediently until he stood before Itzik, casting a shadow that roused the sleeper on the bench.

Itzik bolted upright, hands to his face in panic. "What do you want?"

"You were humming a melody in your sleep. I'd like to learn it." Hillel's deep voice had a seductive graininess to it.

Itzik stared at him, open-mouthed.

"Look, *boychik,* I play music to make a few *groshen.* If you hum that melody again, I'll buy you a meal. You look like you could use one."

"Do you know where is Plac Grzybowski?" Itzik asked tentatively.

"Of course. Everyone knows Plac Grzybowski." Hillel smiled and clapped his hand on Itzik's shoulder like an older brother. "First time in Warsaw?"

Itzik nodded.

"Where are you from?"

Itzik hesitated a moment and, reassured by Hillel's easy manner, said, "Zokof."

"Never heard of it. What brings you to Warsaw?"

"I've come to see my poppa's cousin Mendel the Blacksmith. He lives near Plac Grzybowski."

"Well, if you sing me that melody again, I'll take you to your poppa's cousin, all right?"

Itzik looked confused. Hillel pulled a hunk of bread from his bedroll and handed it to Itzik. Then he picked up the boy's sack and ushered him out of the station.

As the two of them walked the stately streets of Warsaw, I sang snatches of the tune to Hillel, but not so many times that he would remember it and leave Itzik to fend for himself. I sang to him only when Itzik's face wasn't in his sight. That way, it almost seemed as if Itzik was too shy to sing while being watched. Hillel still looked confused, but he succumbed to the melody and began to hum along, his eyes half shut in concentration. That was fine by me because Itzik was so busy gulping in the sight of so many big buildings and wide streets, he couldn't have talked much anyway.

When finally we reached Plac Grzybowski, Hillel made inquiries about

Mendel the Blacksmith. He questioned and wheedled everyone he stopped with all the charm and persistence of a young man used to making his way alone in the world.

"He has a room in that building over there," said a peddler leading a wagon. "Second floor, in the back of the courtyard."

Once again, I gave thanks to the Almighty.

The outdoor passageway to Mendel's courtyard gave off a musty smell, which was mild compared to the stink of cat spray and rotting food in the courtyard. Masses of flies buzzed over a pile of refuse dumped near the outdoor privy in the far corner.

"Mendel's not home," a neighbor woman called from her window roost on the third floor.

Hillel cocked his head to one side amicably as he looked up at her. "Where is he? His cousin here came all the way from Zokof to see him."

"He'll be back. He'll be back," she clucked, resettling her ample buttocks on the window frame.

"Then he'll just wait here on the doorstep." Hillel smiled up at her. The woman smiled back, displaying a gold crown on her front tooth.

"I guess I'll be going," he said to Itzik. "Thanks for the melody. It has a special something, I think. Like a hopping bird. I'll call it the 'Foygl Niggun' — the 'Bird Tune.'"

Itzik looked at him blankly.

"You're a funny one," Hillel said, jostling the boy playfully. "Here, let's see if I can play it on my guitar." He swung the instrument around to the front of his body and began to strum it gently. The bridge was warped, the strings unraveled, but Hillel knew how to coax and caress music out of that guitar's scratched, gouged body. No doubt he could do the same with a woman.

What a joy to hear my Aaron's tune returned to me. When Hillel had mastered it, he began to work on variations that filled me like a cup. I had brought something back to life! And that living thing was keeping Hillel at Itzik's side, even if it hadn't kept Aaron at mine.

He'd left for America just before I married Berel. "I have to go," he'd said. "My parents are crazy from worry they can't pay my way out of the army. My mother goes around saying she doesn't know what's worse, that they starve the Jewish boys or that they feed them trayf." He'd straightened the books he was carrying. I could tell he was getting up courage.

"Besides," he said, eyes downcast with shyness, "I couldn't stay here with you being Berel's wife."

I'd nodded, unable to speak, but for the rest of my life I sang his tune at my window and pretended I still heard him humming it back to me. On my deathbed, people thought I cried out for my husband, but it was Aaron and his tune that I was remembering. My regret followed me even then. That there'd been no child to teach that melody to gave my heart its last anguish.

Itzik sat down on Mendel's doorsill and hugged his knees to his chest. He stared intently at Aaron's guitar as if it were the only thing he could rely on for comfort. Every once in a while, he lifted those great big eyes of his and stole a glance at Hillel, who returned the look with an encouraging nod.

It was nearly nightfall when Mendel finally returned home, bent over and out of breath from poor lungs and overweight. His hands I remember most, black with dirt, fingers broken as tree branches and just as gnarled.

"What's this?" He frowned at Hillel and Itzik, who'd stood up as he'd approached.

"I'm Itzik Leiber, Mordechai the Ragman's son, from Zokof," Itzik said, his words muddled together. Mendel turned to Hillel and raised his bushy brows.

"He's my friend," Itzik blurted.

"You're a Zokofer?" Mendel asked Hillel.

"No, I'm from Łódź."

Mendel nodded. "So," he said, turning to Itzik. "What brings you to Warsaw? Your father knows you're here?"

"No," Itzik answered, lowering his eyes.

Mendel looked hard from one young man to the other. "Do you think I don't know what's what here, boy? Your father gave you a good thrashing and you took off, right?" He eyed Hillel's clean-shaven face suspiciously. "From the look of things, he caught you reading trayf books, right?"

Incredulous, Itzik denied it.

"*Ach.*" Mendel spat disgustedly. "You're all the same. A worthless generation. I've seen your kind before. You boys from the provinces, with your heads puffed up with socialist nonsense, come here to make trouble." He swatted impatiently in Itzik's direction. "What do you think, I'm going to put a roof over your head and feed you while you laze around? Go to America if you want to live in a godless place."

"See here," Hillel interjected. "We only met at the train station. I was just helping him find you." Since Hillel knew nothing about Itzik or why he'd come to Warsaw, he turned to him for support. But Itzik remained speechless, which Mendel seemed to take as proof of his assessment of the situation.

"Your father is a pious man," Mendel said evenly. "I won't play any part in your game, boy. Go back home. Ask his forgiveness and study Torah like a Jew."

With that he pushed past the two boys, opened his door, and went inside. The sharp smell of pickled cabbage escaped briefly from within. I thought to try to go after him, make him reconsider, but something about the man put me off. A man who doesn't listen, who jumps to conclusions, can be a danger. I didn't trust him to take care of Itzik. After all, this was the cousin of a man who'd abandoned his family. I didn't see a wife or children. The situation didn't look good. Not safe. Itzik was better off with Hillel.

Itzik stood motionless, his ears burning dark crimson for all the world to see. Hillel fidgeted with a string on his guitar and began to gather his things again. In an instant, I was at his ear, humming. He had to take Itzik with him. I had to make sure of that.

Hillel's head jerked up at the sound of my voice. He looked quizzically at Itzik, who was too lost in his shame to notice. "Come, Itzik," Hillel said softly, putting his hand around the boy's shoulder. "What do you need with him, anyway? You can stay with me, if you want. We can go to my friend Piotr's house."

Itzik ran his fingertips across Mendel's closed door but stopped when he reached the bronze *mezuzah* on the doorpost. He considered it for a moment, then with a quick hoist of his bundle, turned away. "Are you really a socialist, like Mendel said?" he asked.

"Of course," Hillel answered, as if this was the most natural thing in the world.

"What's a socialist?" Itzik's little face was more animated than I'd seen it. This boy whom I could not reach, whose soul had bolted itself into a prison of anger and resentment, was coming alive before my eyes. And why? Because of a man I'd brought to him, Hillel the Socialist. *Dear God,* I called to the heavens, *do not let this child of mine go.*

Hillel smiled and ran his fingers through his hair. "A socialist is a person who believes that everyone has equal worth and a right to an equal chance in life, no matter if their father was a prince or a peddler."

"Do they have rabbis?"

"No. We believe in mankind, not in God, not in any religion at all."

Itzik's eyes opened so wide you'd think he'd just seen the Messiah.

"Do socialists ask for money from poor people?"

"We share what we have to fight against capitalists who exploit poor people."

That was it for Itzik. With a grin so wide it changed the whole contour of his face, he said, "I'm a socialist too."

"I'm sure you are," said Hillel, laughing, and clapped Itzik on the back. "I'm sure you are."

I'm sure you are a fool, Hillel, I said, *if you socialists think you can drop four thousand years of wisdom into a slop bucket and say that God and Torah are a figment of our imagination.* With dread growing in my soul, I watched helplessly as Itzik and Hillel left Mendel's courtyard and sauntered past the skeletal remains of the day's market in Plac Grzybowski. Near Twarda Street, Itzik ventured a tentative pat on Hillel's shoulder.

"Look over there," Hillel said, pointing to a grand white building. "That's the new shul built by the Nożyk family so they could put their name on something. Do you really think this city needs another shul? Think of what they could have done with that money. Given it to striking workers or hungry mothers."

Itzik looked up happily at his new rebbe. "In Zokof, I used to say the rabbis were all thieves. You should see how they came after my mother when my father left. I had to throw them out of the house."

"So your father didn't throw you out, like Mendel said?"

Itzik shook his head.

"Ha! Mendel was talking to the wrong man. My father's last words to me were, 'Never enter this door again, you Bolshevik!' He didn't care that my mother was screaming for me. I was her favorite, got all the meat she could save up special, and he knew it, the old bastard. Where did he go, your father?"

"He just left. The day before *Shavuos,* two years ago. Said he'd got us through the winter and that's all we were going to get from him."

"What about your mother?"

"She cried. Same as always. And my brother Gershom went running to the shul. Same as always."

"What did you do?"

"I went to work at the mill."

"How was the pay?"

"Terrible."

"The hours?"

"From eight in the morning to ten at night, six days a week."

"You know what that is? That's slavery."

Itzik's face brightened at being understood. "I had no choice," he explained eagerly. "There was no one else to feed the family."

"That's why it's slavery. I'll tell you what's wrong with the rabbis. Instead of fighting slavery, fighting for the rights of the workers, for people like you who have no choice, they tell us to pray. They're all cowards. Nożyk's shul over there is just a shell where weak men run to hide like snails."

Itzik's eyes were shining unnaturally bright. His head bobbed up and down as if he'd just received the revelation from Mount Sinai. His voice grew stronger as he struggled to tell Hillel who he was. Even though I sensed he was shocked at his own candor, he was desperate to nestle under Hillel's warm wings.

I was sick to my core. What had I done? My Itzik was being pulled in by a man who had no respect for a house of God. A man whose philosophy could land him in prison, and Itzik along with him.

They passed Nożyk's shul, contempt written across both their faces. This confidence that Judaism could be taken for granted, insulted even, made me afraid.

A growing wave of anxiety for Itzik overtook me. He was like the Wicked Son they tell of at the Passover Seder. The one who knows the Four Questions he's supposed to ask, about why this night is different from all other nights, but who doesn't want to hear the answers because he wants to keep his distance from Jewishness. My father used to say that the child of the Wicked Son is the Simple Son. He barely understands what's happening at the Seder because his father didn't teach him the tradition and his grandfather, the Wise Son, is gone. By the fourth generation, all that's left is the Son Who Doesn't Even Know There Is a Question. That will be Itzik's grandchild. If Hillel doesn't get him shot first.

7

*I*T WAS A SLOW BUSINESS TO REACH HILLEL'S FRIEND PIOTR'S apartment. The winter had not let go its hold on Warsaw, and the pavements were muddy and gray with slush. There was ice still in some places, and Itzik took a tumble when he slid in front of a porter carrying a load of fabric. The city was filled with such men, carrying their goods on their backs, in their arms, pushing and pulling with carts, but mostly just with their bodies, like beasts. God may live closest among the humble, as my poppa used to say, but better one should suffer from a little pride and have a better life.

I took my chance then, to look around the city. I guessed we were near the Saxon Garden, because I saw with my own eyes, even such as they were, the Zamoyski Palace, the Blue Palace, places I'd read about in a Jewish book of stories from Warsaw. Such a pity that I could not go inside and see those paintings and books and sculptured things I'd read about. This was something I had a hard time imagining, because we never had such things at home. But I was afraid to lose Itzik.

Hillel's Piotr lived in an old tenement near the Saxon Garden. Itzik hung back on the staircase, making like he'd take off if something wasn't right. Hillel went up ahead to the third floor and knocked at the door. It wobbled on its hinges when the man on the other side opened it.

He was a big fellow, with hair that shot out in all directions like a field of mowed hay, and one of those Polish faces, where the nose starts low and shallow and ends in two upturned nostrils, dark as tunnels. This face was worn for someone still in his twenties. "Come in, my brother!" he said to Hillel, and pulled him into the room, where the walls were dirty and cracked. "There's vodka on the table and not enough drunken men in here to fill a privy."

Hillel laughed. "Piotr, this is my friend Itzik. He came in on the train today from the east. Go slow. His Polish isn't as good as mine." Hillel pulled Itzik inside. The boy was nervous as a street cat. "I'll join you in a drink, but he could use a crust of bread, if you have any."

Piotr grabbed Itzik's hand and shook it enthusiastically. "*Pan* Itzik," he said, bowing to him like an aristocrat. "A pleasure to make your acquaintance. Any friend of Hillel's is a friend of mine."

Itzik stared at his own hand, buried in Piotr's grip.

I understood how he felt. I never could make up from down at Polish manners, the hand-kissing, the bowing, the fawning way they call you *Pan* or *Pani,* Mister or Missus, if you please. Of course, only a fool believes any of it. Next thing you know, they give you that sideward glance that says what they really think, that you're one of the "cursed race."

"To the People," Hillel said, dropping his bedroll to the floor and grabbing the open bottle of vodka by the neck. He took a gulp and wiped his mouth with his sleeve. "To the People of the Republic of Poland!"

"To the Republic of Poland," Piotr echoed, accepting the bottle from Hillel. He motioned in Itzik's direction. "Will he eat our bread?"

"He's a socialist," Hillel answered. He winked at Itzik. "He'll eat whatever you eat. Right, Itzik?"

Itzik nodded agreeably.

"Good," said Piotr. "There's kielbasa and bread on the shelf. Help yourselves. I'll light the lamp."

What could I do? With my blurred double vision, I circled the unkosher meat and bread. I tried to knock them away from Itzik's hands. But he grabbed them both and shoved them into his mouth. He was hungry, yes. But hungrier still for Hillel's approval.

It was evening already. Within the hour, the tiny apartment filled with people. A *lumpen* collection of stragglers, if I ever saw one. There was only one chair and a table in that place, so they sat on the floor or leaned against the white-tiled stove. They laughed. They joked. They got louder after they'd finished Piotr's bottle of vodka and started passing around their own flasks. For this they called themselves socialists?

Itzik hid his extra bit of bread, but he pulled out his mother's bottle of kvass and passed it around, to the approval of all. *"Na zdrowie,"* to the health, he toasted. But his hands shook, and it seemed clear to everyone that Polish did not roll easily off his tongue.

"Sing to us, Hillel," Piotr said. "Yes," the group called out. "Sing! Sing!"

I prayed to the Almighty that Hillel not defile Aaron's tune by singing it. I was so grateful when he sang a Polish ballad about a girl in love with a dying soldier, I almost missed someone whispering to Piotr, "As if this *Yid* knows anything about being a soldier."

Piotr cut the man off with a scowl. "Hillel's one of us," he said confidentially. "Don't you forget the Jews fought at our fathers' sides against the Russians in the '63 uprising."

The chastened socialist leaned back against the wall and waved his flask as he recited Adam Asnyk's verse: "*'The heroic Maccabees, If circumstances demanded it, Would fearlessly give up their souls, For their god — capital.'*"

The room grew still. Hillel was not so carefree in the way he moved anymore. Itzik curled against the wall, looking from one face to the next, desperate to know what had just been said.

Poppa had been right, I thought. The intoxicating days of '63, when Pole and Jew had their one moment of brotherhood, were just an accident of history. Nowadays, when you heard a Jew referred to as a "Pole of the Mosaic persuasion," it was with a smirk, not a smile. Better a Jew should stick to his own kind and study.

Piotr spoke up. "You can't blame the Jews for raising money to fight for the cause. When circumstances demand it, don't we do the same? And call ourselves heroes for it?" He clapped Itzik on the leg and offered him a small flask of vodka. "Have some, little brother," he said grandly.

Hillel winked at Piotr.

I watched helplessly as Itzik poured the swill down his throat like water. When he coughed half of it back up, everyone laughed, including Itzik. Good humor was restored. "To the People," he cried triumphantly, and drank some more. Hillel strummed his guitar and nodded approvingly.

But in the middle of Hillel's next song, Itzik did what any boy who'd swallowed a quarter of a bottle of vodka would do. He vomited it all over himself and the floor, with the trayf meat he'd eaten. I can't say I was sorry.

"Forgive him, Piotr," Hillel said as he leaped from his seat and slung his guitar over his back.

"It's all right. A wash and some air is what he needs," Piotr said.

Hillel agreed. "Until later, Piotr." And with a short farewell salute to the group, Hillel grabbed his and Itzik's things, hoisted Itzik by the armpits into the hall, and carried him down to the street, where he lowered him onto a wooden crate that had been shoved up next to the building.

"Why did you drink so much vodka, Itzik? You're too young for it."

Itzik pushed away Hillel's supporting arm. "I'm not too young. *You* were drinking."

"Not so much. I drink so they think of me as one of them."

"What for?"

"Because I have to." Hillel squatted in front of the boy and looked him in the face. "Itzik, the truth is, Poland is still *their* country. Socialism is our only chance for equality."

Itzik picked up a dirty cloth from the street and wiped the vomit from his trousers. "My poppa used to say, 'A Pole is a Pole. You can't do nothing with them.'"

"Well, your poppa was wrong," Hillel told him. "When they see how much they have to gain under socialism, they will change. I promise you."

I thought, what a marvelous thing is a young man's sight. Everything is so clear to him that he cannot even imagine a world clouded and blurred, doubled or darkened by doubt. I pressed myself as best I could against Hillel's clean-shaven cheek and could only wish him well, this darling young man, who had such faith.

He stood up.

I could see he was making himself ready for a speech.

"The Poles will learn that they can't just talk about their honor or their freedom. They'll have to make something of themselves first. They'll have to understand that this is how you become free. And when that day comes, Itzik, we will be able to call ourselves Poles too. There will be true justice. They'll stop treating us like foreigners, even though we've been here for a thousand years."

"You think so?" Itzik asked hopefully. But before Hillel could answer, Itzik's face darkened. "What's so great about calling ourselves Poles?"

It was a fair question, but it clearly stopped Hillel cold, the way children's questions often do.

"What's so great about living like a Jew, like your father and that Mendel the Blacksmith back there?" He waved dismissively in the direction of Plac Gryzbowski. "That's the world you want for the future? You want to continue that golden chain of generations?" He rolled his eyes. "That's nothing but *shtetl* Jews living in filth with their ridiculous notions of superiority. No wonder the Jew is a figure of fun! What else do you call someone who thinks memorizing every page of the Talmud is what man was put on earth to do? That's about as useful as learning to repeat every argument ever made on whether an egg laid on the Sabbath can be eaten. Is that what you believe in? Then go home to them. Go ahead!" He pulled the boy from the crate and gave him a push. "Go back to your momma."

Itzik was close to tears. "I can't."

I could feel his body heat up as it did when he clung to my gravestone. His stomach muscles tightened. His breaths shortened with panic, and the focus of his great round eyes became distant, as if he barely could see the Warsaw street at all. He staggered a bit, then braced himself against the wall. A moment later he sank to the ground and put his arms protectively over his head, as if to block out the blows of the world.

Hillel, I could see, was not prepared for a reaction like this. "Look, boychik," he said gently. He kneeled at Itzik's side. "All those people back east in that muddy town you come from, I know them. I grew up with people like that too. I had a father like yours once."

"What do you know about my father?" Itzik said thickly.

Hillel seemed to consider this. "Itzik, listen to me," he said. "Ever since I came to Warsaw, I've been getting myself an education from a man named Pesha Goldman. Pesha Goldman came also from one of our towns in the east. He has made a great change in his life. Before, he spent his days wrapped up in mysticism. But then soldiers raped his wife, Devora, in front of him. He put away the Kabbalah and took her and their son to Warsaw. He says a Jew doesn't have the luxury to live in the clouds."

I felt a pain, like the cut of an ax, in my heart.

Hillel sank down the wall next to Itzik, who was rigid after what Hillel had just said. "Pesha joined the movement. He became an activist. He got caught organizing striking workers. They put him in prison, but he said they couldn't do anything to him that would change his mind about fighting for a better life here and now. He and his wife take in boarders like me, and he teaches us social history. He's a photographer by trade." Hillel smiled. "He likes to collect pictures too, especially of Indians in America."

Itzik looked at him like a bird in a nest, opening its mouth to be fed. "Why?"

"Pesha says the Jews are like the Indians. We hold to this idea of the greatness of our 'tribe.' They dress themselves in feathers and paint. We dress in caftans and fur. But it's all an illusion, he says, just like the studio photographs with the painted backgrounds. We've both been conquered. The Indians they sent to live on reservations, the Jews to the Pale of Settlement in Russia, to live like rats and starve. Pesha says the only picture that tells the true story is the one a friend of his in America sent him. It's hanging in a frame in his house — a freezing Indian boy huddled between two mongrel dogs, trying to keep warm in the bitter winter on the plain. Pesha says that's what comes from allowing ourselves to be led by superstitious, fanatical chiefs and rabbis. That's what happens to people who insist on being tribal in the twentieth century."

"What choice is there? We're different from other people."

"No we're not, Itzik. If we become kindred to our fellow Poles, stop calling ourselves the chosen people, and insulting them with our kosher eating, they'll stop hating us for being different. We'll be able to live like men in this country. That's how Piotr and I are brothers."

Itzik nodded slowly. Then he began to smile. The color returned a little to his cheeks. "If socialism will get rid of the thieving rabbis, then I'm for it."

"Well," said Hillel, giving Itzik a playful tap on the head, "then you'd better learn how to drink!"

Thwap! I broke one of the strings on Hillel's guitar and kept him turning around in confusion, looking for the cause. What was he teaching my Itzik? *To be kindred to our fellow Poles?* Was he stupid or just willfully blind? When the Poles let us own land and live where and how we want, maybe we'll be kindred as two dignified peoples can be. Blame the rabbis and our traditions for the rules the Poles made for us? What kind of crazy thinking was this? The best thing a Jew can aspire to, after five thousand years of survival, is to learn to drink like a Pole? For shame!

A fog had rolled in, carrying with it the smell of horse manure and sewage, tar and smoke. I hovered over Hillel and Itzik as the two made their way to Bonipart Street through a maze of tiny workshops that gave off their own smells of leather, yeast, sour cabbage, and decayed herring.

We arrived at Pesha Goldman's damp basement apartment. *"Sholem-aleichem,"* Pesha's wife, Devora, welcomed us. *"Aleichem-sholem,"* Hillel answered. She put her hand on Itzik's shoulder and ushered my exhausted boy in, even though Hillel had barely explained his presence. "You look very tired," Devora said to Itzik. "Lie down on that pallet. I'll bring you a cup of tea." Her hair was not covered by a marriage cap, as would have been proper. But even so, I liked her and the care she took to make Itzik, a stranger, comfortable.

Itzik mumbled his thanks and went immediately to the place Devora had indicated for him to lie down. He pulled out the red ribbon his sister Hindeleh had given him and began to play with it, comforting himself by wrapping and rewrapping it first around his fingers, then his wrists and forearms.

Almighty God, I called out. *I think maybe You should take a look at what Itzik the Socialist, the one all of Zokof used to call Itzik the Faithless One, has done with his little sister Hindeleh's ribbon. You see? He can't let go of You. Look how he wraps it, around his hand like a pious Jew laying tefillin.*

The door opened, and Pesha came in, stout but sturdy, squinting slightly through his glasses. "Ah, Hillel. Are Schimmel and Gordon with you?" he asked, removing his coat and galoshes.

"No," his wife answered. "They went to the printer for the leaflets."

"Well, good. Good. They'll be ready for distribution tomorrow then." Pesha rubbed his hands together and nodded agreeably at his wife. Then, noticing Itzik on the floor, he said, "A new student?"

Hillel smiled. "Yes, he's just got off the train from Radom this afternoon, and he's already become a socialist."

Itzik sat up.

"Very impressive," Pesha said warmly. Then, studying Itzik more closely, he said to him, "You have a good face. I wonder if you'd mind posing for me tomorrow."

Itzik stared up at Pesha, so drunk with fatigue he could not speak. Who could blame him, poor soul? In one day, he'd been accused of killing a man, been forced to leave his home and family in terror, and traveled to a strange city, where he'd been tossed from here to there like a dust rag.

Pesha nodded understandingly. "We can talk about this tomorrow. Rest, child."

That night, long after Itzik had fallen into his deep sleep and Pesha's students had reassembled under their teacher's roof, I listened as they ate pumpkin seeds from a paper bag and recounted stories of Jews whose beards had been ripped out from the skin, of women raped and babies skewered on bayonets. What bothered me most was my certainty that they did not share these stories with their Polish "brothers."

I watched over Itzik, so small for his age, so alone. I wondered, could it be that our feeling for faith comes more from loyalty to those who make us feel we belong than from an idea about, or even a need for, God? I knew what my beloved father would say. He would point to Itzik's bound forearm, crisscrossed with Hindeleh's ribbon, ready for prayer.

8

A FEW DAYS AFTER HE'D SETTLED IN AT PESHA GOLDMAN'S, Itzik went back to Plac Grzybowski to find work. Hillel went too. They were listening to a half-smiling organ grinder when all of a sudden Mendel the Blacksmith lunged out of nowhere, grabbed Itzik by the scruff of the neck, and dragged him, with Hillel at his heels, into the darkness of a courtyard entryway.

"What are you crazy, walking around here in broad daylight?" Mendel said, pushing Itzik against the wall. "You want we should all be arrested?"

Itzik, his breath knocked out of him, turned the color of paste. "What's the matter?" he whispered.

"What's the matter? *Gottenu!* You killed a man! The word is everywhere. You think you can just *disappear* in Warsaw?" His eyes narrowed. "Killed a man, you hear me? And not just any *farchadat* peasant, no. You had to pick one whose father saw the Virgin Mary over the Tatra Mountains. Now they got a bishop after you." He cuffed Itzik's left ear with one hand and grabbed him at the chest with the other. But it was fear, not anger, I saw in his eyes.

"You came to my house and let me think you were just another runaway kid I should return to his father. Made such a *tumult,* the whole building was talking about you and your friend there. If it gets out you're the one they're looking for, they'll come and take me in for questioning. And when they find *you,* they're gonna hang you from the nearest tree, believe me."

He shook a jagged finger in Itzik's face, but to me it looked like the hand of the Almighty Himself, scolding me for being so careless with Itzik's safety. What was I thinking, letting him parade around in the open, maybe attracting dangerous attention? I was making speeches to God against the socialists, but they were the only ones protecting him. Them and this louse Mendel.

May you live to be a hundred twenty — without teeth, I cursed myself. Ten thousand times I must have said this in my life, but now that I was without a body to call my own, the effect wasn't so satisfying. *Ach!* Say it plain, you foolish old *yideneh*. If you didn't have children, it's because God knew better than to give them to you. You didn't protect this precious boy, not even from Mendel's hand. You've broken your promise to his mother that you *would* protect him.

Itzik's head hung to one side. He rubbed his bruised ear. "It was an accident with the peasant, Mendel. I swear on my mother's name!"

I felt a blow from inside, and then my sight was gone. I don't know for how long I was like this, but after some time, the pain disappeared and my sight returned, such as it was. Only, I couldn't tell if what I saw was real. I saw Sarah, Itzik's mother, wearing all her clothes on top of each other, carrying her red-haired little girl, Hindeleh, down an empty road, who knows where. I called to her, *I won't leave him!* She didn't hear. God forgive me, but I was grateful when she went away and I didn't have to look at the pity of it. This much I knew: Sarah and her other children were outside my power to save, and they were gone from Zokof. But I promised Sarah again — what I could do for Itzik, I would.

Warsaw returned to my sight, and I humbled myself in gratitude to the Compassionate One.

"An accident? You killed a man!" Mendel scoffed at Itzik. "*Ptuh!* You think you got a city of refuge here? The *goyim* don't care if you did it or if one of theirs did. Don't you know yet they make it all up anyway? *Schlemiel!*" He smacked Itzik on the side of his head. "They make *us* up!"

I slammed a door inside the courtyard to get Mendel to his point.

He checked the courtyard then grabbed the outer door handle, ready to escape if he had to. "There are reports about a pogrom in Zokof. It's all over the Jewish press. Everyone's talking, so now the authorities have to make a show of an investigation. One thing's for sure, you're not going back to Zokof. Understand?"

Itzik's eyes snapped open. "What happened to my family?"

"Do I know? The story is the Russian magistrate over there wouldn't send a detachment of soldiers to stop it. Wouldn't take a bribe. Probably wasn't big enough. Now some landowner named Milaszewski is saying his peasants had to defend themselves from the Jewish devils who started up with them. People are dead, you little shit! All because you had to start up with the only famous peasant in town. What a business!" Mendel waved his free hand above his head.

"Why wouldn't the Russian magistrate send the detachment?" Itzik said helplessly. "Avrum Kollek said they'd come. He had enough for a bribe."

Hillel had been leaning against the wall, graceful but on guard. "It's like I've been telling you, Itzik," he said, pouncing on the chance to make a socialist's point. "The landowners and the Russians don't mind letting things get stirred up now and then. It gives the peasants a little distraction, so they don't get ideas. A few Jews get hurt, maybe even killed, so what? The country's full of them. It keeps the bigger peace." He smiled ironically, for Mendel's benefit, I thought.

Mendel's blackened hands fell to his sides. Encouraged, Hillel went on. "And if things get out of hand, they can always count on the Church, the great Opiate of the People, to call us Christ killers from the pulpits and justify the bloodletting that way. You understand now, Itzik?"

I looked into Itzik's bewildered eyes, so like his mother's. The story was as old as Moses. Every Pesach we tell the tale of our redemption from bondage in Egypt. But if we were still being used for other people's purposes, we were still slaves. Still slaves.

"What should I do?" Itzik whispered.

Hillel sighed, the oratory suddenly gone out of him. "You have to leave the country, Itzik."

No! I cried. *Blessed God, please don't make us leave Poland! He needs Polish soil to grow. I need it.*

But Mendel agreed with Hillel. "Leave the country and things will die down. What else can they do? Kill more Jews?"

Itzik shrank to the stone floor in the shadows of the entryway, scared as a cornered mouse. "Things didn't die down when they found out I left Zokof. They made a pogrom," he said, chin on his knee.

"They can't make a pogrom against all the Jews in Poland," Hillel argued. "Itzik, I have friends. I'll book you passage to America."

"Just get him out of here fast," Mendel said. "And when you get to America, you'd be smart to change your name, like my worthless son Shima the *Gonif* — the Thief. Then no one will ever find you." He sneered. "That's what America's for, a place to send our *dreck.*"

If he changes his name, not even he *will find himself, Mendel!* I said. But of course, he didn't hear me. No one heard me. The Golden Land, they call America. What could such a name mean but that gold is all they value there? God help us, Itzik and I were going to a fool's paradise. Then I cursed myself for dreading it, for resisting God's will. If that was the place where Itzik would be safe, that was where I should gladly go.

"*Zie gezunt* — good health," Mendel said, and walked out the entry door, finished with Itzik forever. *Ach!* A pox on him.

An awkward moment passed before Hillel took Itzik by the arm and led him back into the crowded street to Pesha Goldman's empty apartment. He pointed to a chair by the kitchen table. "Sit down. I'll pour you a cup of hot water," he said.

Eventually, Itzik began to speak. "What happened, I'm not even sure," he mumbled, not taking his eyes off the cup.

Hillel sat down opposite and laid his open hands on the table. "Try," he said very gently, because Itzik looked sure to fall apart.

A mishmash of words came. "The boys had Yudel the Teacher's lantern. It was late. I was on the other side of the road, but I saw Jan, the one with the laugh, the famous one. He had the whip out again. Always he has it out for the littlest ones. But the horse made him fall, not me." Itzik looked up at Hillel, tears all over his face. "Now he's dead."

Hillel waited patiently for him to go on.

"The Poles came after me. I hid in the cemetery until they left. Then I went to Avrum Kollek. He gave me money, and he went for the Russian magistrate." Itzik choked back more tears and collapsed in his chair, a heap of shaking rags.

I sang to him, curled my soul around him, and tried to soothe him as I'd soothed his mother. Nothing. Hillel came around the table and put a hand on his shoulder. "You did what you could." He waited for Itzik to calm. I pulled back. Useless again. Even my gravestone he'd left out. For him, this was nothing. How was I to help this boy if he didn't even know I was part of his story?

Hillel's dreamy eyes had a look of melancholy. Their crinkled corners had lost their laughter. "We'll have to hide you while I organize some papers for you and book the boat passage to America," he said. Itzik hung his head, but Hillel, suddenly excited by his plan, rushed on. "We'll put you in Pesha's darkroom! It'll be safe. It's perfect!" He laughed and coaxed a smile from the boy.

Later, Pesha Goldman, may his name be inscribed forever, agreed to hide Itzik, even though it was a danger.

Itzik didn't take much more on his journey to America than the clothes on his body and the contents of his small sack. The sun shone so bright on the day he left, it reached even the Goldmans' damp basement apartment. Devora filled the sack with freshly baked poppy-seed rolls. "Safe journey, Itzik," she said. Pesha smiled and handed him the two photographs they'd taken the day after Itzik had arrived in Warsaw. They were mounted on cards, with the studio name and address on the bottom right corner.

Itzik stared at one, his portrait. He looked so fine, dressed in the stately studio clothes Pesha had fastened in the back with clips. The second photograph was of him seated, with Hillel standing next to him, his hand on Itzik's shoulder. In the white border below, Pesha had written, *Chaverim — May 5, 1906.*

Hillel glanced at Pesha's writing. "Friends," he said sadly.

"Take them both," Pesha told Itzik. "With what's going on, we can't keep them."

Hillel looked longingly at the photograph of the two of them.

"Thank you," Itzik murmured.

Pesha winked at Itzik. "Don't worry. They'll never recognize the criminal Itzik Leiber under that cap Hillel got you."

This made everyone smile, even Hillel. It was true. The cap was so big, all you could see was Itzik's chin. He tugged nervously at the knots in his sack, and once again his eyes filled with tears. "I'll send you my address when I get to America. I'll send you pictures of Indians."

Pesha nodded and patted him softly on the back, after which Hillel took him by the arm and led him out the door. The two of them wound their way through the back streets of Warsaw to the train station.

As they waited by the train, Itzik said timidly, "I won't forget you ever, or what you taught me."

Hillel chuckled, a little sadly, and rechecked Itzik's papers. "Take your tunes to America. They'll keep you from getting lonely." He bowed his head and let his long hair fall forward so Itzik couldn't see the tears gathering in his eyes.

"I can't sing," Itzik protested, clearly puzzled why Hillel thought he knew tunes. "You keep them and remember me, all right, Hillel?"

Hillel opened his arms and pulled Itzik into a tight embrace. The boy shut his eyes, his face contorted in pain, as if he'd never been held like that before and didn't expect to be held like that again. They clung silently to each other for a long time.

"Go now," Hillel said, pulling back, his eyes still lowered as he turned in the direction of the train. It was ready to leave its berth. With a final squeeze at Hillel's arm, Itzik pulled the photograph of himself and Hillel from his pack and pressed it into Hillel's hand. Before Hillel could protest, Itzik had joined the flow of families with their piles of bundles and fearful faces, all climbing on board for the journey west.

I sang my last song of thanks to Hillel then. He smiled slightly. Such a beautiful face, and the soul of a *lamed-vovnik*. If he was one of them, those thirty-six righteous souls on whom justice in the world depends, I would not be surprised.

The train pulled away from the station. Itzik pressed his hand against the glass to Hillel, who waved until Itzik was out of sight. Throughout that sorrowful ride across Poland's flat farmlands, Itzik stared out the window as if committing every field, every willow, and even the Polish roadside shrines to memory.

Shah, shah, Itzik, I said, *You'll plant your soul in American soil and grow there. It will be fine. You'll be safe.* I said this maybe as much for myself as for him.

Itzik gripped the windowsill and hummed Aaron's tune off key, as if it were the only thing he had left in the world. Over and over he hummed the tune, my tune, until he'd transformed the sweet Hassidic melody into a plodding march. His cap, pulled over his brows, hid the tears that didn't stop until late in the day, when we reached the German border.

The German officials let him pass without questioning the papers that identified him as Leo Rudovsky. It was as if once they saw his ticket for the ship docked in Antwerp, he was no longer of any consequence to them. What did they care about a Jewish boy? they seemed to say as they returned his papers. He'd soon be gone.

When the train left the station, I got *schpilkes* — nervousness I couldn't quiet. At first I thought this was because I didn't want to go. Poland was where I belonged, with generations of my family. But I'd accepted that the Omniscient One had decided Poland wasn't where Itzik belonged, and if this was His test of my loyalty to the child He'd given me, so be it. I made ready for the crossing.

I should have remembered that God responds to our prayers in strange and mysterious ways. When the train crossed the border, a dark whirling cloud came upon us. With deafening noise it swept me from Itzik. My vision, blurred and doubled as it was, faded until I could not see at all. I began to sink, slowly, softly. When my sight returned, there was nothing but the color blue, only blue. I felt a certain buoyancy and tried to speak, to say, Gottenu, where am I? But even my breath was bound, trapped in a liquid universe.

Master of the Universe, I protested. *Is this Your judgment of me, an afterlife of exile in the waters of Your creation? Is this my punishment for breaking the chain of generations? Does it not move You that I repent? The sin of childlessness was mine, not Berel's. I know now what I did not know in life, that the child nurtures Man as Man nurtures God.* Fear made my tongue wag still harder. *Almighty Creator, why did You give me a child, only to take him away before I could put something of You in him?*

God did not answer me. As for Itzik, not a sound from him either. I waited desperately for his prayers, that they might redeem me. Even so, I told myself, surely a God of Justice would not have returned me to the living only to punish my sins. Surely there was a reason He had chosen me, not Ruchelle Cohen, to lead Itzik from Poland. Maybe He only meant I should believe myself condemned to eternal exile so that I would know the full sweetness of redemption when it came.

I clung to this *midrash* — this interpretation — like a drowning person clings to the branch. But I would be lying if I did not say I was also driven nearly mad to find myself floating in that vast blueness, helpless and insignificant as a fleck of dust. I waited, suspended between grief and wonder at the awesome power of God.

Then, without warning, a living soul came to me. It had lost its way to God's great light. This was not Itzik, but someone from our town, one of those rare souls whose flame burns into the world beyond. My father used to tell me some souls suffer so profoundly they transcend the world, but I had not believed him until this one shone on me in the blue.

God the Joker has answered me at last, I thought. I am to guide this soul also, like Itzik, to where it needs to go. And indeed, when I touched that soul I emerged briefly from exile. What that man, that beautiful man, saw of me, I cannot say. I only know that with him, I had some peace, enough to give me hope of return to rest with my body, and some respite from the terror of my entombment in the blue.

The silence in that place was broken only once. The loud echo of a ram's horn passed me like a comet. On its tail rode my father's voice, clear as in life. *Be vigilant and await the coming of Aaron's sister, Miriam,* he called to me. *Return her timbrel and she will make an opening for you to return.*

I waited. I became vigilant. I listened for the shake of a timbrel and wondered what it could mean.

Time passed. Itzik went to his final rest. I felt his uncooked soul return, exhausted, to the firmament. *Master of the Universe,* I prayed, *let it not end here. Let me not end in this blue water.*

PART II

NATHAN

In the tree's higher branches the crows sit,

Seven across, sunlight shining off the black crowns of their heads

They recite their opinions of the dead

Tah! Tah!

Their beaks bobbing over the bones

Tah! Tah!

And with spread wings they descend to earth

To walk among us on two legs

Lingering at our feet.

9

Shortly after he arrived at Warsaw's Okęcie airport in May 1991, Professor Nathan Linden was paged repeatedly by loudspeaker. He didn't respond. Perhaps he didn't recognize the Polish pronunciation of his name. More likely, he didn't listen to the broadcast. At fifty-nine, Nathan had become adept at insulating himself from inconsequential stimuli, and that afternoon he was wholly intent on finding his colleague, Professor Czesław Dombrowski, of the History Department at Warsaw University, who was supposed to meet him at the baggage claim.

Nathan circled the room several times, discreetly attempting to make eye contact with men he thought looked like Polish academics. He began to imagine how he would respond to Dombrowski's words of welcome, and even how he would deflect Dombrowski's apologies for not recognizing him immediately. By the fourth or fifth time around, he was becoming irritable and tense, and all but ready to concede that his wife had been right. This trip had not been worth the trouble.

Four months earlier, the invitation to Poland had arrived at Nathan's home in Cambridge, Massachusetts. He'd found the letter in the foyer mail tray and had called upstairs to his wife, Marion, with the news.

"Poland? Of all places!" had been her reaction.

The Victorian's stairs had creaked like old bedsprings under her feet as she'd descended. He was charmed by his home's idiosyncrasies. After thirty years, its gracious architecture still gave him a sense of accomplishment.

The winter sun had lit Marion's salt-and-pepper hair as she'd stood on the landing. He'd smiled contentedly up at her, his bride. "They've asked me to lecture on constitutional paradigms," he'd said. "It's been a year since the Communist Party's been dissolved. After the Round Table Agreements between the government and the opposition last year, they've had the apparatus of a democracy in place. But they're still living under a Soviet-style constitution. It's a three-day trip. What do you think?"

Marion Linden was used to her husband's pedagogic style of speaking.

She went to him in the foyer and took the letter from his hand. "What about your Prague trip in the fall?" she'd said. "Maybe it would be better to schedule them back to back."

They'd passed through the short hallway to the kitchen. He'd seated himself at the table. She'd heated the water for tea.

"No, I can't wait for the fall," he'd said. "If I wait, even for a few months, the mood could swing in another direction, and they might not be welcoming an American's opinion."

"It's a long way to go for just three days."

"I know. But my suspicion is, the lecture at the university is just window dressing, an introduction. If they're interested in what I have to say, they'll put me in touch with the people in parliament who are drafting the new constitution. That could be pretty interesting, I think." He'd given her the sly grin he knew she loved. "Besides, how can I turn down Dombrowski when he wrote that I was 'Harvard's most justifiably eminent constitutional scholar?'"

She'd laughed. "Nathan, I think you're going to Poland."

But now, as Nathan stood in the airport with his bags collected, no one seemed to be looking for him. "Professor Nathan Linden," the loudspeaker announced again, and this time, he heard.

"I am so terribly sorry," Dombrowski said on the telephone to which Nathan was directed by an airport official. "I had hoped we could have a private talk on our way to your hotel, since that won't be possible at the reception this evening, with all the people who will want to speak with you. Unfortunately, just a few hours ago my father became seriously ill, and I must go to him at the hospital."

"Of course," Nathan said, already bracing himself for the unpleasant task of getting into the city on his own.

Dombrowski was anxious. "Do you think you can find the Marriott shuttle bus, or should I try to find someone else to drive you there?"

Nathan slid his fingers under his glasses and rubbed his eyes. "No, it's quite all right. I'll take the shuttle. I hope your father feels better soon. I'll see you later at the reception."

Outside, the terminal's awning was no protection from the hard, slanting rain that had begun to fall. Nathan opened the mini travel umbrella that Marion, as always, had carefully tucked into the bottom of his carry-on bag, but he quickly became uncomfortably damp.

By the time the Marriott bus pulled up and opened its doors like a pair of arms, he was no longer irritated that his request for a Polish hotel had been ignored. Much as it embarrassed him to look like a garden-variety American tourist staying at an American hotel, the Marriott was at least going to be comfortable, and comfort, he admitted to himself, was what he wanted.

He remembered, with some discomfort, a conversation he'd had with his daughter, Ellen, when he'd last visited her in Manhattan. They'd been having coffee at the café downstairs from her apartment, when a tightly massed group of Japanese had passed by. "A tourist is a silly creature — a duck out of water," he'd commented. "If you travel with a purpose, Ellen, you'll always have the dignity of an insider."

She'd just smiled and made a point of shaking her long copper corkscrew curls, the way she had since she was a little girl. "There's nothing wrong with being a stranger, Dad," she'd said. "No one belongs *everywhere*. You go around the world being met at airports and taken around by academics who make you feel as if you've never left home. Where's the adventure in that?"

He watched the driver load wet luggage onto the Marriott bus and thought, *An adventure like this, I could do without.* That was the kind of thing his pop used to say. But Pop would never have gotten on a plane to Poland. "What do I need with such a place?" he would have said, as if it was offensive to even suggest the idea of traveling. Which was why Pop had never gone anyplace.

Nathan looked out the window as the bus headed into the city. Warsaw's architectural theme appeared to be a harsh display of Soviet bureaucratic power. The drab concrete-block buildings had been dropped, seemingly at random, onto littered, uncut grass, gracelessly traversed with unpaved footpaths. It depressed him even more to see the neon lights of McDonald's and the massive warehouselike IKEA inflicting their new kind of insult upon the city.

Yet he was relieved when the Marriott Hotel, with its lobby brightly lit with chandeliers and done up in marble, turned out to be a replica of its high-end American counterparts, and just as comfortable. As was his custom after overseas flights, he unpacked, closed the curtains of his room, and took a long nap.

He awoke feeling much better and was getting dressed for the reception being given in his honor at the home of someone in the History Department, when the phone rang. Dombrowski again. It seemed his father was now in critical condition. He was terribly embarrassed he hadn't been able to make further arrangements. There was a painful pause on the line; then Dombrowski said he would call someone to take Nathan to the reception.

Now, Dombrowski had been in contact with Nathan for almost five months. Nathan felt as if he already knew the man. He liked him too. "It's quite all right. There's no need to trouble yourself. I'll have the concierge call a taxi," he assured him. What else could he say? Dombrowski was clearly distraught and suffering from conflicted responsibilities. The whole thing was horribly awkward.

Downstairs, the taxi driver, summoned by the hotel, seemed to know the address Nathan handed him on a slip of paper. Even though he didn't speak much English, he had the ramrod posture of a man who knew what he was about. It therefore came as a great surprise to Nathan when after about twenty minutes the fellow stopped in the middle of a collection of gray cereal-box buildings, arbitrarily clumped at odd angles, and left him to fend for himself. "Number eight," the driver said, pointing vaguely at one of the buildings. And as if to clear up any doubt Nathan might have had about what he was expected to do with this information, the driver put out his hand for the fare and added, "You go."

*H*alf an hour after he'd stepped out of the taxi, Nathan was still wandering around, unable to get his bearings. Gray pavement, unadorned by a single tree, stretched before him like a blank canvas. He cursed the taxi driver under his breath. Then he cursed himself for paying him what he assumed must have been a small fortune.

It was six thirty. By now he was supposed to be in building number eight. They were waiting for him in apartment twenty-three. He looked up at the tiny windows of the apartment buildings around him, hoping for some direction. But all he saw was a grid of panes, many of them piled high with disarrayed possessions.

He checked his watch again, dreading the prospect of having to ask someone for help, of being forced to admit his unfamiliarity with the language and the neighborhood. It didn't matter to Nathan that anyone could get lost in a city. He hated to appear unknowledgeable, even about things that he could not reasonably be expected to know. This, and his stubbornness about not being interfered with on such occasions, had driven Marion and his daughter, Ellen, to distraction more times than any of them could recall. But now, even if he had wanted to ask, there was no one around to give directions except a small boy on roller skates who disappeared quickly around a corner.

He began to talk to himself in a monotone hum that disguised the words, an old habit that usually calmed him. "Building number eight. Is this number eight? This is seventeen. Here is four. There's no number on that one." The sun was setting, but sweat gathered around his collarbones in the warm May air. Droplets had already begun a slow descent through the hair on his chest. His ascot stuck to his neck, the silk unmoored from its careful placement at the center of his white shirt under the brown tweed jacket. He reached up to remove it but stopped when he realized that without the ascot he would appear unprofessional. What would they think of him?

"Damn," he muttered. Why had he been so nonchalant? Why hadn't he at least insisted on more detailed instructions from Dombrowski?

He paused to look around again and to adjust his glasses, which were sliding down the thin ridge of his nose. He reached for the keloid scar under the hair at the back of his head, another nervous habit that calmed him. With several short strokes of his fingertips he also combed back some strands at the top of his head.

Four men ambled toward him from across the parking lot to his left, arms clasped around each other for support, bodies sagging from what looked to Nathan like the result of years of too much alcohol and starchy food. Their loud song sent him scurrying toward the protective shadows of a numberless building. It was an instinct brought from childhood. He had always hugged the buildings as a boy, trying to hide his small, skinny frame from the swaggering young toughs, Irish boys mostly, whose fathers had taught them to be proud of their fists. He remembered, as his jacket now scraped against the rough cement, how he'd wished for a father who'd put some manly energy into his son instead of merely spewing sarcastic remarks about life, as Pop did, from his third-story window.

The men drew closer. Nathan felt a sick wave in his gut. It whorled around his stomach and into his chest, as familiar and inevitable as the game of taunts and fists that used to follow. He put his head down and picked up his pace, aware that since his arrival in Poland, he'd felt a certain sense of threat, which he'd dismissed as irritation at not having been treated by his hosts in the usual deferential manner.

"Calm yourself. Nothing's going to happen here. You'll find your way.

You've done it all over the world," he hummed. But he could barely catch his breath.

The drunks were laughing now. He thought they were pointing at him, so he refused to look at them, to give them an opening. He reached a door and pulled himself inside, dizzy with panic.

The men passed, lolling their heads from side to side like bulls. He watched them through the small window in the door until they were gone and it was silent. He stepped back, straightened his ascot, ashamed of the fear that had left half-moon sweat stains spreading in the armpits of his shirt.

The hallway, lit by dim, uncovered lightbulbs at either end, stank from rotting food, like cooked cabbage, he thought. Over a doorpost, like a miracle, he saw the number eight. "Thank God," he said, weak with relief. He hurried up the stairs, found apartment twenty-three, and gave several short knocks. A tall man in a white knit boatneck shirt opened the door and extended his hand. On his third finger, he wore a large ring with an ornate crest.

"Welcome to my home, Professor Linden! We hope you had no difficulty finding us," the man said.

Nathan smiled. "No. No difficulty at all."

I heard the words, saw the two men in the doorway. Such bright lights they had inside. Thanks God, I was delivered from my blue exile! My eyesight was still no good, everything in two's and three's, but I could see that I was not among Jews there. They were beardless men, their clothes strangely cut. And the women — I was ashamed to look at them. Uncovered arms and skirts so short you could not imagine. Why do You send me here? I asked the Almighty.

From Him, I got no answers, but I remembered my poppa calling to me. "Be vigilant and await the coming of Aaron's sister, Miriam. Return her timbrel, and she will make an opening for you to return," he had said. "Why Miriam, Poppa, why a timbrel?" I called out. From him I got no answer either. But what joy, my voice was returned to me at last. I was sure these strangers would hear me, but I needn't have feared. No one turned in my direction.

Nathan Linden, a man whose false confidence already made me nervous, shook the Pole's hand and went inside.

10

*T*HE MAN AT THE DOOR INTRODUCED HIMSELF AS PROFESSOR Stanisław Załuski. "On behalf of the entire History Department," he said, "I wish to apologize for Professor Dombrowski, that he could not bring you to my home this evening and that he will miss our reception. His father's illness, you see."

Nathan adopted a look of concern and nodded understandingly.

"He was looking forward to greeting you personally after these many months." As Załuski spoke he escorted Nathan to the center of the small apartment, where about thirty people mingled, packed together in small groups. The place was uncomfortably warm, and no one wore a jacket. Nathan wished he could remove his own. The cramped quarters, lined from floor to ceiling with books, every available surface cluttered with photographs and knickknacks, had the feel of a temporary storage unit.

"Professor, please let me introduce you to my wife, Anna, and to some members of our faculty," Załuski said.

One by one, with great formality, Załuski introduced his wife, a woman whose delicate face was framed by an elegant pair of amber earrings, and each of the assembled Poles. They all shook his hand and, to Nathan's great relief, greeted him in English. Several people expressed admiration for his theories on constitutional paradigms. Others apologized for Dombrowski's failure to escort him to the reception. Nathan accepted a glass of sherry from a young man in jeans. With a conspiratorial wink, Załuski handed his guest a hot cheese blintze on a delicately decorated china plate. "My wife makes the best *naleśniki z serem* in Poland," he said.

Nathan stared at the cheese blintze, which until that moment he believed was of Jewish origin. He bit into the soft dough and discreetly admired Załuski's shock of thick blond hair, which swept majestically away from his broad, high forehead. The Pole's drooping blue eyes gave him an air of aristocratic ease. You could watch a man like this and be convinced that blintzes are every bit as refined as French crepes, he thought. "They are delicious." He smiled at Anna and followed his host to one of the few chairs that had been scattered about. Załuski motioned for him to sit. Nathan could not politely refuse, although he felt more comfortable observing the gathering from the perimeter walls than from the center of the room.

"I hope you will enjoy your first trip to Poland, Professor Linden. I think you will find we are a more complex people than most Westerners think, Polish jokes notwithstanding." Załuski winked again.

Nathan smiled agreeably as he watched his host light a cigarette and slowly inhale. A moment later he realized that he too was being closely observed. "I think that can be fairly said of all peoples, that they are complex, don't you agree?" he said. "At least, that's been my experience, and it's part of the challenge of devising constitutional paradigms."

"With all due respect, Professor Linden," Załuski said in a voice that resonated throughout the room and caught the attention of all its occupants, "I think you Americans put too much stock in creating systems of one sort or another. I don't think the world can be that easily reduced." Załuski slowly exhaled through his nose. He paused, gazed around the room, and narrowed his eyes. His audience quieted as he continued. "I believe there are irrational forces in all societies that cannot be tamed or reasoned away. They are the enemies of democracy, the dark, magical side of human nature if you will, and a hundred of your perfectly drafted, duly adopted constitutions will not diminish their power."

"Perhaps, but a constitution can control them," Nathan responded without a second thought.

"Only to a point. In your own country, did the post–Civil War amendments abolishing slavery and promising equal protection under the law end the apartheid mentality, if not the practices, of your southern brethren? I think not."

Nathan was not used to this level of skepticism about the foundations of his life's work. He raised his eyebrows in what he hoped would convey a neutral, slightly bemused attitude, and smiled back. But his jaw was locked, and his teeth were clenched.

The two men regarded each other. Then Załuski leaned back in his chair and gave Nathan a half smile. He pulled an ashtray from a bookshelf and twirled the burning tip of his cigarette into the glass until it was crushed. He paused, inspected the stub, then looked directly at Nathan.

"Excuse me for my curiosity, but what kind of name is Linden?" he asked.

A tight, pulsing sensation shot across Nathan's stomach. "An American name," he said.

"But of what derivation?"

"European. American families don't generally come from just one place. My family came from all over Europe." He quickly turned his face away.

"Forgive me," Załuski said, "but I ask you about your name only because I don't recognize its origin, and I have a fascination with such things. In this country, you see, one's origin is of singular importance. My own family, the Załuskis, for example, traces its Polish lineage to the fifteenth century. The name is my Polish birthright, more significant to me than the memory of Germans arresting my father or the Communists seizing our ancestral home to make us outcasts in our own country. We are still Załuskis, of the Kingdom of Poland."

Nathan gave his host a short nod. "I'm aware of Poland's history of invasion," he said. "I suppose it's the lot of a nation that stands between Western and Eastern Europe without the protection of natural borders."

"Yes, an old story," Załuski concurred. "We are the Christ of Nations. But now, about your family?"

"I'm afraid that, like most Americans, my origins are obscure," Nathan offered, hoping to put a quick end to the discussion. "In any case, my origins are not of much interest to me or to anyone else in my family."

Załuski looked genuinely shocked. "How do you know who you are if you don't know where your family came from?"

All around the room people appeared to regard Nathan with new interest. He rose from his chair and fixed Załuski with one of those ironic professorial smiles that worked so well at confusing his students back home. "Perhaps that's the great American dilemma," he said. But as he looked about hopefully for support, not one person returned a sympathetic gaze.

Załuski's wife, Anna, pressed a steaming dish toward him. "Another *naleśniki,* Professor?"

"I would love one," he replied, smiling at her gratefully. But as she placed the delicacy on his plate, Nathan was reminded of the far less elegant blintzes frying in the Brooklyn kitchen of his childhood. He remembered the steam on the window, the fire escape, and the brick wall. He had set the course of his entire life to break free from that kitchen and the boundaries of Brooklyn. To succeed, he had even left his name and his parents, Sadie and Isaac (née Itzik) Leiber, behind. How, in God's name, had Załuski guessed?

11

THE FOLLOWING MORNING, THE HISTORY DEPARTMENT'S LEC-
ture hall was packed with scholars and government officials. Professor
Dombrowski, temporarily freed from his domestic difficulties, introduced
Nathan, in Polish and English, in a warm and highly laudatory manner. To
much applause, Nathan ascended the steps, grasped each side of the
wooden podium, and addressed his respectful listeners.

"The great American philosopher Morris Rafael Cohen once said, 'No
man can stand in front of an audience without pretending that he knows
more than he does.'" He waited a beat, with an expectant smile. "And I am
no exception."

The audience tittered politely. Nathan leaned over his prepared text
like an athlete warming up and launched into his theory of constitutional
genesis and the paradigms for progress, aware of the appreciative sounds
that punctuated his remarks. He focused briefly on the first row, where an
impressionable-looking young woman, seated on the aisle, was making a
point of showing off her superb calves. She needn't have bothered for
Nathan's sake. He was merely using eye contact to assert his dominion at
the lectern. His wife, Marion, was the only woman who'd ever really suc-
ceeded in gaining his sexual attention. And even she suspected that his devotion was almost as much out of gratitude for the way she protected the
sanctity of his study and helped him battle his dyslexia, as for love.

Nathan transitioned smoothly into his discourse on the principle of separation of powers, implied limitations on government, and the fundamen-
tal rights outlined in the American Bill of Rights. The microphone hissed.
He tapped it. "Let me say, in conclusion, that for a Polish constitution to
survive in a new Polish democracy, the common man must believe it is a
living document, not a relic to be paraded around for state occasions." He
watched with satisfaction as scores of hands furiously scribbled his advice,
marvelously unaware that the man who they subsequently applauded had

spent his youth pushing garment racks down Seventh Avenue by day so he could take classes at City College, the poor man's Harvard, at night.

A breeze floated through the hall, rustling papers, causing feet to shuffle. Nathan collected his notes and sensed an unusual charge in the atmosphere. He felt a bit off center, as if one of his ears was filled with water. When he pulled on his earlobe to clear it, he heard what sounded like a far-off voice humming an indistinct tune. Dombrowski stepped up to the podium and shook his hand. People crowded the front of the hall to meet him. But the eerie sensation and the voice lingered and robbed him of his customary post-lecture high.

A faculty member proposed a project between Harvard and a multi-disciplinary group of Polish scholars. He tried to look interested, but he couldn't shake the fluttering sound in his ears. Disturbed, he made his excuses and left the hall, hoping to escape further contact with the Poles until he could reclaim his sense of equilibrium.

"It seems my colleagues were highly impressed with your constitutional paradigms, Professor Linden."

The deep, rolling voice, directed at his back, gave Nathan a start. He turned. The sounds in his ears stopped when he saw Stanisław Załuski standing at the exit door of the lecture hall. Feeling immediately improved, he regarded Załuski with the confidence of a man who'd just bested his enemy. "I guess not everyone shares your belief in the dark side of human nature," he said.

Załuski squinted into the sunlight and lit a cigarette. "Laugh if you like at my way of expressing my opinions," he said, approaching Nathan, "but it is my duty to speak frankly because you are a man of some influence, and I am a man who loves his country."

Flattered and slightly curious, Nathan waited for Załuski to continue.

"You are a Jew, Professor Linden."

An electric sensation stung Nathan at the back of his neck. He clenched his jaw. "What of it?"

Załuski's smile creased the corners of his heavy eyelids. "They say we Poles have a sixth sense about Jews. We always know. So let us understand each other. It is not wartime, after all." He took another drag of his cigarette and gave Nathan a meaningful look. "A Jew should understand what I say. A Jew knows he has reason to fear man's dark impulses."

Nathan went taut with fury. How dare Załuski presume he was a Jew before he was a scholar, as if he, Nathan Linden, had some primitive tribal obligation to represent the Jews.

"In March 1968 this country went into something of an anti-Jewish madness," Załuski continued evenly. "Extremists openly said Jews were German sympathizers during the war. Three million people were responsible for their own deaths, they said. They pushed Jews from their livelihoods. Some they beat, some they robbed. The Jew was used as an excuse to brutalize students who demonstrated for more democracy on this campus." He pointed his finger at the spot where they stood.

Nathan was upset to hear this. But he did not trust where Załuski might be trying to lead him. He cleared his throat. "I certainly remember there was trouble in Poland during that period, but I wasn't under the impression that things were quite as serious as you say."

The lines on Załuski's face deepened with irritation. "Then let me inform you, that when it was over, twenty-five thousand, including almost all the young Jews we had left here, had packed their bags and run. Some of our best minds went out the door that year."

His voice, thick with emotion, attracted the attention of passersby, but he ignored the scene he was creating. "None of this," he said vehemently, "could have been accomplished if it were not for the willingness of an enslaved nation to embrace its dark and ancient hatreds rather than reflect on what they had seen with their own eyes during the war, the genocide against the Jews."

Flushed, he took a drag of his cigarette and exhaled sharply. "It has been my life's work since that time to say to anyone who will listen that if the Poles don't begin to question themselves they will always be slaves, downtrodden and spiteful. I say this, you understand, out of love for my people. They don't know it, but to be rid of this mania about Jews would be a relief."

Nathan was at a complete loss. "What does this have to do with me?"

Załuski's face hardened. "We are at the beginning of a new era in Polish history. We have achieved sovereignty. This we paid for with our blood and centuries of unimaginable suffering. You, Professor Linden, were invited here to speak to us about creating a constitution. But what I say to you is that we don't need Utopian schemes that will send us back into the grip of the tyrants. We need someone who understands that the Poles' dark impulse to lay the blame outside enslaves *them*. Build individual responsibility, a presumed duty to reflect, into every corner of your constitutional paradigm and we will have something useful from you, a real contribution to history." He took a long, uneven drag on his cigarette.

Nathan knew what Pop would say to this. He'd say, "Listen, Mister College Professor, a Pole is a Pole. You can't do nothing with him unless he's a socialist. Then he's a brother." Pop had a whole arsenal of truisms like this, one more obscure than the next.

"So, until tomorrow then?" Załuski said.

"Tomorrow?"

"I am to give you a tour of the city."

"Actually," Nathan said, hoping to conceal his distaste for the plan, "I think I'd rather get out of the city and take a look at this country of yours. Can you arrange for me to have a car and driver for the day?"

Załuski smiled. If he'd been surprised or disappointed by Nathan's request, it didn't show. "If you would prefer, I'm sure this can be arranged," he said with a slight bow. "I'll call you with the details later this evening." Then he headed off in the direction of Kazimierz Palace, smoke fanning out behind him like a cloud.

12

WARSAW! BEAUTIFUL WARSAW! THAT CITY WAS NO MORE. I could not find the Great Synagogue on Tłomackie Street, or mark my way to Plac Grzybowski by the smell of hot chickpeas. But still sweet was the smell of grass growing in Saxon Garden.

Warsaw's air smelled of a burnt stew of elements Nathan could not identify. It was also permeated by dust and gasoline exhaust, which irritated his eyes. But after the morning's events, he felt so agitated he decided to take a walk, despite the added threat of rain. He passed under the university's decorative wrought-iron gate, with its Polish eagle on top, and walked north, intending to visit the Gothic postwar reconstruction called Old Town. He had read somewhere that although small in size, it was quite charming.

But somehow he managed to take a wrong turn, and he found himself instead at a pleasant but unremarkable park identified in his tour book as the Saxon Garden. According to the book, a building called the Blue Palace could be found on the far end of the Garden. The name intrigued him, but the guide said the original building, with its extensive art and book collections, had burned during the war, that it had been rebuilt as the headquarters of the municipal transport enterprise and now wasn't worth a visit.

Nathan retraced his steps, and with a sudden desire for the taste of something sweet, he drifted south toward the cafés on the elegantly reconstructed Nowy Świat. He sat down in a café that had a large display of doughnuts in the window. Of all things to find in Poland, he thought. He ordered a sugar-sprinkled one with a tea, in the best Polish he could manage from his tour book.

The waiter looked sympathetic as Nathan struggled to pronounce *pączek,* the word for *doughnut.* "That is very good Polish," said the waiter, although it was clear to them both that Nathan had just about reached the limit of his abilities in the language.

"You speak English," Nathan said gratefully.

"A little," the young man offered.

Nathan noted how even in jeans and a T-shirt, the Pole retained that intangible difference that marked him as non-American, as if some trace of ancestral formality prevented his wearing casualness well. "Can you tell me what that church is over there with the two towers?" he asked.

The waiter bent slightly at the waist as he set up the table. "That's *Kościół Świętego Krzyża,* the Holy Cross Church," he said. "Inside it was almost destroyed, from bombs, in the Second War. During the great Warsaw Uprising there was much fighting there between our people and the Nazis."

"Well, it certainly is beautiful on the outside."

The young man straightened proudly. "Before the war, all Warsaw was beautiful. It was the most beautiful city in Europe. Not like this." He motioned vaguely at the city beyond the reconstructed zones of Nowy Świat and Old Town. "Horrible, no?"

Nathan knew better than to agree. It was one thing for a Pole to disparage his city, quite another for a foreigner to do so. "It's no wonder you love your beautiful churches then," he said amicably.

The waiter seemed surprised. "But of course, we always love our Mother Church. Every Pole does."

He went about his duties as if nothing could possibly be added to this observation. When he returned with the doughnut and the glass of tea, Nathan was still debating with himself whether the young man had meant that a Jew could not be a Pole. Perhaps he should have devoted more attention in his speech to the issue of separation of church and state, made a reference to the case he'd just won against the evangelical Christians who'd proselytized at a public high school.

He took a bite of the doughnut, which was soft and delicious, and remembered how Ellen had teased him about that win.

"You really are the son of a flaming socialist," she'd said.

This had peeved him. "There is a difference between the law and Pop's ideology," he'd said primly. That she had laughed at this had hurt his feelings.

A young couple approached the table adjacent to Nathan's and smiled shyly at him as they sat down. He smiled back, and resolved not to allow Jewish paranoia to mar any more of his first impressions of the country. It was ludicrous to imagine the Poles had nothing better on their minds than Jews and Jew-baiting. Aside from the usual quotient of kooks, why would they put energy into disliking a people who were no longer part of their daily world? Annoyed with himself for having to articulate the self-evident, he decided the Jewish issue had been blown out of all proportion by his encounters with Załuski. The man had an agenda, that's all, he decided.

The waiter returned. "You find Frédéric Chopin's . . ." He pointed to his chest.

Nathan grinned from a sense of vindication at the young man's friendliness. He took a last sip of his tea. "Chopin's heart?" he guessed.

"Yes. In the church. Look on the left side, in the, how do you say?" He made a gesture with his hands as if circling something long.

"I don't think I understand."

"If you go, you will see," the waiter assured him. Nathan thought it somewhat strange that the church would keep only Chopin's heart, but he said, "Chopin is one of my favorite composers."

The waiter nodded approvingly, as if he'd had some part in Chopin's genius. Nathan paid his bill and, with a short wave good-bye, left the café.

At Holy Cross Church, he lingered outside, admiring the Baroque design. When he sauntered through the open front doors, it was with the confidence of having visited hundreds of churches in his life. Inside, he was moved by the statue of Jesus, which had been painstakingly arranged to produce a martyred but majestic effect. He remembered Załuski's reference to Poland as the Christ of Nations and felt sympathetic. What a horror it must have been for the Poles during the Nazi invasion, he thought, knowing their Russian allies were sitting just outside, on the banks of the Vistula, mocking them, allowing the city to burn.

Chopin's heart, it turned out, was contained in an urn that had been placed in one of the Church's pillars. Nathan stood before it reverently, grateful to Chopin for études that recalled for him tender evenings spent reading and drinking tea before the fireplace with Marion, shuttling between recordings of Rubenstein and Horowitz.

A German tour guide approached the pillar and delivered a prepared speech to his elderly charges. Nathan wondered how these Germans thought about the ruin still evident in the Church and surmised they might prefer to focus instead on the long-dead Chopin. He did not meet their gazes, offended somehow by their unrepentant air.

Suddenly his ears filled again, muffling the ambient sounds of the church. From somewhere inside his head a woman's voice said, "Gottenu," one of his father's favorite expressions. He turned around to see who was speaking and was struck by dizziness and an inexplicable unease at being in a church. Disturbed, he hurried out to the street, where, to his relief, his ears cleared immediately. The sky, too, had cleared. He decided to continue his tour.

Heading south down Nowy Świat, then west toward the monstrous Soviet-built Palace of Culture and Science, he came upon a swarm of portable stalls displaying cassette tapes, videos, watches, and hand-painted signs offering foreign currency exchanges. He was drawn to an unmanned stall of Polish folk music recordings and decided to wait for the proprietor to return so he could buy one for Marion. Next to a box of tapes, he noticed a set of hideously ugly wooden dolls, presumably for sale.

Picking one up, he realized to his horror that they were all caricatures of Hassidic Jews, complete with bulging eyes, beaked noses, and expressions of lusty greed. One figure held a fiddle, another a prayer book, but the one that shocked him most held a scale piled high with gold in front of his big belly, and an unmistakable leer on his face.

Shaken, Nathan looked around, hoping for a benign explanation for why the dolls were on display, or why anyone would want to buy one. But when no answer immediately presented itself, he threw the Polish folk tape back on the table and took off at a brisk pace into the park that surrounded the Palace of Culture and Science.

When at last he felt composed enough to take his eyes from the pavement, he noticed a young woman in a pink cardigan about fifty paces ahead of him. She held a sleeping little girl of about four or five in her arms. Sunlight flickered through the light veil of trees. For a split second it lit up the child's ringlets and reminded him of Ellen at that age. His heart began to beat wildly again at the thought of what sort of people they would have become if his self-assured daughter had grown up in Poland, exposed to such filth as he'd just seen, where he would have been unable to protect her.

The young mother in the pink cardigan changed paths and headed toward the other side of the Palace. Nathan turned away from the building and resumed his walk westward until he reached Emilii Plater Street. He followed it north to a small street called Twarda, which led to an almost empty, nondescript little square marked Plac Grzybowski. Set off at an angle from the street, a graceful neo-Romanesque white stone building, with tall arched windows of leaded glass, caught his eye. Above its doors, engraved in Hebrew, were the Ten Commandments, crowned by a Star of David.

He hesitated, unsure whether to investigate further. Anyone could visit a church, he reasoned. But to enter a synagogue was tantamount to a confession of faith. In a country where a Jew looks to the locals like one of those dolls he had just seen, who would visit a synagogue but a Jew? And even then, he'd have to be religious, which quickly brought Nathan to the question of who would be inside. He felt no identity with the ranks of men who wrapped themselves in blue-and-white prayer shawls, who rocked back and forth, muttering incomprehensibly. He scraped the pavement nervously with the side of his Timberland shoes, as if something distasteful were stuck there.

"The synagogue is a place where weak men run to hide," Pop had always said. "They run to the synagogue to pray instead of fighting for a new social system, for a workers' state."

"What's so great about socialism, Pop?" the thirteen-year-old Nathan had asked. "It seems to me that the system's only as good as the people who practice it. Just like religion." He was never sure why he got such a rise out of Pop by teasing him that socialism and religion were interchangeable. But it never failed.

"What do you know about it, Mr. Fancy American Boychik?" Pop would fight back. "You don't know *bubkes* about it. You know books. You don't know from work. I was a slave in that country. I was like a dog from the time I was eight, living in a hole, working six days a week, sixteen hours a day."

Every few minutes the Leibers' one-bedroom apartment under the El would vibrate with the ruthless cacophony of passing trains. From the kitchen, Nathan's mother, Sadie, would bang her pots as a warning not to argue with his father, but he would press on, carefully tracing the cracks in the living room's linoleum with his fingernails as he spoke.

Nathan's conversations with his father invariably took place in the evenings, some time after Pop awoke at six o'clock and before he went to work at eleven at Rubenstein's Bakery around the corner. Back then, Pop worked six nights a week at Rubenstein's. He didn't get home until seven in the morning. During the day, his mother guarded his sleep. Noise from Nathan or his sister, Gertie, was not tolerated. "Your father breaks his back for you, and this is how you repay him? Take a piece of *mandelbrot* and go outside," she'd say.

What little was left of his waking time, Pop spent barricaded behind his beloved newspaper, called *The Forward* in Yiddish, ensconced next to the window in the brown upholstered living-room chair that had taken on the shape of his squat back and wide seat. Nathan learned early that he could get his father's attention only by sending verbal darts through that newspaper. He always knew which article his father was reading because Pop talked to the paper as if it would answer him. So Nathan would throw out an English response for every comment his father made in Yiddish. Like most immigrants' kids, he could understand Yiddish but couldn't speak it. Eventually, in frustration, Pop would come out of his newspaper cave, growling like a bear whose sleep had been disturbed by a flea.

Yet on *Yom Kippur* mornings, when Nathan and his father cooked up a batch of onions so the whole neighborhood would know that Sadie Leiber's husband and son were disgracing her and God again by not fasting, or on the evenings when Pop invited him to play gin rummy around the kitchen table with Lou Gersh from down the hall, a penny a game, and on all those Saturdays when the family went to Coney Island and Pop bought hot dogs with sauerkraut and tickets for the rides at Steeplechase, Nathan loved his father deeply and hungrily. He especially loved the ferocity of Pop's belief in socialism and his equally ferocious hatred of all things Polish. They alone transformed the tired drone who sat like a sack of potatoes staring with his big, sad eyes out the living room window. He became passionate, alive. And when Pop came alive, he'd reach out to his son to teach him what he cared about. For Nathan, the magnetic ties between socialism, Poland, and Pop were an intricate puzzle he could never piece together and which his father would never explain.

Nathan looked at the tree shadows rustling across the white stone walls of the synagogue. Suddenly, half a dozen voices echoed the singsong of Jewish prayer off the high walls inside. He pulled out his tour book. "The Nożyk Synagogue," it said, "is the only remaining synagogue of the Warsaw Ghetto and the only functioning synagogue in Warsaw. The Great Synagogue on Tłomackie Street, which held up to three thousand people, was blown up by the Nazis. The Nożyk was gutted for use as a horse stable during the war and reopened in 1983 after a complete restoration. It is open to tourists from ten until three o'clock on Thursdays."

Well, that's that, Nathan thought. It's not Thursday.

A Pole wearing a blue cloth jacket and workman's overalls rounded the corner of the building. After he'd gone, Nathan noticed that one of the front doors of the synagogue was slightly ajar. He climbed the steps and entered the foyer, telling himself he was only interested in the building's historical significance.

In the large, high-walled sanctuary, graceful brass chandeliers shone in the white light that poured through the windows. Nathan was taken aback by the room's elegant simplicity, by the beauty of the iron grille work and the delicate intricacy of the canopy over the *Aron Kodesh,* where the Torah was kept. For him, a synagogue was a graceless place, festooned with plaques naming big, immodest donors and lit with garish, multicolored lights. This is refined, he thought. Beautiful. He felt a bit mischievous. He'd have loved to tell Pop he'd been to synagogue in Poland. *That* would have sent him spinning!

A small group of men stood praying around the bimah in front of the *Aron Kodesh,* terms he remembered from his Bar Mitzvah. They glanced repeatedly at him. Ignoring them lest they try to include him, he brushed his hand across the leaf pattern of a bas relief along one wall and felt a sudden, small flutter of delight, like the feel of Marion's bare shoulder as he caressed it.

One of the men, his head covered by his prayer shawl, turned around. Nathan had no choice but to return his gaze. The man's egg-shaped face and his worker's hands startled and touched him because he could have been Pop's brother. He beckoned to Nathan, as if to invite him under the protective wing of his prayer shawl. Something in the man's expression put Nathan at ease. He's *haimish,* he thought, surprised that the Yiddish word came to him instead of the English word *warm* or *cozy.* The man's face was as warm as the pastrami-on-rye sandwiches he secretly indulged in whenever he was in New York.

"We need a *minyan,*" Pop's look-alike said in Yiddish.

Nathan froze. How could he, a nonbeliever, join in prayers he'd never learned? Out of a desire to spare the man offense, he smiled, pretended not to understand, and hurried toward the door.

Outside, he immediately regretted that he had not spoken to the man, had not taken that small step that might have led him into an interesting and informative exchange. If pressed, Nathan also might have admitted that he wouldn't have minded some Jewish company that day.

He walked around the other side of the building. Spray-painted on the white wall, next to a large, sloppy red Star of David were the words "Fuck the Jews." That these three words were written in English made Nathan feel as if the defacer had taken a knife to *his* skin. His throat constricted. He could barely breathe. The fury painted on that wall was as incomprehensible as the Hassid dolls, or the Irish boys yelling "dirty Yid, dirty Yid" through the streets of his childhood.

Shah, shah, a female voice whispered in his ear. *A kluger vaist vos er zogt, a nar zogt vos er vaist.* Nathan ran his fingers over the keloid at the back of his head. The words comforted him so much he translated them under his breath. "A wise man knows what he says, a fool says what he knows."

13

*T*HAT NIGHT NATHAN HAD A DREAM.

In Harvard Square, the Hassid doll with the gold coins balanced on his scales danced and screamed on the roof of the Coop, limbs flying akimbo like in one of Ellen's modern dances. The sound of a reckless, screeching violin reverberated over the square, where a crowd of Nathan's colleagues, students, neighbors, and acquaintances had assembled. The whole lot craned distortedly to make out the Hassid's words. Hawkers stopped hustling. Street musicians stood, mouths agape, silenced by the mad figure swaying precariously above. "Give me! Give me blintzes, Jew!" the Hassid roared, his voice finally distinct.

On the other side of the square, from the great arched window of a synagogue, Pop sat watching with hooded eyes. Still and remote, his slumped torso barely rose above the windowsill. Below him, the blue neon light of a bookshop pulsed indifferently. REMAINDERS, it said.

Nathan crouched under the subway awning in the center of the square wearing nothing but thermal underwear, the crotch puckered from misbuttoning. Everyone was looking at him. Slowly, they raised their fingers and pointed. "He's the Jew!" they whispered to one another. Nathan cupped his genitals protectively and looked around, anguished.

The Hassid careened toward the ledge of the Coop and held out his scales, the fringes of his blue-and-white prayer shawl wafting into clouds of smoke. He had Załuski's mocking face.

Nathan cried out, "I have nothing to feed you! There's nothing left." He turned to Pop for reinforcement. But his father shrugged and looked away. The Hassid howled again for blintzes. Nathan screamed with terror as the frenzied crowd closed in on him.

Suddenly, an oddly dressed old woman with a strong, beautiful face floated down like a dandelion seed. "Little Zokof, little town. How I miss you so," she sang, midair, to Pop in his window. He ignored her. She turned her attention to Nathan. She was coming closer when he woke up.

*   *   *

The next morning, a young man of about thirty, medium build, in a black leather jacket, approached Nathan as he sat over his fourth cup of coffee in the hotel café.

"Good morning, Professor Linden," he said pleasantly, with the bare hint of a bow. "I hope I am not too early for you. I am Tadeusz Staszyc, your driver. The car is in front, if you are ready." The young man stuck out his hand.

Nathan shook it. "Thank you for agreeing to drive me on such short notice," he said, thinking the boy's dark-blond shag could have used a wash. He followed Tadeusz across the sumptuous quietude of the marble lobby, through the revolving doors that pushed them unceremoniously into the gray haze, noise, and smell of Warsaw.

Nathan regarded Tadeusz's toy-size Peugeot and wondered whether he should sit in back like a taxi or in front.

"Please," said Tadeusz, motioning to the backseat. "You'll be more comfortable there." This pleased Nathan. In the backseat he could sink freely into his thoughts without feeling the need to keep up his end of a conversation.

Once seated behind the wheel, Tadeusz draped his arm casually over the front seat. A thick black digital watch hung from his hairless, pale wrist. "Where would you like to go?" he asked.

Until that moment, Nathan had planned to visit Kraków. But without even quite knowing why, he said, "I'm doing some research on your small towns. I was told Zokof would be a good choice. Do you know it?"

"Sure, it's between Radom and Lublin. About an hour-and-a-half drive. How long are you in Poland?"

"I'll be leaving tomorrow night," Nathan said, as distracted as he was amazed that the young man could drive him to Pop's hometown, the way some people are amazed that a jet can take them to the "Holy Land."

Tadeusz started the motor. "Two days in Poland and you want to be in Zokof?" He shrugged and edged the car into the traffic. "I could take you to Lublin, or better, Kraków. Beautiful medieval city, Kraków."

Nathan blinked rapidly, jittery from too much coffee and sorry for it. "I'm sure I'd like to see them both sometime," he said. They soon crossed a bridge over the Vistula to the Praga District, as Tadeusz informed him. He had to fight the dread that overwhelmed him when he saw the cement buildings, the primitive dirt footpaths, and the uncut grass. They hadn't even left Warsaw. What was he going to find in Zokof, some backwater mired in poverty and superstition? The place wasn't even listed in his guidebook.

Just outside the city, Tadeusz slowed to avoid a farmer in a horse-drawn wooden wagon. But for the rubber tires, Nathan thought, the wagons probably looked much the same in Pop's day. He again wondered anxiously about Zokof. As long as he could remember, the town had stood between him and Pop in a way that seemed different from other immigrant fathers and their sons. Other fathers placed proud hands on their American sons' shoulders and enchanted them with stories of hometowns whose names stuck in the throat. These men didn't become enraged at the mention of Poland, as Pop did.

It wasn't that Pop was cold or unloving. But Nathan always knew that some part of him was so distracted he couldn't seem to pay sufficient attention to America. And that distraction was felt most deeply by Nathan, his American son. It made him feel helpless and invisible. As a boy, he'd tried to get Pop's attention by working to make the highest grades in his class. He'd even made president of the debate club, shy as he was. But his successes never made much of an impression. Long after Nathan had become an internationally acclaimed professor of constitutional law at Harvard, Pop still referred to him as "mine son the meshuggener law teacher." When Nathan received a MacArthur Grant he'd said, "*Feh!* We had plenty of hair-splitters like you in Zokof. Teachers and rabbis, a *choleria* on them all! Not one knows from how to earn an honest day's living."

Nathan had gulped with humiliation and fury. He hadn't even bothered to tell his father that the grant came with a significant monetary award. "How can you compare me to a rabbi?" he'd snapped, blaming Zokof for his father's peculiar craziness.

But other times, Pop's passion about his hometown invited Nathan to come a little closer. In those magical, suspended encounters, the boy's questions and the father's answers felt like a tentative embrace.

"What was it like there in Poland?" the boy, Nathan, would begin.

"Slavery. It was slavery."

"Tell me about your town, Pop."

"What's to tell? It was a town. A few people, some buildings, the dogs the Polacks set on us. It was a town from nothing. A town you should never have to see. That's all I know."

"Did you have enough to eat there?"

"Eat? Bread and onions we ate. Soup."

"Chicken soup, like Mom makes?"

"*Agh!* What are you talking? If a poor man ate chicken in Zokof, one of them must have been sick."

"How was it when you came to America?"

"It was slavery."

"But better than Poland, right? In America, you had freedom."

"In America, Rockefeller has freedom. A worker like me has slavery. Capitalism is capitalism the whole world around," Pop would instruct with a twisted smile and a gentle, almost rabbinical wave of his hand that seemed intended, to young Nathan, as a gesture of fatherly love.

*T*hey were heading southeast on a two-lane highway out of Warsaw. "Are you from the Big Apple?" Tadeusz asked, lighting the first of a chain of cigarettes in a hand-cupping, one-eye-squinting, Marlboro Man style.

"I'm from Cambridge, Massachusetts," Nathan said, sniffing, irked by Tadeusz's slang because it reminded him that he could not converse without embarrassment in a foreign language. He smoothed his hair and caught sight of Tadeusz studying him in the rearview mirror. "What part of the country are you from?" Nathan said mildly.

"My family is near Katowice."

"What do they do there?"

"They're farmers, since the time of King Zygmunt II. You know, the great Polish king?"

Nathan stroked his chin thoughtfully and nodded, although he hadn't any idea of what King Zygmunt II's claim to fame had been. "What brought you to Warsaw?"

Tadeusz hissed a mouthful of smoke from between his teeth. "I wanted an education, to be a civil engineer. So my father let me go."

"He didn't want you to be a farmer like him?"

Tadeusz turned and gave Nathan a smile. "No. He said, 'Get educated.' He used to read books he took from a man he worked for. He didn't want me to sneak around like that."

Nathan gazed at a couple of black-and-white cows grazing in a field and thought it refreshing to hear of a farmer who hadn't been afraid to embrace his son's intellect.

"My father says sneaking is for Gypsies and Jews."

Nathan's hand dropped stiffly onto the door handle as if it had been knocked from his chin.

"But I don't know Jews," Tadeusz continued matter-of-factly. "There aren't many of them anymore. At least, not ones who call themselves Jews."

Nathan coughed nervously but couldn't resist asking, "What else would they call themselves?"

"They hide, like they did in the war. We don't know how many there really are. There could be thousands, maybe even millions. Our parents say they recognize them. A lot of them are in the Party, the Communist Party, yes? But mostly they're capitalists. My father always said, the Poles own the land but the Jews own the houses. It's a shame, really, but we never mixed well."

Nathan stared at the back of Tadeusz's head, stupefied, unsure how to, or even if he should, argue. The opinions being offered as fact were like deadly viruses that would simply mutate if he revealed himself as a Jew. He thought briefly of Załuski and said nothing.

"There's a lot of strange stories the old people tell about Jews," Tadeusz said, apparently oblivious to Nathan's discomfort. "My grandmother used to say they killed Christian children for their Easter bread."

"Jews don't kill Christian children," Nathan said, hoping to at least convey annoyance.

Tadeusz turned around and offered him a friendly look. "I don't say they do. *She* said it was in their religion. My grandmother said that when the Nazis came to our town, the Jews cried out, 'Let Christ's blood fall on our heads and on our sons' heads,' and they accepted their punishment."

Nathan tensed from his neck through his shoulders and down his back. He studied his reflection in the window, disgusted at his gratitude that his looks had always allowed him to hide. He yearned to know the strength of a man who could say to Tadeusz, "Here now, fellow. I am a Jew."

They were on Highway 7, the road to Radom. Neither driver nor passenger spoke. The flat Polish landscape, with its thin-striped fields of potatoes, cabbage, and corn plowed by horses and men in caps, rolled on mile after mile. In the early morning sun, the soft willows and poplars, forsythia and white-blossomed apple trees that crowded along the unfenced boundaries blew in unison. They passed a group of peasants gathered in the middle of a field. Nathan wondered, as he watched the village priest bless the earth, if the Christians realized they were following an ancient pagan rite.

14

NATHAN! WE ARE HERE! THESE FIELDS WHERE I CROSSED WITH your father on our flight to Radom. Here, we saw Nahum and his horse. There, your father slept beneath the trees and I had a vision of our town, of every man awakening to pray, generations I saw though not, God forgive me, the pogrom they had made in the night. Nathan, look! This is your Zokof!

When at last Tadeusz's car passed the black-and-white road sign to Zokof, Nathan rolled down the window and craned his neck for a fuller view of the town. The road was lined with willows and apple trees. A warm breeze, laden with the sweet smell of spring grass, rushed into the car and tousled his hair like the fingers of a fond old aunt.

Zokof began with a small white shed and a blue-gray wooden house at the edge of a field. After that, the two-lane highway narrowed to a main street of two- and three-story postwar houses, their casement windows hung with white curtain sheers. Each story, being constructed of different building materials — stone, brick, cinder block, or stucco — gave the impression that these houses had been built over a period of years.

They passed a man in a horse-drawn cart, a couple on foot, a young girl on a bicycle. From the shabbiness of their clothing, Nathan guessed the town had not enjoyed much prosperity in the new capitalist era. Near the main square, the already decaying postwar apartments rose to four stories, their balconies hung with plants and laundry. Tiny automobiles buzzed across the main street from narrow side lanes, but the town did not have a traffic light or even a stop sign.

"Where do you want to park?" Tadeusz asked.

Nathan pointed at the town's main square, with its war memorial in the center. "Over there." Decorative black chains trimmed each of the square's corners, but it seemed uncared-for, no more than a large patch of land cut diagonally with footpaths and dotted with small trees and trodden grass. From the far side of the square, the brick church's spire, a stiletto point atop an onion bulb, accented the town's otherwise flat skyline. Nathan wondered what Pop would have recognized about this place.

Tadeusz pulled the car onto the curb and turned off the motor. "Would you like me to come with you, to translate?"

Nathan got out of the car. "Perhaps a little later," he said, tired of coping with the tension the young man provoked in him. "Why don't you get an early lunch and meet me back here in an hour."

"Sure," said Tadeusz, locking the car door with one hand, searching for the extra pack of cigarettes in his pocket with the other.

Nathan crossed the street to get a closer look at the older buildings that lined the square, all of which had shops at street level. He wondered how much of the town had survived from Pop's era. At the corner, just before heading down a side street, he glanced back at Tadeusz, leaning against the car fender, smoking with the offhanded assurance of a native son.

For a quarter of an hour he wandered, not knowing what he was looking for. The stares of passersby made him feel his strangeness in their midst. Was it the stranger or the American they saw? he wondered. Or was it the Jew?

He walked on, scanning the street for clues about the past. A crow cawed from a nearby tree, then swooped crazily close to him and flew down a curved lane. The lane, with its low-slung sheds and shacks, was the only one that didn't conform to the town's gridlike streets.

Curious, he followed it until he came upon a small wooden house with a weathered, overhung roof. Moss crept unevenly up its unpainted walls, as if nature were already reclaiming it. Above the windows, the remains of a fiery red-orange paint peeled and furled.

A grass-scented breeze again blew against Nathan's face, surprising him. As he stared at the old house, certain that it dated from Pop's time, the front door opened. From the shadows of the doorway, a small, thin, quite elderly man slowly stepped out into the late-morning sun. His beard and long hair were the color of smoke, and the deep wrinkles around his enormous sagging eyes framed his face like barbed wire.

Nathan saw the yarmulke and the long gabardine coat. His heart began to hammer. Part of him wanted to draw back, repelled by such an extravagant show of religiosity.

Years ago, the mere sight of his niece, Laura, with a Star of David around her neck had had almost the same effect on him. "Since when have you felt the need to wear your religion around your neck?" he'd admonished her at a family dinner. His sister, Gertie, had given him a murderous look.

"I bought it because I'm proud of being Jewish," Laura had said, with all the pomposity that adolescence is capable of mustering.

Pop had been there. He'd laughed, cackled actually. "You think the world won't remind you you're a Jew?"

"Yeah, sure," Laura had said, seemingly impervious to the cut. But the next time he'd seen her, the Star of David was gone, although whether it was because of Pop or because she'd found another cause to make her proud of herself, Nathan never knew.

He studied the figure in the doorway. What kind of madman would dress like this in Poland? He was within feet of him now, about to pass by the house, when it occurred to him this might be the only remnant of Pop's world he would find in Zokof. It was a take-it-or-leave-it opportunity. But if he took it, how could they communicate? If the man spoke to him in Yiddish, he wouldn't be able to answer, even if he understood.

Then he remembered his regret at not having spoken with the men at the Nożyk Synagogue in Warsaw, and in a moment of inspired unselfconsciousness, he said the only word that came to him. *"Landsman."*

Because the word, with its connotations of tribal kinsmanship, was such an odd and difficult choice, Nathan pronounced it as softly as a confession. He'd always used a soft voice to dull whatever traces remained of his Brooklyn Jewish accent. Still, he felt out of character, alien to himself for having said it.

The old man regarded him carefully and nodded. Nathan nodded back, his equilibrium off again, as it had been in the lecture hall and in the Holy Cross Church in Warsaw. The man remained rooted to his place in the doorway.

"*Bist a Yid?* Are you a Jew?" The voice had a gruff quality that suggested impatience.

Nathan cringed at that word, *Yid.* He could barely stand to answer in the affirmative, to call himself the equivalent of a spic, a nigger, a wop. But the man seemed to require some kind of confirmation before he would go on.

"Yes," he said tightly. "Do you speak English?"

"A *bissel,* yeh."

Nathan was deeply relieved. "That's wonderful," he said. "Where did you learn it? Here? I would think German, Russian, perhaps, but not English."

"I learned what I had to learn," the old man said impatiently. "We have

Voice of America, BBC. I read lots of books, yeh? What else is for me to do? You from America?"

Nathan was glad for the opportunity to explain himself. "Yes, I am," he said, with unaccustomed eagerness. "I'm a professor of constitutional law at Harvard University in Cambridge, Massachusetts. Actually, I was invited here to lecture at Warsaw University. They gave me a car and a driver so that I could see a little of the country."

"The government sent you?"

"I'm working with your government to develop a constitution," Nathan said, surprised that his account seemed to anger the old man.

"Government," he scoffed. "I have no government. What for did they send you here?"

"They didn't send me."

"Then why do you come to a town like this?"

Nathan was taken aback by the man's coldness, by his suspicion. But then, he had never spoken to a religious Jew before. He'd always assumed such men — other than the violent zealots who lived in Israel's West Bank settlements — were docile because they kept to themselves, because they never looked up to meet the eyes of strangers. He took this as a sign of weakness, that they must live in fear of the next assault.

"Nu?" the Jew said impatiently.

"I don't understand."

"What's to understand? I asked a simple question. Why have you come here?" The old man glared at him like an angry teacher who had been given the wrong response and resented having to repeat the question.

Nathan's chest contracted in alarm at the man's tone, and at his own inability to articulate his thoughts or the seriousness of his purpose, much less to impress the man with his credentials. He gave it another shot. "I thought I'd try to get some feeling of my roots."

"Feeling? Gottenu! What's wrong with you? What does feeling got to do with it? Feel you're a Jew? You're a Jew or you're not a Jew. That's that."

The old man spoke with such force, Nathan was afraid to question him further. He waited a moment, hoping the man's anger would abate.

"I suppose I also came to see my father's birthplace," he offered.

"Who is your father?"

"Isaac Leiber."

The old man seemed to take offense. "*Isaac?* What is *Isaac?* Itzik!"

"Yes," Nathan said, recalling the name his mother used when her husband displeased her. "My grandfather was a rag peddler," he added, frustrated that he didn't know his own grandfather's name.

But the old man showed no sign of recognizing the name Leiber, which gave Nathan the numb, disorienting sense that he was an orphan, that his lineage began in Brooklyn. "Maybe they were here and you just didn't know them," he suggested hopefully. "My father left in 1906, when he was fourteen years old."

A few crows cawed from a distance. The old man seemed to sag a little. He looked down at his feet and took a deep breath. "I know who was your father. You been to the cemetery?"

Nathan shook his head, no longer knowing what to expect from this man.

"A Jewish grave is a sacred trust," the old man said. "'Generation to generation,' it is written in the holy books. You must honor our cemetery. Come with me." Stepping from the doorsill, he grabbed Nathan roughly by the forearm and began to lead him out of the alley.

"Where are we going?"

"To visit the graves. That's what you came here for, isn't it?"

Nathan wrested his arm from the old man's tight grip. He resented being made to feel like a truant schoolboy, and he hated cemeteries. He'd never even been back to his father's grave after the funeral. "Look, I'd rather meet the living than the dead. I'd rather see a bit of the town," he said.

The old man scowled. "Living? Who's left living here? They're all gone. Who's left is in the cemetery." He pulled again at Nathan's arm, but Nathan resisted so much he had to let go.

"Why are you here?" the man demanded. "You want to collect the names of the last Jews of Zokof to give to the government? That's what they asked you to do?"

"Why would they ask me to do that?"

The old man was simply furious. "To erase us from the ledger, like they erased three million. Don't you know, Leiber? The Poles are worse than the Germans. They've never settled their accounts with us." He shot Nathan a piercing look and raised his hand to his beard.

Stunned, Nathan watched the fingers, curled and thickened with age and arthritis, disappear into the smoky strands.

"You want to see your roots, Leiber? I'll show you roots. Come with me," the old man commanded.

A farm truck rumbled past at the far end of the alley.

"Come with me," he repeated, his voice stern, authoritative.

Nathan hesitated. "I don't understand this. With all due respect, I don't care to see the cemetery. Why do you insist?"

"I am Rafael Bergson, the head of the *Chevra Kaddisha* of Zokof. The Burial Society, you say in English. There is no other position for me. We don't have a shul. I am the leader of a community of one."

"You're the last Jew in Zokof?" Nathan couldn't believe it.

The old man nodded slowly. "Before the war, we were five thousand souls. Five thousand of us and five thousand Poles. Now it's their town, like we were never here. Even in the cemetery." His voice trailed off. "Ach!" he burst out, waving his hand against the still air as if to push aside an annoying pest. "Come, I will show you."

Nathan, sensing that Rafael Bergson would not relent in this matter, bent his head in submission. "It's far to walk," Rafael said. "Where is your driver?"

That's all he needed, Nathan thought, to walk up to Tadeusz and have to explain why he wanted to go to a Jewish cemetery. His teeth ground familiarly against one another, producing an ache that could not distract him from the debacle that was about to take place. "The car's in the town square, but the driver isn't there. I told him to get some lunch." He was frantic.

"We'll go first to Jerzy."

"I thought you said you were the last Jew?"

"Yeh. Jerzy's a Pole. A good man, a mensch. If he's at home, he'll take us in his car."

Relieved beyond all reason, Nathan allowed himself to be led a block from the main square, into a cement apartment building whose ground floor and balconies were painted a faded yellow. Every balcony had a different type of railing, and each of them had been woven with a different colored material, presumably to give their owners more privacy. But instead of lending a measure of gaiety, as they might in a Latin country, Nathan thought the colors here merely added to the aura of dirt and decay that seemed the hallmark of modern Polish architecture.

A woman wearing a blue-flowered smock over her housedress hung her wash over the balcony railing on the second floor. She stared down at the two men, taking in every detail about them. But she said nothing. Didn't even nod.

Rafael walked slowly to the end of the apartment's dark entry corridor. A baby babbled. A television announcer's voice boomed through a closed door. The hall was dusty, the walls a patchwork of rutted cracks. He tapped on a door at the back, softly, as if not to alarm the residents within. When no response came he slowly turned, and to Nathan's great discomfort announced, "We'll use your driver."

15

Tadeusz had left Zokof's main square, but Nathan's re-lief was short-lived. Almost everyone he and Rafael encountered stared at them with disturbing intensity. Some returned his nods, but not one of them responded to his smiles, modest as they were. He checked his watch ceremoniously, as much for the time as to publicly indicate that his presence would, by necessity, be brief. "It's eleven thirty. I have no way to find my driver for another half hour," he said. "We should wait for your friend to return home."

Rafael shrugged, not with resignation, Nathan thought, but like a man who knew he had the upper hand. "It's not such a big town. If he's a Pole, he's at an inn," he said. "Come. We will find him." The subtle lift of his brow seemed to suggest amusement at Nathan's discomfort.

Nathan had never been less charmed by the singsong cadences of a Yid-dish accent, which he had always found coarse and embarrassingly overfa-miliar.

"Come," Rafael repeated. He pointed to the far side of the square and suggested they cut across. At the war memorial in the center, wreaths of fresh flowers had been laid before the bronze soldier holding a cross.

Just off the square, Rafael stopped in front of a rough cement building. Three or four bicycles leaned against the outside wall. "In here." He pulled Nathan by the sleeve into a filthy, undecorated room. Shouting drunken men careened into one another across the open floor, dull-eyed, faces red with the bloom of intoxication. The place stank of sweat, cigarettes, and beer.

Nathan's fear at the sight of so many men unleashed by alcohol was magnified by what Rafael's religious garb might provoke in them. He was as frantic and ashamed as a man being made to walk naked in public. He felt certain the men would surround him and Rafael. He saw himself on the floor, crawling to the door, the innkeeper turning his back. The disgrace of it, the indignity. His skin was on fire, as if he were being horsewhipped.

Pop! he cried inwardly. *I came back. God, why?* Instinctively, he retreated to the wall, terrified of impending violence.

Rafael stood a few steps inside the door, patiently waiting for Nathan to identify his driver. Despite his fear, Nathan took a look at the old man. He had to admit, there was something almost noble about the way Rafael met the gaze of every person who approached him. Since meeting Rafael, Nathan had regarded him merely as an unenlightened version of secular Jews like Pop, who had outgrown the superstitious religion of the shtetl. But Pop had never been as strong a presence as this man.

From across the room, a heavyset Pole, his features stretched across his face as if someone were pulling at his cheeks, swerved toward Nathan. "My driver's not here," Nathan said. He seized Rafael by the arm and rushed them both out the door before the man could accost them.

Outside, Rafael calmly turned to Nathan. "Then we try the other inn, Leiber."

Nathan couldn't tell if Rafael meant this as a test or a taunt. He only knew the man, a complete stranger, had seen how frenzied fear made him. "Look, I'm sure my driver will be back soon. I suggest we go to the square and wait for him," he said quickly.

Again, Rafael shrugged. They returned to the square and waited against the car's locked doors.

Minutes later, Tadeusz sauntered over. He barely glanced at Rafael. "Found what you were looking for?" he asked evenly.

Nathan thought to make introductions, but then remembered the old man's paranoia. Besides, what could he say? What possible professional reason could he give for keeping company with an Orthodox Jew? Worse, how could he explain why the old man addressed him as "Leiber"?

When Rafael had first called him this, Nathan had been too embarrassed to correct him, hadn't wanted to expose himself to scorn for having Anglicized his name. But he'd begun to feel an odd camaraderie the name conferred on him in Rafael's eyes. *Leiber,* not *Linden,* gave him legitimacy, like a password to Pop's world. He held on to it now, like a talisman. "Please take us to the place this man will direct you," he said, deciding not to explain anything.

Tadeusz nodded perfunctorily, as if he and Nathan had not spoken during their ride to Zokof.

Slowly, heavily, Rafael folded himself into the left backseat of the tiny Peugeot and pulled his long coat in with him. Nathan followed. When they were both settled, Tadeusz gave Nathan a quick glance in the rearview mirror and lit a cigarette. He squinted into his outdoor rearview mirror, raced the motor, and sent the car lurching off the curb. No apology was offered.

Nathan wondered if Tadeusz was acting out of embarrassment at what he'd said, or if he was angry at Nathan for letting him go on about Jews. The young man kept working at his cigarette with quick, aggressive drags, apparently trying for an appearance of indifference about Rafael. For his part, Rafael seemed equally intent on ignoring Tadeusz.

Despite his uneasiness, Nathan saw something childish, almost comical, about two grown men refusing to look each other in the face, as if afraid of what they might say. He settled nervously into his seat. Rafael looked straight ahead, hands on his knees. They drove on in silence, punctuated only by Rafael's terse directions in Polish. He led Tadeusz out of town, in the opposite direction from where Nathan had come. To his right, Nathan saw a maze of vertical lines that were the trunks of young birch and pine trees. The slender trunks, lit through the lacy canopy above, struck him as somehow delicate, almost feminine, not at all like an American wilderness.

After about a quarter of a mile, they turned left onto a dirt road. On their right, a rye field swayed, open and buoyant with sun. On their left, more birch and pines. "Stop here," Rafael said in English.

I had been afraid to come here, to see nothing changed, the stones criss-crossed in a dome over our House of the Living, our cemetery. As I feared, as I knew, God had not forgiven me. Nathan's return had not moved a single stone.

*N*athan fairly leaped from the car, only to feel embarrassed by his obvious haste to escape Tadeusz's domain. He reached for the keloid scar at the back of his head and thought he heard the sound of horse hooves. Startled, he spun around. A peasant, seated on a horse-drawn wagon, squinted down at him from under the brim of his gray cap. Nathan stared back. Involuntarily, his hands balled up, as he found himself unable to break free of the man's insolent stare. The peasant raised his reins. Nathan threw his arms up protectively.

"*Geyyah!*" the peasant yelled hoarsely. The horse jolted forward, and the wagon's wheels grumbled with the sound of earth and rocks being crushed beneath them. The peasant never took his eyes off Nathan, who slowly lowered his arms with all the dignity he could muster.

To Nathan's chagrin, Rafael appeared to be smirking. "He thinks you are here to make a claim on his property," he said. "His daughter lives in Yaacov Hertzberg's house in town. He is afraid a rich American Hertzberg will come back and make trouble. Come." He shuffled around Tadeusz's car, grasped Nathan's arm, and led him slowly across the road to a narrow forest opening strewn with broken bottles. Nathan stepped carefully over the debris and was surprised to see a long, weed-choked path of large stone pavers stretching deep into the woods. He glanced around in confusion and wondered if this was the cemetery itself or the way to the cemetery. He looked back at the car. Tadeusz sat rigidly in the driver's seat, staring straight ahead, as if contemplating his next move. "Wait for us here," he called to Tadeusz. But he wondered if he would.

Uneasily, he followed Rafael down the path. A loud caw, followed by three or four others, echoed from above. He looked up at the great canopy of the tall, thin-limbed trees. Scores of twiggy, round crows' nests hung like huge dust motes from the uppermost branches. The cawing intensified, harsh, coarse, and guttural. The birds swooped from tree to tree, their two-foot wingspans setting up waves of clattery motion in the branches.

A single lamppost rose from the green underbrush, a solitary indicator that nature had once been dominated here by the will of man. The path led to a paved circle from which other stone paths unevenly radiated, like the bent spokes of an abandoned wheel. Two scrawny dogs, heads and tails hanging, loped by and disappeared into the foliage.

Rafael stopped at the central circle and observed Nathan carefully. "This is the Jewish cemetery of Zokof," he said.

"Where are the gravestones?"

"There are no gravestones. What the Nazis didn't destroy, the Communists took to build roads and walls. *Farshtaist?* Understand?"

Nathan was too shocked to reply.

"What? This surprises you, Leiber? Where have you been?"

"I had no idea it would look like this," Nathan said. He thought of Mount Zion Cemetery, where his father was buried, a city of the dead that stretched for miles over prime Queens real estate, overlooking smokestacks and billboards with ads for Coppertone sunscreen and Dominic's

Auto Service. He hated Mount Zion, with its specific Jewish reference, its long rows of stones sticking out like so many taunting tongues.

But here, the very absence of Jewish gravestones made him realize the pettiness of his dislike for Pop's resting place. *"Tah! Tah!"* the crows screamed back and forth above, denying even silence to the dead.

Rafael pointed his two twisted forefingers to the earth. "What they did here doesn't change *bubkes*. This ground is sacred for eternity. Bodies of pious people are resting here! Men over there." He pointed to the left. "Women over here."

He fixed his gaze on a small pile of stones about thirty feet away. "Some of them rest, eh, mine Freidl?" he muttered.

Nathan held his tongue, presuming Freidl was Rafael's deceased wife.

Rafael cleared his throat and turned abruptly back to Nathan. "The Poles say magicians are buried under the gravestones that used to be here. They say the stones were covered with 'strange codes.' That's what they call the Hebrew letters." He shook his head disdainfully. "It's been less than fifty years, Leiber. The stones are gone, but these meshuggeners have turned us into their own fairy tale."

"They *actually* believe in magic?" Nathan said.

"Ach!" Rafael responded with yet another dismissive wave of his hand. "They *actually* believed we put poison in their church bread, the bread they call the Host. I ask you, do *we* care what they eat in church? They make up these stories, Leiber, so they won't be haunted by us, or by truth."

"Which truth would that be?" Nathan asked, indulging in his old professorial trick of denying the objectivity of truth.

Rafael held up his hands in fists. "The truth that we used to be their neighbors." His thumb shot out, signifying he counted this as the number one truth. "They called us by name." He raised his forefinger. "They knew our children." Another finger. "They bought our goods. They sold us food from their fields. They shared with us our daily life in this town. And then . . . out like a light, Leiber. Out like a light. They let the darkness take us all. On purpose they forgot our names. That's the truth." The fingers of Rafael's hands splayed out before him, pointing their indictment to the heavens.

For several minutes the two of them stood together, silenced by a renewed round of screeching from above. The agitation of the crows was palpable now. The black birds hung from the branches, waiting.

Rafael lowered his hands and walked slowly to the pile of stones.

Nathan followed, nonplussed. He wondered how many of his ancestors were buried here. He couldn't name even one, having long ago given up trying to get any information out of his father. Over the years, Pop's refusal to discuss his life in Poland had simply worn Nathan down. Even as a kid, he knew he wouldn't get anywhere if he asked about his relatives. Perhaps this was why he regarded genealogy as a hobby for people who had no serious interest in history, who reduced it to the merely personal. Genealogy was for nostalgic aristocrats like Załuski, he thought, people who hoped to bootstrap greatness to themselves through the imagined noble exploits of their forefathers.

Still, he couldn't help wondering, what were their names, those other Leibers who came before him and Pop? He turned to Rafael, thinking he might enlist his assistance to research the Leibers' history in Zokof. Perhaps there was something in the city records. The thought gave him the distance he needed from the oddness of his present situation. He toed the earth with the tip of his shoe and tried to calm himself, retreating from the disturbing well of anger at Pop that so often churned his gut. His father had had a secret, that much he knew. There was too much rage. Why didn't he even have a picture of his parents, like the one Marion's mother had of her parents, somber as can be, sitting in their silver frame on the mantel with their shoes sticking out from their stiff clothes, scuffed and black?

"You want to know about my father?" Pop would glare at him whenever the boy Nathan asked. "My father was a no-goodnik you shouldn't know from. What's to know from a man who doesn't make an honest living for his family? A man who wastes his time in shul instead of putting bread on the table. Such a man, who left his family and never came back, you don't have to know. May his name be blotted out."

They'd reached the little pile of stones marking the grave of the woman Rafael had called Freidl. By then, Nathan was trying to reconcile Pop's rejection of his father's religiousness with the performance he gave every Passover. "You want I should come to your Seder? What for?" Pop would demand, his English sputtering out like a candle, making way for the fiery Yiddish that took its place. "A Seder is for the lazy no-goodniks who want to tell fairy tales."

"But, Pop, you're the only one who can read the Hebrew," Nathan's sister, Gertie, would plead.

"From my childhood I know Hebrew from that stinking *melamed* that drove it into me from when I was three years old. But from my head, as a thinking person, I know something else."

Every year Pop would refuse to participate in the telling of the story of exodus from slavery in Egypt, the *Haggadah*. But the grandchildren, Ellen and Gertie's Laura and Josh, would clamor for him to read the Hebrew. They had a fascination, somehow, for the sound of the language. Maybe they were hungry for the religious education their parents hadn't given them. Every year, on the pretext that he couldn't refuse his grandchildren, Pop complied.

Like a shaman, he would begin the incantation he knew by heart. After about three or four minutes, he would lay the book back on the table and begin to cry. The family would sit transfixed, watching the tears flow down the lines of his cheeks until they dropped off his jowls into his lap. When he finished his recitation, he would pull his large white handkerchief from his trouser pocket and wipe his lashless eyes dry. Then he would look at his family in silence, as if he were a foreign child among strangers.

Everyone but Nathan came to regard Pop's tears as part of the service, as eagerly anticipated by the children as Elijah's visit for his cup of wine. For Nathan, tears that came from a childhood his father wouldn't discuss with him felt like rejection. So he interrupted these moments by clearing his throat and calling on the next person to read.

"Maybe he's just sad about not believing in God anymore," Ellen had suggested one year as the two of them turned out the lights at the end of the evening.

"He wouldn't cry about that," Nathan had muttered.

But now he was not so sure. He recalled Załuski's words of two nights before. *How do you know who you are if you don't know where your family came from?* At the time, the question had seemed tinny and clichéd. But since he had come to Zokof, propelled by mere casual curiosity, he felt the vastness of a loneliness he could not name, the disconnection his father's rejection of his God had somehow caused for him. He wondered if a connection was even possible anymore. What did he know of the things that drove the lives of his family generations before? He didn't know enough about their God to cry for his loss as Pop had. He didn't know about God at all. He'd been a seed tossed on a foreign shore, left to grow wild by his own father. "Damn him," he said, under his breath.

And yet Nathan felt a sweet tug in his heart at the thought that people who lay buried here, halfway around the world from the place he called home, surely shared the same genetic propensity for long, tapered toes and narrow-bridged noses that he had inherited from Pop and had passed on to Ellen. He took a deep breath of the forest's penetrating smell.

What *are* their names, Pop? he thought. Did you think I'd become religious if you told me their names? Were you that uncertain a socialist that you had to make your family disappear?

A group of older Poles ambled down the path toward them, murmuring softly, nodding to one another as kindred souls do. They skirted Nathan and Rafael carefully, averting their eyes when Rafael said, in Polish, "It is written in the Talmud that a cemetery should not be used as a shortcut." When he repeated this in English, Nathan was horrified, but also impressed at the risks the old man took in provoking his neighbors.

He looked down at his plaid shirt, blue tie, and Timberland shoes. Anywhere but in Poland these clothes and his mundane face simply identified him as an American. Just an American, not "the Jew" he felt he'd become here, a tag that had affixed itself to him. The more he tried to pull away from it, the more it stuck, making him feel like a specimen, a bug on a board.

He took in an uneven breath and wished he were home, safe among the harmless squalls of academia. But when he remembered his dream of Załuski in Harvard Square, dressed up as the Hassid doll, pointing at him, trapping him with that accusatory scale of gold, he knew Cambridge would never again be an entirely safe haven.

Rafael raised his head. "It's time to say *El Molei Rachamim* for her. She must rest." He swept his arm in an arc around the cemetery, a gesture Nathan took to mean that the prayer was for every Jew buried there. Rest? The dead are dead, he thought. He felt a hot wave of embarrassment break over his face at the idea of taking part in a primitive religious ritual. He didn't know any prayers, and he'd be damned if he was going to make an ass of himself in front of passersby just to satisfy an old Jew. There, he'd said it, *that* word, even if only in the privacy of his head. Not the genteel *Jewish,* but *Jew.* Immediately, he felt deeply ashamed.

"I thought the prayer for the dead is called *Kaddish,*" he said, hoping to steer the discussion on to a more rational plane.

Rafael stared, as if unsure Nathan could be this ignorant. "Kaddish? A

Jew doesn't say Kaddish without a *minyan,* ten men." Something about Nathan's blank expression must have convinced Rafael he didn't understand the distinction, because his tone softened as he explained, "*Kaddish* means *holy.* It is an ancient prayer, Aramaic, a prayer in praise of God."

"Then why is it said at funerals?" Nathan asked, remembering how Lou Gersh had stepped forward and said it for Pop.

"Because at the funeral a man might think to blame God, reject God for the loss. But at such times he needs to remember what God has given us and to praise Him, out loud, with others. Kaddish a son says for his father, every day for eleven months after his death. Saying Kaddish for the father shows a man has done his work well, raised a son worthy of his name."

Nathan nodded, painfully aware that Rafael knew he had not done this for his father.

Rafael stroked his beard. "El Molei Rachamim is the prayer for the dead. You know what's meant by 'sacrificing to the idols'?"

The question seemed a non sequitur to Nathan, but he grabbed it, hoping to forestall reciting El Molei Rachamim. "No, I've never heard the expression."

Rafael nodded. "One of the great Talmudic masters, Rabbi Bunam of Pzhysha, said, 'When a devout and righteous man sits at table with others and would like to eat a little more but does not because of what people might think of him — that is sacrificing to the idols.'"

"I see," Nathan said.

"What do you see?" Rafael demanded.

"That . . . I . . . well . . ." Nathan looked away, thinking, Damn it, he's playing me for the schoolboy again.

"It means it doesn't matter if there are two Poles in here, defiling this cemetery like it was their park, or two hundred. It doesn't matter if they look at you like you're a meshuggener. They all think I'm a madman. What does it matter? It only matters that you do what a Jew has to do, whether you believe in your God or not. You say El Molei Rachamim for your Jews who lie buried here. Generation upon generation of them, flesh of your flesh, bone of your bones. Have you no respect? They haven't been defiled enough? Say your prayer, Leiber. That's what you came here for, isn't it?" The hard look of suspicion returned to his face.

Nathan's cheeks burned with the shame he suffered when he felt a teacher's disapproval. It always made him want to work harder, achieve more. Looking up at the trees, he felt trapped in the birdcage cemetery. How could he satisfy this man while retaining some semblance of his own integrity? His eyes fluttered down to the pile of stones at their feet. *A Jewish woman is buried there,* he thought. *Her stone, with her name on it, has been destroyed. She could be a Leiber, for all I know. Maybe I could do this, a show of respect for Pop's world, for everything they destroyed.* The raucous cawing of the crows continued. "What a strange sound," he said.

"Phff!" Rafael spat. "Those birds scare the Zokofers plenty. They think they're the voices of our dead. They come here at night with bottles of vodka. Over there, at the entrance, they get *shikkered* and make wishes. They're afraid to come inside after dark."

"Why?" Nathan was intrigued by what might frighten the Poles about an empty cemetery and astonished at the idea that they would wish for something from Jews.

"Because every one of them knows the story about Freidl. They're afraid of her ghost. She scares them even more than the magicians." The hint of a smile crossed Rafael's face.

"Who is Freidl?" The crude pile of stones hardly looked like a grave marking, much less the home of a ghost.

Rafael's face fell like a clump of earth. "Are you really Itzik Leiber's son?"

Nathan's heart leaped when Rafael said his father's name. "Of course I am." Feeling slightly annoyed with himself for not having thought of it sooner, he reached into his coat pocket and handed Rafael the photocopy he'd made of a cardboard-mounted sepia photograph. "This is a picture of my father just before he left Poland. I found it in the strongbox in his bedroom wardrobe after he died."

He pointed to the writing on the bottom of the card. "Here's the name and address of the photographer. Pesha Goldman, 23 Nalewki, Warsaw." He looked up at Rafael. "Do you recognize him?"

Rafael cradled the photograph between his hands and stared at it for a long time. Then he closed his eyes, tilted back his head, and began to hum a disjointed tune. His body swayed in concentration.

Nathan was afraid to interrupt him.

Finally, the old man straightened, opened his eyes, and turned the photograph toward the pile of stones. "God is merciful, Freidl." Nodding approvingly, he handed the photograph back to the startled Nathan. "It is enough. *Dayenu.*"

Nathan didn't know what to say. The man before him seemed to be on speaking terms with a woman who had known his father more than eighty years ago. Had he been driven mad by living as the last of his kind in a town that was clearly hostile to him? He touched Rafael's arm. "Please understand, my father never told me anything about his life in Poland. He was very secretive about it. He never mentioned a woman named Freidl. I don't even know the names of my relatives buried here."

Rafael looked wounded. He seemed to be struggling to compose himself. Finally, he said, "So, Leiber, you must do better than he did. You must finish what he left unfinished. She must rest. It is your duty as Itzik's son to help Freidl rest."

"What did my father have to do with this woman? Who is she?"

"Later, Leiber. I'll explain later, when it's over. When you have said your prayer and we can say Dayenu."

Nathan mulled over the word *Dayenu,* which he recognized from the song the family sang at their Passover Seder. *Dai-dai-yenu,* they would chorus, over and over, because they didn't know the Hebrew stanzas. He remembered that when Pop was alive, he never sang it with them. "That word, *Dayenu,*" he said. "It means *it is enough for us,* isn't that right?"

Rafael nodded. "For the rabbis, this is a special word, *Dai.* They say when we look at the name of God, Shaddai, it is really two words. *Sha,* which means *that,* or *that says,* and *Dai,* which means *enough.* Together, it means that ours is the God who says enough. He is a God who defines by walls, the beach that separates the water from the land, the six hundred thirteen commandments he gave to the Jews to bind them to His law, and the wall separates us from Eden, where there is the tree of eternal life. The rabbis say it is the walls that define us."

"Interesting," Nathan said, professorial again.

"But not so interesting as what you want me to tell you about Itzik, yeh?"

Nathan smiled. "Yeh."

Rafael turned his palms upward, resignedly. "So sit," he said, pointing to what appeared to be the remnants of a stone wall, fifteen or twenty steps away. His command, authoritative but inviting, comforted Nathan. It reminded him of his beloved law professor Irwin Feingold, preparing to do battle with an idea in the Jewish way, indifferent to chivalrous conventions. And like Feingold, Rafael shared with his student a sweet, conspiratorial look.

Nathan, feeling more in control standing than sitting, braced one leg against the stones. A sharp rod of restless anticipation jabbed at his gut. That great luminous wall of glass that Pop had stood behind all his life, which had reflected but refused entrance to his son, was about to be shattered. And he, Nathan, was going to splinter that glass with his questions until he'd broken a hole big enough to let the stagnant Polish air out. And let him in.

16

*T*HE TWO OR THREE FEET OF STONE WALL TO WHICH RAFAEL HAD pointed had almost been reclaimed by lichen and moss. Rafael seated himself slowly and tamped the earth to set his footing. His black shoes were dirty and scuffed. The rays of the noontime sun shone on his long black coat, revealing that it too was worn. Nathan glanced at the cuffs, the unraveling threads and the frayed material beneath, and could hardly stand to imagine what it would be like to live as an uncared-for man.

"There is a story they tell in Zokof about a farmer called Jan Nowak," Rafael began, his voice gruff but vigorous. "The Nowaks were here since the days when they belonged to the landowners. Rough people, illiterates, you understand?"

Nathan understood. But he hoped Rafael would quickly get to the point because he was acutely aware that his time in the cemetery was being measured on Tadeusz's clock.

"The Nowaks were not just another peasant family. Jan Nowak's father, Karol, was famous all over Poland. One day, plowing his field, he said he heard a voice. It told him to go to the Tatra Mountains. This from a man who had never left Zokof in his life. But he went. When he came back to Zokof, he said the Virgin Mary appeared to him in the mountains. He said she gave him a wooden cross to wear around his neck. Naturally, people believed him."

Nathan affected that special skeptical look he'd perfected from years of teaching.

"What, Leiber?" Rafael snapped at him. "So you don't believe. A Virgin Mary and a cross is nothing by us. But let me tell you, a story like this you don't dismiss either. It has a life of its own."

Nathan hadn't expected that his skepticism would so offend Rafael. "I'm sorry. Go on," he urged, relieved to know Rafael understood that the story's importance lay in its context, not in some literal belief.

"After Karol died, Jan wore the cross. One night, when Jan and his wife rode home in their wagon, people say he came upon the devil himself.

Only that night, the devil was disguised as a fire inside a lantern — a lantern, I should tell you, carried by three Jewish children."

The collision of the words *devil* and *three Jewish children* took Nathan by surprise. "What did you say?" he asked.

Rafael turned his attention to the tips of his scuffed black shoes. "It is said that the children danced around the lantern, called out prayers to the devil in tongues. Jan raised his whip. 'In the name of the Father, the Son, and the Holy Ghost,' he said. Then he beat the children without mercy, until they dropped the lantern. Jan reached for it, to smash it and put out the evil flame. But the devil was too quick for him. He jumped from the fire and turned himself into a young Jew. The Jew grabbed Jan by the arm and threw him beneath the wheels of his own wagon. The horse bolted, pulled the wheels over Jan's head, and killed him."

Nathan thought this sounded like a Sholom Aleichem story. He was intrigued that Pop had really lived in a world like that. But he was also feeling edgy at the time being lost.

"All this time," Rafael continued, "Jan's wife stayed in the wagon. She said the Jew tore the cross from Jan's neck. She said he spoke in the devil's tongue and howled with joy when he broke the cross in half. Then he ran here to this cemetery."

"Is this kind of story common in Poland?" Nathan asked.

Rafael glared at him. "Stop with the questions, Leiber, and listen to what I'm telling you."

Chastened, Nathan held his tongue.

"When the people from town heard about Jan's death, they gathered to avenge him. They lost their fear of the magicians buried below. They followed the sound of the boy's howling to this cemetery. They looked everywhere, but the Jew had vanished. In his place, a menacing old Jewess appeared over her gravestone, which lay broken in two. She chased the townspeople from the cemetery. They say one brave peasant grabbed the top part of her gravestone, on which her name was written, and carried it out. He thought if he smashed the stone, he could destroy her. But the spirit pulled the stone from his arms. It fell into a stream, where it was covered with leaves and lost. They say that gravestone is why the stream dried up and that the old Jewess's spirit is still here in Zokof."

"That's quite a story," Nathan said patiently. "But what does it have to do with my father?"

"Quite a story, you call it? Yeh. Every mother and father in Zokof knows it by heart. To their children they say, 'Watch out, the old Jewess will come for you in the night!'"

Nathan laughed.

But Rafael was angry. "What? You think this is some kind of game we're playing here, Leiber? I read the papers from Warsaw. You American Jews come to Poland to dig around for roots. This is no museum for you to pretend everything is in the past. Let me tell you, nothing is past in Poland. For us, the past is more unfinished here than anywhere else. Here, every story has a consequence. Understand?" He rose unsteadily and rubbed his temples with both hands as he took a few steps in the tangled underbrush. "Oy, Gottenu," he said, then sighed.

"Look," Nathan said, "I don't deny that people retell myths about their past, it's just that I want to find out more about my father's life." But he was shaken at hearing the word *Gottenu* again. The last time he'd heard it was at Holy Cross Church in Warsaw.

Rafael wound his fingers into his beard. "Then listen to what I will tell you, Leiber. The boy, the one they say had the devil in him. *Him,* the Zokofers remember especially. His name was Itzik Leiber."

Nathan stared. "My father?"

"Yes. He was here! Your father."

"In this cemetery?"

"In this cemetery. On the night Jan died. Yeh. The only question to ask now is, is there any truth in it? I told you the Polish story. Now I will tell you the Jewish story, as it was told to me."

Nathan, not knowing what else to do, sank onto the bough of the fallen tree and waited.

"The Jews always began the story like this." Rafael held up his hands, as if about to conduct an orchestra. "When Itzik Leiber's father abandoned his family, the boy drove the rabbis from his mother's house. People said it was because the father, Mordechai the Ragman, beat his wife for the whole town to see, but made a *tsimmes* of his piety. In time, they called the boy Itzik the Faithless One."

"That's him!" Nathan said, proud that his father had earned a nickname in town, although he couldn't imagine Pop actually throwing a rabbi out of the house. The man he knew ranted and railed against rabbis, put on a real performance for the family, but only behind closed doors.

Rafael again studied the tips of his shoes. "Everyone knew the Leibers didn't have two kopeks to put together. But after Mordechai left, Itzik refused help for his family from the shul. Imagine!"

Nathan may have been shocked that his grandfather was a wife beater, but he was not surprised that his father would not take help from the shul. When Nathan was a boy, his father had refused help from the shul during a bakers' strike. His mother had to accept the money in secret and put it into her "private account," as she called it. Nathan had called it her "protection from Pop" money.

Rafael looked at him. "Now, my legal scholar from Harvard University, tell me, what *should* a Jew think of a man like Mordechai the Ragman, who boasts of his devotion to God but violates his obligation to his family?"

Nathan thought about it. "I'd think he was a hypocrite. But" — he frowned — "I'm not a religious man. It would be my guess that religious people would think his first obligation was to God."

"Then they'd be fools, like your grandfather," Rafael retorted. "Listen to me, Leiber, pride in piety is a sin in the eyes of God. A Jew's obligation to his fellow man is higher than his obligation even to God! God is not diminished by your failure to observe His Sabbath or to keep a kosher home. If a man sins against his children, who is made unholy? God?"

"That's a Jewish belief?" Nathan asked. He'd never given much thought to the relationship a man was supposed to have with God.

Rafael nodded. "There is a proverb. Proverb twenty-two. It says, 'Teach a child in the way he should go, and even when he grows old he will not depart from it.'"

Four or five caws echoed overhead. Rafael stroked his beard. "Mordechai Leiber practiced the worst kind of impiety," he said. "He made his son hate God. A child learns more from deeds than words."

"Actually, he made Pop an atheist," Nathan said.

"Your father was no atheist, Leiber. He was angry. His father was a hypocrite. But he didn't deny God."

Nathan was incensed. "How do you know? He was *my* father. As long as I can remember he always said there is no God." Of this, he was certain. But he was no longer sure what Pop may have secretly believed. The image of him slumped tearfully at the Seder table haunted him now. He put his finger on the bridge of his nose and adjusted his glasses, trying to ward off the sense that he had been dragged into a slow-motion, underwater world that was fissuring and crumbling the pillars of his life. He opened his mouth and tried to pull more air into his lungs. Deeds, not words, he thought. The word *hypocrite* kept coming back to him. When he was young, Pop used it so often he'd assumed it was Yiddish.

"What are you, a hypocrite rabbi?" Pop would say when he found the young Nathan lazing around the house on Saturdays.

"What's wrong with a day of rest?" his son would say, defending himself. "You had one when you were a kid."

"Rest? What rest? You think my father let me rest on that day? My father dragged me to the shul to sit with the *alter kockers* with garlic on their breath and chicken bones in their mouths. Even on Yom Kippur they ate the chicken bones."

"Weren't they supposed to fast on Yom Kippur, Pop?" Nathan would tease, knowing Pop would go for the bait.

"Of course they were supposed to fast. And the rabbis, the *hypocrites,* were supposed to love God. They *davened* plenty. A regular show they made with their praying. But while they were carrying on, they had their hands in hardworking people's pockets." Pop would slide his hand into Nathan's pocket and grab his leg until he screeched, delighted at the unexpected attention. "Took money for *schnapps,* money to build shuls, to make themselves important. *Bah!*" And with that, Pop would retrieve his hand, snatch up his newspaper, and drop into the old brown upholstered chair by the window.

The lesson Nathan learned from these encounters was that making fun of rabbis was a sure way to please his father.

"I'm no hypocrite," Pop had said a few years later, when his wife had insisted Nathan be called to the Torah as a Bar Mitzvah.

"Don't you argue socialism with *me,*" she'd said. "This has got nothing to do with you and your ideas. A tradition is a tradition, and I'm not going to be the shame of the whole neighborhood just for Mr. Marx's sake."

So week after week Nathan toiled over his Torah portion, without comprehension. To his every question about the text, the sour Rabbi Menken would respond, "Your job is to recite, not interpret." Filled with a newfound sense of solidarity with his father about rabbis, Nathan had pleaded, "Pop, do I have to become a Bar Mitzvah?"

"It's important to your mother. So you do it. That's all," Pop had answered, cutting short a rebuttal with the flick of his open newspaper.

On the day Nathan was recognized as a man before the whole community, it was Pop's face he looked for in vain among the congregation as he plodded flawlessly through the Hebrew. But Pop had stayed home in protest, just as he'd promised. "I'm no hypocrite," he'd said.

Rafael squinted at him. "What do any of us know about what goes on in the privacy of a man's heart? But one thing I know is your father was a believer. Not because of what he said, but because of what he did."

"What did he do?" Nathan wanted to know.

"The Jews said that on his last night in Zokof, he scrambled on all fours through this cemetery, in fear for his life. His cries were so terrible they could be heard even by the souls of the dead. Next to the walls that used to surround this cemetery, the souls of suicides and criminals heard him. Itzik's cries were hard as rock, flint. They lit a holy spark in him."

"Why did he come here in the first place?" Nathan asked, barely able to contain his shock, to reconcile the boy in the story with the man he'd known all his life, a man who moved with the slowness of pulled dough, a man who avoided the troubles of others if at all possible. This Polish Itzik Leiber and the man he knew as Pop didn't match.

Rafael held up his hand, signaling that he would not be moved off course. "That holy spark lit Itzik's way to the grave of a woman named Freidl Alterman, *aleha ha sholem* — may she rest in peace." He turned his head and looked off into the cemetery for a moment. "Itzik held on to her gravestone. It was a new one, unsteady in the earth, you understand? And in his terror, it was to God that Itzik the Faithless One turned to plead for mercy."

Nathan was so overcome with this strange image of Pop that everything slowed. His world became very quiet and heavy. Lifting his hand was an effort; he felt as if he were being carried away, unable to control where the story of his father's childhood was going, much less what its consequences might mean for him. "Why did he have to plead for mercy?" he asked.

"Because that night he had committed a sin so great he knew he had to repent immediately and with complete sincerity. Without excuse. Without anger at his father or the rabbis." Rafael brushed some bark from his coat. "The story is told that Itzik the Faithless One prayed so hard for mercy, he pulled Freidl's stone over. Broke it in two." Rafael gestured with his hands as if breaking something. "They were after him that night. They chased him all the way here. But she protected him. She scared them away."

"The menacing old Jewess spirit?"

Rafael nodded. "Freidl. She left her grave for him and became a wandering soul. She knew he needed her, and she, a childless woman, needed him."

A tractor made its way down the road outside the cemetery.

"But what sin did my father commit?" Nathan asked. He ached with frustration at having to interpret the facts of his father's life through the superstitious prism of a religious imagination.

He asks what sin his father committed? He knows nothing, the past is blotted out? I flew from tree to tree, upsetting the crows.

17

RAFAEL WAITED FOR THE CAWING BIRDS TO SETTLE. HE SEEMED PER-plexed by Nathan's question."Itzik never told you why he left Poland?"

Nathan shrugged. "I always thought it was because he wanted a better life." He ran his fingers through his hair, searching for more of an answer. "My father said he'd been like a slave here, that he'd worked sixteen hours a day."

"*Ptuh!* That had nothing to do with it. He left because of Jan Nowak."

Nathan was aghast. "You mean to tell me there really was a Jan Nowak?"

Rafael narrowed his eyes, assessing the effect the name Jan Nowak had had. "Yeh, Leiber, those stories I told you don't lie. There *was* a Jan Nowak in our town. The night your father left us, Jan and his wife were in their wagon, on the road where your driver is parked." Rafael indicated the entrance of the cemetery with his head.

"They saw three of our *kinderlach* on their way home from cheder, and Jan started in with that crazy laugh of his. The children were so afraid of him they didn't move. Then it was too late to run. He brought the whip down on their feet to make them jump. His wife yelled he should do it faster, and he did, laughing with the blows, I tell you."

He shook his head with a heavy sadness that made Nathan wonder why in the world this man had remained in Zokof.

"Your father was coming home at that time, and he saw what Jan Nowak was doing to those children. He ran to the wagon, grabbed Jan by the arm — a *chutzpah* for a skinny stick of a boy when the peasant was two heads taller than him and strong as an ox."

Nathan flushed, surprised and impressed that daring had once accom-panied Pop's rage. "How can you know that this happened? What proof is there?"

Rafael raised his palms upward and shook them meaningfully. "I know what I know. It's not often that God intervenes in the lives of men, Leiber. But that night, God intervened. Jan Nowak slipped on a handful of grass and fell from his wagon. His horse went *meshuggeh*. That's what killed him. The wagon rolled over his head."

Nathan could not think of a way he could combat Rafael's certainty. Instead, he became alarmed. "But the man's death was an accident, wasn't it? No one could accuse my father of murder."

"*Ptuh!* This is Poland, Leiber! In Poland, a Jew who gets caught in such a business, they call a murderer."

Horrified, Nathan tried to imagine the scene. "What about the children?"

"The youngest one recognized your father. He called out, 'It's Itzik Leiber!' A terrible mistake. Terrible!" Rafael grimaced. "The wife heard. 'Itzik Leiber is the devil himself!' she shouted. What could Itzik do? The Poles would come after *him* now, not the children. All three kinderlach were holding tight to his legs. 'Run home safe,' he told them. But they wouldn't let go of him. The wife took hold of Jan's whip. No one waited for the blows. The children ran. Itzik ran. He jumped over the cemetery wall."

Nathan looked around for a wall, trying to imagine his slow, round Pop jumping over it like a hunted animal. But except for the remnant on which Rafael had sat, there was no wall.

"He crawled on all fours over the graves, until he came to Freidl's resting place over there." Rafael pointed. "What made him stop, I'm sure he himself couldn't have said. He wrapped himself around her gravestone like he was trying to climb into her arms."

Nathan looked at the pile of stones to which Rafael pointed, intrigued but skeptical. "Couldn't he just have been out of breath and didn't know where else to go?"

"Exactly, Leiber. Out of breath," Rafael commended him, although Nathan didn't know why.

Rafael placed his hands on his knees, much as Nathan himself placed his hands on a lectern. "In the Torah," he began, "the word *breath* is connected with the soul, with God Himself." He smiled. "You are right. You *could* say he was out of soul, out of God, when he came to Freidl. He *didn't* know where to go. So he stopped."

Nathan recognized the teacher in Rafael appealing to him. But he couldn't grasp what he was being expected to learn.

Rafael pouted slightly. "I will admit, it was not such a wonder that her stone fell over when Itzik put his arms around it. A stone, newly unveiled and not so steady in the earth. Of course it fell. Broke in two pieces, as I said."

Nathan fought not to show his disbelief. "Are you telling me the broken stone is a historical fact?"

"That's right." Rafael nodded with satisfaction. "After it broke, the Poles ran from the cemetery. Who knows, maybe they saw a ghost?" His eyes widened with mock amazement, and his laugh was deep, gravelly as his voice, but oddly pleasing.

Nathan smiled, reassured that Rafael's metaphysical beliefs had limits.

"Later, Itzik crept like a thief back to town. He went to the house of his employer, a rich miller who bought wheat from Jan Nowak. Avrum Kollek was his name." Rafael shook his head. "Avrum Kollek made your father beg for every zloty he gave him. As if it weren't a sin to shame the poor."

Nathan took the studio photograph from his jacket, of his father as a boy. He tried to imagine all this. Begging took a willingness to be vulnerable, an attitude wholly absent in Pop's familiar defiant expression. Only fear for his family could have made him bend so far against his nature. He looked down at his feet, ashamed for Pop.

A horn blasted twice from outside the cemetery. A moment later, it blasted again, then again.

Rafael looked over in the general direction of the noise. "It is your driver. He wants to go."

"Well, he'll have to wait. I'm not ready to go yet." Nathan was surprised at his own vehemence. They waited for the horn to stop. He could not get it out of his mind that Pop had really crawled on all fours in this cemetery. "You said he begged for money?"

"For his mother, Sarah," Rafael nodded. "Sarah, mother of Itzik. Strange, no? Another Sarah. Another Itzik. Another sacrificial lamb. Poor woman, half dead already from hunger and overwork. And because of what happened that night, she had to leave Zokof too."

"With him?"

"No."

"He left alone?"

Rafael nodded. By then, Nathan's shoulder muscles were knotted so tightly they were causing him the kind of pain only Marion's massages could undo. He was gripped by the thought of his father losing his home and his family at the age of fourteen.

Rafael looked toward the car. Nathan looked at the old man's worn shoes and realized that he needed the ride back to town. He stood up. "I'll go talk to him."

"Nah. He'll wait," Rafael said brusquely. He picked up a dead leaf and rolled it gently between his fingers. "Sarah left Zokof at dawn. By then, her other children were in danger. In those days, Leiber, Poland wasn't so bad as Russia. They didn't push Jews into a Pale of Settlement and let them starve to death. But it was bad enough. It wasn't safe for her to stay."

Why the hell didn't Pop tell me any of this? Nathan wondered. He rolled his shoulders, trying to stretch his tight back muscles. "What about his employer, the miller? Couldn't he have done something?" he asked irritably.

"I'm coming to that. After he sent Itzik off, Avrum Kollek went to the Russian magistrate and offered him gold, that he should protect the Jews of Zokof. But there were sensitive matters involved with a local nobleman, and the Russian refused to send a detachment of soldiers. The Poles knew what that meant. They made a pogrom like the Jews hadn't seen for years. For his trouble, Avrum Kollek himself fell under their boots. It took five men at least to hold him down while they pulled out his beard, tied him up like a chicken, and put a trayf sausage in his mouth. They hung him, in front of his daughter, Shuli. Ach! The things that were done here, you don't know. You can't imagine."

Nathan got nauseous. "Did my father know what happened?"

"Nah, not until later. He heard there was trouble when he was already in Radom. How many details he got, I don't know. All night he'd been walking, hiding in ditches along the road, sleeping through the morning with his head on the bundle his mother, may she rest in peace, packed for him. In his pocket he had a red ribbon his sister Hindeleh gave him from her hair."

This last bit of information startled Nathan. "I found a ribbon in the strongbox where my father kept all his important papers. It was tied around the photograph I just showed you. It was more pink than red. It must have faded. How did you know about that ribbon? How do you know about any of this?"

"There are things I know, Leiber. Let's leave it like that, for now," Rafael said.

Overcome, and still grateful for all this information, Nathan was willing to give him the benefit of the doubt, for now. "How old was Pop's sister Hindeleh?" he asked.

"Four. A little beauty. Thick red curls. And her face, a perfect oval. Light-brown eyes."

"A Modigliani girl." Nathan blurted one of his pet names for his Ellen.

Rafael shrugged. "The only Leiber who returned to Zokof after the pogrom was Gershom, the eldest boy. But that was years later."

Nathan stared, literally open-mouthed, at Rafael. "Did you know my father's brother?"

"Of course I knew him. A sickly man. A bachelor. He showed up around 1930 and went to work for Chaim the Baker's son. Kept to himself. Slept on the flour sacks at the bakery. Spent all his spare time in shul, though his beard was always covered with flour. The families took turns inviting him to *Shabbos* dinner."

This wasn't enough for Nathan. "What else do you remember about him?"

Rafael brushed a fallen leaf from his shoulder. "It is written, the less a man talks, the nearer he is to holiness. If so, your uncle Gershom was a holy man." He raised his bushy eyebrows ironically. "He was the last Jewish baker in Zokof. Bread like his will never be made again here — pumpernickel, rye. . . . Oy, for a taste of one of Gershom's *challahs*. The Poles don't know from making egg bread."

Nathan vowed he'd find a way to get Rafael a challah. "My father used to say no one in America knows how to make bread either."

Rafael smiled. A squirrel chattered and scampered through the underbrush.

"You were saying, about Gershom?" Nathan prompted.

"From Gershom we learned what happened to Itzik Leiber's family."

"So Gershom was the one who told you what happened to my father that night?" This made sense to Nathan, and he was relieved at the logical explanation.

"Nah, from Gershom I know what happened to Itzik's *family.* They went through forests and towns. They hid from the authorities who were looking for Itzik. In Lublin, he said, they went to the Old Cemetery, the one that's high on the hill. They pushed *kvitls* under stones around the Seer of Lublin's grave. You've heard of him, maybe. They called him 'the Iron Head.'"

Nathan shook his head, no.

"They called him that because he had the *Gemara,* the whole thing, in his head, like an encyclopedia. Gershom wrote the kvitls on thin slips of paper he found along the road, all their prayers for Itzik's safety, for some shelter and food. About this, he was poetic. He said the kvitls fluttered like butterfly wings until the rain came and pinned them down, erasing the letters drop by drop."

Rafael looked at the sky. "Many times I myself have wondered, does God read these messages? If He does, how could He have been so indifferent to the fate of this poor woman and her children? And what of the Seer of Lublin? Even with those famous eyes — they say he had one much bigger than the other, and that they saw through time and space — did they see Sarah Leiber?" He shook his head. "She wandered east toward Chelm and died of a fever."

Nathan shrank inside. "My grandmother died on the road?"

Rafael nodded.

"What happened to Hindeleh?"

"Taken to a Jewish orphanage in Chelm."

Nathan tore at the bark of the tree. "What about the other children?"

"As it is written, they were scattered like straw that flies before the wind."

Even in his anguish, Nathan was taken with the poetic phrase and wondered if it was biblical. "Did any of them come back to Zokof after the war?" he asked.

"Nah. The war swept us all away from here. They didn't come back."

Nathan looked at the photograph of his father again and wondered what had happened to Hindeleh. How could it be that a faded hair ribbon was all that was left of a person, that it could remain intact years after she had disappeared? It was enough to make a man regard faith in a Supreme Eye on the world as something too painful to share with his children. Maybe that's what Pop had thought. Nathan imagined him alone in his window, silent except when he talked back to the radio, silent as he read his socialist newspaper. Not like his holy brother Gershom. Just silent because that was all he had to say about God.

He ached for his father now, ached that they'd lost their chance to speak plainly with each other about Zokof, just as he'd ached for years that he couldn't apologize to him for having made such a travesty of his funeral service. It turned his stomach to think of it.

Rafael stood up. "Come. It's time to pray."

Nathan looked around the unmarked cemetery. "I don't know how to pray. I don't know what is really even meant by *God,*" he said, surprised that he was ashamed to admit this. "After my father died, I never even visited his grave because I didn't know what I'd do when I got there. Is that a sin?"

"What do you think?"

"I thought it wouldn't make a difference to him anymore, if I came or not. He was gone."

"But it made a difference to you. Why does a man pray, Leiber? To ask God to produce presents for him like a magician, or that He should grant wishes? This is for children!"

Nathan was impressed.

"A man prays so he can speak to his own still small voice. He prays to make *himself* change. In the beginning, the words mean nothing. Imagine a boy in the back of a shul, without a prayer book, reciting the Hebrew alphabet. When asked why, he says, 'I don't know how to pray, so I'm offering God the letters. I hope He will arrange the words.'"

The parable appealed to Nathan as an academic, and he smiled appreciatively.

"A man who spends his life working at those letters can learn to arrange the words himself. And if he needs help, he turns to the prayers of his fathers and they become a minyan, reciting as one voice across centuries."

"And what if he doesn't believe in the words?"

"Then he asks God for help — like your father, that night in the cemetery."

Nathan quickly took issue with this. "My father didn't believe in prayers. He didn't believe in God."

"Listen to me, Leiber. Your father believed. He lit a holy spark inside himself in this cemetery, the spark of man touching God. It was nothing less than that. Understand?"

"With all due respect," Nathan insisted, "what you call a holy spark is what I would call a moment of inspiration. There's no need for God in the picture."

Rafael smiled indulgently. "Inspiration without understanding to sustain it lasts as long as a bubble of soap. The understanding that lasts is when a man realizes God's presence in the world. A man who is touched by such understanding is changed, not for an hour or a day, but for a lifetime. He has crossed the bridge to what we call having the proper *kavonah* — paying attention to the meaning and the direction of one's prayer."

"I'm not sure I'd ever be constitutionally able to recognize the presence of God," Nathan said, in his most professorial manner. "It goes against my whole rationalist orientation toward life. Awe at natural beauty is about as far as I go."

"So, maybe for you it will be more difficult. So?"

"So, if I pray, I guarantee you it will be gibberish to me today and gibberish ten years from today, no matter how many times I say the words. To me, the prayers will always just be words, conversations with myself, at best. But there's no God in that."

Rafael smiled again. "And you are so sure that nothing could ever change your *orientation,* as you call it? You are the measure of all things and you are immovable? I can only say, if this is so, Leiber, then you have a problem bigger than not being able to pray. You live in a very small world that allows only for small wonders."

Nathan hesitated before answering. How could a man so immersed in his religion as Rafael understand him? "I just don't need to put a God in the picture to explain life, much less to thank Him for it."

"The rabbis say a man who takes the fruits of the world but offers no thanks is a thief."

"The rabbis have a vested interest in making sure people keep believing in God."

Rafael laughed. "You sound like your father."

"I learned from a master." Nathan smiled back.

"A master of forgetfulness."

Nathan stopped smiling. "What does forgetfulness have to do with believing in God?"

"Your father had the right kavonah that night he was here. It had nothing to do with those rabbis he hated so much. I'll tell you something you don't know. Your father loved God — he'd felt His breath. He knew how to pray. But praying from the heart takes a lot out of a man, especially when his heart is heavy. When Itzik found an excuse not to pray, he stopped."

"What excuse?"

"Socialism."

Nathan knew in his gut there was something to what Rafael was saying. After all, Pop had used socialism as an excuse not to do a lot of things. "I can't change what my father did," he said dejectedly.

"Yes, you can. It is almost enough for us that you returned here, after so many years. Now, be a Jew and learn to pray."

Nathan's ears burned at being put on the spot. But the thought of praying excited him in a way. What had he lost, he wondered, when the chain of generations had been broken, the yarmulkes and the identifying Jewish names removed, all so that he and his family could hide like chameleons among the Gentiles? Was that really all his father's socialist Utopia had been for, to hide from a demanding God because the enlightened world had allowed it? Or were he and Pop just trying to buy a little peace from the boots of the bullies and the butts of their guns? What kind of people hand their legacy over to their enemies for a fairy tale? Socialism. He was depressed by his questions. He was becoming tired, and the crows were getting on his nerves.

"We'll stand by Freidl's grave," Rafael said. "You can pray for her soul. We can say a special blessing to thank God for saving Itzik from imminent danger in this place. There is a special prayer for this." Rafael took a few steps. The heel of his shoe caught on a root and he stumbled. Nathan sprang forward and caught him in his arms. He'd had a similar incident with Pop losing his balance once, at the Adirondacks cabin. "You need some fresh air in your lungs," he'd told Pop, trying to persuade him to leave his newspaper and take a walk.

"What do I need with fresh air?" Pop had said. "I got all the air I need in here."

The road outside the cabin, rutted and lined with pine needles, was one of the things Nathan liked best about the Adirondacks property. But he and Pop hadn't gone twenty feet when Pop twisted his ankle. Nathan couldn't catch him in time to break the fall.

"What kind of place is this where they don't know how to put cement on a road? Feh, it's like Poland!" Pop had spat, his soft, doughy body defying all Nathan's efforts to lift him.

Nathan released Rafael and helped steady him.

"Thanks, Leiber." He chuckled. "The roots here. I got caught in your *roots*. Heh!"

Nathan smiled. He was moved enough by what had passed between them to follow Rafael to Freidl's grave. All right, he thought, I'll try to do what he wants, for his sake. Their coats swayed gently in tandem as they walked the short distance, hands clasped behind their backs. "Shouldn't we be wearing prayer shawls?" he asked.

"Not here. We don't wear them, out of respect for the dead, who can no longer join us in prayer."

..hen they reached the foot-high pile of small stones, Nathan felt a bit sheepish. "What was the name again of that prayer you recite?"

"El Molei Rachamim."

"Can I say it for all the Leibers that are buried here?"

"One person at a time, Leiber. This isn't a party."

"But I told you, I don't know their names."

Perhaps the upset in Nathan's voice persuaded Rafael to back down. "All right, so if you don't know the names, then say it for the family. God will survive it, I'm sure." He did his customary shrug. "But if you're going to say El Molei, you should at least understand what you're saying."

Nathan nodded gratefully.

"It means, *God of mercy, You who dwell on high, may the souls of our loved ones find perfect rest beneath the wings of Your divine presence. And we say, Amen.*"

"It's only the God part I have trouble with," Nathan said.

"That's not trouble, that's a beginning. Say the words with me, Leiber. Bring them into your heart." He closed his eyes.

This is craziness, Nathan thought, even though he'd always secretly admired the elder statesmen of the faith, the way they proudly recited the anthems of their nation. They were men of undeniable power. Lou Gersh, Pop's card partner, was one of them. Who could forget him at Pop's funeral as he'd stepped forward, without warning, and broken the awkward vacuum by saying Kaddish. The mourners had gazed at Lou with gratitude they had not shown Nathan when he'd delivered his eulogy. He had stared at the memorial booklet, embarrassed that he was unable to follow even the transliteration of a prayer he knew was knit into his father's heart.

After the service, Lou had put his arms around him and patted him on the back. "Don't worry about it, Nathan," he'd said. "You made your father proud when it mattered, when he was alive." But Nathan was not convinced. He'd felt more distanced from Pop than ever.

A crow cawed directly above. Nathan and Rafael stood shoulder to shoulder, their heads bowed before the jumble of unremarkable stones that marked Freidl's grave. Nathan rubbed his eyes under his glasses. As a younger man, he'd held on to the hope that one day he could become someone who experienced life more fully. God knows, he'd never had a talent for letting go of himself. Every time he'd tried, it had ended badly. There was that time he'd jumped off the rock ledge at the Adirondacks lake, hoping against hope that he'd fall harmlessly into the water below. He'd gotten seventeen stitches in the back of the head for his trouble, and the keloid would always remind him that he was a bound man, a man who toppled over into undignified states whenever he tried to break free.

He ran his fingers once again over the keloid scar, ashamed and disgusted at himself. But before he could work himself over with further self-recrimination, he remembered Rafael's admonition not to sacrifice to the idols. He commanded himself to stop worrying what the whole damn world would think of him if he prayed out loud for the boy who'd once crawled on all fours in this cemetery — his father, Itzik the Faithless One. He'd pray, damn it, not to let go for himself, but for his family buried here, because he'd never done it for Pop.

"*El Molei Rachamim,*" Rafael said. He signaled Nathan to repeat after him.

"*El Molei Rachamim,*" Nathan whispered, praying for brevity and the strength to go the distance.

"*Shochain ba'm'romim, hamtzai m'nucha n'chona tachas canfai Ha'Sh'cheenah.*" Nathan repeated the Hebrew, phrase by painful phrase, methodically forcing himself to ignore his skepticism about what he was doing. The tactic proved successful. After four or five repetitions, he began to feel oddly enfolded by the rhythm of the words, immersed, carried away by them.

"*. . . sh'ha-lach l'o-lo-mo . . .*" A wave of images came to him. Pop reading Hebrew at the Seder table, Ellen and her cousins listening to him, entranced. His mother in the kitchen serving the matzo ball soup, her ankles and feet puffed up like a soufflé. There they were. The Leibers.

"*. . . b'Gan Edan t'heh m'nu-cho-so . . .*" With each repetition, his voice grew more steady and his eyes met Rafael's less often, until he realized that Rafael had closed his eyes and begun to sway, returning to correct Nathan only when he stumbled, repeating and repeating the phrases patiently until he got it right, nodding, moving on, guiding him gently aloft.

"*. . . v'yitz-ror bitz-ror ha'cha-yim es nish-mo-so . . . ,*" Rafael chanted. Something about the phrase sounded familiar to Nathan, reawoke images of his Bar Mitzvah, his childhood, of that long-ago time of stoops and stickball.

"*. . . v'ya-nu-ach b'sholem al mish-ka-vo . . .*" Nathan's voice caught. For the first time in years, he felt that heat behind the eyes that precedes tears. They came, slowly at first, then spilled over the rims of his lower lids, blurring his vision, washing down over his cheeks and emptying into his mouth, salty as seawater. Like Pop at the Seder table, he realized at once. And in that moment, he understood the power of prayer, that it linked the man with his community and tunneled deep into his hidden self. He understood how even a Jewish socialist could not resist it, could not forget that despite everything he was a Jew first, even if he could not admit it to his son. So there in the Zokof Cemetery, standing over the unmarked bones of his ancestors, Nathan acknowledged it for them both, at last. "... *v'nomar, amen.*"

From your lips to God's ear, Nathan, son of Itzik. Amen.

18

AFTERWARD, NATHAN'S STOMACH GROWLED. HE STAMPED HIS feet to disguise the sound and brushed away the tears that remained on his cheeks. His sense of otherworldliness fell away, and he now felt exposed and embarrassed at the passion with which he had recited El Molei Rachamim.

What had he been thinking, praying like a primitive to a God he knew did not exist, suspending his powers of reason and critical judgment? He stamped his feet again and fought the sudden desire to flee.

A cloud obliterated the pools of sunlight that had filtered through the forest only minutes before. He sneaked a glance at his watch. It was after two o'clock. Time seemed to have looped itself in circles around this day, slowing its progress with all these detailed observations of the past.

When his stomach growled again, he realized he hadn't eaten since early that morning. He cleared his throat to announce it was time to go, but Rafael suddenly knelt and seized two pebbles from the underbrush. "We put stones on graves as a sign that we were here, that we remember." Rafael laid one pebble on top of the pile and rose with difficulty as he handed the other to Nathan.

No harm in that, Nathan thought, hoping this would be the last rite he would be expected to perform before returning to the car. As he leaned over and balanced his pebble next to Rafael's, he was already thinking about what he would say to Tadeusz.

"It's not enough," Rafael said, "but it's all I can do. I had to do something for her. She deserves a monument, but if I made one, God knows what they might do to it. Better it should be like this."

It sickened Nathan that even now a gravestone wasn't safe in this cemetery. He wondered how long it had taken Rafael to build his memorial, pebble by pebble, prayer by prayer. He wondered if it had been built out of respect for the memory of a real woman or if Freidl was just a folktale, buoyantly carried through time by the stream of stories that flowed from this town. Several crows cawed high above him. Their claws crackled the thin branches of the birch tree where they alighted. "How do you know if this woman Freidl ever existed?" he asked. "There's no gravestone to prove it. Have you checked the municipal records?"

Rafael did not lift his eyes from the pile of stones. "I know almost everything about her."

"How?"

"She told me."

Nathan became alarmed. "How could she tell you anything? She died before you were born."

"Freidl has her ways. The dead often do. We understand each other, Freidl and me." Rafael sighed. "Sometimes she speaks. Sometimes she sings me a *niggun,* a tune, you know?" Closing his eyes again, he swayed back and forth, as if listening to music.

Nathan felt his confidence in Rafael slide out from under him like a chair. He'd been a dupe, a kid seduced by a magician's charm, by the excitement of secrets revealed.

"You know what's magic?" Pop had once said when the boy Nathan had offered to perform a card trick for him. "*Gornish,* nothing. Nothing but the sleight of hand. A magician's like a rabbi. He pretends to make something out of nothing. And from the nothing he makes his living!"

Nathan tilted back his head. What the hell *did* Rafael want from him? He was no longer sure if he could trust anything the old man said, especially about Pop. For God's sake, he thought, I've spent the precious few hours I had in Pop's hometown with a man who thinks he communicates with a dead woman!

He stuck his hands in his trouser pockets and tried not to think about Załuski's cynical smile upon hearing Tadeusz tell him that Professor Linden, who did not care about the origins of his name, had followed a crazy old Jew into a cemetery.

"Come, we'll go back to town," Rafael said, taking Nathan again by the arm. "We'll go to my house. There's more I have to tell you."

But Nathan had had enough.

Rafael turned to him. "Nu?" He raised his eyebrows. "We'll go now." Abruptly, he tugged Nathan in the direction of the car. "She'll be pleased."

The forest reverberated with the batting of crows' wings. Nathan glanced around at the rush of shadows. Somewhere in the distance, several men shouted to one another. He shuddered. If Rafael's story had even a glimmer of truth to it, Pop had heard something like that the night he had come here. His sense of vulnerability increased with the loss of his faith in Rafael.

"Rafael, please understand," he said as he felt himself being dragged like a child out of the cemetery, "I would like to visit your house, but I am expected in Warsaw. At five o'clock I have a meeting scheduled with some colleagues at the university. Perhaps another time." It sounded so obvious to him that there would be no other time that he felt guilty. He told himself he was only trying to spare the old man's feelings.

Rafael's eyes flashed with the angry suspicion that Nathan had seen earlier.

"Also, I'm expecting a call from my daughter in New York," Nathan quickly added. "I would like her to meet you one day," he said, hoping to make amends. But having said this, he realized how much Ellen would love Rafael's stories, especially the ones about Freidl. He thought it a miracle that he'd produced a child who did not suffer from his infirmities, who jumped through life feet first, bouncing back unharmed from her mistakes, as if tethered to some magical elastic cord.

Nathan sighed inwardly, utterly exhausted and depressed by his own rigidity.

By this evening, he told himself, everything would be fine. He would eat downstairs at one of the Marriott restaurants, swaddled like a babe in the familiar folds of an American enterprise. The recollection of the hotel's plush comfort filled him with an almost giddy gladness. Poland, with all its unrepentant meanness, would be kept at bay outside the hotel's revolving doors.

Rafael bowed his head and said, "Freidl needs you, Leiber. *Farshtaist?* Come tomorrow."

"I'll try," Nathan said weakly, knowing he would not. What a life he must have had, he thought. Why doesn't he leave Zokof? What's here for him?

They had begun their return to the cemetery's entrance when Rafael stepped off the path and rubbed his chin thoughtfully. "I think there are several Leibers buried here," he said.

Curious, Nathan joined him. Standing there, he felt a pang as he remembered the day, just after he and Marion were married, when they had opened the telephone book to the L's and picked the name Linden. They weren't hiring Jewish professors at the University of Colorado that year.

Nathan had decided that signing his name *Leiber* wasn't important enough to ruin his career over. He remembered Pop's anger on the telephone.

"A name is not like grass. You don't pull it out by the roots and say that's that. It's a *shonda,* a shame on your head that the family name, a proud Jewish name, will die with me!"

"What's the difference, Pop?" Nathan had argued. "Since when do you care so much about having a Jewish name?"

"What do you know what I care? I care plenty that I'm a Jew. I don't need a passport to prove it to anyone. I have my name. I know where I come from. Did I change my name when I came to this country?"

Nathan remembered feeling shocked by Pop's outburst. Illogical, he had thought, for a socialist to harbor that kind of emotion for a discarded faith.

Marion had sat in silence throughout the whole conversation. At no time during that telephone call or after did she admit to Nathan's mother or father that the name change had originally been her idea. From the day they got engaged, she had balked at the idea of losing her ambiguous maiden name, Ross. "Leiber is just too difficult a name for people to spell," she'd said. "And think of our children, what they'll have to go through if you give them a foreign-sounding name like that. Really, Nathan, it's not fair."

He had succumbed to her reasoning without protest because he just couldn't see the point of clinging to a Jewish identity when it stood in the way of his marriage and his professional advancement. They had chosen the name together. Their married name, they called it, until Linden slid off their tongues as if it had always been theirs.

Near the cemetery entrance, he caught sight of the nose of Tadeusz's car, still parked by the side of the road. But his relief that he had a ride back to Warsaw was tinged with renewed anxiety about his driver. He dreaded having to pull on his academic mantle to keep Tadeusz in his place.

At the lone lamppost near the end of the path, Rafael suddenly reached down and pulled up a handful of grass. "It is customary, when leaving a Jewish cemetery, for mourners to take a handful of grass and throw it in the direction of the grave." He handed some blades to Nathan. "We say, 'May her soul sprout from this place as the grass sprouts from the earth.' You must say this, Leiber. Maybe if it comes from you, it will help her rest."

Nathan glanced at the car. Assured that no one was watching, he accepted the grass from Rafael. "May she, uh, sprout from the earth as the grass sprouts from this place." He gave the grass an underhand toss in the direction of Freidl's grave, calculating that overhand might look disrespectfully athletic.

Rafael grunted his approval as, with a gentle swing of the wrist, he too tossed grass toward Freidl's grave. He put his hand on Nathan's shoulder. "There is something else you should know, Leiber. *Grass* is the last word your father said in this cemetery."

Nathan paled.

"Maybe he meant the grass God put in Jan's wagon to make him slip and fall, but Freidl said he dropped two handfuls of it on her grave." He paused. "She said he was frightened by it, that he kicked the blades when they fell. But still, it helped her. It reminded her of her favorite saying from the Talmud. You know of the Talmud, Leiber?" Rafael raised his eyebrows.

"I know of it, yes," Nathan said. But his mind was still trying to process how Rafael would know what Pop had said to Freidl. A fiction, he decided. It can't be anything else.

"Listen to me now," Rafael said with such vehemence Nathan was startled. "The Talmud says, 'Every blade of grass has its own guardian star in the firmament which strikes it and commands it to grow!'"

"Very interesting. What do you think that meant to her?" Nathan asked, employing his old technique of getting others to explain themselves without having to admit that he hadn't understood them.

"It means that every living thing has within it a holy spark. Once lit, that spark will guide it toward growth." Rafael turned back and surveyed the cemetery. "On the night Itzik left here, his soul was on fire. That I'm sure. If he kept that flame alive in America, if he grew, well, you would know better than us. But one thing I will tell you: your father had a soul from the earth. Freidl always said it was like an uncooked potato."

Nathan looked up at the trees. If Freidl was a creation of Rafael's loneliness, he thought, how did she, or he, know so much? He saw Pop sitting in his Brooklyn window, all round and white, his large oval eyes trained on *The Forward.* He felt indignant. What had he expected to get from an uncooked potato? Respect? Appreciation for his accomplishments? To his surprise, he laughed. "That's him," he said, shaking his head. "She got that right. He was an uncooked potato until the day he died!"

"It's a shame. She'll be disappointed."

Nathan didn't feel like arguing. "I don't mean to be rude," he said, "but it's hard for me to imagine being in the presence of a dead woman's soul."

"What are you talking about, Leiber? You yourself were in her presence last night, in your dream! She sang a tune, 'Little Zokof, little town.' Remember? Remember?"

Nathan blushed and admitted it was so, though for the life of him, he couldn't remember having told Rafael about his dream.

"Your problem isn't imagining, it's admitting what you can't explain. Easier to forget, yeh? All those moments when the past and the present become one thing. Like a few minutes ago, you felt Itzik here with you, in this cemetery. I could see it on your face. Don't try to deny it. This is how God intervenes in our lives, Leiber. Pay attention. Stay awake!" He clapped his hands in front of Nathan's shocked face. "She followed him out of this cemetery, all the way to Warsaw and beyond, until he left for America." He cast a penetrating look at Nathan, then took his arm and resumed guiding him toward the cemetery entrance. "I know what I'm saying," he added confidently.

They stepped out into the hazy sunshine, where Nathan was taken aback at the sight of six or seven peasants, men in their fifties, in tattered overalls, standing beside Tadeusz's car. A white-haired old woman with a green-patterned scarf tied under her chin was also there, her fingers curled tightly over her cane. She wore a long yellow sweater over her gray dress, even in the heat of the day. The little group jostled one another as if waiting for a show to begin. At the other end of the car, Tadeusz fired pebbles into the tall grass with one hand and cupped a lit cigarette with the other.

With Nathan and Rafael's approach, the Poles fell silent. They stared, but their eyes were empty of expression. Nathan swallowed hard and kept walking, his eyes on the latch of the rear door. He was halfway across the road when he realized Rafael was not at his side. He turned back and watched in horror as the old man raised his arms above his head and, in a voice that could be heard by all the congregants at the car, said to him, "The Jews have been in this country for over a thousand years. Once, there were more than a thousand cemeteries like this in Poland. One for every year, yeh?" Rafael swung his arms out wide and punched the air for emphasis.

Tadeusz stopped throwing pebbles. He turned to the Poles and translated what Rafael had said. The Poles did not stir. Neither did Nathan. His focus skittered between them and Rafael, and he felt he had become the unwilling fulcrum in their game of Polish seesaw.

"Right here, in our little town of Zokof, we have graves that date from the fifteenth century," he said.

Tadeusz took a nervous drag on his cigarette. The old Polish woman shouted something in a hoarse, high-pitched voice and seemed to be trying to enlist the others' support. Nathan was revolted. She was toothless. Two of the men nodded in agreement. Nathan would have liked to have asked what they were saying, but he was afraid of igniting the situation further.

"She's saying the Jews are always crying about how they suffer," Rafael said, with a curt nod in the peasants' direction. "They say we suffer because of what we did to Jesus." Rafael raised his eyebrows again. "Imagine how Jesus, a Jew, son of a Jewish mother, would suffer if he saw this house of eternity, this *beis oylom,* this cemetery of his people. He would ask, 'Where is the wall that used to be here?' He would ask, 'Where is the house to prepare the bodies for the grave?' He would ask, 'Where are the tombstones, the *matzevot?*'" Rafael narrowed his eyes. "Such beautiful things, those matzevot of the Jews. We had them carved with lions, eagles, trees, books, with candles and creatures and words, words, words. On those matzevot we made the hands of the *Kohanim!*" He split his fingers into pairs of twos, demonstrating the pose of the priestly hands. "Wouldn't Jesus ask 'Why is there not a single sign of respect for the dead? What kind of people are these who come here to drink and pick mushrooms?'" He glanced at Nathan and said, as an aside, "It's a Polish *bubbe-myseh* that the best mushrooms grow here."

The Poles, having heard and understood everything, thanks to Tadeusz, shouted short responses. Then one of them smiled, revealing a gold tooth. The others began to laugh and make jokes.

Rafael addressed himself to Nathan. "It's up to you, Leiber. To them, I'm an old meshuggener. They don't bother with me anymore."

Nathan looked at Tadeusz, who now seemed perplexed. He looked at the Poles. What seemed frighteningly evident was that his name, Leiber, had had a powerful effect on all of them. The grins had dropped from their faces. They stared at him. But what could the Poles hold against the Leibers now? It was a generation later, after all.

Suddenly, he heard a whooshing sound and felt as if he was being lifted high above the scene. As he hovered there amorphously, someone, a woman, began to hum a tune. Terrified, he looked down at Rafael for help.

"Leiber, remember what I have said," Rafael responded. "For all our sakes, remember her."

On the ground, Nathan saw his own body sway unsteadily.

The Polish woman thrust out her cane and beat her chest with her other hand. "Leiber!" she cried out.

He fell, graceless as ever, back to the place where he'd stood at the edge of the forest, between the madness of a lone Jew and the Poles who were his neighbors.

A gaggle of gray geese ran by, honking loudly as their owner herded them down the unpaved road.

Nathan took advantage of the short distraction and walked briskly to the car. "Rafael, we have to go now," he said, trying to camouflage his fear with a measured look — distinguished, weighty, but with a glint of appeasement. He clasped the rear door latch, opened the door, and swung himself inside, deeply relieved that the Poles had inexplicably backed away and that Tadeusz was moving toward the driver door. He willed himself to check Rafael's progress toward the car, afraid that he might have to intercede on his behalf.

Without a word, Tadeusz started the motor. Rafael got in and looked straight ahead, hands on his knees. Tadeusz turned the car back in the direction of town, holding himself unnaturally straight in his seat, his arms rigidly angled on the wheel. The car churned up the gravel on the road. Nathan threw his whole body around to look out the rear window, at the Poles who stared back at him.

I felt his hesitation at saying El Molei Rachamim. I felt it when he threw the grass. A vigorous head doubts, my father always said. But a man Nathan's age should doubt with a certain wisdom that can tolerate the unknown. He was too full of fear. What he could not explain he would not hold in his heart. What hope could I have that God would respond to such a short-lived kavonah as he had? I was desperate that Rafael should have another chance with him, to teach him, to open the way. When they came outside the cemetery, I sang the tune. I flew close to his ear and begged him to believe Rafael. What did I do but make him more afraid?

19

THAT EVENING, NATHAN LAY ON HIS BED IN DROWSY COMFORT after a hot shower and the steak dinner he had permitted himself after such a difficult day. The jacket he had worn to Zokof lay draped over the chair. A stray blade of grass hung limply from its outer pocket. Nathan looked at it sadly.

He was no longer sure what had happened earlier that day, how much of what he'd seen or heard was real, how much an exaggerated perception of reality. Was Rafael an extraordinary man or just a man so different from himself that he'd seemed extraordinary? As for Pop and Freidl, the less he tried to rationalize what he'd heard about them, the better. He turned out the light.

Sometime during the night, a woman's voice hummed the tune he'd heard at the entrance to the Zokof cemetery, the same tune he'd heard in his dream the night before. He opened his eyes.

A lantern flickered in the distance and grew, illuminating a life-size copy of Pesha Goldman's photograph of the fourteen-year-old Itzik. Itzik's pale, hungry face contrasted vividly with his borrowed studio clothes. He stared at Nathan, his big, sad eyes unblinking.

"You didn't retie Hindeleh's ribbon," the boy Pop said from the photograph. "You were supposed to retie it, like this." He held up his arm. The ribbon twisted around it like tefillin.

"How was I supposed to know about the ribbon?" Nathan said. "*You* never even told me you had a sister."

The boy looked off. "She had hair for three people, my mother used to say." His eyes sought Nathan's. "Just like Ellen's."

A round wooden table and chairs materialized. Pop, Ellen, and a little girl with wild red hair sat playing cards.

"A penny a game," said Hindeleh, laughing.

"Nine takes five," Ellen said, happily slapping down her cards. She was about eight years old.

Lou Gersh, Pop's old card partner from Brownsville, appeared from the shadows holding the lantern above his head. "A penny a game!" He laughed with the girls. "Follow me," he said to Nathan.

Nathan followed Lou until all that remained of the card players was the muffled sound of their far-off voices. The lantern swung between them. Nathan reached for it, and Lou laughed. "*Yit-ga-dal v'yit-ka-dash.* Remember when I said Kaddish for your father?"

Nathan nodded, feeling safe as ever beside the Beanpole, as the kids used to call him. "Where are we going, Lou?"

"Back."

"Back where?"

"To Zokof."

Nathan stopped walking. The darkness engulfed him. He felt as if he were choking. "Why do I have to go back? What for?"

"Because it's not finished, what your father left there. The graves are blocked, a maze of cut stones. The dead need peace, Nathan. They deserve better."

Nathan turned away from Lou. Sheaves of grass and mounds of stones welled up before him. Once again, he heard that sweet, slow melody, gorgeous as a Chopin nocturne.

Out of the emptiness, an enormous female figure appeared, face covered, wrapped in a heavy, triangular plaid blanket. Her posture was regal. When she lowered her arms, he saw the face of a wise-eyed da Vinci Madonna. She looked him up and down and smiled, revealing the contours of her high cheekbones.

A gust of wind blew and turned her into an old woman, the same woman who'd sung to him in his dream the night before he'd gone to Zokof. Now she wore a square white cloth on her head, tied in knots at its four corners.

"It's a lovely gift," she said.

Her accent was Yiddish, but the rich timbre of her voice was strangely pleasing to him.

She removed the handkerchief from her head and untied the knots. It floated in her hand, filled with light.

Nathan suddenly recognized it. "That's my father's!" He lunged forward and tried to snatch the handkerchief away.

The woman shuddered noticeably, but she recovered her composure. "I am Freidl," she said. "I knew your father."

He stared.

Her smile returned. "In town, the people called him Itzik the Faithless One. But your father had faith plenty, I can tell you. So much it broke my gravestone in two."

Nathan still could not speak.

Freidl began to sing her melody.

Lou was gone. His lantern shone faintly in the distance.

"What do you want?" Nathan said.

She held Pop's glowing handkerchief high above her head and beckoned him to follow. When he didn't, she faded away, leaving Nathan alone in the night.

*A*t seven the next morning, the telephone rang.

"Dad, I have fantastic news!" Ellen said.

Nathan rubbed the sleep from his eyes.

"We did my new dance piece tonight at the Ninety-second Street Y. Mom came. It went really well. Greg Moore heard I have a shot at getting that New York State grant I told you about. It could fund me for half a year. Isn't that terrific?"

Nathan put on his glasses and sat up in bed. His daughter was now twenty-five. But when she told him about her work, her voice still rushed and tumbled the way it had when she was five. "That's wonderful news!" he said, with as much enthusiasm as he could manage. Despite her fervor, he still wished she'd pursue a career more in line with her intellectual capabilities. Time and again he'd asked her how long this playing at being a dance choreographer would go on. She was jeopardizing her future stability, rejecting the help he could provide, to prove what? That she was her own person?

"It's Ellen's prerogative to make her own life," Marion repeatedly warned him. "If you keep this up, you're going to sour your whole relationship with her."

He knew she was right and tried to hold his tongue, hoping that Ellen would eventually decide to move on.

"How did Mom like the performance?" he asked.

"She said some of it reminded her of Bread and Puppet Theater pieces, but that it had my stamp on it. By the way, I asked her to tuck Grandpa's handkerchief into your suitcase. She didn't understand why I wanted it to go to Poland with you. Did she do it anyway?"

Nathan was stunned. "I have no idea. Just a minute." He stumbled over to his open suitcase, trying to imagine how Pop's handkerchief had been transported from his dream to his waking life. Marion had indeed planted the handkerchief in the crimped pouch at the back. The sound of Ellen's childhood voice in his dream returned to him. *Nine takes five.*

Flattening the crumpled ten-inch square on the bed, he recognized the raised lines on the fabric. He picked up the phone. "It's here," he said shakily. "What do you want me to do with it?"

"I'm not sure. Remember how once I told you Grandpa cried at the Seder because he was thinking about his childhood? That's why I sent it. It's the only thing I have of his, and since he never got the chance to go back, I thought the handkerchief could go back for him." She laughed. "Big symbolism, right?"

Nathan wondered if Ellen really believed Pop had never returned to Poland because he hadn't had the chance. Could she be so naive about the political and social realities of Jews in Eastern Europe? Of course she could. And whose fault was that? After two generations in America, he'd made sure she was an insider. She had no idea what it was to be a Jew in a hostile country.

"Actually, I thought there was something poetic about sending part of Grandpa back to Poland," Ellen said, "especially since his handkerchiefs always reminded me that he was from Europe. I mean, Americans use Kleenex."

Nathan remembered how his mother used to scrub the daylights out of Pop's handkerchiefs before she ironed them into perfect squares. "Elli, *everyone* used handkerchiefs in Grandpa's day. Kleenex weren't invented yet," he said.

She giggled. "Remember that time you made Grandpa come with us to the Adirondacks? He tied knots in all four ends of his handkerchief and put it on his head to protect his bald spot from the sun. He said that's what they did in Europe."

Nathan's heart hammered as he remembered the knotted handkerchief in his dream.

"Dad?"

"I'm here." He looked at the handkerchief, anxious yet amazed at the coincidence.

They spoke about other things after that. He carefully avoided mentioning his visit to Zokof. He didn't want to excite her until he'd been able to get some perspective on his experience there. He told her instead about the interesting church he'd seen, where they kept Chopin's heart in an urn. She liked that.

After they had hung up, Nathan held Pop's handkerchief under the night-stand light and shifted it slowly over the prongs of his fingers. He thought about what an odd, loving pair Pop and Ellen had made. With Ellen, Pop had been childlike, knotting his handkerchief into animal shapes, manipulating it as a shadow puppet. With her, he'd been a prankster, tugging her hair and pretending someone else had done it. Nathan had envied their ease with each other, though God knows how she'd ever understood Pop's heavily accented English. That she didn't know a word of Yiddish hadn't mattered at all when they had played the card game *pisha paysha,* laughing themselves silly for hours.

The last time Ellen had mentioned playing pisha paysha was at Pop's funeral. He had given the eulogy because Pop hadn't wanted a rabbi. In the hospital he'd said, "My whole life I kept those parasites away from me. They're not going to get me after I go." After his death, Nathan had closed himself off in his study and tried to find a suitable inroad to the map of his father's life. He worked all night, but by dawn he was terrified the ideas he'd written down would not come together when he got up to speak. By the time he'd arrived at the funeral hall, his fear had made him manic. Who had he been fooling, thinking he could suddenly speak extemporaneously after a lifetime of memorizing all his addresses, word for word, to give his audience an impression of ease and jocularity?

Every face in the hall had lifted when he'd stepped forward to speak, as if certain that Isaac Leiber's Harvard-professor son would give his father a eulogy to remember. He had watched those faces bloom with astonishment as he'd used the words *unformed, uneducated,* and *dogmatic* to describe his father. Soon after, the expressions of people he loved had withered with embarrassment and disappointment. They stared dejectedly into their laps.

His mother had slumped in her chair and twisted Gertie's silk sleeve until the funeral director had interrupted Nathan and announced it was time to leave for the gravesite. His mother had refused to let him into the limousine reserved for the immediate family.

On the long ride to Mount Zion Cemetery in his car, he'd sat rigid with guilt.

"It wasn't your best speech, but you're not used to this," Marion had consoled him. To Nathan, *this* meant religious ritual, and he'd felt a surge of gratitude toward his wife.

But Ellen hadn't been so forgiving. "Oh, God, Dad," she'd moaned from the backseat. "'Uneducated?' How could you say that about Grandpa? He wasn't uneducated. He read that Jewish newspaper all the time. And besides, he was a terrific grandfather. Why didn't you say that? Why didn't you say that he taught me how to play pisha paysha?"

Marion had promptly turned and corrected her. "That's *up and down*."

"That's what *you* call it. Grandpa and I called it pisha paysha." Ellen began to cry. Nathan had tightened his grip on the wheel, knowing that she had gotten it more right than his wife had.

The sun was rising over Warsaw. Nathan stared at the white handkerchief, still dazed from the effects of his dream and his conversation with Ellen. He showered and dressed, shamed anew at having dishonored both his father and his daughter at Pop's funeral. Tucking the refolded handkerchief into his pocket, he went downstairs to make arrangements with the concierge.

In life, I did not concern myself about what captures the hearts of children. I would have guessed the past is of little interest to them, especially if they are healthy and without real cares, as Itzik's granddaughter seemed to me. But now, heeding my father's warning to be vigilant, I took her interest in the handkerchief as a sign. What it signified, I did not know, but it gave me hope.

20

ONCE IN THE CAR, ON HIS WAY OUT OF WARSAW, NATHAN changed his mind. It was madness to spend his last hours in Poland in Zokof, making poetic gestures for his daughter, giving himself over to the lunacy of a dream. They were crossing the Vistula River. He leaned forward to instruct his driver to return to the Marriott Hotel. But it was too late to go back. His hosts were already affronted that he'd cancelled the appointments they'd made for him. Rescheduling would only compound the insult.

He slid back in his seat and absentmindedly wound Pop's handkerchief around his fingers, grateful that at least this driver spoke little English. When they arrived in Zokof, he used his guidebook Polish and asked to be dropped off at the far side of the main square, thinking he might as well take a last look at the town. As he emerged from the car, a stocky man on a bicycle, in a cap and wool jacket, wobbled to a full stop a foot in front of him. The man narrowed his eyes, but the horizontal line of his thin lips did not move. Nathan awkwardly brushed past him and made his way toward the church, intending to follow the square around until he reached the side street that led to Rafael's house. A pair of skinny teenage girls with bleached hair giggled as he passed, hiding their red-lipsticked mouths with their hands. Nathan kept his head down.

When he reached the side street he was looking for, a tractor lumbered by, pulling a trailer packed with standing men. Every pair of eyes on it was trained on him, so he thought, and not one showed the slightest indication of a greeting. He hurried down the narrow lane, past the fenced yards, the sleeping dog chained to a tree, to Rafael's house. He mounted the splintered wooden steps.

Next door, behind a chain-link fence, a stout, kerchiefed woman with chafed, swollen hands watched him slyly as she raked the dirt in her yard, chickens squabbling at her feet. He knocked purposefully for Rafael, eager to be let in. When Rafael did not immediately respond, he felt a swell of panic that the old man might not be home. Where in God's name would he go? Nathan wondered, shuddering at the thought of having to look for him.

Moments later, the door opened slightly, and Rafael's familiar thick fingers beckoned him. "Come! Come inside! I was expecting you back," he said brusquely.

Perplexed, Nathan crossed the threshold and blinked rapidly as his eyes adjusted to the dim light of the entryway. He jumped aside as his left shoulder touched a metal ladder, which extended up through a hole in the low ceiling. A repulsive, musty odor permeated the house. "How could you have possibly known I was coming?" he said.

Rafael arched his eyebrows. "From Freidl. Who else?"

Nathan's temples began to pulse. Surely Rafael was playing with him. He slipped his hand into his pocket and felt reassured by the presence of Pop's handkerchief.

"You saw her," Rafael said.

"No, I didn't see her," Nathan said firmly. "I just had a dream."

The remark seemed to so amuse Rafael that Nathan felt compelled to explain himself further. "It's not surprising that I would unconsciously try to imagine Freidl, after everything you told me yesterday at the cemetery."

Rafael's eyebrows rose again. "From a dream a man can know his destiny. From a dream a man can accept what his rational mind cannot. You look frightened, Leiber. So, you saw her. You're not the only one." He beckoned Nathan again. "Come."

Nathan followed the old man uncertainly through an interior door, into the yellowish, dust-filled haze of the long main room of the house. To his right, on the street side, a treadle-based sewing machine sat below a window hung with closed curtain sheers. Along the opposite wall were rows and rows of shelved books, which leaned floppily against one another, their bindings mostly broken, like a community of tired elders. In the spaces between the bookcases hung five or six extraordinarily intricate pictures made of paper, from which Hebrew lettering, *menorahs,* trees, animals, buildings, and designs had been cut. "What are these?" he asked.

"Oissherenishen," Rafael said. "Paper cutouts."

"Where are these from?"

"From my factory," Rafael replied, with a puckish smile. "I have ten workers." He showed Nathan his fingers. "The Talmud says we must observe His commandments with beauty. *Hiddur mitzvah.* So I took up the penknife and the board."

He shuffled a few steps farther toward the round table at the far end of the room, then turned back to Nathan and looked again at the paper cutouts. "I'll tell you, in my youth I didn't have the interest. To my father I said, it is for the scholar to waste his time on such detail. But later, when I came back to Zokof, what did I have but time? And details, I didn't mind. It took the mind off other things, you understand?"

Nathan nodded, assuming it impolite to question the connection between cutting paper designs and scholarship.

Rafael clapped his hands. "For us, this was always man's work. But I, I learned from Freidl. She made oissherenishen all her life. Her secret children, she calls them."

He smiled, dismissing Nathan's obvious confusion. "You didn't come back here to talk of paper cutouts." He motioned to the two tall cane-backed chairs at the far end of the room, which stood beside a round table covered with a stained oilcloth. "Come, sit."

Nathan sidestepped the piled books balanced precariously on several footstools and joined Rafael. On the table lay a closed leather-bound book. A white kerosene lamp glowed weakly next to the copper samovar. He sat down and felt the samovar's heat. Rafael sank heavily into the chair opposite.

"I didn't come back only because of the dream," Nathan said.

"So why?"

Nathan removed his jacket, stalling for time to compose himself. "I didn't have the chance yesterday to thank you for telling me about my father's town." He hung the jacket on the back of his chair. "But I have to admit, I still don't understand why it made him such a rabid socialist."

He glanced at Rafael, unsure whether the old man could understand what he was talking about. "I don't imagine Orthodox people know much about socialists," he said. These exchanges with Rafael seemed to him like two strangers shouting across a wild river. They could see each other, but neither could entirely understand what the other was saying.

A checkered cloth, bordered by brown tassels, lay across part of the table. Nathan rolled a tassel in his palm and found it soft and reassuring.

Rafael gathered the strings of his *tzittzit* and combed them with his fingers, from the knots down. His dry lips parted slightly, and he rapped the cover of the book on the table irritably. "There is nothing so embarrassing to the secular Jew as a man like me."

Nathan flushed, recalling all too well how he'd felt when he'd first laid eyes on Rafael.

"And why do I embarrass you?" Rafael persisted. "Because of what it might make the Gentile think of you." He nodded, as if Nathan's appalled expression was all the answer he needed.

"Let me tell you something I've learned in my life, Leiber. A Jew should not accept anyone else's opinion about himself. You're too afraid. We don't stir up anti-Semitism by being pious, by wearing the tzittzit and the *payess*. Anti-Semites don't need us to stir themselves up. They're already stirred up. This *mishegoss* has nothing to do with us. If a man hates Jews, he'll find a reason to hate the secular one as much as he hates the religious one."

"I suppose you're right," Nathan said, although he knew this would not change his embarrassment at the sight of a Hassid in the street.

"The question, Leiber, is what kind of Jew are you going to be when you go home?"

Nathan wondered why this would matter to Rafael. "I have to admit," he said, "I don't think I'll have changed that much, despite all your patient efforts yesterday. I'm a Jew by birth. That's all. I still don't understand your religiousness or what kind of God you believe in." He didn't think Rafael would understand if he said he'd always regarded his Jewish identity as having almost no weight or texture at all, something that could be stuffed into his back pocket, like a handkerchief, and pulled out at will for meals of lox and bagels or for the Passover Seder.

Rafael tipped back his head and roared with laughter. "All my life it's been like that with me! My rebbe at our yeshiva, may he rest in peace, didn't understand what kind of God I believed in either. A lot of *tsuris* I gave him."

This aroused Nathan's interest. "How so?" he asked.

"The rebbe always said we were God's chosen people. This troubled me. We have a relationship with our God. Fine. But what good comes from calling ourselves *chosen?* Our God wants that we should make people resent us, or worse, that we should suffer for His vanity? It's a chutzpah of God, really, don't you think?"

Nathan smiled. "That's a rather secular analysis."

"My rebbe thought so too. A *klop* on the head he gave me for such questions. Feh!" Rafael squinted. "But I asked them. I had to know why I should suffer for such a God."

This man would have been a star at City College, Nathan thought. "Maybe you should have asked your rebbe why being one of the chosen people was so important to him," he said.

Rafael nodded approvingly. "For a man like my rebbe, a man of that generation, we were chosen because it is written in the Torah and that is the word of God. But now, as I think about it, we Jews in Zokof always knew the delicacy of our position, even as children. Maybe teaching us we were God's chosen was the rebbe's way to teach us to be strong, that a Jew must set God's example." He laughed. "Me, I had my own ways to show my strength."

"How so?"

"I'm a fighter." Rafael sat back, smiling mysteriously. "I remember, when I was maybe ten years old, some Polish boys stopped me on the street. They made a circle around me and called me a dirty Jew. To them, a Jew was a coward, and they expected me to hang my head. I told them, 'Leave me alone. I'm a clean Jew.' It surprised them, you see. One of them grabbed my shirt. 'You killed Christ,' he said. As if I did it, yeh? When I laughed, he punched me in the chest, hard, but I didn't fall down, because I grabbed him back. I said, 'You killed my Aunt Tzeitl,' and punched him for everything I decided he'd done to her, hard in the chest, too."

Rafael leaned toward Nathan. "You should have seen this boy's face. All confusion. 'I don't know your Aunt Tzeitl,' he said. 'Well, I don't know your Christ,' I said. 'So leave me alone.'"

Rafael shook his head. "Of course, they didn't leave me alone. Oy, did they beat me that time." He sighed. "This is how my rebbe was right to try to protect us. A Jewish child is vulnerable. He gets wounded. He never forgets the moment when he realized he is an object of hatred simply because he is alive. It pulls the earth out from under, no?"

Nathan flushed and looked down at the table, thinking briefly of Ellen, glad now of her naïveté. "In my old neighborhood, it was the Irish boys who came after us," he said. "Why do you blame secular Jews for wanting to avoid that kind of punishment?"

"Because you can't avoid the punishment. They beat you with or without the yarmulke."

Nathan's ears burned.

"The truth is, the Gentiles can't leave us alone," Rafael said. "And us. We can't leave them alone. We're tied together by the tail like two dogs, snapping at each other for two thousand years. And in places where there are the Muslims, it's three dogs tied together. I ask God if this amuses Him, that we should spend eternity biting at each other's hindquarters. Are we not men?"

"And what does God tell you?" Nathan asked, genuinely interested in the answer.

"Bubkes!" Rafael laughed.

Slightly disappointed, Nathan smiled. "Now you sound like my father."

"Of course I sound like your father. Before the war, Leiber, I was a socialist too."

"How could that be?" Nathan protested. Try as he might, he could not imagine Rafael beardless, much less young and wearing normal clothes.

Rafael calmly raked his beard. "Back then, in the twenties and thirties, I had to show the world I was no dog! I joined *Brti Hachayal,* to defend us from the anti-Jewish riots. I ran around with Zionists. We were young. We'd had some trayf education. Our fathers' world was no use to us anymore. The world was changing. Back then, on Saturday nights, the sidewalks in Zokof were crowded with political speakers." He smiled, his face awash with memories.

Nathan felt a gush of comfort. "In Brooklyn, where I grew up," he said, "we had political debates on street corners too. On Saturday nights, the communists would take one corner, the socialists another, the Bundists too. They would all preach to the crowds and to one another, as if they could convert each other. Up and down Pitkin Avenue you'd hear them. My father used to go all the time, to heckle the communists." He laughed awkwardly.

"Two Jews, twenty opinions!" Rafael said.

"And membership in fifteen organizations," Nathan joined in.

Surprised by their spontaneous humor, the two of them laughed.

"We all wanted to believe in those fairy tales," Rafael said. "Such a happy ending. All of us one big family. The *goyim* calling us brothers, not devils. Wonderful." He teased Nathan with a smile. "And you know, socialism is so Jewish!"

Nathan stopped laughing. He didn't want to hear this. Pop's union affiliation had forced Nathan to have to dodge McCarthy's 1950s communist witch hunt at his university. He'd come close to hating Pop for that. "Socialism is not Jewish," he said. "Only anti-Semites want people to believe there's an international Jewish socialist conspiracy."

"Ach, don't make speeches. It's just you and me here, Leiber. You want to know what socialism was for your father? It was Judaism for the twentieth century. It had a Messiah, even, the guarantee we'd be a free people among the nations. It set us on fire!" Rafael looked elated and wistful at the same time. "When the Poles cursed us and said, 'Jews to Palestine,' we cheered for their enemy, socialist Russia. You understand? We needed to believe in the socialist dream to go on living here, Leiber. Only later we saw that socialism was our Sabbatai Tzvi."

Nathan had never heard of Sabbatai Tzvi, but he was encouraged by the surprising fullness of Rafael's body of knowledge.

Rafael must have realized an explanation was required. "This was a false Messiah, in the seventeenth century. People followed him, but the End of Days didn't come. It was the same with the socialists. In the end, they were corrupted, and we saw they were only men pretending they didn't need God."

A dog barked outside. Nathan rubbed his chin. "My father used to say, 'A man is greeted by how he is dressed, but bidden farewell according to his wisdom.' I owe you an apology, Rafael, for judging you by your orthodoxy first. I wasn't raised to respect men of faith. I underestimated you."

"Your father quotes Talmud."

"No, that's a socialist saying."

"Feh! Stolen wisdom." Rafael raised his hands resignedly. "What can you do?"

Nathan was amused at having discovered the origins of one of Pop's favorite sayings. "At law, we require that people cite their sources."

"You'd have made a good Talmudist."

"My father would have disowned me."

Rafael frowned. "Where do you think your ideas of right and wrong come from, Leiber? Do you have the chutzpah to believe that you and your father made them up?"

"I take your point," Nathan said, aware that he was becoming increasingly confused about Pop's relationship with his religion.

Rafael rose and shuffled toward the closed door on the wall with the bookcases. When he opened it, a ray of sunlight from the window lit the worn elbow of his white shirt, revealing the bony fragility beneath the cloth. Nathan noticed how Rafael's shoulders, which yesterday had assumed definition under his black coat, now slumped under his misshapen gray wool vest, and how his trousers bagged at the knees. Through the open door, Nathan saw the corner of a white-tiled wood stove. He considered the hardship of gathering wood for the stove, of bending nearly to the floor to shove the logs through the metal door, of struggling to get it lit. How much longer could Rafael go on like this?

Rafael pushed aside a dented enamel pot on top of the stove and produced two glass cups. "Tea?" he asked, returning to the table. He poured a cup from the samovar for Nathan and one for himself. "Forgive me," he said. "There is no sugar."

Nathan waved this off, but Rafael seemed extremely embarrassed at not having it to offer. It occurred to Nathan that during wartime, sugar was a precious commodity. That it was still precious for Rafael suggested that the war had never really ended for him. He thought of his own crammed pantry at home, where grains, pastas, and cereals were always spilling from their boxes, waiting to be swept into the trash with Marion's next housekeeping frenzy. When he returned home, he would send a check. He'd make a little joke so it wouldn't look like charity. Something with the word *sweeten* in it. Something expressing his gratitude. He'd finesse it, give it a dignified sound.

"Look," Rafael said, removing a small wood-framed photograph from the wall. "One of my neighbors found this in his attic and brought it to me."

Nathan studied the photograph of about fifteen smiling young people casually posed on a hillside — a pretty girl in a checkered dress, a pair of clowning boys. Their faces looked so familiar, like his college friends. He smiled and handed the photograph back to Rafael.

"The house where my neighbor lives used to belong to a Bundist named Lazer Weitzman. When we were young, I argued day and night with Lazer. He said we shouldn't need to go to Palestine. We don't know from living in deserts anymore, he said. For a thousand years we've lived here in Poland — what we call *Poyln* in Jewish — that means, *here, we rest. This* is our country. We have a right to say so already." Rafael shrugged. "I said different. But he was a good man, Lazer. They all were. Good hearts." He thumped his chest and nodded back at the picture. "Not a single one of them survived the Annihilation."

Nathan looked again at the photograph and tried to imagine those promising faces in a concentration camp, especially the earnest-looking young man in glasses, so like himself at that age, so like Pop, too, perhaps. He looked at the wall where the framed photograph had hung. The fleur-de-lis wallpaper was faded. Its edges curled downward from the ceiling, as if exhausted from fighting gravity for so many years with so little paste to hold it. He felt depressed. He wanted to go home.

Rafael carefully returned the photograph to its place. "After the Destruction, Leiber, we had no right to play games with our Jewishness."

"But I don't understand why what happened made you more interested in finding God," Nathan said. He pointed to the photograph on the wall. "It would only make me want to bring their killers to justice."

Rafael shrugged. "The guilty ones don't interest me anymore. I'm too old, too tired to fight them. I save my strength for wrestling with God Himself, for asking what is the nature of His will."

"But wouldn't you think it's God's will that the guilty be judged? How do you reconcile the slaughter of innocents with God's will?"

Rafael took a deep breath and slowly exhaled. "Leiber, there is evil in the world. It comes from the darkness that existed before God's creation, and it remained after God brought forth light and life. If I believed evil is there by God's will, then I would also have to believe that it is God's will that the innocent are slaughtered. A God like that cannot withstand my accusations. I do not accept Him any more than I accept the God of Choseness."

Nathan was surprised and impressed at such candor from a religious man. For him, the matter had always been much simpler. To believe in God, any God, was for the soft and immature, people with a childish need for pat answers about life.

"I believe there is only one God," Rafael continued. "He is the One who lights our souls at birth with a holy spark and watches how we burn our way back to Him. That is God. The rest is what we think He wants from us."

Nathan again sought the handkerchief in his pocket, stirred by the first compelling argument he'd ever heard about God. "How did you come to this point of view?"

Rafael rubbed his knee, which seemed to pain him. "Freidl," he said, as if this was the most natural answer in the world.

Nathan reached for his keloid. The sour taste of disappointment filled his mouth. He'd allowed Rafael to seduce him with an idea of God. And where had it taken him? Headfirst into the mushy pit of mysticism.

Outside, a group of men passed the house. Their muffled voices penetrated Rafael's closed window. Again, he wondered why Rafael had remained in Zokof, the last of his kind, literally *wearing* his Judaism every day.

If Rafael noticed Nathan's upset, he didn't acknowledge it. "When I came back to Zokof in 1945, the summer after the war," he said, "I had nothing left in me. I was like a dead man. Skin and bones and no heart, no desire. Freidl came to me the same way she came to you, in a dream. She said to me, 'A Jew must join in his own traditions or his children will suffer in the darkness.'"

"My father would have said that raising children to believe in God is the same thing as letting them suffer in darkness," Nathan said curtly.

Rafael twirled the long ends of his mustache. "Leiber, a man who forgets God withers. His roots wrap around a heap of stones and his life is drawn from rocks. The holy light goes out."

Nathan closed his eyes and saw Pop, crying at the family's Seder table. He dug his hand into his pocket again and clutched the handkerchief. "In my dream last night, the woman who called herself Freidl held a light in her hands."

Rafael exhaled loudly. "In the dream she had a handkerchief, all lit up, yeh?"

Nathan opened his eyes. "How do you know about the handkerchief? Even I didn't know I had it until this morning."

"Freidl showed it to me."

"But *I* have the handkerchief." He produced it from his pocket and laid it on the table.

Rafael barely glanced at it. His whole focus was on Nathan. "You have the handkerchief. But the light that made it so beautiful stayed here in Zokof. It's your father's light. This is why you returned. You know this, Leiber. It's in your bones."

"What does light have to do with my father?"

Rafael leaned back in his chair and let his hand rest on the leather-bound book. "It's his holy spark."

Nathan was determined not to let Rafael think he would accept easy, fanciful answers to his questions this time. "There's nothing left of my father. He's been dead for years."

Rafael shook his head impatiently. "When a man dies, his holy spark returns to God. The light you saw in your dream was an image of your father's spark, the same that woke Freidl from the grave."

Nathan wondered how the spark had gotten into his dream when he didn't even believe in God.

Rafael stroked his beard. "Leiber," he said quietly, "I'm not so far from the days when death will sit on my nose. I want you to know something before I go. I remember the night your father's spark took flame."

"When we met yesterday you acted as if you hardly knew my father!"

Rafael laughed. "I didn't know you yesterday."

Nathan suddenly felt shaky and weak. He gripped the sides of his chair. "What do you remember about my father?"

Rafael rubbed his thumb over the leather-bound book authoritatively. He regarded Nathan briefly. "In the cemetery," he said, "I told you stories about the night your father left this town. You remember the three kinderlach — those little boys, walking home from cheder that night?"

Nathan nodded.

"They had names also. There was Tzvi Baer. The other was Chaim Apt. The third one, the three-year-old, carried the lantern. He was the one attacked, whipped on the face and hands by Jan Nowak. He was the one who called out your father's name and blackened it forever in the minds of the Poles in Zokof. That boychik with the lantern, Leiber. That was me."

I knew who he was from the first time he appeared in my blue exile. His guilt at betraying Itzik had led him there to me. The start of the dark night of his soul. That is what Rafael called the cold spring night when Jan Nowak died and Itzik fled to my grave. Many times I asked him, Rafael, what did the events of that night have to do with Miriam? Why Miriam? It was a shame, really, that he never had an answer for me.

21

NATHAN WAS SHOCKED BY RAFAEL'S CONFESSION, BUT HE COULD not make sense of it. He could accept as fact that if Rafael was three in 1906, he was eighty-nine now. But to comprehend that Rafael had known his father, that the story of Jan the peasant's death was true, required more imagination than he could immediately summon. He said nothing.

Rafael smiled. "I have remembered your father all my life," he said. "Itzik Leiber came out of the night like an angel — an angel with no meat on his bones." He pointed to the other side of the room and shook his finger emphatically, as if Nathan should be able to see Pop there as clearly as he did. "He did not have to save us. He was safe, hidden in the dark. But he ran to our lantern, to that *cham,* Jan the peasant." He shook his head. "Ach! You should have heard him. The man laughed like a devil. I was the first to see Itzik coming to us. Even in that dark, I saw he had a fury in him, a fire. How such a skinny boy could refuse to be afraid, this I would never forget."

Nathan tried to imagine it. But the only fire he'd ever seen in his father was when Pop argued that one-note philosophy he called socialism and reduced every situation to the same equation. The strong oppress the weak. The weak have a duty to organize and to throw off the tyrants' yoke. Increasingly, Nathan had found his father's views intellectually irritating. Once, he stood up and left the room when Pop started in.

"What? You think this has nothing to do with you, Mr. Big Shot Professor?" Pop had called after him.

Rafael reached over and grabbed Nathan by the wrist. "Like this your father stopped Jan from bringing the whip down on me!" He yanked the startled Nathan's arm above his head. "The horse went up on its back legs, took the wagon with it. Jan fell under a wheel. It crushed his head. He was finished. We couldn't believe it. Itzik said run, so we ran. We left them there, Jan and him. Two dogs tied at the tail, yeh?" Angrily, he waved the thought away, releasing Nathan's wrist. "I never saw your father again."

Gingerly, Nathan touched a corner of Pop's handkerchief and, with some difficulty, said, "He never told me about you or this man, Jan." A truck rumbled by the house, briefly blanketing the room in shadow. In the closed, dusty corner where they sat, Nathan felt a chill. "I'm sorry," he said, adjusting his glasses, "I had no idea, and it's hard for me to see my father the way you describe him. He became a very different sort of man. As long as I can remember, he always had plenty of meat on his bones." He cleared his throat. "Pop argued with radio announcers and at the newspaper he read. He talked as if his socialist propaganda was going to change the world, but he never stood up for anything or anyone in public. When he wasn't working, what I remember him doing most was sitting at the window." He paused, recalling the image of Pop in his chair, like a photograph. His face burned with embarrassment as he realized how inappropriate it was for him, at this moment, to reveal the level of his bitterness and resentment toward his father. Nervously, he flicked the soft tassels of the checkered cloth around his fingers, anxious at how Rafael would respond.

"Freidl always said Itzik had the soul of a potato," Rafael said quietly. "So it seems his soul didn't grow in America. It's a *shonda* — a shame. A man may only have one moment in his life when a spark flames in him. If this he doesn't protect, it dies. But even so, Leiber, what your father did for me was the lesson of a lifetime. That a man must have courage to do what is right in the eyes of God, no matter the cost."

"But my father didn't think in terms of God," Nathan insisted again.

"Yes, he did. He was one of us. It is in our bones to think of God as the Measure of Righteousness. Maybe Itzik would not say this, especially after he met Hillel, but that is how he thought about it."

"Who was Hillel?" Nathan wanted to know. "Someone from Zokof?"

Rafael frowned. "Your father never told you about Hillel?"

Nathan shook his head. The only Hillel he knew was Hillel Gelbart. Gelbart was now a well-known MIT physicist, but to Nathan he would always be the gangly kid who hid out at the Leibers' to avoid practicing the violin. Hillel Gelbart was the only one of his childhood friends who Pop joked with and listened to, a fact that Nathan somehow held against Gelbart, despite all his achievements.

Rafael clasped his hands patiently and recounted, at length, how Itzik and Hillel had met at the Warsaw train station.

"Where did you hear this?" Nathan asked.

"Freidl told me," Rafael said, with a confident shrug. "This was the part of Itzik's story that made her laugh. She told it to me many times. 'Imagine,' she said, 'Itzik the Faithless One and Hillel the Socialist walking the streets of Warsaw, with me singing Aaron Birnbaum's tune in Hillel's ear!'" Rafael sat back in his chair and laughed. "What a group! 'Better a Jew without a beard than a beard without a Jew.' That is what she said about Hillel. Ha!"

The afternoon sun lit the curtain sheers until they appeared opaque. Nathan gazed at them, thinking Rafael had now lost all restraint about Freidl, as if he had secured Nathan's confidence to the extent that he could speak of his conversations with a dead woman and expect to be believed. A slow, painful pounding began at his temples.

"She said Hillel took Itzik to find Mendel the Blacksmith, a cousin of your grandfather's. He lived near Plac Grzybowski."

Nathan's heart leapt. "Plac Grzybowski, is that spelled *G-R-Z-Y*?"

Rafael nodded.

"I was there the other day!" he said, glad for a means to direct their attention away from Freidl. "I found a synagogue. The name begins with an *N*."

" Nożyk, yeh. The last synagogue in Warsaw. By the Nożyk Synagogue your father became a socialist. Hillel told him a synagogue is a place where weak men run to hide."

"My father used to say that all the time! How did you know?"

Rafael shrugged again. "I told you. Freidl."

Nathan knew there was no point in arguing. "What happened to Hillel, after my father left Poland?"

"Ach! Stalin's gulags."

"Did my father know?"

"In America? Nah! When a man went to America, it was for us like he fell off the earth. And during the war, Itzik wouldn't know what happened here."

Nathan noticed that Rafael suddenly looked distressed. He asked him why.

"I once had a photograph of the two of them, your father and Hillel. He was such a handsome boy, Hillel."

"Where did you get the photograph?" Nathan asked excitedly.

"During the war."

"You came across a picture of my father taken in Warsaw, during the war? That's unbelievable."

"Unbelievable? Nah. Always, my life was full of coincidences about your father and that night Jan died." He touched his yarmulke.

"What do you mean?"

"In the beginning, it was just small things. Once, when I was a boy of nine or ten, I saw Jan's old horse in a field. No one around. I tell you, that animal looked at me and went up on its back legs, just like on that night. Now, I think she did that. God knows how. She left me signs, put things in my path so I should remember Itzik."

Nathan was becoming annoyed that Freidl was showing up at every turn in Pop's story. But, not wanting to insult Rafael, he played along. "Why did she want you to remember Itzik?"

Rafael gave him a reproachful look. "Understand, I didn't go looking for Freidl to be in my life. I heard the story about her frightening the Poles away from Itzik in the cemetery, sure. Everyone in Zokof knew it. But I didn't believe it. I was there that night, remember. I saw him, full of his own strength. He had a chutzpah. I thought he made a commotion for the Poles, to scare them — threw a rock, made sounds. Of our cemetery, they were already afraid. It wouldn't take much for him to do it."

Nathan was relieved to have some of his confidence in Rafael restored.

"But you understand, Leiber? After us boys ran away — Tzvi, Chaim, and me — what I heard about him I heard from Freidl. No one else heard nothing — *gornish* — after he left Zokof."

Nathan didn't want to conjure with that statement. Instead, he considered how to delicately steer the conversation back to the photograph of Pop and Hillel. The photograph, at least, offered some kind of evidence of Pop's history, by someone other than Freidl.

But Rafael persisted. "Think what you like about Freidl after, but listen to me. Most of my life I have felt someone with me, putting people, things, events in my way. A thing like this you don't talk about. You live with it."

He pulled at his vest. Nathan noticed several buttons missing on the shirt underneath, and realized how uncared-for Rafael was. It made him ashamed to try to take away his faith in Freidl, and his apparent companionship with her. He toyed resignedly with his glass of tea and hoped Rafael would not detect his disbelief.

"I'll tell you how it was with Freidl," Rafael said. "Until 1939, these coincidences she made happen didn't matter so much. Then, the Nazis were at our doorsteps. I got Polish papers, which wasn't easy, with this Jewish face of mine." He displayed his profile with a weary playfulness.

Nathan wondered how well his own looks would have protected him if he'd lived in Europe at that time.

"The night I got the papers, I put some clothes in a bag, a few zlotys in my shoes, and I ran. I escaped to Soviet Russia, Byelorussia they called it then. The plan was, my wife, Chana, would follow with the baby."

Once again, Nathan was stunned. "Your wife and baby? You had a family?"

"I wasn't always an alter kocker, Leiber. I was a young man in those days. I had a family." Rafael wiped his face with his cuff. "What did I know it would happen so quick after I left them? We had a plan to meet later. How could I take them to live in the forests? With what food? What shelter? You can't imagine what kind of people they had running around in there too. I was hiding in haystacks in the fields, all the time moving east, away from them in Zokof." The corners of his mouth tightened.

Nathan touched Rafael's arm to comfort him. "I'm sorry if I upset you by asking," he said. A painful stillness settled on the room. He squeezed the old man's arm lightly and felt the bones.

Rafael nodded appreciatively, now restraining his emotion with obvious difficulty. "Even now, I see my daughter Sonya's fingers pulling at my jacket. Just them, the little fingers."

He stood up and shuffled to the wardrobe near the window. He pulled a small wrinkled piece of paper from one of its drawers and handed it to Nathan. It was a photograph of a big-cheeked baby in the arms of a dark-haired young woman. Their features were obscured by the scores of folds in the paper.

Nathan studied the photograph with all the horror of knowing he was about to hear that something terrible had happened to this mother and her child.

"Every time I thought I was finished, some coincidence came my way," Rafael said. "One time, a Russian caught me stealing eggs. He raised his gun. I don't know why, but I said, 'Have pity on a father. I have a daughter, eighteen months old.' 'What's her name?' he asked me. I told him, 'Her name is Sonya.' He put down the gun. 'My sister's name is Sonya,' he said, and he walked away."

Nathan returned the photograph to Rafael, who put it back in the drawer. "Things like this happened to me all through the war. Two years I wandered through Uzbekistan, Kazakhstan, wherever the work or the trains took me. In October 1942, I came across some Polish partisans in the forest. These sorts of fellows I knew. Sometimes they turned in Jews, so I hid from them. But I stayed close to catch what news I could. I heard them talking about Zokof, my town. And the news! My God! The Nazis had taken all the Jews — rounded them up from a ghetto they had made there, shot them in the streets, drove them like cattle to the trains. My Chana and my Sonya! That night I lay facedown on the forest floor like an animal, my open mouth full of dirt, not even free to howl my grief."

With slow, careful control, he folded his hands. "For my family," he said, "there were no coincidences. They sent my wife and my daughter to a killing place, deep in the forest. Treblinka. The ones who went in there didn't come back."

Nathan couldn't bear to look at Rafael. He imagined himself, an urban intellectual, alone in a forest, hearing that his girls, his Marion and Ellen, had been taken away and murdered. But hard as he tried, it was impossible for him to get the feel, the depth, of such a loss. His best guess was a sense of insurmountable helplessness against ongoing pain. He wondered how a human being continued to live after that.

Then he thought of his father, who never knew what had happened to his family in Poland, but who had managed to carry this burden alone all his life. He wondered if a monstrous protectiveness had kept him from telling his children about his past.

Rafael returned to his seat. "After I heard what they did in Zokof, I joined the exiled Polish army in Russia. They had a general there who was looking for recruits. I wanted not to feel anymore, to be frozen, to take orders. What better place for me? The Poles made me an officer, put me at a desk. For me, it was a blessing not to be *the Jew* for that time. They knew, but they never said."

Nathan cringed at how the word *Jew* could be one's most significant trait in the eyes of other people.

Maybe Rafael saw this. "You are your father's son," he said. "You know the Four Sons we tell of at the Passover Seder — the Wise Son, the Wicked Son, the Simple Son, and the Son Who Doesn't Know What to Ask?"

Nathan admitted he vaguely recalled reading this in the Reform Haggadah from which his family freely skipped whole sections in their flight toward the meal.

"Freidl always said Itzik was like the Wicked Son who asks, What does this night mean to *you?* Not *us* — as if he does not belong to the community." He smiled. "She said the same thing about me too, after we got to know each other. You see, we have all been Wicked Sons, Leiber."

"I suppose you're right," Nathan said. "But tell me, what's this all about, this business with Freidl?"

Rafael sighed. "Yeh, it's time. I will tell you. One night in Russia, I was on my way from one camp to the other. An old man in rags stepped out from the shadows. He spoke to me in Jewish, quietly. He told me I had to help him. He was starving, and the local people were treating him rough. Why waste food on an old Jew? I said all right, I would bring him food, but he would have to meet me outside the camp because if anyone saw, we would be shot for certain. He thanked me. Then, he said, 'He who saves a life, saves the whole world.' You know this expression?"

Nathan said he'd heard it before, but it hadn't meant much to him. A platitude.

"I was in no mood for pretty words either," Rafael agreed. "I said, 'You're talking to a man whose world is already dead.' And this man, half-dead himself, takes me by the arm and says, 'I also had a wife. I had four children. We are not here to make a perfect world, just a better one. That is what's required. That is why, even in the gulag, I played tunes on my guitar, and when there was no guitar, I sang.'

"I did not want to know from his tunes or his gulags. I told him, 'A guitar you won't find here. I'm done with believing human gods. I'm done with Karl Marx.'

"This man said to me, 'Marx? Are you meshuggeh? That's Talmud, *chaver* — my comrade, my friend.' Then he made a face. 'But, what's the difference?' he said."

Nathan remembered their earlier conversation about Marx and the Talmud. This time he didn't argue.

"Leiber, I tell you, right then, in the middle of an open field with nothing but snow for miles around us, the idea of Marx and Talmud as the same, it was like God's idea of a joke. We fell on each other, this man and me, like we were lost family. We cried and we coughed until we were bent in two. I gave him the crust of bread I had in my pocket, and he gave me his name — Hillel."

Nathan got white as the curtain sheers. "The same Hillel as in the photograph with my father?"

"The same. And it was no coincidence. It was Freidl, making a *shiddach* — a connection between us."

"What kind of connection was she trying to make?" Nathan asked.

"I didn't know. I fed him. I did what I could to get him a roof over his head. We were a comfort to each other. He always had a tune. But later that winter, he was finished. Before he died, he gave me the three photographs he had kept with him always. There was one of his family, and one of an Indian warrior in America, a proud face. The last one was of your father, with him. I recognized Itzik, of course. I asked him, 'How did you know this boy?' He told me how he met Itzik and how Itzik went to America. Even with the war, all the disorganization of our lives, where I thought nothing could surprise me anymore, I was left without words, to hear this man, Hillel, bringing Itzik Leiber back into my life again. It was fantastic. Impossible. What was I to think?"

"Where are his photographs now, the one with my father?"

"I'm sorry, Leiber," Rafael said. "They were stolen from my coat on the way home — a story to itself. It's a shame. I would have given it to you."

Nathan's hope for hard proof sank. "Thanks anyway," he said.

Rafael took a sip of tea. "I am not yet finished. You asked me about Freidl. There is more to tell. After the Annihilation, I came back home to Zokof. I didn't have anywhere else to go. Maybe, I thought, there'll be someone left, someone I know. You have no idea how hungry I was to see a familiar face! Five thousand Jews we used to be here. There had to be someone.

"The first night, I hid in the forest near the cemetery. You see, we returning ones, we were afraid. We heard stories about Poles killing Jews when they came home. This happened. I knew people who died like that."

Nathan believed him.

"The next night, I crept like a thief to Jewish houses in town and saw Poles were living there. For three nights I made my inventory. On the fourth night I knew I was the only one left. My life wasn't worth a sucked egg." He sighed.

"That night, while I slept in the forest, she came to me. Freidl. A beautiful woman, with such a voice — so strong and full of feeling."

"An alto," Nathan said absentmindedly, remembering his dream.

"'Do not leave Zokof,' she begged me. My heart bled. To hear the sound of Jewish for the first time in months and here, in my hometown. 'Who are you?' I asked. She answered me with words I remembered from my child-hood. *Lamentations,* it is called in English. What we recite on the holy day of *Tisha Bov,* the day we remember the destruction of the Second Temple in Jerusalem." He checked to see if any of this registered with Nathan.

Nathan only nodded at Rafael to continue.

"Freidl said to me: *'He has blocked my ways with cut stones. He has made my paths a maze.'* I knew the words well. I said, *'He has walled me in; I cannot escape. He has made my chains heavy, and when I call and shout, He shuts out my prayer.'"*

Tears began to roll down the crisscrossed tracks of Rafael's face. "This woman knew what it was to suffer. She knows the dark night of the soul. By morning she was singing tunes to me. The old tunes. *Little Zokof,* we called our town."

Nathan sat up straight. How could it be? How? He could hear the song Freidl had sung in his dream and at the cemetery. His ears once again felt as if they were filled with water. He felt unbalanced, faint. *Little Zokof, little town. How I miss you so.*

Rafael did not seem to notice Nathan's distress. "I was so glad to have her there," he said, "someone to keep me from a loneliness you cannot imagine. There was nothing I could do to thank her, a lost soul. The stones, you un-derstand, they were blocking the way to her grave. She could not rest. There was no peace for her." He paused, stroked his beard. "She said she always knew that I would help her, for Itzik's sake. But I was too young when Itzik left for America. She had to wait, and follow me. And now, it was time."

Nathan was so moved by this, his resistance to Freidl, to the idea of her, began to weaken.

"You understand, something prevented her from going to America," Rafael said. "I never knew what. But it seems I was her only connection back to that night, back to her gravesite, to peace. I did not know how to help her. I said to her, 'I am angry at God. Please don't ask me to appease Him. He thinks His people are so weak they require suffering to remain true to His word. Just because I remember the words of Lamentations from my childhood does not mean I say them today as a man who bows his head before God.'

"She said, 'I am a woman who had to wait until I was in the grave to meet a child, and a man, whose lives I could touch. But still I believe in my God. And you must believe also.' These were her exact words. I remember, because they made me weep. She tried to comfort me. She said, 'You were saved by a boy named Itzik! Itzik means *laugh.*' And she laughed and laughed until I laughed too."

Nathan smiled, and continued to be drawn in, even charmed, by Rafael's story.

"The next morning, she found a way to bring Jerzy to me. You remember Jerzy? We went to his apartment yesterday."

"Yes, I remember. The apartment at the end of the hall," Nathan said.

"'You're still here?' Jerzy said to me. I didn't know if he meant I had the chutzpah to still be alive or that he was surprised I came back."

Nathan shuddered at such a rude homecoming.

"But he was a mensch," Rafael said. "He told me, 'The town needs a tailor, Rafael. Be our tailor, and we will live in peace. There's a house I know for you.'

"So I became a tailor, a good one even, and the people here have always let me be." He glanced at the sewing machine beneath the window. "And it is not such a bad thing. You see, God has provided. I have even made my own linen shroud."

Nathan looked stricken.

Rafael waved away his concern. "No one escapes the boundaries of death, Leiber. Not even Moses, whom God favored. Not even he could persuade Him to set aside the sentence."

"And Freidl?" Nathan asked. "How has she escaped that sentence?"

"Freidl is dead, Leiber. She crossed the boundary. Her body lies inside the cemetery, walled in by God, even if the gravestones and the wall are gone."

Nathan knew full well that he was crossing the boundary of his own beliefs, but he couldn't resist asking, "But how does she participate in your life?"

Rafael pulled nervously at the ends of his beard. "When I moved into this house, I was haunted for many years by the memory of my wife and my daughter. The Poles began to call me the 'crazy Jew' because I wandered the streets. What did they know what I was looking for? Could they imagine what it was to be homesick in my own town? I would walk to the marketplace on Friday, just before Shabbos began, and see Shima walking the streets, shaking the birch whisk, calling, 'Jews to the bath.' It was terrible. I was making myself sick with grief.

"Freidl came to me. She said, 'To the cemetery.' I thought she wanted me to do something for her. But she said, 'Pick up stones. Put them on the graves.' And I did. I began to talk to them, the buried ancestors, as if we were family. It was craziness and I knew it, but it consoled me, stone after stone. After, she began to come to me at night."

"In dreams?" Nathan guessed.

"Dreams, yeh. But not like dreams. We talked. She told me her life, and what came after, and about Itzik and Hillel. There was more between us too, but of this you do not have to know." He gave a little shrug. "I needed her. She needed me. We are alone here. But she never forgets your father." He looked at Nathan.

"She wanted so much to know what happened to him. Why he did not return when the danger was past. Why didn't she feel his prayers? Did he remember her? Did his children pray for her? She is in terror that she will never be able to return, to rest again in her place in the cemetery. Don't look so skeptical, Leiber. You are fortunate that such a woman of valor is bound up with your life. This is a great woman, wise, and a scholar, like you. The daughter of the famous Rebbe Eliezer of blessed memory."

Nathan felt lost. "How do you expect me to believe it could make any difference if my father or I prayed for her?"

Rafael laid his hand on the table. "Because to pray is to understand and to understand is to heal."

Platitudes made Nathan impatient. "That's a very nice statement," he said. "But with all due respect, that's the kind of thing I hear from my students who fancy themselves Buddhists."

"Then let me explain it like this. The night when I first moved into this house, it was the eve of Tisha Bov — the ninth day in the Hebrew month of *Av.* Freidl said we must read. Lamentations. This I explained to you before."

Nathan nodded.

"I could not refuse her. In the beginning, as we davened, for me, it was just *narrishkeit* — nonsense. Empty words. Two thousand years ago the Second Temple was destroyed. What was that to me, after what I'd been through? But I was glad for her company, you understand?"

"Yes."

"But from repetition, all through the night, I began to listen. This prayer said what was in my heart. Without Freidl, I would not have found it — my way back from the dead. *'Yahweh, remember what has happened to us;*

look on us and see our degradation. Our inheritance has passed to aliens, our homes to barbarians.'" He had closed his eyes and begun to sway as he said the words, first in Hebrew, then in English. "*We are orphans, we are fatherless; our mothers are like widows. We drink our own water — at a price; we have to pay for what is our own firewood.'*"

He opened his eyes. "She helped me to heal what could be healed. That is what I prayed for. Now, you ask why I stayed here, Leiber? For her, I stayed. Because of her, I became observant. The way I thought about it was this: whether God thinks we are His chosen people does not matter anymore. I choose to be a Jew, like her. Let the world think what it likes. It's nothing to do with me. I grew payess, put on the long coat and the yarmulke, and this comforts me. In time, the people in town began to call me 'our little Jew.' I don't mind." He took a sip of his tea and wiped a few droplets from his mustache.

Nathan looked at him incredulously. "You would have left Zokof and lived a secular life if not for her?"

"Maybe. Yeh. Probably I would have gone to Warsaw. There, at least, there were other Jews. Maybe I would have left Poland, gone to Israel. I had a cousin there, may he rest in peace. Who knows what might have been? It doesn't matter. I lived my life here, with her, almost a full life, if you understand me, and I'll die here."

Nathan shifted in his chair. Even if Freidl was a creature of Rafael's imagination, he thought, a ruse to reconnect him with his life after the war, he lived with her. They had a world. He actually felt calmer about her now, less alarmed at how Rafael knew details about Pop's life that could not be explained without her — Pesha Goldman's photographs; Hillel saying, "the synagogue is a place where weak men run to hide"; Hindeleh and the red ribbon; the light in Pop's handkerchief last night.

He looked around the room and noticed that a fair number of Rafael's books on Judaica were in English, which explained the ease with which he spoke the language. What would happen to these books when he passed on? He imagined the neighbors turning from the deathbed, eyeing the contents of this house. They'd want the wardrobe, the samovar, the meager furniture. But who would care for the books, the photographs, the artifacts of Jewish life in Zokof?

For a painful moment he thought that perhaps he should offer to do

something about this. Part of him dreaded the thought of such an entan-
glement, but part of him almost hoped to be asked. In the end he decided
that if Rafael wanted him to do something for him, he wouldn't be shy.

Rafael took another sip of tea. "What tormented me, through the years,
was that I could do nothing for her. Can you understand what that was for
me? For her, there was only the blocked grave and the broken stone."

He looked down at his lap and sighed. "Last night Freidl came to me,
happy. Happy! She told me you brought back Itzik's handkerchief." He
looked hopefully at Nathan. "All these years we waited. And now, my
prayers for her are answered. You are here, and this business will be
finished at last. Look at me, Leiber. I am an old man. I can't last much
longer."

Nathan was ready. "What would you like me to do?" he said.

"I want you to help return her soul to rest with her body, as it was the
night Itzik disturbed her."

Nathan, who had already formulated a plan to donate Rafael's books to
worthy institutions and to erect some sort of memorial in the cemetery, had
no idea how to respond to this request or even what it meant. His nervous
fingers searched for the scar at the back of his head. He took a breath.
"How would I do that?"

"Wait here." Rafael almost jumped from his chair, then crossed the
room and disappeared into the entry hall. Nathan heard the creak of the
metal ladder against the wooden ceiling as it was being mounted. He
rushed to the foyer. "Let me help you!"

"I go up and down this ladder all the time, Leiber. It's nothing. Go sit. I
will be down soon." By then, Rafael was already at the top rung.

Reluctantly, Nathan returned to his chair. He stared at the floor. The
linoleum had worn through, exposing wide, uneven planks of rough wood.
He heard footsteps along the attic floor. A chair squawked as it was being
dragged. It creaked, as if bearing weight. Not long after, Rafael descended.

He paused for a moment in the doorway, clutching to his chest an odd-
shaped object about two feet long and a foot and a half wide. It was
wrapped in cloth. In the muted light, Nathan thought Rafael looked like a
prophet, like Moses descended from Mount Sinai with the tablets.

Rafael brought the object to the table and gently laid it down. "For almost forty years I have this," he said, slowly unwinding the long strips of
cloth that bound it. They came off in layers of different colors and textures.

First, a rough cotton, then some blue muslin, under this a bit of lace with a blotch of brocade peeking through. Nathan watched the unveiling with fascination. A piece of green-and-orange silk fell away.

Rafael loosened the last piece of fabric, a black-and-white-striped prayer shawl. Its soft weave gripped the object beneath it and relinquished its hold with pops and tearing sounds. He lifted a fold of the cloth and revealed an irregular piece of stone, about two inches thick, rounded at the top, broken off at the bottom.

Nathan leaned over it and saw two Hebrew letters at the top. Below them, inside a half circle, was a bas relief of a bird in a tree, its wings spread as if ready to take flight. The rest of the stone was covered in block-shaped Hebrew letters, bordered on each side by a candlestick with candles. "It's Freidl's *matzevah,* her gravestone, Leiber. The top piece that your father, Itzik, broke off. It was in the riverbed."

The two men stood side by side before the stone. Nathan trembled at the thought that Pop might once have held this object in his hands, might even have been responsible for its having been broken. "My God," he whispered. He bent to look at it more closely. "What does it say?"

Rafael pointed to the two letters at the top. "This is the *peh* and *nun,* that represents the words *here rests.*" He touched the letters below, from the right side. "It begins with a verse from Lamentations. *'My eyes are in tears. Far from me is any comforter who could revive my spirit.'* Then it says, here, *'The pious Freidl, daughter of Rebbe Eliezer, of blessed memory, master of the Torah, scholar of the holy community of Lublin, and dutiful wife of Berel the Butcher, of blessed memory, of our holy community of Zokof.'*"

Nathan dared to put out his hand and trace the candlestick along the left side of the stone.

"Candlesticks show a pious woman, who lights the Sabbath candles, who brings God's spark into the home," Rafael explained.

"And the bird in the tree, here on top?" Nathan pointed.

"The bird is, for us, the soul. The birds are on many stones, especially for the women. But here, when you see a bird with wings spread, like this, making ready to fly," he said, pointing to the carving, "this is not so usual. This is a sad thing. It comes from the psalm, 'I watch, and am as a sparrow alone upon the housetop.' That she was alone in death, without children or family. That is what it means."

"W-what are you going to do with it?" Nathan stammered.

Rafael smiled. "Still playing the Wicked Son, yeh? Well, Leiber, I'm giving this stone to you. Take it to America."

Nathan's throat tightened. When he swallowed, his glasses slipped down his nose, blurring his view of the letters. He pushed the frames back into place. "Rafael," he whispered, "how can I take this last remnant of her away from you?"

But as he passed his hands over the stone's rough inscription, he realized he wanted to take it home. He even started to worry how he was going to get it through customs. Hell, it must be against the law to take an old gravestone out of the country without permission. He could imagine the humiliating scene, an eminent constitutional law scholar caught stealing property of the Polish Republic. He could imagine Professor Załuski's smug amusement at having to come to his rescue. But then he saw Rafael, gazing at him with a tenderness sons long for from their fathers.

"Leiber," Rafael said softly, "understand this. There is nothing left of us from Zokof but bones and remnants."

Nathan felt weak. "Where is the other part of the stone?"

"The bottom half is at Wladek Głowacki's farm. Freidl saw the cham steal it from the street in town. It was there, facedown, since after the war. They made pavement from our stones, where people should walk. Ach! Take this part and pray for her eternal rest."

Nathan stepped back from the table. "You want me to pray over it? I'm still not a believer, Rafael. How can I pray without being a hypocrite?"

"You don't have to believe to pray, Leiber. You think even now, I don't have my doubts about God?" He shrugged. "It comes with being a Jew. But, you repeat the words. You try to understand them. Meaning comes. It will come. It's like a *cholent*. It needs cooking. A lot of cooking." He smiled.

Nathan smiled back, but he was tense. "What would you want me to do with the stone?"

"That, I don't know. It is Freidl who wants that you should have it. Pray, and you will know what to do. Maybe not now. Someday." He nodded encouragingly. "You will know. Besides, after I go, there is no one left to take care of it."

Nathan felt sick. He looked at the stone and remembered how Rafael had described its shielding Pop from harm. How could he leave it behind?

This was a thing to be cherished. And even if it turned out that Freidl was only a story, it was one that belonged to Pop.

He lifted the stone to his chest. It was lighter than he'd expected, as light as Ellen had been, he thought, when she was ten or eleven months old. He closed his eyes and, overcoming a moment of acute embarrassment, hugged it tightly, as if it were Pop himself.

Rafael folded his hands before him. "Freidl says this stone is our witness. May God watch between us when we are out of sight of each other. *Farshtaist?*"

Nathan nodded, his eyes still closed. "*Farshtaist,*" he said. "I understand."

It was my hope that the scholar in him would drive Nathan to learn to read the words of my stone, and with that beginning, he might develop a taste for Torah and a prayer for me. As it is said, if the world is to be redeemed, it will be through the merit of children. But it is also said, fruits take after their roots. When Nathan left for America the next day, only God knew which would prevail, the scholar or the son of a man with a soul like a potato.

PART III

ELLEN

Although my eyes cannot now see you,

Knowing your house — and the trees of the garden, and the flowers,

My mind's eye knows where to paint your eyes and figure,

Between which trees to look for your white cloak.

From "Separation," by Juliusz Słowacki, 1809–1849

22

ELLEN LINDEN HAD THE RADIO TUNED TO A JAZZ STATION WHEN the call came, late in the afternoon on December 11, 1992. A sax was playing a pared-down version of "White Christmas." Her mother was on the line. From her frantic, disjointed telling, Ellen gathered that during the annual *Marbury v. Madison* lecture, her father had raised his hand to the back of his head and collapsed over his podium in front of a roomful of second-year law students. Forty minutes later, he was pronounced dead at Massachusetts General Hospital. The doctors said the heart attack had been so massive it was unlikely Professor Linden had realized what was happening to him before he succumbed.

Only three weeks before, Ellen and her father had had their long telephone conversation about her career. It had begun with an odd, unrelated event. Just after Ellen said hello, a crow had plummeted through the air shaft of her apartment building on Ludlow Street. Its cries echoed off the brick walls and were carried away by cold gusts of wind.

She had pulled the cordless phone from her ear and listened for the bird's call. Hearing none, she crossed the studio in two or three quick steps, to see if it had indeed fallen five floors to its death. The wind rattled the chicken-wire windowpanes. She'd craned her head downward, but in the blue-gray light she could only make out shadows.

"What did you say, Dad?"

"I said, I don't know why you're taking his offer so seriously. This Pronaszko fellow isn't promising anything more than a performance of your work in a park."

"It's not a park, Dad. It's an outdoor cultural festival that gets a lot of attention in Europe." She looked out the window again. No sign of the bird.

"Well, I think you should reconsider leaving New York City for almost three months. You're just starting to get critical notice."

His strategizing pleased her. Given his skepticism about her career, it was actually reassuring. She returned to untangling the mess of laundered leotards and tights piled on her dresser drawer. The carved mahogany monstrosity dominated her studio the way it had once dominated her grandpa Isaac and grandma Sadie's bedroom. Ellen liked to say it was so *ungepotchket* it was beautiful. Her grandfather had always said that word to make her laugh.

"What kind of salary is he going to pay you?" her father asked.

She folded a leotard and laid it in the drawer. "Pronaszko said they'd cover my transportation and board. I think there's a per diem stipend too, like when I was with Gayle's company. I'm not sure."

"You're not *sure* about the terms of the agreement? How can you be unsure about something that would control your circumstances halfway around the world?"

She bit her lip, angry at him for pointing this out and embarrassed at her own lack of professionalism. "Dad, it's not a big deal. I just got the offer. I'll work it out."

She expected him to interject. When he didn't, she reminded him that she didn't have a lot of bargaining power in the first place. "You know the market for dance choreographers. If the artistic director of a prominent company asks me to do a piece, I pack my bags and go. End of story. And by the way, Eastern Europe is going to be the next new place. Everyone knows that."

"I've never heard of this company."

"Right. And if Professor Nathan Linden hasn't heard of it, it doesn't count?"

"I didn't say that."

"Then what are you saying, Dad?" Now she was irritated that he presumed to know the subtleties of her field — who or what was in, or out.

"With or without the salary, I don't think their offer is significant enough to warrant so much of your time and effort. You have that grant from the New York State Council on the Arts this fall. That is significant. You should be focusing on what you're going to do with it."

The wind tore again through the narrow air shaft. She shivered as she crossed the room to make herself a cup of tea and to consider what this conversation was about.

"Actually, Dad, I think you've seen Pronaszko's work. He choreographed that piece for the Paul Taylor Company, with the dancers swinging and hanging from ropes and pulleys in a huge black box. They had about fifty spotlights on them. We saw it about a year ago at City Center, when you came down with Mom to visit Aunt Gertie. Remember? The one with the poems about shadows and light and prison and freedom."

"Vaguely. Oh, yes," he said.

"I've liked his work for a long time. I've never seen his company, but I've heard they're well trained. Solid technique makes the choreographer look better, right?"

"I suppose."

She poured a cup of tea and returned to the window, folding herself comfortably into the old armchair she'd re-covered with wads of fabric scraps. Nothing, she realized, not even her father, could minimize the simple, amazing fact that Konstantin Pronaszko had chosen her as his summer choreographer in residence.

"I still don't understand how you could have told him you were coming without discussing it with us first," her father said.

Her skin prickled with anger. "Dad, I'm twenty-six years old! Why are you giving me such a hard time? I've just been offered an opportunity that could make my career, and you call it dancing in a *park?* Why would I hesitate for a second, much less turn it down?"

He sighed heavily. "I have my concerns about your going to that country. This matter needs more serious thought and discussion. I don't like the idea of your being there alone. I just don't like it."

Here we go again, she thought. She stretched her legs, admiring their length and taut muscles. Ever since his trip a year and a half ago, he'd had some kind of mysterious *thing* about Poland. He'd never come out and say just what it was. He'd just drop snide remarks, like the one he'd made at the Lerners' dinner party, that the Poles were too primitive to ever embrace a constitutional democracy. Their architecture was distasteful, he'd said, and their cities dirty. He had a barrage of petty grievances against the people he'd met there.

"He's annoyed at the way he was received," her mother had confided in her. "He'd never admit it, but he feels insulted that the Polish government hasn't contacted him for advice. He's even let the book drop. It's not that Polish professor's fault. The man has tried again and again to solicit essays from Polish and American scholars. But your father doesn't seem interested in doing his part. He just gives him the runaround. I don't understand it."

It had gotten dark by the window. Ellen flicked on the Indonesian lamp beside her. The light glowed through its bark shade. "Dad, don't worry so much," she said, knowing just how useless the admonition was. "If you'd just tell me what's the problem with Poland I'll at least know what to expect."

"Didn't you think it would have been prudent to wait until you'd had a chance to ask me about Poland before you said you'd go?" he said tensely.

"Why? You don't answer me. Do you realize that every time I've asked you about Poland, you've turned it into a joke about family ghosts coming out to haunt you? I'm not a kid."

She felt around for a few ringlets at the top of her head and slowly wound them around her fingers. "Dad," she said gently, "this is really a great opportunity. I'm the first American and the first woman Pronaszko's asked to produce an original work for the Pronaszko Dance Theatre. I'll be perfectly safe, and Pronaszko said Kraków's a great city."

Her father sighed. "I'd like you to take the train up to Cambridge."

"Is that really necessary?"

He insisted it was.

"All right. I'll come up on Friday."

"Don't you have windows to dress?"

She rolled her eyes. "Hey, don't make fun. My dressing windows pays the rent. Besides, it's a noble tradition among artists."

"I know," he said. "Merce Cunningham and Robert Rauschenberg did it too. If I've heard that once . . ."

"Right. And David Gordon."

"Oh, yes, the one who used to be with the Judson Dance Theater. You see? I am capable of assimilating this information."

She smiled at the shy way he had of making amends. To her, it revealed how painfully aware he was that he appeared pompous and awkward.

"So, I'll see you Friday?" he said.

"Okay. I'll bring you a thick-sliced corn rye from Irv's bakery. Just so it won't be a total loss."

They said their good-byes. Ellen turned to lower the bamboo window shade. Outside, nestled on the ledge, was the crow. Delighted, she reached for the loaf of bread near the sink and tore off a piece. The bird cocked its head, as if surprised by the gift, and with an abundant rustle of wings, flew off.

23

A COLD WIND FLICKED AT ELLEN'S LONG CURLS AS SHE CLIMBED the Harvard Square subway station stairs that Friday afternoon. In front of the Coop, a draft lifted the silk scarf from around her shoulders and tossed it skyward. She plucked it from the air and hurried down Massachusetts Avenue to her parents' house on Lancaster Street, followed all the way by swirling gusts and sunlight illuminating the copper cast of her hair.

She liked to kid her father that the house on Lancaster Street was his other child. That year, he'd fussed over the choice of colors for the outside — the right shade of wine for the windows and the cream trim against the chocolate siding. He'd spent months poring over paint samples, while the shrubs and flowers her mother planted spilled and sprouted in the front yard and along the brick walk as if driven by some internal force to do their best at enhancing her father's pride and joy.

He came to the glass storm door, looking pleased to see her, in his usual restrained way. He kissed her cheek and shook his head doubtfully at the row of tiny beaded hoops ringing her left ear.

"Like them? I added a few new ones." She laughed and hugged him hard. "Where's Mom?"

He gave her his playful, mischievous look, the one from the corners of his eyes. "She went to Fresh Pond. Something special for dinner, I think. Come on in."

Ellen laid her embossed leather backpack on the foyer table and unbuttoned her coat. Her father lifted it from her shoulders, as he always did.

"Your mother had a coat that flared from the waist like that, a calf-length aubergine wool," he said. "Forty years ago."

She smiled at his enjoyment of what he called her "opera getups." He said that even in her lace-trimmed jeans, she looked dressed for the Met.

The sun poured through the oversized living room windows onto the little bronze Indian god Shiva — the Lord of Dance, her father liked to remind her — who balanced, one-legged and many-armed, on the coffee table. She went in and sat in the Eames chair, loving the thrill she still got from seeing his treasures — the giant turtle shell that leaned against the fireplace, the African thumb pianos, the masks, the ancient ceramic pots, the rugs. Her father had brought each of them home with an elaborate acquisition story. "Ellen's legacy," he called the collection.

She unlaced her high-heeled boots and curled her feet under her, wondering what promise he was planning to extract from her with this dutiful visit.

From the arched doorway, her father cleared his throat. "When you're ready," he said, "I'd like to talk to you upstairs in my study."

She did not protest that they hadn't yet had lunch. A meal with him would be a lot more pleasant after they'd finished this business about Poland.

The old wood creaked as they climbed the stairs. She brushed her hand over the Moroccan camel bag on the stair wall to release the hint of its animal smell, then followed her father down the narrow hallway to the back of the house. Her heart beat with anticipation and a slight sense of dread at having to take him on. Growing up in this house, there were times Ellen had so wearied of her father's insistence on discussion and analysis, she'd almost envied Tommy Brant down the street, whose father resolved family conflicts simply, with a strap.

Her father opened the door to his study. "Have a seat," he said, indicating the couch.

She didn't like his sudden formal tone, as if he were speaking to a student. But her displeasure was short-lived. On her father's desk, framed and prominently displayed, was the sepia-tone photograph of her grandpa Isaac as a teenager. This was surprising, as he'd never before shown much interest in the photograph. It was Ellen who had ritualistically unearthed it from the family album, always fascinated that this skinny, tightly dressed European boy had become her round old grandpa Isaac, a man who wore undershirts tucked into baggy trousers and black leather slippers with socks — an unkempt, working-class look that always seemed to embarrass her dad.

"Why did you frame Grandpa's picture?" she asked, settling herself slowly onto the hard Danish sofa. She hadn't remembered just how sad the boy's distinctive large eyes were. By the time he'd become her grandpa, his eyes had acquired the droopy sweetness of a hound dog.

Her father regarded the photograph with a tight expression. "We'll dis-cuss that presently," he said. He seated himself in his brown leather desk chair and pressed the tips of his fingers together. It reminded Ellen of how Grandpa Isaac used to say, "A man who holds his cards too close to his chest is hiding a bad hand."

"Ellen," her father said, turning to her, "I'm really very glad you came." He reached for a paper clip on his desk and slowly bent its tongue back and forth. "It's important we have this discussion face to face." He set the paper clip down meaningfully, then pressed his fingers together again, as if considering the course of his lecture.

Ellen recognized these gestures as his way of asserting control over the conversation, and her usual response would have been to rile him until he loosened up. But something, perhaps a sense that he was upset, made her hold her tongue.

"You may know," he said, "or maybe you guessed, perhaps Mother men-tioned it, my trip to Poland was . . . well, it was problematic." He sniffed, as if trying to lend authority to his scattershot phrasing. "I haven't felt the need to burden you with the details. There wasn't anything I needed to . . . you see, there wasn't a point. But since you've come up with this idea of going to Poland . . ." He paused, as if disturbed anew by the thought. "I feel it's only right, as your father, to give you some facts to consider."

She leaned on the arm of the couch, unused to his being so nervous and unsure with her.

He cleared his throat. "The main thing is, I visited Pop's town, Zokof, when I was there."

She glanced at the photograph again. "You never told me that," she said uneasily.

Awkwardly, he put his hand to the back of his head.

She knew the more tense he was, the more stilted his movements became.

"It was an awful place. People looked at me as if I was some kind of a suspicious character." He raised his brows skeptically. "Can you imagine?"

For all her discomfort at her father's secrecy, Ellen had to smile. It was no surprise to her that, outside Cambridge, people might find him odd. He belonged to that set of academicians who wore ascots and Russian fur hats, who paired rubber-soled shoes with dress slacks, blithely unaware of the violence they did to normal ideas of fashion. They were dear men, darling to her, actually. But to the outside world, they did look strange, maybe even suspicious.

He pressed his fingers together again and assumed a serious expression. "Do you remember when I went to southern China in 1982?"

She nodded, wondering what one thing had to do with the other.

"Everywhere I went, people surrounded me and stared. Hundreds of people." He spread his arms wide to demonstrate. "But at no time did I ever have a moment's fear for my safety. They were just curious. They'd never seen an Occidental before. But in Zokof . . ." He glanced at the photograph of his father and shook his head. "To this day, I don't know what to make of those people's faces. They had no curiosity." There was an awkward silence. He seemed to be struggling with himself. "Horrible," he said.

Ellen could feel his tension ratcheting again.

"If your grandfather was here, *he'd* tell you about those people."

"*Those* people? Since when do you talk like that?"

He shot her an angry look.

"I bet Grandpa would be thrilled if I went to his town. He'd have loved for me to see where he came from."

Her father tapped a nervous finger on the desk. "Your grandfather wouldn't have wanted you anywhere near that cauldron."

She wrapped one of her longer curls around her finger and studied his agitation. Her father looked ready to explode, yet the ominous conversation seemed to be lurching around without a focus. "I think maybe you're being a little paranoid."

"No, I'm not," he said angrily. "People will look at you, and they won't be kind. This isn't just any foreign country!"

"What are you talking about, Dad? I'm a dance choreographer. What are they going to look at?"

A look of panic suddenly crossed his face. "Did you tell Pronaszko anything about Pop?"

"I said my grandfather was Polish," she said, unused to such an open display of panic from him.

He considered her answer, as if assessing the information's potential for harm. "Well, don't tell him anything more than that. He doesn't have to know."

"Know what?"

"To them, you'll be a Jew!"

Ellen paled. He'd never talked to her like this, and he looked scared.

"Dad," she said gently, "what is this — saying I'm Jewish as if there's something wrong, and *those* people, and calling a town a *cauldron?* All my life you've taught me not to judge people like that." Her voice wavered.

Her father worked the muscles on the sides of his face like a man readying himself for a dangerous leap. He reached for the blue Venetian paperweight on his desk and rolled it in his palm. "You don't have any experience with this," he said finally.

"With what?"

"Anti-Semitism." He looked directly at her. "What are you going to do when they start in?"

This seemed to her less a question than an expression of his anxiety. "Come on," she said, trying to soothe him, "do you think it comes as some big surprise to me that there are people who don't like Jews? Should we all convert, to make morons happy? And what, exactly, would we Lindens convert to, Dad, since we're not much of anything in the religious department?" She thought this would make him smile, but it didn't. His jaw just clamped tighter.

He sniffed. "It wouldn't help."

She tried again. "Look, you worried when I went to Indonesia. Remember? You worried when I went to Peru. You've always said the world isn't a safe place, especially for women. I know that. Dad, I'm very careful. Trust me, I wouldn't walk around Zokof or Kraków with a Star of David around my neck, though, come on, I wouldn't wear one anywhere. How tacky is that?" She smiled at him hopefully.

"It wouldn't matter," he said tensely. "They'll know you're Jewish. They just do."

She was utterly exasperated with him. "So what?"

"So, you can simply not put yourself in that situation. Pronaszko can find someone else, and you can do better."

She tried to control her anger. "No, I meant so what if they know I'm Jewish? I want this job, Dad. I'm going to take it. It's in Kraków, not Zokof, if that's what you're worried about. And if anyone in the company asks, I have no problem telling them I'm Jewish because, here's the thing, they're not going to care. No way are Polish dancers going to be different from American dancers. They're going to be obsessed with their love lives and their bodies. They're going to be worrying about getting work and how they're going to pay the rent." She waited a beat, for emphasis. "Believe me, my being Jewish is not going to make a blip on their radar."

He was looking out the window as if he wasn't listening to her at all. A clod of icy snow, a remnant from the last storm, fell from the fir tree outside his window and startled them both.

"Do you know why your grandfather came to America?"

She was surprised by this change in the conversation's direction. "He told me it was because they were so poor in Poland."

"Well, that's not why. Your grandfather came here because he had to, because one night in 1906, he saved three Jewish children from being whipped by a Polish peasant." He turned to her with challenging, narrowed eyes. "Can you even imagine such a thing? A grown man in a wagon beating five-year-olds? *That's* your grandfather's Poland. You think he'd want you to see that? I say he wouldn't. And neither do I, because it hasn't changed. Nothing's changed."

Ellen felt paralyzed. Her father's voice, raised and angry, was as terrifying as the crazy story he was telling. She wanted to jump in the car and drive to Fresh Pond to look for her mother. Her mother would calm things down, lend some perspective.

Her father disregarded her unease, if he'd noticed it at all. "Pop grabbed the peasant's whip," he said as if he'd witnessed the act himself. "The man fell under his wagon, and the wheel ran over his head. Killed him! Your grandfather had to run away from Zokof. All he took were some things his mother packed for him and a hair ribbon his sister Hindeleh gave him." With an unsteady hand, he picked up the framed photograph and waved it at Ellen. "This was taken just a few days later, in Warsaw. The clothes aren't even his!"

"Why didn't anyone ever tell me this? I didn't even know Grandpa had a sister!" Ellen said, deeply wounded and shocked. It wasn't as if her grandfather hadn't told her anything about his childhood. He'd slept on top of the oven when he was little, he'd said. It was the warmest place in the house. "And you didn't get burned?" she'd asked him repeatedly. He'd just smiled at her indulgently, leaving it to others to explain that his oven wasn't like the one in the Lindens' kitchen.

Nathan regarded his daughter carefully. "I didn't tell you about Hindeleh because I didn't know about her either. He never told us a lot of things. It seems his mother and her four other children left Zokof because of what happened that night. Only his brother Gershom made it back." He tapped his desk, musing. "Strange," he said, "Gershom became a baker, like Pop."

"What's strange," Ellen said tersely, "is that in a year and a half you haven't bothered to tell me any of this."

Now Nathan looked wounded. "I wasn't sure if it was true. I'm still not. I'm not!" he insisted as if he didn't think she would believe him.

Their eyes met.

"But you're right," he conceded. "It's time I tell you about it. God knows, time hasn't made anything clearer to me. I can't understand how he went through his whole life without telling anyone about his mother or this little Hindeleh, or the rest of his family. How?" Her father looked desperate.

"Dad . . ." Even in her anger, it scared Ellen to see him so distressed. "Are you okay? Maybe we should take a break."

"No. I just can't stand the thought of your going there."

"How do you know his sister gave him a hair ribbon?"

"*He* told me," her father said softly.

"I thought you said Grandpa didn't tell you about her."

"He didn't."

"Then who?"

Her father grimaced. "The last Jew in Zokof."

The phrase was powerfully evocative to Ellen. She recalled a black-and-white Roman Vishniac photograph of a peddler in the snow, half his face in shadow.

"That's right, he's the only one left," her father said sharply. "His name is Rafael Bergson. I'm sure I don't have to tell you what they did to all the other Jews of Zokof. The ones Nazis didn't kill or chase out during the war, the Poles finished off after."

He was wound up so tightly she didn't dare interrupt. Almost reluctantly she asked, "How did you find this man?"

Her father's face softened, and with a sad, secretive smile, he said, "Call it a coincidence."

24

ELLEN WAVERED BETWEEN CURIOSITY AND ANGER AT HER FATHER for never having mentioned Rafael Bergson. "Tell me about him," she said.

Her father leaned back in his chair and laced his hands behind his head. "There's a Yiddish word — *beshert.* Pop used to use it. Know what it means?"

She was mildly annoyed by the professorial pose. "Not really," she said.

"It suggests that something is meant to happen. Fate, if you will." He studied her.

She doubted he believed in fate. She assumed he just had something to tell her that he couldn't bring himself to say outright — like the time he'd insisted they go ice-skating in a snowstorm, to discuss the subject of *love,* he said, when what he meant was she could not sleep under *his* roof with the college boyfriend she'd brought home that weekend.

The pause in their conversation threatened to become awkward.

"I was walking around Zokof, without any idea of what I was looking for," he finally offered. "I had an unpleasant driver, and no one I saw seemed approachable. I told you how they looked at me."

She nodded, losing a notch of her anger at the thought of him walking around a rural village in his galoshes.

"So I just wandered. I happened to take a certain lane, and there he was."

Ellen didn't really think this rose to the level of *fate,* but she wasn't going to argue the point, yet. "How did you even know he was Jewish?" she asked.

Her father smiled indulgently. "That would be hard to miss. He wears a yarmulke and the long coat. And a beard, of course. The whole bit."

She noted his use of the present tense, as if he was preparing her to recognize Rafael Bergson when she met him.

"When I established that he spoke English, I told him Pop was born in Zokof. He insisted I come with him to the cemetery."

"That's pretty weird."

"I thought so too, and I didn't particularly want to go, but he made it difficult for me to refuse." He drummed two nervous fingers on his arm-rest. "I just thought I'd pay my respects and that would be the end of it."

Ellen leaned forward excitedly. "Wouldn't people from our family be buried in the Zokof cemetery?"

"That's really why I agreed to go with him. I thought I'd see some of their gravestones, something connected to Pop." He shook his head. "But there's nothing to see. The place doesn't even look like a cemetery. It's a forest, with a few overgrown paths running through it. And a lot of crows."

"Crows?" Ellen repeated, briefly recalling the crow at her window.

"They're in the treetops. They make quite an unsettling racket."

"What happened to the gravestones?"

He pursed his lips. "Rafael says the Nazis and the Russians tore out the stones and used them for building projects. Apparently, you can find Jewish gravestones all over Poland — on the undersides of sidewalks, in building foundations, even cut for manhole covers. You can even find a few in the cemeteries. But not in Zokof."

She recognized the sarcasm. It was just like her grandfather's.

"Of course, the Nazis and the Russians were only the first to desecrate the graves. After them, came the Poles. Their neighbors' gravestones." His fingers stopped drumming, and he looked at her sharply. "You see what I mean about them? Why should you help the Poles look good?"

She considered his question. "Is that why you've refused to work on that book with the Polish professor?"

He seemed surprised she knew about this. "Maybe that's part of it," he admitted.

"But, Dad, if Rafael Bergson stayed, there must be some decent people around."

"That's *not* why Rafael stayed!"

"Why then?"

Her father rubbed his eyes under his glasses. A couple of kids ran by the house, their shouts a sharp contrast to the silence that had fallen over the study. He picked up the paper clip on his desk and began to work at straightening it.

"Rafael stayed in Zokof because of a woman buried in the cemetery."

"His wife?"

He shook his head and tilted back the photograph of Isaac on the desk. "No, this woman was already buried when Rafael was a child."

Ellen smiled. "Like the love story Mary Aiken told us, about the man who lived across the road from a graveyard in the Adirondacks? Remember? He wouldn't sell the house because the poem on one of the gravestones made him fall in love with the woman buried there."

He looked at her blankly, even though Mary Aiken was a close friend and Ellen knew he'd been in the room when Mary had told the story. Typical Dad, she thought. He hadn't listened to a word. The subject was beneath his attention. "What did Mom say when you told her about Rafael?"

"I haven't told Mom much about Rafael," he said stiffly. "I think I might have told her I met a man who showed me around Zokof. She's not particularly interested, and I didn't want to make a cocktail story of him. We've had some correspondence since I got back. He's an extraordinary intellect." He hesitated. "Well, it's been sporadic. It's hard for him to write letters and get them mailed."

"I'll look forward to meeting him then," she said confidently. "Don't you think it's incredible that this opportunity has come up? I mean, what are the odds that I'd be chosen by a *Polish* dance company director?" She was sure that would get a rise out of him.

Her father picked at his fingernail. "Actually, I haven't been able to get that very thought out of my mind. Of all the young people this director of yours met — not to belittle your talent, Ellen — but from all those people, he chose you, Isaac Leiber's granddaughter. It's like it was, well, beshert."

"Yeh, right, fate." She was sure he was kidding.

"It's even stranger than that," he said, glancing up at his shelves. "Last month, a book about Jewish cemeteries in Poland fell out of a remainder bin onto my foot at some bookstore on the square. I'll show it to you later. I meet people who tell me, unasked, they're from that part of Poland. They name towns I passed through in the car. Your mother and I went to a concert a few weeks ago and I heard music . . . I can't describe it, but it's from there."

For a moment, Ellen felt the way children do when they see their parents drunk for the first time, acting out of character, out of control, and it scared her.

He stood up suddenly, walked over to his wooden cabinet, and slowly opened it. He lifted out a big lumpy object covered with cloth and cradled it in his arms. "It all comes back to this," he said, carefully laying the lump on his desk. He began to unwrap it.

"What is that?"

"This is the top of the only surviving gravestone from the Zokof cemetery. It belongs to the woman for whom Rafael stayed in Zokof. Her name is Freidl."

She jumped off the couch. "How did you get that?"

"Rafael Bergson gave it to me."

"Why?"

"Because, he told me, after the peasant was killed, Pop ran into the cemetery and hid behind this stone. Rafael said it's broken because Pop pulled it over."

"*This* is the stone Grandpa broke?" She was stunned.

Her father nodded.

She looked from the bundle to the photograph of her grandfather, trying to figure out where to start unraveling this story. "Why didn't Rafael put the stone back on her grave?"

"I don't know exactly. Probably, he was afraid of vandals. But when I went to his house, Rafael gave this part of the stone to me, in trust, to do something appropriate with it."

"Why you?"

"He says the stone belongs with us. Because of Pop."

"Well, do you really think it's appropriate to keep it in a cabinet?"

He looked embarrassed. "I don't know what to do with it. I even tried reading from the bible, *Tanakh,* it's called. I thought maybe I'd find a clue there because he and Freidl are religious." In his agitation, he stopped in midsentence, and only then did he seem to realize his daughter was looking at him as if he'd lost his mind.

"*Are* religious?" Ellen said. "You said she's dead." He seemed so lost, so distraught about the stone and what he was supposed to do with it. She squeezed his arm gently and asked, "Didn't he tell you what he wants you to do? Why didn't you show it to me?"

He pushed his glasses onto the bridge of his nose. "I wasn't ready to show this to you. And your mother wanted to make it an art piece." He looked at the stone. "It's not art. I won't hang it on a wall." There was a certain defiance in his voice.

Curious, she asked, "What weren't you ready for?"

Ellen watched her father as he continued to unwrap the stone. From the sure way his hands moved, she knew he'd wrapped and unwrapped it many times before. At last, he removed a black-and-white striped piece of fringed cloth and revealed a gray stone tablet, rounded at the top, broken off at the bottom. He gazed at the stone. "Come, take a closer look at this," he said.

She approached the tablet and instinctively ran her hand over its face and sides. It was about two inches thick. She dipped her fingertips into the rough hollows of the Hebrew letters and wondered what they said. Her only contact with the Hebrew alphabet had been playing the *Hanukah dreydl* game in elementary school during the holiday season. Every year, one of the other Jewish parents would come to class and explain the meaning of the letters on each side of the dreydl. She didn't remember the letters' names. Her parents didn't play the game. They had a Christmas tree.

"What does the stone say?" she asked.

"I can't remember how to read Hebrew. And I wouldn't understand it even if I could," her father said. "But Rafael told me it says she was the daughter of a famous Talmudic scholar from Lublin."

Ellen found it somehow offensive that the woman had been defined in death by her relation to someone else. "What else?"

"She married a man from Zokof and died there in 1905, at the age of eighty-three."

"No, I mean who was *she*?"

He seemed pleased, relieved actually, at her interest. "She was a scholar; she read Hebrew. That was unusual for a woman in those days. But since she was childless, apparently they didn't mind what she did with her time."

"Did Grandpa know her?"

"Why do you ask?"

"Because you seem to know a lot about her."

He shrugged. "Everything I know, Rafael told me. Grandpa never said a word about her. I don't know what he knew."

She looked at the photograph. Her father rested his hand on the stone and looked down at it again. "There's only one memorial in the Zokof cemetery. It's the pile of remembrance stones Rafael made for her."

"Where's the rest of the stone, the bottom?"

Her father sighed. "He said that after the war, it was laid, facedown, as pavement in the town. Then a farmer stole it. It's still there, at his farm." He looked away. "It's terrible," he said. "I still don't like the idea of your going there."

"Well, I'm going."

Their eyes met again.

"I just don't think it's appropriate," he said.

Ellen could no longer conceal her anger at him. "I don't think you're in a position anymore to tell me what's appropriate. You've been back from Poland all this time, and you never thought it might be appropriate for me to hear about this? You didn't think I might like to know what happened to *my* grandfather?"

"I didn't think you'd be interested," he said weakly.

"Oh, come on, Dad. I've asked you many times about Poland. You just blew me off! You pretended it wasn't even worth describing. Now you tell me you went to Grandpa's hometown and met someone who lived there when Grandpa did. You've been to the cemetery where people in our family are buried. And this Freidl thing. How can you call that nothing? If Pronaszko hadn't invited me to Poland, I would never have known about any of this. You wouldn't have told me. I can't believe you!"

His face was rigid. He studied his fingers. "I didn't know you'd feel this way about it," he said. "I didn't think you'd care. You wanted me to bring his handkerchief back there. I thought that was enough for you."

"That's because I didn't know there was anything more!"

"There was nothing more I could have told you then. I didn't understand it myself. I still don't. You know I don't identify with all those religious rituals. He wanted me to pray in the cemetery. Can you believe it?" He looked off again. "Why should you have to be burdened with such things?"

"What prayer?" she asked, uncomfortably aware she wouldn't know one from another.

"El Molei Rachamim, it's called. Pop would've died all over again if he'd seen me."

"You mean, you actually did it?"

He nodded.

She couldn't imagine how anyone could talk her father into praying. He who affected a look as if he'd been sprayed with a bad odor whenever the subject of God came up. "I've got to meet this guy Rafael," she said.

He rubbed his eyes under his glasses again and turned wearily to the stone, as if for a sign of approval. "I suppose you do. He was one of the children the peasant was beating that night. He feels responsible for what happened to Pop because he called out his name. That's how the Poles knew it was Pop."

Ellen was having trouble processing this information.

"I want you to promise me something," her father said.

"Sure," she said weakly.

"Promise you'll call me before you go to Zokof. And I don't want you there at night. It's not a place you can wander around after dark. The men drink, and they're not used to foreign women, especially women traveling alone," he said, not returning her shocked stare. "Poland's not that big. Actually, it's about the size of New Mexico. Zokof is in the eastern part of the country, and you'll be in the south. I suppose you could take a day trip there." He said this quickly, as if by doing so she might not notice that he had capitulated.

"Pronaszko won't need me every day. I'll have time," she said cautiously, not understanding his change of heart but not wanting to argue.

He patted the back of his head awkwardly. "I'll handle getting you a driver. I've made a few calls, as a precaution, in case you insisted on going." He looked a bit sheepish. "In Warsaw, they have something called the Lauder Foundation, to help Polish Jews. It's funded in the States, by the cosmetics heir Ronald Lauder. I was told they'd know someone reliable. But I want you to promise me you'll stay close to him."

"I'll stay close." Ellen smiled, delighted she'd be going to Poland with his blessing after all.

*T*hree weeks later, he was dead.

On December 21, more than three hundred people attended the service for her father at Harvard's Memorial Church, many of them arriving in Cambridge from all over the United States and abroad. In the entryway, they filed past the enlarged photographs of Nathan, including the one where he posed, in his ascot and trench coat, with President Carter, and one of him reading in the hammock at the Adirondacks house.

In lieu of a rabbi, Ellen and her mother had asked several friends, colleagues, and former students to speak at the gathering. Each recalled a slightly different aspect of the man. Nathan the champion of law as social policy; Nathan the friend of foreign students; Nathan the no-sense-of-direction tour guide in Cappadocia, Turkey. From Ellen, they heard about Nathan the father, who taught himself to ice-skate — badly — so that she, an only child, would always have a partner.

Afterward, the family took the urn with his ashes to Mount Auburn

Cemetery and buried it in a shallow hole below a modern abstract sculpture. Her mother politely refused her father's old friend Mort Grinberg's offer to recite Kaddish. "Nathan wasn't a believer. Why be hypocritical?" she said.

Ellen hadn't disagreed. But she felt the absence of ritual at the burial site, as if they had not done right by him somehow, that the job of laying him to rest was unfinished.

Later, when they all returned home, she excused herself and went upstairs to her father's study. She opened the cabinet with the gravestone. Wedged next to it, she found a round Plexiglas canister on which a meadow scene had been painted. Inside was a tightly sealed bag and a note addressed to Rafael. Seeing her father's almost impenetrably tight script again brought tears to her eyes. It read, "I am sure you will find my daughter Ellen a more winning student than I of your impressive body of knowledge. Here at home, I am finding the meadow and planting a seed. In the meantime, I hope you both enjoy this sugar for your tea."

She took the canister and note from the cabinet, realizing he had intended her to take it to Poland. Underneath it, she found a manila envelope containing several documents. They appeared to be some kind of trust account, with Rafael Bergson as the beneficiary of a monthly stipend for the remainder of his life. She also found a paper, signed by her father, that seemed to indicate that although he was the sole source of these funds, the beneficiary had been given to understand that they had been collected from "elderly Bundists in America." Her father, it said, preferred that this understanding not be corrected in the event of his incapacity or death.

Although Ellen had no idea what *Bundists* were, she began to weep. "Oh, Dad," she said, muffling her cry with her hand. She scanned the shelves for the two books she had come to his study to retrieve.

"I want you to take a look at this book," her father had said at the end of their last session. "It's called the Tanakh, the Jewish bible."

She had taken the book from him hesitantly. "Why do you want to give this to me?" she had asked, believing a history of Poland might have been more useful.

"Read it. You'll recognize a lot of the stories. I think you'll find it useful when you meet Rafael. Read the section called Lamentations. You'll be amazed. It's pure poetry. Actually, I've been surprised at how much our orientation to the world is based on this one book." He had reached into the top drawer of his desk and taken out a blue booklet.

"What's that?"

"It's a prayer book. I picked it up at Sol Litvak's funeral a few months ago. El Molei Rachamim is in here, the prayer for the dead. You might want to recite it in the cemetery."

She had opened the booklet. Next to the transliterations, it was filled with indecipherable Hebrew letters, punctuated by dots and dashes. Her grandpa Isaac was the only one in the family who could read this stuff, she thought, and he had called it crap — the Opiate of the People. She could still hear him saying it.

"Wouldn't Grandpa go nuts if he knew we were reading this?"

"I'm not so sure," her father said.

She had managed to forget to take either of the books home with her that day. Maybe, if she had to be perfectly honest, she had done it on purpose. The idea of her father giving her religious books gave her the creeps. Now, with a terrible sense of guilt, she gathered them both in her arms to take with her to Poland.

On the train ride back to New York, she wrote Rafael a letter informing him of her father's death, and asking him if he would meet with her when she arrived in Poland that summer.

25

In early July 1993, Ellen left for Poland. She awoke during the descent to Warsaw's Okęcie Airport, eager to follow her father's path into the city. She had even avoided looking at photographs of Warsaw so that she could begin her trip by seeing what he had seen. At the baggage claim, she expertly bungee-corded her duffel to the top of her enormous wheeled suitcase, amused by the curious glances her blue cowboy boots were attracting. Then she boarded the bus to the city center and took a window seat.

Her first impressions were not promising. Along the wide boulevard she saw imposing but unremarkable gray apartments, a dirty glass-and-concrete building crowned with the yellow IKEA logo, and the strangely inert, fatigued faces of commuters in passing red trolleys. By the time she was in view of the Palace of Culture and Science, she had jettisoned her father's warnings and had categorized Warsaw as one of those drab, if practical, cities populated by people dressed ten years out of date, but as safe and bright as an electric bulb.

In the underground passageway leading to the Central Railway Station, she dropped a few dollars into the hat of a street musician as a gesture of her goodwill to the country. Then she boarded the express train for the two-and-a-half-hour ride to Kraków.

From the doorway of her second-class compartment, an elderly couple observed her struggles as she stood on her seat, hauling her luggage onto the rack.

"*Czesc.* Hello." Ellen smiled down at them, glad to at last make use of her Polish language tape.

Rather doubtfully, the couple smiled back, then took their seats opposite as Ellen continued to push her bags into place. The man's shirt and jacket were worn, but his wool vest and wide tie lent him a certain old-fashioned propriety. He opened his newspaper. His wife spread a white doily across the width of her prodigious lap and began to crochet, her thick fingers moving with the unconscious assurance of habit.

Ellen took her seat and thumbed through one of her Polish tour books, hunting for information about the route from Warsaw to Kraków. The book pictured a historic Poland, but when the train emerged from the tunnel on the other side of the Vistula River, she was disappointed to find herself in an industrial area that more closely resembled Newark, New Jersey.

Not long after, she caught the elderly woman stealing glances at her. When Ellen smiled, the woman burst forth in a profusion of Polish. Ellen looked at her regretfully. "*Nie mówie po polsku* — I don't speak Polish," she said. She opened her father's Polish phrase book and gamely attempted to explain that she was an American and that she was going to Kraków for two months.

The woman pointed at Ellen's blue cowboy boots, which seemed to amaze her, and offered an apple. *Dziękuję bardzo,* Ellen thanked her, and in her best sign language, she admired the woman's crochet work. The woman's face flushed with pride, and revealed a faded blue-eyed prettiness. They smiled at each other several more times and ate their apples. In pantomime, the woman asked if Ellen had sewn the filmy green layered skirt she was wearing. She reached forward and fingered it approvingly when Ellen nodded yes.

Soon after, Ellen closed her eyes and drifted off, dreaming of a misted forest filled with melodies, all in a minor key. The pleasing romance of it lulled her to sleep.

When she awoke, the train was cutting across lush, soft hills dotted with black-and-white cows and lopsided, unpainted barns. She saw wooden villages and farmers on horse-drawn wagons plowing oddly thin strips of land, bordered in the distance by the delicate outline of birch trees. Utterly charmed, she felt her faith in her tour book's Poland restored.

The elderly woman tapped her on the knee. Her husband had pulled bread and sausage from the basket planted between his feet. He pressed some into her hand with an encouraging nod, and she accepted. "*Dziękuję. Dziękuję,*" she thanked him, and told him the food was delicious. She wondered how they saw her, an American girl, with her perfect white orthodonture and the shadows under her "Linden family eyes," as her mother called them, artfully covered by liquid concealer.

The woman somehow communicated they were going to visit their son, who lived in Nowa Huta, outside Kraków. Ellen showed them her tour book and looked up the town, only to learn that Nowa Huta was an ecological disaster, a postwar steelworks built by the communist government. "Over decades, Nowa Huta's intensive industrialization has turned the region's rivers into sewers and filled the air with smog in nearby Kraków as well, where its gases and acid rain are methodically eating away at the city's stone," the book said. She looked up at the couple's expectant faces and smiled, not wanting to insult their civic pride. "Nowa Huta," she said, with growing concern at spending two months immersed in so much pollution. She pointed to the town's name in the book. Pronaszko certainly hadn't mentioned the problem.

They passed a massive cross planted along the road, its base strewn with bunches of flowers. She wondered if there was a memorial like that in Zokof for the Polish peasant her father said had died at her grandfather's hand. She was glad she had not heard this when her grandfather was alive. As it was, she had always suspected he'd had secrets. He'd been so difficult to know. The way he turned serious questions about his life into jokes had always made her feel he was evading her, that he didn't trust her, or even that he was laughing at her for some reason.

But then, her father wasn't exactly a trustworthy reporter either. He got so distracted by his own tension that he often misunderstood facts and circumstances. Worse, he misread people. For all she knew, Rafael Bergson might just have been telling him some local tall tale about the death of a peasant. She wanted to know the real reason he had given her father the gravestone. This was what she meant to find out when she met him. The thought of it excited her. Turning from the window, she closed her eyes again and was comforted by the gentle sway of the train.

By afternoon, the church spires of Kraków's skyline rose like graceful fingers in the distance. As they drew closer, Ellen was thrilled by the sight of its green copper and rust-colored roofs, and the stone facades. At the station, she said good-bye to the elderly couple and dragged her ridiculously heavy load from the platform. The hazy air had a distinctive burned smell she could not identify. She assumed it was some vestige of Nowa Huta.

She found a driver to take her to her hotel. On the way, her concerns about pollution dissipated at the sight of so many architectural collisions — medieval battlements beside stately eighteenth-century townhouses, domed churches nestled beside the Baroque exteriors of stylish modern boutiques.

The entire center of the city seemed to be surrounded by a greenbelt with benches and paths for strolling. She sat back, happy to have found her way to a city of human scale, to a place more beautiful than anything she had been led to expect.

The taxi slowed at a small square. Bright modern-art posters hung from the buildings in marvelous juxtaposition to the stuccoed friezes that decorated the eaves. Ellen sensed a tremendous free-floating creative energy about the place.

Her driver didn't speak English. But moments later, when they pulled up to the Palace Residence Hotel, he pointed down the block. "*Rynek Główny* — Market Square," he said, nodding meaningfully, in what she took as a proud attempt to orient her to his city.

She had worked out an arrangement with Pronaszko to stay at this hotel, rather than at the less costly room in a private home that he had originally offered her. She would have preferred the room because it afforded an opportunity to meet local people. But its location had sent her mother into a state of extreme anxiety. "I want you to stay in the center of the city. I've talked to people who've been to Kraków. It's the safest area," she'd insisted.

The Palace Residence Hotel, as it turned out, was a respectable turn-of-the-century European establishment, which, behind its white-stone facade, had a small, modest lobby. Ellen checked in at the front desk, accepted the porter's offer of assistance with her bags, and noted the hotel's one truly palatial feature — a sweeping marble staircase better suited to women in evening gowns than American girls in cowboy boots.

They took the elevator. On the third floor, she followed the porter down a wide hall to her room. She liked the architectural detail of her door, tucked inside a niche. Inside, the entryway was almost blocked by an enormous armoire with a large oval mirror. As she squeezed past it, she took a quick look at the rudimentary kitchenette to her left, next to which was a small bathroom equipped, in the European manner, with a bidet and a poorly located showerhead.

The bedroom had an extremely high ceiling, which had the effect of dwarfing the low, lumpy double bed. Angled at its foot was an upholstered wingback armchair.

The heavy decor might have put Ellen into a funk if the French windows hadn't opened onto a view of flower boxes on the rococo building across the way. Best of all, on a small table below the window was a gorgeous flower arrangement with a welcoming message from Konstantin Pronaszko. He wrote, "I imagine that after your long journey you will want to have a quiet evening. If you are not too tired, may I suggest you take a short stroll to Rynek Główny before you retire. It's quite a nice introduction to our city." He closed with directions to the dance studio, where she was to meet him and the company the next morning at ten o'clock, and his best wishes for their collaborative efforts.

Delighted, Ellen called home. "Mom, I *love* Kraków! The hotel is great. Perfect location. Konstantin Pronaszko sent me flowers! I'm going over to the studio at ten tomorrow!" She said all this practically in one breath, not caring at all that she sounded like a ten-year-old. She wanted her mother to understand that her father had missed seeing a whole other Poland. She only wished she could have told him so herself. Again, as it had many times over the past months, the finality of his loss hit her hard.

"So the trip was all right? You managed to get to the train without any trouble?" her mother asked.

"No trouble. Just a lot of *schlepping*," Ellen assured her, enjoying her grandpa Isaac's word.

"That's good. That's very good." Her mother sounded relieved. "Call me again tomorrow, after you meet the dance company. And, Ellen, be careful in the street. I hear they drink heavily there."

Her mother's worry only reminded Ellen of her father's ceaseless protectiveness, so especially fierce about Poland, and how much she actually missed it now. She still imagined him so easily, in his robe in the study, fiddling with the blue Venetian paperweight, and a longing for him passed over her with the strength of someone seizing her from behind.

That evening, when she walked the few blocks to Rynek Główny, she was not disappointed by Pronaszko's recommendation. Strings of tiny lights hung, jewellike, on the trees that lined its perimeter, creating a soft glow over the elegant cafés. The square was bisected by a long, ornate building with huge arched arcades along the ground floor, and crowned with an intricate parapet. According to her tour book it was a Renaissance Cloth Hall, now filled with tourist shopping stalls. On the other side of the Cloth Hall was a massive statue of someone identified on the plaque as Adamowi Mickiewiczowi. Ellen stopped for coffee at Café Malma, and read that Adam Mickiewicz was a national poet. What an extraordinary people, she thought, to erect a statue of a poet in their main square. She wished she could have told this to her dad.

The clock tower pealed high above the square. From a church tower diagonally across, a bugle played a sharp, high melody that stopped in midnote, apparently to commemorate a guard who sounded a warning of a thirteenth-century Tartar invasion and was silenced by an arrow in his throat. They called the tune the *hejnał*, according to her tour book. She walked back to the hotel, bouncy with happiness at the city and excited about the next day.

Early the following morning, she rolled the sides of her leotard over her tights to her hip bones and knotted her batik silk dress in a handful of places so it would billow slightly when she walked. Finally, she pulled on a pair of beige high-heeled boots, determined to show Kraków a bit of style.

At 9:00 a.m. she was out the door of the hotel to get an early look at the dance studio and to warm up before meeting the company. The warm humidity had heightened the smell of pollution in the air. She walked through the smoggy haze that had settled over Rynek Główny and entered one of the narrow streets on its far side. A few blocks farther, she located the stucco facade of the address Pronaszko had given her and opened the wrought-iron gate. Before her was a short, dank passageway, permeated by the smell of old vegetables. It opened onto a bright cobblestoned courtyard where the last thing she expected to see was a video shop. But there it was, complete with the Polish version of *The Terminator* in the window, next to a weird little store with clothes that looked like bridal dresses for children.

Ellen entered the wide, open doorway at the back of the courtyard and began to climb the stone stairs. The risers listed to the left, and the tread of feet, marching up and down over centuries, had left little hollows in the steps. Thick wads of dust bunched in the curves of the iron banisters.

On the fourth floor, the lion knocker on the studio door might once have been a fine wood carving. But it had been painted over so many times it now looked merely globular. An old woman with reddened hands mopped the landing floor. A wisp of gray hair dangled down the middle of her broad forehead. She seemed to have expected Ellen because, with a few muttered words, she unlocked the studio door. *"Dziękuję,"* Ellen thanked her.

Alone, she stripped to her leotard and tights. Warped mirrors ran the length of the wall opposite the courtyard windows. They swelled and shrank her five feet seven inches every three or four steps. She clipped up the copper-colored mass of her hair and sat on the floor to stretch and calm her nerves.

The morning sun shone through the long windows. Legs wide, she reached sideways, head facing up, and noticed that whole chunks of molding were missing from the white ceiling. It reminded her of a certain studio where she used to take class in New York, above a pawnshop on Eighth Avenue in the Forties. It had the same dry smell of accumulated dirt, the same sooty windows and water bugs.

She stood up and brushed the wooden floor slats with the soles of her bare feet, trying out some movement sequences. After the long flight, it felt good to move again, to watch, with a certain detached pride, how well her body responded to the demands of the art.

She began a series of jumps and rolls, but dizziness overtook her. For a moment, everything looked a little green. Her ears became plugged, as if she was underwater, and she was forced to sit down, cross-legged, and rest her head in her hands. Quavering, distant sounds, almost melodic, rippled through her ear canal. She'd never had an experience like this before and wondered if it was jet lag. For several minutes she listened, out of breath, her heart racing in the silent room. Gradually, the dizzy sensation stopped. She lay down on her back, in the yoga position of repose, and closed her eyes.

At nine forty-five the door opened and a blond girl in a mauve raincoat walked in. She was about a head shorter than Ellen. In her pink leotard and tights, her hair pulled into a tight bun, she looked like a ballet dancer. Ellen, who had regained her equilibrium by then and was stretching at the barre, thought she must have startled the girl because, for a second, the girl just stared. But then she smiled and shuffled to the mirror to unpack her things. In profile, her flat, wide nose was almost saddle-shaped.

Assuming the girl might not speak much more English than she spoke Polish, Ellen said, "Ellen Linden," and pointed to herself. She brushed away several long, corkscrew tendrils that had escaped from her hair clip.

The girl smiled. "Yes, from America," she said in a child's voice. "Genia Slabczyńska," she said, pointing to herself.

Ellen wasn't sure she could even repeat that last name, much less remember it, but to relieve the awkwardness, she nodded enthusiastically and returned to her stretches. Again the door opened. This time, a tight cluster of dancers entered, two slight, fair-skinned young men and a gamine-like girl with a short haircut and an elongated neck. The girl was laughing. They all paused when they saw Ellen. One of the young men waved. The others smiled in her direction.

Pronaszko had assured her that most of his dancers knew some English but that he would have a translator available for her. At that moment, though, she felt badly handicapped at not being able to make small talk. In her experience, dance companies were tight, intrigue-packed worlds. The choreographer who ventured into their midst always had to tread carefully.

Several more dancers filed in, each of them announced by the walloping sound of the door closing, until the company, in various stages of peeling down to their leotards and sweatpants, was assembled. Some stretched against the wall; others chatted in pairs or in groups. Ellen smiled whenever one of them looked her way. They smiled back, but none of them approached her. She continued her stretches. It was all very awkward.

At long last, Konstantin Pronaszko sauntered in wearing a cape, a particularly odd form of apparel given the warm temperature. He was talking to an ash-blond young man with a gelled angle cut and the face of a god. Ellen went to greet Pronaszko.

Pronaszko turned abruptly from the young man. "Ellen! You've arrived! God be praised!" he said, rather more for the benefit of the company than for her, she thought.

The phrase struck Ellen as peculiar, and she laughed, wondering what God had to do with her arrival. Pronaszko looked at her quizzically. His eyes were deep blue. Inscrutable. He took her hand, to shake it, she thought. But before she could say a word, he bowed slightly, like some character out of the nineteenth century, and kissed her right above the knuckles. She stared down at the crown of his head, at the fading blond hair of his princely bowl cut, more alarmed than charmed at his greeting — especially in front of the entire company.

The ash-blond god put his things down and walked over to them.

"Please," Pronaszko said to her, with his now-signature bow. "This is Andrzej. He is the translator I promised to make available to you." He smiled and, with a hint of gleeful mischievousness, said, "But not too available, yeh?"

"Of course not," Andrzej interjected, in a manner both amused and detached. He turned to Ellen. "Nice to meet you," he said. He had cigarette breath, but a beautiful smile.

"Nice to meet you, too," she said.

"Of course." His eyes lingered, in the manner of men used to flirting.

Ellen thought he could be the quickest route to making an ass of herself. Looks were already flying between members of the company. Andrzej turned to them and made a short remark. Everyone but Ellen laughed, since he smiled at her but did not translate.

No way, she thought, and shrugged at him good-naturedly.

Pronaszko, meanwhile, apparently found this exchange quite amusing. He called the class to order, then formally introduced Ellen to the company, with much flourish over her choreographic accomplishments. Andrzej translated.

Ellen thanked Pronaszko, said she was looking forward to working with him and with the company, and apologized for her inadequate Polish. "You'll be amazed at how much English they know, when it suits them." Pronaszko winked at her. "Isn't that so, Henryk?"

The short muscular fellow grinned. "Oh, yes," he enunciated slowly.

Ellen felt better. She decided it would be more politic to participate than to watch class, and Pronaszko approved of her joining them.

His class was a smattering of Martha Graham and Cunningham techniques, ballet, and a dash of Twyla Tharp–type frenetic kinetics. He was showing her what they could do. All through class, he pounded out syncopated rhythms with a heavy, carved wooden cane and recited odd but affecting poetic phrases in his big, dramatic voice.

They were good dancers, some of them very good. But she could see that every one of them had begun with ballet. They had that look that afflicts all ballet dancers, a sort of articulate puppetry. Ellen wondered if they would be willing to give up their technique and go with what she would want from them, or if they would resist her ideas of postmodern choreography.

Near the end of class, when the studio smelled richly of sweat and towels hung limply around dancers' necks, Pronaszko announced, "Today, in honor of our American friend, we will do some improvisational work."

The group rustled, exchanged looks. They seemed a bit agitated, but Ellen didn't know why, since improvisation was pretty standard fare for modern dancers.

Pronaszko surveyed the class, clearly enjoying the drama he was creating. "You will each improvise the movement in a work of art," he said.

Ellen hoped her face didn't reveal that she thought the assignment trite. Kids' stuff. She sat cross-legged on the floor, assuming he wouldn't volunteer her to be first. She had no idea what he had in mind, and anyway, she didn't want to serve as an example of what was good or bad. If he liked what she did, it would put more pressure on the company and they'd hate her. If she was bad, she would lose credibility as a choreographer.

"Ellen, perhaps you'd like to begin."

Annoyed, she walked to the middle of the floor, stood in thought for a moment, then gathered Adam Mickiewicz's imaginary robes around her, cupped his book in her hand, and executed a series of her trademark movement phrases. When she finished, the dancers glanced at one another nervously and began a slow, polite applause. Ellen thought this odd. Applauding improvs was not part of her world's etiquette. Pronaszko winked at her.

She turned to Andrzej. "Please tell everyone I was the statue of the man who's standing in Rynek Główny."

He looked at her, all amusement, and translated. The poet's name was repeated around the room. But instead of having the effect of warming her to them, they seemed to regard her with some suspicion.

She spent the rest of class watching the others perform their improvisations. They did so with varying degrees of success but with increasing humor, most of which she didn't understand. Then Andrzej took his turn. He clearly took special pleasure in performing some very dated hip-hitching jazz moves, which he seemed to think sexy but which, to Ellen, were just funny.

When class ended, he came up behind her. "You should have done an American," he said flatly.

"What's wrong with Adam Mickiewicz?"

"We call him Adaś," he said coldly. "Nothing is wrong with him. But how can an American dance to the poet of Poland's spirit? This is like a deaf person pretending to hear music or an atheist pretending to know God."

Ellen's face became very hot. "I didn't mean to insult anyone," she muttered, quickly gathering her things.

Pronaszko interrupted. "Ellen, I would like to invite you for lunch."

"I'd love to," she replied, unsure if he had heard what Andrzej had said but grateful for his intervention.

"Unfortunately, today I have an important meeting with one of our benefactors." He pronounced the last word with gravity.

She smiled gamely. He asked her how she liked her hotel, and they discussed the living quarters he had arranged for her. "I promise, we will have our lunch," he said. "A dinner would be better. More expensive, anyway." He winked at Ellen's deflated face. "Go, have a look at our city today," he encouraged her. "Come back fresh to us tomorrow."

By this time, the company had already dispersed. She slowly walked back to her hotel, not knowing what to do with herself for the rest of the day. As a hedge against her anxiety, she began to study the street more closely. Pollution had blackened the buildings, pocking and wearing away their facades and bas reliefs. But the pair of old wooden entry doors, hanging awry like broken arms, filled her with shame at her loneliness.

26

*U*PON RETURNING TO HER ROOM, ELLEN CALLED HER MOTHER.
If her father had been alive she would have admitted that her first day with
the company had been difficult and that she was pretty depressed. But she
had learned that the death of a parent creates an imbalance that is less forgiving of normal family complaints.

"Today was fine. Really fine. It was a good class, just a little weird in Polish. I couldn't talk much to anyone," she said in her bright upper register.
She described the cobbled streets, the courtyards, the hejnał, the amber
earrings she'd just bought at the Cloth Hall. Taking a small risk, she said
she wished Dad could have seen all this too. The silence that followed this
remark made her add, "This afternoon I'm going to visit the castle in the
middle of the city. It's on the top of a fortified hill."

"By yourself?" Her mother sounded alarmed.

"Yes, by myself. It's totally safe." What Ellen wasn't going to admit was
that she felt unmoored, that she'd have preferred to work, to connect, not
to loll hours away on tourist attractions. "You know how I am when I
travel. I like to scope out a city alone. Anyway, this place is called Wawel."
She cleared her throat and affected a deep tourist guide's voice. "This was
the seat of Polish kings for five hundred years."

"I see," her mother said.

"No, really, there's a whole museum complex up there, and a cathedral." She was aware of working too hard for her mother's approval.

"Don't you have work to do with the company?"

From the careful tone her mother used, Ellen knew she had detected
something was wrong. "Today is sort of an off day. There's nothing scheduled until tomorrow." She hoped her mother wouldn't ask why because
she had no answer, which, in itself, was worrisome.

"I thought there'd be some sort of reception for you tonight," her
mother suggested.

Ellen crumpled into a ball on the lumpy bed and tried to keep her voice even. This was something her father would have said. Receptions for visitors were the specialty of academicians. They were something her mother, who'd traveled often with him, had grown to expect. Meanwhile, she hadn't even thought about how she was going to get through the evening. "They don't do that kind of thing," she told her mother, in what she hoped was a casual voice.

"But some kind of welcome would seem appropriate," her mother insisted.

Tears popped over Ellen's lower lids as if they'd been waiting in the wings for their cue. They dripped sloppily off her nose and onto her pillow. She wiped her eyes. "Pronaszko said he wanted to take me out to lunch but he had some kind of fund-raising meeting. We're going to do dinner another day." But even this now seemed tenuous to her.

"I see," her mother said, in a way that sounded doubtful and judgmental of Pronaszko. For that, Ellen loved her fiercely. She gripped the phone hand piece, straining to be closer to home. Finally, she realized she had to let go. "Mom, this is costing a fortune. I'll call you tomorrow night, okay?"

"So everything's fine?"

"Everything's fine."

They said good-bye.

She threw on a pair of jeans and the comforting blue cowboy boots. On her way out the door, she grabbed some scarves and her short mustard silk jacket from the armoire.

By the time she'd reached the impressive sight of Wawel Hill, some fifteen minutes' walk from her hotel, she felt much better, even though it looked like rain. The wind had picked up. She began the climb up the narrow stone ramp that led to the complex of buildings on top. To her left, dark redbrick fortifications supported the hill. On her right, a steep, lush embankment plunged to the street. About halfway up, under a tree, a costumed Polish folk group was playing for a scattering of German tourists. She stopped to listen. Raindrops began pattering onto the leaves of the tree, but she stayed where she was.

The music reminded her of her mother, who'd brought home ethnic recordings ever since Ellen could remember — obscure Russian balladeers, Nana Mouskouri, Odetta, and Miriam Makeba. She'd spent much of her childhood dancing to foreign tunes, wrapped in scarves and loopy ensembles, banging a tambourine while her mother stomped along behind her, clapping and encouraging her to dance and dance and dance.

Ellen slipped some zlotys into the musicians' basket and continued up the steep incline. The city's street sounds receded. The spire of Wawel Cathedral rose directly above her. At the top of the hill, she joined the small groups of visitors passing through the castle gate, heading left the short distance to the entrance of the great cathedral.

Inside, the smell of burning wax from hundreds of flickering votive candles permeated the gigantic vaulted space. Her boots echoed on the stone floor. She walked slowly down a side aisle, rolling her heels to muffle their sound in the hushed atmosphere.

The ornate chapels, many of them closed off with grilles, looked to her like miniature stage sets. She peered into one and saw a painting of Saint Sebastian. As a child, she'd pulled her mother from room to room in the Metropolitan Museum of Art in New York, looking for all the paintings she could find of the saint. Her mother had thought her ghoulish for counting the number of arrows stuck in him at every painting — under the armpit, in the thigh, through the ribs. She'd had no idea who he was. Years later, finding him again in the galleries of European museums, she'd realized it hadn't been fascination with his torture that had drawn her to Saint Sebastian. It was his peculiar nakedness, so unnecessary for a man being executed by arrow. The unspoken secret in all these portraits, it had seemed to her, was how many painters had used him, of all the saints, as a model for the suggestiveness of a beautiful young man, tied helplessly to a tree. But now, as she stood looking at the painting in the Wawel chapel, she sensed from the dense Polish iconography that some other allusion to the saint was being made, that a conversation among Poles, something about martyrdom, was under way in that space. Intrigued, she moved down the nave toward the central altar, instinctively running her hands along the cold stone smoothness of the royal carved sarcophagi as she went.

She noticed a middle-aged couple seated in a pew. Their faces, lit in profile by the votive lights, flickered in and out of shadow like a Rembrandt painting. Ellen sank onto a bench and scanned the twenty or thirty faithful bowed in prayer throughout the cathedral. Stout, ruddy peasants and urban sophisticates alike, on their knees. What did these people think about in that pose? she wondered. Were they forming words of atonement or reciting wish lists to God?

This need to pray had baffled her since she was eight years old, the night her parents went out for the evening and Grandpa Isaac had told her the rocket story. She remembered how he had shuffled into her room and stood at the foot of her bed, not knowing where to put himself in the glow of her nightlight.

"Your grandmother sent me up to tell you a story. I don't know from stories," he'd said.

Maybe he'd thought she'd let him go, send him back downstairs with a good excuse. Instead, feeling very grown up, she'd patted the coverlet and said, "Sit on my bed, Grandpa. You can read me a story. Dad's been reading me *Hans Brinker.*"

"Oy, Gottenu," he'd said, which meant no. She didn't yet realize that Grandpa Isaac could barely read in English. He'd rolled his big dark eyes upward and sat down. Ellen had always loved her grandfather's eyes. She used to think he stored wisdom in the great domes of his lids. "What kind of story you want to hear?"

She chose carefully. "Tell me about heaven," she'd said. In the Linden family, this was the equivalent of asking about sex. Her parents wouldn't talk about it. Whenever she asked, all they wanted to know was who put the idea in her head. Once, she told them her friend Mary Sorentino had said God lived in heaven behind pearly gates. They were speechless. "We, we don't believe in that," her mom had finally stammered.

"What do we believe?" Ellen had asked.

"In nature," her dad had said.

"You don't have to *believe* in nature," Ellen had argued. "Nature is all around us. You can touch it. What if God made nature?"

"There is no such thing as God," her father had said.

She knew she'd hit the outer wall of what could be discussed. And that night with Grandpa, she knew she was taking a chance asking him about heaven too. The thing she didn't understand was why they got so upset with her for asking.

"Oy, Gottenu," Grandpa had said again.

Then they were both quiet. She had stared at his bald head. Its shape reminded her of an egg.

He'd cleared his throat. "The only story about heaven is there is no story."

"How come?"

"Because if they shot a rocket up in the sky that could go forever, it would never reach anything."

"You mean no gates? No walls? Nothing? Just more space?"

"Yeh."

His certainty had amazed her.

"That's scientific," he'd continued. "Heaven is for the stupidstitious."

"Stupidstitious!" She had laughed, edging her way into his orbit.

Grandpa Isaac had laughed too, which was rare. She'd wrapped her arms around him, basking in his precious warmth until, without warning, he'd stood up, put his hands in his pockets, and startled her by walking out of the room without delivering his usual clumsy kiss good night. She didn't try to call him back. Even at that age, she knew her grandfather's power to dispense love was limited.

Ellen never asked Grandpa Isaac to tell her another story, and he never did. But ever after, she could not believe in God. That would be "stupidstitious."

Years later, in high school and in college, she would lie awake, working out arguments for believing in a Supreme Being. But even when she'd decided it was as plausible for there to be a Supreme Planner behind the Big Bang as for matter and energy to create the universe on their own, she'd found herself returning to the image of Grandpa's rocket, hurtling through an infinite universe without a God or heaven capable of blocking its way. A cold, lonely feeling would come over her, as if she'd been left alone in the dark.

By the time Ellen descended Wawel Hill, the rain had stopped. She ordered a coffee at a small café at the base, unable to face the long evening alone in her room. Families and couples went by. No one spoke to her, or even met her eyes. They were all engaged in the earnest business of living daily life. Only she had to pretend a purpose in being in Kraków. She felt anxious again, and horribly lonely.

The July air was warm, and a feathery light brushed the city. She wandered south along the riverbank, intending to make a slow, wide circle back to the hotel.

On a whim, she turned inland and noticed immediately that the neighborhood, identified as Kazimierz on her map, had changed. The architecture seemed duller, in a late-nineteenth-century way. Many windows were shattered or missing panes. Her pulse quickened with excitement at being off the beaten path.

At a nearly deserted marketplace a few blocks east, several old women in nylon kneesocks and cotton skirts stood under canopies gathering single eggs, small bottles of milk, apples, and garden greens from makeshift tables. They didn't try to sell Ellen anything. She passed through, feeling invisible.

She walked beneath a stone archway and eventually came to a shadowy street called Józefa, no wider than a compact car. For some reason, the name caught her eye. Probably because, unlike most Polish names, it was so easy to pronounce. As she ventured down it, the bustle of human activity disappeared so quickly, she wondered if she'd entered an area closed for renovation.

There was almost no one around. The carved double doors lining the street were falling off their hinges, their stately wooden crests almost worn away. She noticed long, deep gouges on the right sides of doorposts and wondered what this meant. Window glass was broken or missing, the empty spaces crudely covered with nailed plywood. Whole sections of stone facade were exposed, revealing dark, rough wounds in the buildings.

A thin middle-aged man, his jacket and trousers frayed and out of shape, swept dirt from a cobbled corner lot pockmarked with sand pits. Wordlessly, a stout woman with a thick cotton scarf around her head bent over a dustpan, brushing in refuse. The smells of desolate, musty alleyways wafted into the shadows of the street, gathering pungency with the dust. Ellen's cowboy boots echoed on the narrow sidewalk. This silence, in the middle of a city, unnerved her.

The street ended at a large, rectangular plaza, with cars parked in the center. It was marked "Szeroka." She noticed a little grassy island on the north end, circumscribed by a black wrought-iron fence and heavy chains, and was attracted to this welcome break from the stone cityscape. A large, irregular stone, embedded with a plaque, jutted from the earth, breaking the symmetry of the fence.

Ellen was surprised to see a Star of David at the left corner of the plaque. Three paragraphs followed, each in a different language. The first paragraph looked like Polish. The third was Hebrew. The middle one, in English, read: "Place of meditation upon the martyrdom of sixty-five thousand Polish citizens of Jewish nationality from Kraków and its environs killed by the Nazis during World War II."

Realizing that she had apparently stumbled into an old Jewish neighborhood, Ellen pivoted a half circle and stared down the length of the empty square. The buildings, uneven in size and material, must have looked the same when the Nazis were there, only perhaps less dilapidated. The sky reflected in every window, like a series of framed photographs. She was shaken by the thought that fifty years ago, on an evening perhaps just like this one, they might have reflected the sky like this, camouflaging the last Jews hiding inside.

She knew it was crazy for her to become overwrought about Kraków's Jews, to be carried away imagining the presence of dead souls. But the little plaque, understated and seemingly forgotten, had touched her like a human hand. She felt off kilter and disturbed, vaguely aware that her identification with the Jews might just be a way of creating a surer sense of herself than what Pronaszko had given her that morning.

On her right, she noticed a white stucco building with Hebrew letters engraved in a half circle over the arched stone doorway. She wondered if this might be a synagogue, although she couldn't see inside because the arch was blocked by black iron doors. Just then, one of the doors opened from inside, and an old man in a cap, his distended belly filling a ragged pea-green sweater, came out. He quickly shut the door behind him, as if protecting the place from intruding eyes.

Ellen now felt foolish. What did she have in common with a man like that, a man who lived as a Jew? Her Jewishness was an absence, not a presence, a hollow corner of her being with no more to fill it than Grandma Sadie's chicken soup and the songs of *Fiddler on the Roof.* She had no idea what it meant beyond that. Except for friends' Bar Mitzvahs, she'd never even been to a synagogue service.

All her life, when asked about her heritage, Ellen had always said "American," even when she knew she was being asked if she was Jewish. She didn't see the point of labeling herself something that didn't interest her. Dance and art were all the religion she'd ever felt she'd needed.

A sweet-scented breeze blew in her face, carrying the sound of live music to her. Drawn by the beauty of the melody, she followed it toward the southern end of the square, where a massive, fortresslike building sprawled behind a great expanse of paved stone.

At first, Ellen thought the music came from this building. But the breeze directed her toward the adjacent side of the square. There, above a newly renovated whitewashed building with flower boxes in the windows, hung an interesting calligraphied sign that read *ariel*. Below this, *restauracja café*. She debated whether to go inside for dinner or whether to take the tram back to the hotel before dark.

The slow, rhythmic tune appealed to her. It was familiar somehow, lulling, comforting, and warm. Suddenly, she realized this was the tune her grandpa Isaac used to hum when he played the card game pisha paysha with her. Of course, his version of the tune sounded more like a march, and he wasn't much good at staying on key, but she recognized it just the same. "What's the name of that song?" she'd once asked him. He'd laughed, in his *heh, heh* way, and said, "That is the 'Foygl Tune,'" as if this was some kind of joke. Ellen hadn't minded. She'd thought he'd called it the "For-a-Girl Tune," and remembered it fondly, believing he had made it up for her. Only, years later, when she'd asked him to hum it for her again, he'd looked at her blankly when she'd called it the "For-a-Girl Tune."

"The 'Foygl Tune,'" he'd said, when he finally understood her. "A *foygl*, that's a bird," he'd said, as if anyone should know this. She had been so disappointed that she'd misunderstood him all those years that she hadn't even asked him why it was called the "Bird Tune."

Just as she reached the arched threshold, the music stopped inside the café. She went in, unsure what she was pursuing but knowing she could no more walk away now than if her grandpa Isaac himself were there.

A young woman in conservative blouse and skirt asked her if she'd like to sit in the front or in the back room.

"Who was playing that music?" Ellen asked.

The hostess smiled shyly. "They are our musicians. They are on break, for dinner. But soon, they will play again."

From the vestibule, Ellen could see a second room, where several long tables and a few smaller ones had been beautifully set with white linens and lit with candles. A well-stocked bar ran along the back wall. "I'll sit in the back room. That's where they'll play, right?"

The hostess nodded and led Ellen to a cozy corner table. Noting the paintings of dancing Hassidim on the walls, Ellen asked, "Is this a Jewish restaurant?"

"Jewish-style," the woman said.

Ellen must have looked confused because the hostess quickly added, "It is not kosher. We have no one for that, to make it kosher. So . . ." She looked apologetic.

"It doesn't matter to me," Ellen interjected. "I'm not kosher."

The hostess smiled and handed her a menu. "Many of the tourists are disappointed with us."

"Do many tourists know about this restaurant?" Ellen asked, slightly disappointed that tourists had found the place at all. She wanted to believe she'd discovered a bit of hidden Kraków.

"Oh, yes," the hostess assured her. "We are well known. In fact, there is a group of Americans coming soon. You should stay."

Normally, Ellen probably would have headed for the door at the mention of American tourists. But she wanted to hear more of her grandfather's music. And she was lonely.

Ten minutes later, about fifteen Americans crowded into the tiny back room, stereotypically loud and aggressive about where they wanted to sit. Ellen knew them all without knowing any of them. The Uncle Mervs from New Jersey, the Sylvias from Brooklyn, the perennially searching single Debbies and Stacys, each with her own self-conscious *look.* But as she listened to the way they joked and complained to one another, Ellen actually felt relieved to be in the presence of people who sounded like home.

During her second course of chicken with mushrooms, the musicians filed in, bearing a viola, a bass, and an accordion. Each wore a fedora that hid his face. In their white shirts, vests, and black trousers, they looked strangely like Orthodox Jews. The bass player towered over the other two. He opened their set with a tune whose slow upbeat brought to Ellen's mind a line of men brushing their feet off the floor in unison, their arms around each other's shoulders. It didn't quite sound like Jewish klezmer music. She wasn't sure if this was because the wild, laughing clarinet was missing or because of something else.

"I heard the musicians are all goyim. Fake Jews!" one of the Americans said. The group laughed.

Ellen became annoyed with them again. "I'll have some tea, please," she told the waitress. One of the Mervs from New Jersey turned to her. He was a tall man, strongly built, with glasses and salt-and-pepper hair. A lawyer, she guessed. "Where you from?" he asked.

"Massachusetts. But I live in New York."

"So do I. Upper West Side. So what's a nice Jewish girl doing all by herself in a country like this?"

Before she could respond, he reached out his hand. "Sy Messner," he said jovially. A few of the people seated around him turned to her and offered greetings.

Ellen smiled back, unsure whether to be pissed off that Sy Messner assumed she was Jewish or touched by the way he talked as if she was a family member. With a certain reserve, she told them about her stay in Kraków.

"We belong to Temple Beit Tikva in New York," Sy told her. "A few of our congregants are Holocaust survivors. They wanted to return to Poland, and we came along for support. Let me tell you, I could use some support myself right now. We just spent the last six hours at Auschwitz. Have you been there yet? It's less than an hour west of here."

The barman suddenly lifted a menorah onto the counter and proceeded to light its seven white candles.

A woman named Esther shook her head. "Oh my God. It's Friday night. They think they're lighting Shabbos candles!" Looks of mocking incredulity were traded around the table.

Ellen looked away. Far from causing her offense, she thought the candles had been lit out of respect.

Soon after, the tall bass player traded his instrument for a guitar and played her grandpa's "Foygl Tune." Again, Ellen marveled at how he had transformed the march into a hauntingly lyrical tune, slow and soulful, but airy and somehow playful too. He had dropped in little hops so that the tune seemed to totter and almost fall, only to be caught at the last moment.

She looked up at the guitarist and was surprised to see that from under his hat, he was watching her.

The melody repeated and built speed. The guitarist turned his attention to his fingering and added decoration, folding in new melodies, new rhythms, until the tune wildly crescendoed to an end. By the time he'd finished, even the Americans had stopped talking. But the guitarist quickly left the stage, barely acknowledging their applause.

Ellen stood up and walked to the vestibule, hoping to see him.

He soon emerged from a side door. Lithe and graceful, he slid past the cluster of tables toward her.

"Do you speak English?" she asked him.

He lit a cigarette and tipped back his head, revealing a long, elegant neck and a strong jawline. "Yes, some English."

She thought he sounded wary, but interested.

He took off his hat, and she was struck by his unusual looks — a face long and oval as a Modigliani, with dark-brown eyes and taut, pale skin. His wavy shoulder-length brown hair was combed straight back. In one ear, he wore a thin gold earring, and the middle of his chin, just below the lip, was punctuated by a reddish tuft, about the size of a dime. He eyed the row of gold hoops in Ellen's left ear with obvious approval.

"Your music is fantastic," she said, hoping her attraction to him wasn't overly obvious. "I heard you practicing that last song before I came into the restaurant. You gave me a real shock. My grandfather used to sing that. Do you know anything about the tune?"

He looked at her carefully, eyed the rings in her ear again, then smiled shyly. "I don't know what it's called, but I like that one very much. It has something in it, I think."

She thought he had a beautifully shaped mouth. "Where did you hear it?"

"In the street, on my way home one night. I never found the person who was playing it. But I have a good memory for tunes, and I like to research them. It is difficult work. There is not very much written down."

Ellen tilted her head to the side and smiled up at him. "One of the people at the other table said that none of you are Jewish. Can I ask you, what makes you interested in this music?"

His expression hardened. "Must you be Austrian to be interested in Mozart?"

"Of course not." She laughed, hoping he wouldn't think she'd meant to insult him, although the analogy seemed odd. Everyone knew Mozart, but playing obscure Jewish music in a country without Jews just seemed strange.

"Actually," he said, "the accordion player in our group had a Jewish grandfather."

"Does he consider himself Jewish?"

"No." He frowned. "He's a Catholic, like me. We just like Jewish music." He pursed his lips. "Of course, my parents would prefer that I play Mozart."

"Why?"

"Because to them, this is low folk music, simple. It's not serious. They think I am wasting my time."

Ellen smiled. Despite the slight to Jewish culture, she sensed she was in the presence of a kindred spirit. "I know what you mean," she said.

"The older generation, they always think this way," he continued, clearly having given the matter considerable thought. "They want you to be a serious person so they can be proud. This isn't music my parents know. It does not make them proud. But"— he shrugged and smiled shyly again —"I like it. I do not even know why. It feels good to play it." He laughed, and Ellen laughed with him, enchanted by the warmth in his eyes.

"I'd love to have a tape of that tune," she said. "Do you have a recording of it?"

"Not yet. But, if you like, I could make you a cassette. Can you come back here sometime?" He raised his eyebrows questioningly.

"I could," Ellen said, enjoying his flirtatiousness. "That would be great!"

They smiled at each other, each knowing some kind of a beginning had been made.

"By the way, my name is Ellen Linden," Ellen said, extending her hand.

"Mine is Marek Gruberski," he said, returning her handshake and cupping it with his other hand. She liked the feel of his skin, smooth and intimately warm.

27

THE NEXT DAY, ELLEN WENT TO THE STUDIO TO OBSERVE THE company and to make notes on their dance styles. During a break, Pronaszko took her aside. "I think we should begin to discuss your piece. Can you meet with me this evening?"

"Of course," Ellen said.

"Seven thirty at Café Malma in Rynek Główny then. We can walk from there to a restaurant."

At the appointed hour Ellen, armed with her spiral notebook, arrived at Café Malma to find Pronaszko rolling an almost-finished glass of beer between his hands at an outdoor table. "Would my young colleague like to join me for a drink or shall we go on to dinner?" he asked.

Ellen remained standing, having noticed that he had already had a few beers. "Dinner would be great," she said.

He swerved ever so slightly as he made his way through the maze of small tables. There weren't many people in the square. Pronaszko led her along its eastern flank past the squat, domed church planted peculiarly in the pavement.

"I might as well ask you now," Ellen said. "The company doesn't seem exactly thrilled that I'm here. Is there something I should know?"

Pronaszko threw back his head dramatically and looked up at the uneven double towers of Saint Mary's Church across the square. "They are not thrilled that you have joined us. Not thrilled at all."

Drunk or not, his bluntness hurt her. "Why?" she said.

"They had the idea I should pick one of them to choreograph a dance, not someone from outside, especially not someone from America. I disagreed, so they are upset." He shrugged, as if the company's desires were merely a nuisance.

They passed a small bakery. Ellen caught a glimpse of their reflection in the glass and thought of her grandfather. He would have called her a scab, working for Pronaszko when the company wanted to do its own choreography. "You're a parasite of the boss," he'd have told her.

"You must understand," Pronaszko said, "under communism we had no worthwhile cultural exchanges, nothing was permitted in the open. The country was a suffocating hole. How difficult it is to grow as an artist in such an atmosphere. My dancers don't understand that. They are too young to understand that my job is to give them fresh air."

Ellen studied her mentor's profile — the short nose, the strong chin jutting out resentfully — and wasn't sure if it would serve any useful purpose to argue with him about communism. But she was troubled by his attitude toward his dancers. "Maybe they feel they also have a right to make choices," she said.

"And what would they choose? These are, almost all of them, children from the country. They are not city people. When I take them on tour, they stay together like sheep and don't go out to explore the places where they have been so fortunate to have been taken. Do not be fooled by their modern clothes. If I let them, they would choose this dead, stupid Soviet ballet. That is what they know. But I know what we need. We need fresh influences, new passions. So I do not care what they want."

"I understand what you're saying," Ellen said carefully. "But do you think the company will give their best creatively if they're so angry?"

"That is for you to work out. Certainly, they will resist you. You don't know the Polish character as I do." He stopped and turned to her. "For all our European pretensions, we are a peasant people. Subservient. A people deformed by invasion. You want to know why they smile at you in class one minute and whisper about you the next? It is because they are all two-faced servants." His eyes flitted up to the statue of Adam Mickiewicz as Ellen tried to recall when the dancers were whispering about her.

"Ellen." He ran his forefinger back and forth over the length of his nose. He seemed hesitant. "You remember your improvisation of the statue, of Adam Mickiewicz?"

She rolled her eyes. "That was a big mistake."

"No. I have given this some thought. You have a sense. You could not have chosen better, even without knowing him. Mickiewicz is the national poet, yes. Ask any schoolchild. And this is because when the nations around us cut us into parts and made Poland disappear from the map of

Europe, we needed to believe in the poems of this man, our Polish pa-
triot." He squinted, as if appraising the statue in Rynek Główny. "But the
truth is our national poet lived abroad most of his life. He died in Istanbul.
The statue of him in the main square, that is our little Polish joke. Because
Mickiewicz was never in his life in Kraków." He lowered his voice, as if
others might be listening. "And the rest of the joke? That is for you to enjoy. Now that our communist friends are not rewriting history anymore, I
can tell you that it has long been believed that our Polish Shakespeare, our
hero to the faithful, had a Jewish mother. Ha! There is something they did
not tell us when we were memorizing *Pan Tadeusz!*"

Ellen was conscious of holding her breath, of not wanting to misspeak
in the face of a man's rebuke of his own people.

But Pronaszko apparently did not share her sense of delicacy. "We are becoming free to say the truth," he said, with some belligerence. "And truth can
be very difficult for Polish people. We operate in the fantasy of ourselves."

Ellen didn't think there was a politic way to respond to this, so she
merely offered a smile.

He gave her a wink. "Nothing is what it seems, yes?"

She nodded weakly at this man with whom she still felt so awkward.

He took her by the elbow and began walking again. "They do not like
strangers. What they don't know is that they need them. The stranger will
teach them who they are. Hundreds of years ago, strangers built our econ-
omy. Our princes, our King Kazimierz Wielki invited them to come here,
from Germany mostly. Just as I invited you."

Ellen was unsure how much of this speech was being randomly driven
by drink and how much was his trying to tell her something he thought was
important.

"And ever since the Jews left this country, we have suffered, even
though some of them who survived were very powerful in the government.
Jewish communists are the worst, you know. They really believe."

She felt the pressure of his fingers along her arm, and prickles ran up
and down her spine. She remembered her father's warning not to tell
Pronaszko that she was Jewish. But was he an anti-Semite? What did he
mean, she wondered, by the phrase "since the Jews left"? Had he meant
the Jews who had emigrated, like her grandfather, at the turn of the century, or was he referring to the Holocaust? And if he meant the Holocaust,
how could he call that *leaving?*

At that peculiar moment, she noticed that the taller of Saint Mary's two towers was ringed by a gilded royal crown. It made her think of the odd phrase on the plaque in Szeroka Square —"*sixty-five thousand Polish citizens of Jewish nationality.*" She hadn't been able to articulate what had bothered her about it. But now, looking at the tower, she realized that in a country where church and state were one, a Polish Jew was regarded as having a different *nationality.* She felt cold.

They turned off the square, onto the narrow stone sidewalks of a side street, and headed toward Mały Rynek, the small market square behind Saint Mary's. Ellen listened to the rhythm of their feet on the pavement and worked hard at pulling herself together so that she could face what she knew was going to be a difficult dinner.

"Ah, well." Pronaszko sighed, waving their subject away. "All this is for another day. Tonight, perhaps I am more pessimistic than usual." He guided her toward a wood-gated doorway, which led to a rough cubbyhole of a restaurant. "The food here is excellent," he said, dismissing the plain surroundings with the easy manner of a connoisseur.

The restaurant's owner, a short man with a mustached face as round and red as an apple, greeted Pronaszko with excited deference and seated them at a center table where, unfortunately for Ellen, the cigarette smoke seemed thickest. The place was crowded with locals, a few of whom stared at Pronaszko, then at Ellen. Pronaszko leaned toward her and said softly, "You see, some of us recognize an interesting beauty when we see one!"

Ellen took this as encouragement, not as a come-on. "Thanks." She smiled and examined the jeans and thick-soled black shoes on the young Poles at the next table, wondering if Pronaszko's dancers didn't have a point in objecting to an outsider choreographing for them. Maybe it wasn't outside influences they needed. From New York to Kraków, everyone was starting to dress alike, as if they were all shopping in the same friends' closets. In a way, there was something sweet about it, but she had an uncomfortable sense they might all be surrendering too much of themselves.

"I'll order you the beetroot soup and the pierogi. They are specialties here. You will like it." Pronaszko called the owner over and with great élan, and without asking her permission, ordered their dinner. She was offended but, for the sake of the subject they were about to discuss, she let it pass.

"How do I get your dancers to loosen up and try things?" she asked him.

"This is their problem," he said, frowning. "They know same, same,

same. No color, no variety. I wanted you to make them see how you use improvisation in your choreographic work, to show them the process."

Ellen smiled, relieved to know the reason he had chosen her to do the first improvisation. "How do you get to the point where you don't mind their resentment?" she asked.

"You ignore it. You do what is best for the company, for its art. You do not need them to like you. You need them to work so that they learn to live with the terror of creativity."

She laughed at his dramatics. "And you call yourself an anti-communist?"

He answered with what she thought of as the European continental smile, head bowed in a show of false modesty, while the eyes reveal a practiced cynicism. "So, what do you have in mind for us?" he said, jerking his head up suddenly and returning to his professional demeanor.

She pulled out her notebook and began to flip nervously through the pages. "The piece I worked on for you in New York is called *Four Corners*. It has the sound of something very basically American to me, like the old town squares up in New England, or an Amish quilt pattern, or square dancing. I like the idea of superimposing that on a Polish sensibility. Obviously, a lot will get influenced by the way your dancers move."

Pronaszko nodded slightly.

"My idea is to pull images and sounds of very different types of people from the four corners of the stage. They appear successively, each interacting with one or more of the other corners. I have three hip-hop types coming together with a superslow whirling dervish, each with their own music. There's interplay with the music too. You get one style, one beat, then the other. The volume of each musical identity goes up and down and fuses as they interact."

Pronaszko's eyebrows rose, but Ellen couldn't yet tell if he was interested. "I have leaping, tumbling gymnastic types who dance to Japanese Kodo music. They come together with smooth, gliding types, dancing to country-western music. The whole piece plays with the idea of diversity."

Pronaszko played absentmindedly with his silverware. "Unfortunately, I do not believe in the melting pot," he said, sniffing. "I like the title *Four Corners*. It evokes something. But to just introduce types and treat them like puppets, what is the point? This sort of thing is done all the time. I don't like it. I think we should try for something bigger."

Ellen wasn't prepared to have him brush off her work without more discussion, but she liked that he was pushing her. "Not big enough?" she repeated, amused. She took a sip of water.

Pronaszko sighed and pulled out a cigarette. When their dinner arrived, he became more interested in extolling the virtues of the sour beetroot soup with minced-meat raviolis — ears, he called them — and the wild-mushroom pierogis, than he was in hearing about the thought process behind her work. He cut a pierogi in half and pushed it around his plate. Then he put down his fork. "I want to hear a point of view," he said slowly. "I want to hear a cry of passion, a subject from your soul. You talk about *types*. I am not interested in types for types' sake. I did not bring you here to play with mere concepts. That is for the timid." He slammed his open palm on the table, jangling the silverware, startling her. "I am interested in evoking response."

"Response to what?"

"That is for you to decide."

A silence fell between them. Pronaszko studied her face. "Ellen Linden, I chose you because you have a certain pure American fire. You do not know how that looks to us, how exciting, how alive. You have that gift of passion without intellectual self-consciousness. We cannot get enough of that here."

Ellen was surprised to hear a European admit this.

"All right." He lifted his hand slightly from the table and returned the two of them to a lesser state of tension. He pointed his forefinger at her. "I want something new out of you. I want something freshly dug." He returned to his food, stabbed a few pierogi, and bit them off his fork. "When you have worked out an idea and you want to see how it looks on some dancers, let me know."

Ellen realized she would have to start over. The pressure felt like a knee against her spine. Yet she was exhilarated.

They exchanged careful smiles.

"How about a vodka?" he said.

How confidently she raises her glass and drinks to him in Polish. This Ellen Linden is no fool. Not for her to make herself sick with vodka like her grandfather. Poor soul, trying to impress Hillel and that Pole Piotr in Warsaw.

28

THAT NIGHT IN HER HOTEL ROOM, ELLEN FOLDED HERSELF INTO the formidable wingback armchair at the foot of her bed. For a long time she hugged her knees and rocked back and forth, hoping for inspiration. But the longer she rocked, the harder focusing on her piece became. A few indistinct themes flickered through her head, but she dismissed them quickly as dry and lightweight, nothing that would impress the sort of people who'd created the fabulous posters plastered all over the city.

At one in the morning she gave up and went to bed, disgusted and scared at her own emptiness. A half-moon shone through the open French window, and a soft wind blew at the curtains. She closed her eyes and listened to the hourly trumpet call, the hejnał, from Saint Mary's Church. Its regularity was now almost a comfort. But the thought of the church's spire and the crown gave her a chill again.

Eventually, she fell asleep and dreamed of Marek Gruberski, the musician from the Ariel Café. He appeared in a swirl of sand, his features emerging like a developing photograph. The long brown hair fell gracefully at his shoulders. When he saw her, he began to sing the "For-a-Girl Tune." They approached a wide river, the Vistula perhaps, but with a classical setting, like a painting. Marek held a rod over his head and beckoned until she came to him, wearing bells and harmonizing the song. Together, they stepped into white light; then Marek was gone. Ellen's foot hit a cobbled stone on Szeroka Square. She ran to the Ariel Café, but the door was locked. She sang the "For-a-Girl Tune" at the clouds that floated in the windows around the square, trying to call him back.

On the second floor of a brick building, at an open French window, sat a striking gray-haired old woman wrapped in a fringed plaid blanket. The woman rocked back and forth in time to the "For-a-Girl Tune." She nodded and smiled at Ellen. The room behind her was filled to the ceiling with bright-green cut grass.

"From your mouth to God's ear," the woman said. The Yiddish accent was thick, but clear enough for Ellen to understand. "Such a lovely voice you didn't get from Itzik."

*E*llen awoke the next morning so perplexed by her dream she was determined to return to Szeroka Square that day.

It was late afternoon by the time she arrived. She walked the perimeter of the wide, rectangular street, searching for the French window where the old woman had sat. She couldn't find it, or not the exact one. Instead, she noticed that even in Jewish Kazimierz, the highest airspace was silhouetted with church steeples, not synagogues. She wondered if the architectural dominance was intentional, or if she was becoming as paranoid as Sy Messner's tour group.

She walked over to the Ariel Café.

A paunchy older man was doing paperwork at the reception table. "Are any of the musicians here yet?" she asked him.

A chair in the second room scraped the rough wooden floor, and Marek looked around the partition. A smile sprang to his face. "Hello again!" he called to Ellen.

"Hi!" Ellen couldn't believe her luck at finding him.

There was an awkward pause. Neither of them seemed to know how to pick up from where they'd left off.

"I'm just replacing a string," he said, holding up his guitar with its hanging string as if proof was required. "You came for the tape?"

She remembered how slowly his face had come into focus in her dream. "Sure, if you have it!" she said. She liked his street clothes, the blue jeans and the black T-shirt.

He looked hesitant. "One of the members of our group is bringing it, but he will not be here until later."

"That's okay." She smiled. "I can wait. I'm going to be in Kraków for about two months."

He tilted his head with a happy look. "That is a long time for a tourist."

"I'm working with the Pronaszko Dance Theatre."

He looked puzzled.

"I'm a visiting choreographer," she explained. "I'm working on a piece for the company. They'll be performing it, I hope, at the end of August."

Marek tugged at the tuft of hair in the middle of his chin and smiled broadly. "I thought there was something different about you. You are not like the other Jews who come here."

"What do you mean?" she asked testily.

"I don't know," he said, averting her gaze. "Most Jews come here to cry. They don't see Poland. They see Auschwitz."

She wondered if this was his payback for the remarks about the menorah, or the survivor, Mr. Landau, saying, "All Poles are anti-Semites. It's in their blood." Maybe he also heard that woman, another survivor, say, "The Poles were worse than the Germans!"

"I'm sorry," she said. "Not all Jews think that way."

He shrugged. "There were a lot of Poles in Auschwitz too. Jews don't own suffering. In my family, we also had people there."

Ellen didn't like the way he seemed to be challenging her to condemn Jews for complaining. "Have you ever been to Auschwitz?" she asked, as a kind of defense.

"Sure, I went when I was in school, but I don't go to those places now." Marek waved the subject away. He turned back to his guitar and began to thread the string through the peg. "American Jews say we are anti-Semites, but that is not how it is with us at all."

Genuinely curious, Ellen asked, "How is it then?"

"I will tell you one thing," he said, turning the peg. "After the war, we stayed, with the Russians and everything. The Jews left."

Ellen lost her attraction to him. "What do you mean *left?*" she said, remembering Pronaszko's same use of the word.

"They could leave. They could go to Israel. But the ones who stayed here, we did not hate them. There was a Jewish boy in my class, Kopelman. He was not our good friend, but it did not matter. The truth is, he kept to himself. He was not one of us. It was as if he could not hear us. So what Kopelman said to us also did not matter." Marek raised his head and looked at her. "I am not saying this was a good thing, but it is not like these people think."

Ellen tried to imagine what it would be like to live among people who did not see or hear her. "To me, that would be an unbearable way to live."

"Then don't come to Poland," he said.

She could not believe how brutal the conversation had become.

He sighed. "I'm sorry. I am not explaining it very well. To me, it is sad that Poland lost its Jews. It is a different country now than the one my grandparents knew. My grandmother says, 'The spice is gone. Now we all taste like potatoes.'"

She was surprised by the sweet smile that appeared when he spoke of his grandmother.

"My grandmother's best friend was a Jewish girl," he said. "From when I was very young, she told me about this girl and her family. The stories of the Jews are her best stories, how they played together and how wonderful it was, and the Jewish festivals. It was my grandmother who sang me their songs. She did not know the words, only the tunes. Maybe there were no words. I don't know."

Ellen was amazed and touched by this. "Do other people like your grandmother's stories too?"

He nodded. "People don't know how to say it, but in a way, I think they miss the Jews. Our generation does not have these Jewish friends like my grandmother had."

Ellen heard the contradiction between this sentiment and the anger he had expressed toward Jews like his schoolmate Kopelman, and toward others whom he somehow held responsible for depriving the Poles of their full measure of martyrdom during the war, and for being able to escape to Israel. She wasn't sure he realized this. "What do people miss about the Jews?" she asked him.

"I don't know. For some people, it is nostalgia for another time. For me, it is something I hear in their music. It is very powerful, this emotion they had. I hear prayers in the notes. And these prayers are hidden everywhere, like the covered-over Jewish words, Hebrew street signs, and store names on the doors in Kazimierz. You have seen this?"

"Sort of," she admitted. But what he was saying made her uncomfortable. It was as if the Poles, now free of the constraints of real relationships with Jews, were enjoying a romantic, unthreatening *Fiddler on the Roof* fantasy of who they wanted them to be. It was creepy, a form of necrophilia.

A round woman, her hands and apron covered with flour, poked her head out of the kitchen and wiped her wide brow with her wrist. Her eyes were short slits in the heavy mass of her face. She said something to Marek in Polish.

"I have to eat my dinner now, before people start to come," he told

Ellen. "Would you like to join me? The cook says she will make you a plate too. We can sit over there." He pointed to a small table next to the kitchen door.

"I'd like that very much," Ellen said, relieved that they had made peace, however unsettling.

While Marek went to get their food, Ellen sat down at the table and inhaled the smells of Grandma Sadie's kitchen, the chicken and onions, the chopped liver, and the fried chicken skin her grandparents called *griebenes.* How she missed them.

Marek returned bearing two heaping plates of roasted chicken and cooked vegetables. Ellen liked the way he enjoyed what she used to call "Grandma food."

"*Smacznego,*" Marek said as they began. "That is Polish for *bon appétit.*"

"*Smacznego,*" Ellen repeated.

"Not so bad, for an American." He smiled.

"The chicken's very good," she said. "But speaking of very good, how do you know English so well?"

He smiled slightly. "My mother teaches English. Also, when I was nineteen, I was sent on a special program to a music conservatory in London. I learned more English there, and I made friends. We are still, as you say, in touch." He smiled.

She wondered if the *friends* included a girlfriend and felt a jab of jealousy. "Have you traveled much?"

"Not so much as I would like. Not enough money. Too much politics. It is not easy, being from Poland." His smile seemed less certain.

"I understand," she said. "Being American has a way of making traveling easier. Of course, there was the time I was the one American around for an anti-American demonstration in Lima. That was a treat." She rolled her eyes, enjoying the admiring way he now looked at her. It seemed the right time to ask him on an adventure. "Marek, have you ever heard of a town called Zokof?"

He seemed surprised but not displeased with the question. "No, I do not know it. What province is it in?"

She pulled her map of Poland from her purse and pointed to the town.

"Oh, yes," he said brightly. "It is near Radom." He leaned over her and the map with a gentle familiarity. "It is very possible that your song was from there. They were famous for their music in that area."

"My song?" She laughed, feeling the warmth of his skin. "It sounds a lot better as your song, believe me. My grandfather used to murder the tune."

Marek laughed for the first time since she'd arrived. She liked the sure, masculine sound of it.

"Your family is from Zokof?"

"My grandfather was born there. When my father was in Warsaw about a year and a half ago, he visited, just to see it." She was careful to add, "It was sort of a last-minute thing," because she didn't want Marek to think of her father as one of those mourning Jews. "He met an old man who lives there."

"A Jew?"

"Yes, why?" Ellen's nervous defenses rose again.

"Because I have never met a Jew from that region. I think they are almost all gone."

Ellen was relieved he didn't say they'd *left*.

"He might be able to tell us something about your grandfather's song. Did you tell your father that you heard it here in Kraków?"

"My father died last December." It was still hard for her to say this, and she was grateful when he put his hand on hers in a consoling way.

"I am very sorry," he said.

"Thanks," she responded quickly, having become unhappily used to the etiquette of condolence.

"Maybe this Jew in Zokof remembers some music from the old days. That would be very interesting," Marek said hopefully, as if trying to cheer her.

"Maybe," she said halfheartedly.

"The only way to learn about these songs in the small towns is to talk to people who remember them," he pressed on gamely. "In the cities it is easier. For example, I can find a lot of information about the music of Mordechaj Gebirtig because he was from Kazimierz. You know Gebirtig?"

Ellen looked at him blankly.

"The man who wrote the song about the town on fire, 'Undzer Shtetl Brent.' It is very famous. I am certain your grandfather sang that to you too."

She felt foolish. "No, he only sang the 'For-a-Girl Tune.' That's what I called it. I'm sorry. I've never heard of Mordechaj Gebirtig."

Marek shook his head. "You should know about this history as much as you know about Auschwitz. It would give you something to be proud about."

Ellen made a face. "It's not like I know so much about Auschwitz either."

"Well, you are not going to learn that from me. But I could teach you something about Jewish music." His smile teased her.

"I bet you could."

"We could go together to Zokof. I could take you in my car," he said. "A week from Tuesday maybe?"

Ellen nodded yes, her insides fluttering.

29

DURING MONDAY'S CLASS, ELLEN LEANED AGAINST THE STUDIO wall, thinking of Marek. Thinking of Marek had by then become something of a pastime, and a tension-easer. She replayed and reexamined their conversations, minus the moments of disagreement. She thought about the tab of beard he wore under his lower lip, the warm look of his eyes, his lovely accent, the smooth, inviting feel of his skin. This is the stuff of high school. Too much distraction, she told herself. To no avail.

Pronaszko rose from his chair. "Ellen," he said, with a suggestion of a bow, "the class is yours to finish." He smiled, gracious as a prince.

She hopped to her feet, having almost forgotten that she had asked for a half hour to work with the company that day. "Sure!" she said, annoyed at herself for sounding like an eager kid.

The company stirred warily.

"Let's start one at a time across the floor." She pointed to the far corner. "Work with the idea of weight, how it pulls your body forward, backward, or sideways." She waited out Andrzej's translation, making circles on the floor with her pointed toe, purposely not demonstrating. She wanted to see how inventive they were, what ideas they had about movement. The only instruction she added was, "As you cross the floor, increase your weight-edness."

The dancers slowly began to move, en masse, toward the designated corner, where they wadded themselves together like prisoners trying to avoid notice. Ellen saw in their improvisations a resistance to venturing past the boundaries of their classical training. They approached the task given them without joy or curiosity. It was evident to her that their cooperation rested entirely on Pronaszko's heavy presence in the room. When he finally stood and called class to an end, both he and the dancers quickly gathered their belongings and left the studio.

Andrzej the translator stayed where he was, posed in what he must have imagined was the perfect Bob Fosse jazz stance. Ellen found this disconcerting, especially since nothing in the flat, pale blueness of his eyes gave her any indication of why he was lingering. She needed the time to work alone, and rifled through her bag for another pair of leg warmers, hoping he'd get the message. Finding them, she sat down.

Andrzej stared at her. "How do you choreograph from that chaos you made with us?" he half whispered, clearly not wanting the few stragglers near the door to see him questioning her.

Ellen, appreciating the delicacy of the moment, bunched her striped blue leg warmers around her ankles and slowly pulled them up. She waited for the other dancers to leave. "I let things get wild so I can get to the outer edge of what I'm going for," she told him. "Then I shape the movements and layer them with music and words and the set. You know what I mean?"

Eyes on the door, he nodded, but Ellen thought he looked unsure. "This is interesting," he said, not unkindly. He stole a glance at her in the mirror. "I thought perhaps we could go for a coffee after class tomorrow."

The invitation was so tentative it was almost endearing. Still, there was a calculated guardedness about him that Ellen did not like or trust.

"Thanks, I'd really like that, but I have plans." She smiled, anticipating her day in Zokof with Marek. "Actually, I won't be here tomorrow."

His eyes widened at the rebuff, then narrowed as he seemed to consider whether to believe her. "Some other time," he said, his lips flattening into a smile without mirth.

"Definitely."

He stretched into second position on the floor. "I am curious about the dance you are making for us."

Ellen closed her dance bag and crossed the floor, hoping he would leave so she could get started. "I'm still working on it."

He didn't seem interested in leaving. "Do you choose your principal dancers from the improvisation technique?"

"No, I choose them by the type of movements they do best. When I need those kinds of movements, I put those dancers in." She knew he was lobbying for a lead part, and she hoped he had the political sense not to ask her.

He shook his head suggestively, letting the angle cut of his hair fly. "You have ideas about how I move best?"

"Not yet," she said curtly. "Actually, I was planning to work on the piece now."

It was clear from the momentary tightness in his face that he understood he was being dismissed, but he tried once more. "Maybe I could show you how the movements look on a man."

She smiled at recognizing this old dancer ploy, that once she saw his interpretation of a movement she would be more inclined to give it to him. She couldn't resist teasing him. "I always like seeing how a movement looks on a man."

"So do I," he said slowly.

She realized this was a confession when he jumped nervously to his feet and muttered a quick good-bye.

After the door had closed behind him, Ellen faced the mirror and led herself around with an outstretched arm, like Marek in her dream, holding the rod above his head, beckoning. She began to hum the "For-a-Girl Tune."

30

*Y*OU HAVE A MESSAGE," THE FRONT DESK CLERK TOLD ELLEN when she returned to the Palace Hotel later that afternoon.

> My group is playing in Łódź tomorrow. Last-minute engagement. Sorry. Sorry. Sorry. Maybe we can go to Zokof again another day. I hope you have a good visit with your friend. Call me at the Ariel Café, if you like.
> Marek.

Ellen called the Ariel Café.

"Marek is not here," the receptionist said. "I am sorry. I do not know where you can call him. The musicians are separate from the restaurant."

"Could I leave him a note?"

"Of course," the woman said empathetically.

Within an hour, Ellen had delivered it to her. It said:

> Marek,
> I'm sorry too. I was looking forward to our going to Zokof together. Until we meet again, I'll be humming the "For-a-Girl Tune" and thinking of you.
> Ellen.

She added her telephone number and hoped the message sounded more jaunty than needy.

Now she was sorry she had ever mentioned to her mother that Marek was driving her to Zokof. That had set off all her mother's alarms. "What do you know about this boy?" she'd demanded, as if her daughter hadn't any street sense of her own.

Ellen wasn't having any of it. "Mom, he plays klezmer music every week at the Ariel Café. That's as close to a nice Jewish boy as you can get in Poland." She could hear her mother fretting on the other end.

"Why couldn't you hire a reputable driver through the hotel?"

"Mom, stop worrying about Marek. I haven't gotten myself raped or killed yet."

Her mother emitted one of her exhausted sighs. "Don't be smart with me. You don't know where this boy is from or how he thinks. Ellen, you know better. A woman alone over there is a target."

"That's why I'll feel a lot safer going to Zokof with him than with a strange driver." To her relief, her mother was temporarily stumped by this argument and let the matter drop.

Now, as Ellen stood outside the Ariel Café, the sky had clouded up over Szeroka Square. The first fat drops of rain had begun. Ellen knew that in Kraków this meant a thorough soaking was coming and that she needed to find shelter until the storm passed. The weather was a setback in getting things together for her trip. She'd sent Rafael a letter telling him to expect her. She had to buy fresh produce, pack up the provisions she was bringing him, and make sure she brought the traveler's checks she'd bought with funds from her father's trust account, the balance of which she intended to give him in full. Her memory of the trust's language — *in the event of the incapacity or death of the undersigned* — gave Ellen a moment of raw grief so painful she had trouble breathing.

She crossed the square in the rain, over the great expanse of paved stone, tears flowing, her body hurting. She thought she'd take a shortcut to the tram stop, through a street behind the square. But her path was blocked by the strange fortresslike building that stood at the southern end. She didn't know what it was.

The stone architecture was a confusion of rectangles, arched doorways, buttressed walls, and a parapet. On its left side, the whole edifice seemed to have been torn apart and was collapsing like a classical landscape into a deep grassy pit the size of a city street.

She noticed a recessed doorway on the far right side of the building. The rain had begun to fall in sheets, and she ran to it for shelter. There was a sign near the entrance door: THE OLD SYNAGOGUE, MUSEUM OF HISTORY AND CULTURE OF KRAKÓW JEWRY.

Tentatively, she opened the door, walked into a darkened vestibule, and found herself in an almost bare sanctuary, inexplicably bathed in white light. The light so reminded her of her dream of Marek and the old woman in the window, she hesitated before taking a few cautious steps farther. A cool draft blew her wet hair.

In the center of the hall stood an enclosed circular balustrade. Its delicately crafted wrought-iron bars curved to a pinnacle on top, like a giant birdcage. Despite the sunless sky, the white light poured through the windows around the chamber, illuminating the ceiling's rib vaults, which flowed delicately onto several slender stone columns. The whole effect was elegant, yet intimate.

Ellen's cowboy boots echoed on the stone floor, reminding her of how carefully she'd tried to walk in Wawel Cathedral to soften their sound. But this white place was nothing like the dark, ornate Wawel, which had made her feel dwarfed amid the outsized sarcophagi and the soaring heights of its walls.

Near the entry wall stood a short, stocky woman in a brown nubby suit, one stiff hand curled protectively over the other.

"Excuse me. Do you speak English?" Ellen asked her in Polish.

With a restrained smile, the woman nodded.

"Do you know anything about this place?"

The woman nodded again. "This is the prayer hall of the oldest Jewish religious building in Poland, dating from the fifteenth century. It was once the seat of the Jewish community. Several hundred people could worship here together. Some of the outer walls rise to about seventy feet and were part of the city's walled defenses." She spoke methodically, with a British accent, as if reading from a tour book.

"Well, it's gorgeous," Ellen said, looking around. "The sign outside says it's a museum. It's not used for worship anymore?"

The woman eyed Ellen carefully and shook her head no. "During the war, the Nazis used it as a warehouse. Later it was torn apart and looted."

Ellen found the woman's calm demeanor jarring. "Really?" she said, unable to think of a fitting response. She noticed that in various places the whitewashed walls had been gouged, exposing the brick beneath.

"Eventually, the building was restored and became a museum," the woman continued. She motioned for Ellen to follow her as she walked toward the birdcage structure. "Please," she said when Ellen hesitated. "This is the bimah." Again, she gave Ellen a careful look. "That is the Hebrew word for the platform used for ritual observance and for reading from the Torah. Over there, on the eastern side of the room, facing Jerusalem, is the original Aron Kodesh, or the Ark of the Covenant, the ornamented cupboard where the Torah scrolls are kept. That wall," she said, pointing to grilled windows on the entry side of the room, "is the *me-chitzah,* the divider between the men and women's sections. As you can see, the eternal light is located above the Aron Kodesh." Her tone remained polite but distant. She paused, as if testing for some reaction.

But Ellen, utterly unfamiliar with the terms the woman was using for the ceremonial objects in the sanctuary, could only comment on their beauty.

"Over there, to the side of the Aron Kodesh, is a chapel that also served as a *kiddush* room."

Ellen noticed the woman did not translate this word, and she was embarrassed to ask what it meant.

"Today, the kiddush room is used to display Jewish artifacts. For example, there are silver cups that used to contain salt for sanctifying the bread before a meal. In the next room," she continued briskly, "we have many ritual objects and Jewish decorative art on display." Again, she assumed her cupped-hands position. "I think it is unfortunate, really, that we have placed them under glass," she said, almost confidentially. "When the Nazis planned their Museum of the Extinct Jewish Race in Prague, this is exactly how they intended to display Torahs, kiddush cups, and prayer shawls. Under glass."

Ellen's skin crawled. "A Museum of the Extinct Jewish Race?"

"Yes." The woman's expression did not change.

The whole hushed, whitewashed atmosphere of the synagogue now gave Ellen the chilling impression that Jews were extinct. "How long have you worked at the museum?" she asked, assuming now that the woman was a docent.

"I don't work here, but I am from Kraków," the woman said. "Today I am leading a group from Canada. They should be here any minute. I only thought you might be interested in more information about . . . our past."

Ellen realized she had just been asked if she was Jewish. She smiled awkwardly, troubled that the woman had not felt she could be direct. "I appreciate it. Thanks," she said.

"Not at all. Forgive me, but you are what my father, of blessed memory, would call a shayna maidel." She smiled, more warmly.

Ellen remembered her grandma Sadie calling her that — a beautiful girl. But now the words made her feel odd, somewhat exposed actually, as if the genetic Jewish remnant that linked her to Poland was so obvious, like a naked body through a sheer dress.

"I always think of my father when I come to this shul, this synagogue," the woman continued. "He used to daven, to pray, here. Now I give people tours in his name."

Ellen shivered, remembering how her father had told her he'd prayed in Zokof's cemetery, for Rafael's sake. She felt tears coming on again. Uncertain of her ability to maintain her composure, she walked over to the Aron Kodesh. In front of it was the biggest menorah she had ever seen. She forced herself to focus on the eagle that stood poised at its center, its powerful spread wings conveying to her a disturbingly misplaced sense of entrenchment and authority.

A group of English-speaking people threw open the door of the synagogue. The woman smiled. "Those must be my Canadians. There is an upstairs exhibit. You *must* see it before you go."

"I will," Ellen promised. "Thanks again."

The woman nodded graciously.

Ellen moved on to the adjoining room, where she admired the engraved ritual cups, the collection of old Torahs, the pointers and *shofars*. Although she wasn't exactly sure how they were used, she was impressed that these objects represented the work of hundreds of hands over hundreds of years.

In the upstairs gallery that the woman had said she *must* see was a horrifying display of Holocaust photographs. Ellen was unprepared for this. So much so, she was tempted to leave, angry somehow at not having been warned.

But a large picture of a pretty young woman, about her own age, with a stylish pageboy caught her eye. The photograph had been taken in the midst of chaos in Szeroka Square. What Ellen found most disturbing about it was that the young woman, clutching a bundle to her chest and clearly frightened, was wearing beautiful black suede pumps. The shoes, so like a pair she'd once rescued from her mother's Goodwill pile, drew her into the room.

She approached the photograph, curious to know where the young woman had walked after it had been taken, where she'd slept that night, and what had happened to her, and to the shoes. Her jaw ached. She realized she was grinding her teeth.

After several minutes, she moved on to the next photograph, identified as having been taken at the Podgórski Market in Kraków. In this, and in every photograph after it, she found the odd human details the most painful — the bent old man hiding a handful of bread and a pair of scissors, the woman on Krakowska Street who had chosen to take only an empty bookshelf into the ghetto, the child with the adultsize hat covering most of his face, with only one weary eye staring into the camera.

When at last she arrived at the end of the exhibit, Ellen felt the need to place her hands against the sturdy walls of the synagogue and to offer comfort. She was keenly aware of the presumptuous grandiosity of this gesture, that she was not the kind of Jew who would make the former congregants of this synagogue feel secure about the future of their faith. But she felt a powerful impulse to comfort them, to assure them they at least *had* descendants.

She thought of Marek, of how much she wanted to talk to him about this place, until she realized he wouldn't have had much patience with her being so upset. Marek, who had no use for Jews who came to Poland to cry. This incensed her. How dare he pretend he could love Jewish music without loving the people who wrote it? Ellen's legs shook as she descended the stairs. She held tight to the banister, alarmed at the intensity of her own fury.

As she left the Old Synagogue a few minutes later, a mass of sparrows took off from the roofs into the now-gray but rainless sky, as if swept away by an impatient arm. She stopped and watched them scatter, still waiting for her legs to steady.

She heard a tune, the "For-a-Girl Tune," but slightly different than Marek's, coming from a battered brick building at the other end of the square. She began to walk toward it, her pace quickening every few steps, until she was practically running. She passed several people, but no one seemed to notice the music.

The tune brought her to a tiny bookstore behind an arched stone doorway, then faded away. Above the shop, she thought she recognized the window where the old woman in her dream had sat.

The shop was empty of customers. Its proprietor was arranging books on a long table.

"Were you just playing some music?" she asked.

The man, shabbily dressed, looked at her questioningly over his bifocals. "This isn't a music store," he said in Polish-accented English. "We have books here."

"But did you hear music playing in the square?" Ellen persisted.

He looked at her but didn't respond.

Embarrassed and confused, Ellen scanned the titles on the long table. They were mostly in Polish and English. A few had Hebrew writing, maybe Yiddish, she wasn't sure. She picked up a book of Yiddish proverbs, one about Kazimierz, and another about the synagogues and Jewish cemeteries of Poland. By the time she left the bookshop, with an uncomfortable good-bye to the owner, she had purchased a small library of Holocaust literature as well.

That evening, in her room, she didn't give a single tormented thought to her choreography, or to Marek. She called downstairs and made arrangements through the hotel concierge for a driver to Zokof. Fired by her experience at the Old Synagogue, she opened one of the new books and began to read the chapter titled "The Zenith of Polish Jewry (1556–1648)":

> The royal authority, weakened by conflicts with the gentry, could not always prevent the hostile legislation of the city magistracies. Thus at Posen the limits of the ghetto were strictly defined; only forty-nine houses were allowed to the Jews, so that it became necessary to raise the height of many dwellings by additional stories. The magistracy of Warsaw refused to admit Jewish settlers, and Jewish merchants, visiting the city on business, could not tarry longer than two or three days.
>
> The warfare of the Catholic clergy against Reformers and Anti-Trinitarians, led by the bigoted Nuncio Ludovico Lippomano, incidentally resulted in turning the battle against the Jews. The usual weapon was seized upon. A rumor was set afloat that Jews of Sochaczev had procured a sacred wafer and desecrated it by stabbing it until it bled. Before the king could intervene, three Jews and their supposed accomplice, a Christian woman, were burned at the stake. The Jewish martyrs stoutly professed their innocence, protesting that the Jews do not believe that the host is the divine body nor that God has either body or blood (1556).

Ellen put down the book and stared at the wall, stunned by the thought that Jewish ghettos had existed in Poland so long before the Nazis. As for desecrating the host, she couldn't understand what this was all about. That Jews could be killed for a Christian ritual that had no meaning to them seemed to her more a sign of a Christian need to assert power and dominion. But to what end she could not imagine. Why did they care so much about Jews? Why go through such irrational religious posturing? This bothered her so much, she found it difficult to fall asleep. People who don't think things through logically are dangerous, her father always said.

"Dad, I miss you," she whispered.

In the night I came to her, covered with my plaid blanket. I sat in the big chair by her bed, like a living person; and knew I had to speak to her, to strengthen her nerve.

"My eyesight is not so good," I began. "These days, twos and threes I see of everything. But a shayna maidel, a beautiful girl, I can recognize." My voice was not my own, a clatter of high and low pitches, but I thought she could hear me. She had opened her eyes.

I pointed at the book of history on the table by her bed, the one she had been reading. "A lot of narrishkeit the goyim have said about us," I told her. "No one can deny it. But, shayna, better you should fill your head with the words of Rabbi Nachman of Bratslav, than your heart with such an anger. Rabbi Nachman said you should put your anger in your pocket and take it out only when you need it. What do you need with such anger? All of life is a struggle. So?"

She was looking at me, a little bewildered, I thought. "I am here," I said. "Yes, your eyes do not trick you." She said nothing. I suggested it wouldn't hurt that she study a little Talmud and Torah, like I did at my father's knee, may the Almighty preserve his name.

She seemed to smile. "My father studied with me," she said in a child's voice, not her own.

But I did not care to speak of Nathan Linden, who had betrayed my trust. "I understand," I said. "A terrible loss, your father."

"Can you talk to him?" Again, the child's voice. The girl could break my heart.

"Talk to him? I am talking to you. That is all I can do."

But I could not ignore her obvious unhappiness at my answer. "Your father is not here," I explained. "Maybe others are together, but I am alone. That is my share."

"You never see anyone else?" she asked, not without sympathy.

"Once," I told her. "My father came to tell me I should be vigilant." I did not know what more to tell her than this. "Stop torturing yourself already," I said. "I saw you at the shul. That girl with the shoes. I saw."

She looked off, sad but thoughtful.

I wanted she should understand me. I said, "Who knows, even when life is past us, what it was God intended? I myself might have been a mother in my lifetime. I took my regret at my childlessness with me to the grave. And yet, had I children, as God had commanded, the Smoke and Fire would have been their fate. That girl with the shoes could have been my yiches, *my legacy. What am I to think of this? I will tell you. I think at the end of tragedy, there is a story, and a story needs a storyteller. Maybe someone like you, from the outside, can tell it best."*

Her mind was elsewhere, I could tell. I said, "He's a langer loksh, *this Marek of yours."*

"What?" she said.

Now I had her attention. "A long noodle, what we call a tall, thin person. But I will admit this is a good-looking boy, a kind face. About him you shouldn't worry. Of course, it would be better for us both if he was frum.*"*

"Frum?"

She never heard this word? What kind of Jewish girl does not know even that much? "Frum, what you call observant, religious," I said.

She seemed to understand me. I said, "Also with your grandfather I had this problem, to find a frummer mensch *to take him under his wing. I said then, and I say now, if you can't have both, take the* mensch. *This boy Marek is a* mensch, *like Hillel was a* mensch.*" I gave her a nod. "Another day he'll take you to Zokof," I said. But she stopped me there.*

"Were you the one who sang the tune to Marek?"

It seemed she did not know what was what at all. I tried not to worry myself. I said, "I sing the tune always. Your langer loksh *heard it, that is all."*

"But why a tune, why not speak to him?" she insisted.

"With what word, what language?" I asked her. "Polish? Jewish? A tune everyone understands. A tune is like the apple your old bubbe *cut for you in pieces just the size of your mouth. It makes you cry, because she is gone and you miss her."*

I gave her time to think about this. "A tune touches the heart." I put my hand to where my breast had once been flesh. The lantern appeared between us. Its brightness grew, until the white light blotted us out to each other. I knew she was trying to see my face again, to look around the light. But it was impossible. I was being drawn back into the blue.

Quick, a last word, I thought. "Ellen, you should understand, before the

Smoke and Fire most of the Jewish people in the world lived in this country."
My voice sounded thick to me now. It echoed in the room.

She looked alarmed. I wanted to calm her, but I did not know how much
longer I would be able to remain with her.

*E*llen awoke with a start and lay rigid for some time. She had had a dream, that much she knew. There was a voice, a woman, or an idea of a woman in a blanket. There had been conversation, snatches of which she began to recall. She was sure Freidl, the gravestone Freidl, was the woman. But she couldn't piece it together. In frustration, she half rose and reached for the telephone to call her father. When she remembered that he too was gone, she rolled over and wept.

31

*A*T NINE THE NEXT MORNING, A MIDDLE-AGED MAN WITH A RE-
ceded chin and a sallow complexion introduced himself to Ellen in the hotel lobby. "I am Krzysztof, your driver," he said. He pointed to the small
Renault outside the window, as if to offer proof of his profession.

She shook his hand, told him she appreciated his being on time, having
by now observed that punctuality was not a Polish trait, and asked him a
few questions about the route to Zokof. "I need to be back here by late afternoon," she said, heeding her mother's warning to leave the town before
dark. "No problem," Krzysztof assured her. Ellen wondered why Euro-
peans found this phrase so attractive.

She slipped into the front seat of the Renault. Within ten minutes they
were out of the city. The light-green hills and meadows, the scattered,
sunken thatched huts, would have enchanted her had the car not been permeated with the sour smell of Polish cigarettes and Krzysztof's sweat. She
rolled down her window. There was no point in trying to make conversation. It had soon become apparent that Krzysztof's English was limited,
and in any case, he seemed rather withdrawn.

Squinting into the wind, she remembered Freidl's advice not to focus
so much on the Smoke and Fire, but she couldn't resist imagining Nazis
streaming across the sunny striped fields. The phrase *Smoke and Fire*
lent her a comfortable sense of insulation between the past and the bright,
normal-looking present.

Twenty minutes after they'd passed the tall cement high-rises of Radom,
the sight of Zokof township's black-and-white road sign made her nervous
to be entering her grandfather's hometown and finally meeting Rafael.

When they arrived minutes later, Zokof was not the charming hamlet she
had hoped for. Even the onion dome and the long, graceful spire of the
church on the town square could not soften the dilapidated impression
made by the surrounding uncut, haphazard grass and the cement apartment

buildings, with their raggedy laundry hanging from the balconies. She wondered if the town had been this depressing in her grandfather's day.

Krzysztof parked in front of a pharmacy on the square. Ellen pulled her
bulky backpack onto her shoulder and then unfolded the rough map to
Rafael's house that her father had sent her the week before he died. "I don't
know how long I'll be," she said as she got out of the car. Krzysztof nodded with the amiable indifference of a man whose services had been hired
for the day.

Her English attracted the attention of one of the pharmacy's customers,
an ill-shaven man in a threadbare jacket, who came outside, right up to the
car's front bumper, to stare at the newcomers. Ellen evaded him, but as
she proceeded around the square, she became increasingly aware of other
people's stares — some sidelong, others with a certain lack of expression,
which, to her, seemed excessively cold. She remembered how she had
mocked her father when he had told her how in China, surrounded by
hundreds of people craning to see his Occidental face, he had not experienced the sense of threat he'd felt in Zokof.

She quickened her pace. A block south of the square, away from the
noise and the stares, she stopped to look again at the map. A white-haired
woman, perhaps in her sixties, approached her. She carried a basket of
eggs on her arm, the handle buried in the folds of a heavy knitted sweater.

"*Przepraszam* — excuse me." Ellen showed her the map.

"*Tak, tak, tak.*" The woman adjusted her clear-rimmed glasses and
chucked her head agreeably. But when she looked at Ellen, her pinched
brows suggested she had no idea what the map meant.

"Rafael Bergson?" Ellen ventured.

The woman brightened. "*Pan Bergson ten Żyd?*"

"*Tak,*" Ellen said, startled that the woman had appended *Jew* to Rafael's
name.

Speaking rapidly in Polish, she took Ellen's arm and led her across the
street, down an alley, and up to the front door of a battered wooden house.
Ellen recognized the red-orange color her father had described. The paint
was blistering and peeling. Around the foundation, whole sheets of siding
had been eaten away.

"Here is Mr. Bergson's house," the woman chirped in Polish.

"*Dziękuję!*" Ellen thanked her.

"Proszę. Proszę." The woman bobbed her head again and continued on her way. But when Ellen glanced back at her, she saw the woman had stopped three doors down and was watching her intently. It made her nervous. She knocked on the door, hoping Rafael would answer quickly. When he didn't respond, she began to worry that maybe he hadn't received her letter. Maybe he wasn't home. She might have to wander around Zokof alone and return another day.

The sagging house did, in fact, seem shut. The white curtain sheers were drawn, the windows closed despite the warmth of the day. She fidgeted with the strap of her backpack and shuffled her feet on the worn boards that served as a doorstep, nervous too at how he would receive her if he was home after all.

When at last the door opened, she forgot about the woman in the street. She was facing a very old man with large brown eyes set deep in a wrinkled face. His lips, puckered like drawstrings, were barely visible beneath the awning of his mustache. A large black yarmulke capped his head, from which shoulder-length white hair trailed into a long ashen beard. He seemed so exotic, almost unearthly, that it was difficult for her to grasp that this man had been the boy who reset the course of her family's life, who had made her very existence possible.

They shared a lengthened moment of mutual appraisal. It did not escape Ellen's notice that he seemed to tense as his eyes passed over her bare shoulders, visible under her loosely crocheted jacket.

He beckoned her inside, his fingers thick and awkwardly angled with arthritis. "So you are here, Ellen Leiber. Come in."

She thought his deep, gruff voice unexpectedly robust, and he surprised her with a small, courtly bow. But as she thanked him, she wondered why he had called her *Leiber.* She crossed the threshold into the darkness of the vestibule and was repelled by the dust and the heavy human smell imprisoned in the house. She took his swollen hand, which he had not offered. "I'm very glad to meet you, Mr. Bergson," she said. "You had a very special place in my father's heart."

He acknowledged her greeting with a half-smile and several small nods, but gently drew back his hand. "May his memory be for a blessing." He rocked slightly. "You said in the letter he went quickly. Thanks God, at least he did not suffer."

Ellen looked away. Even after all these months, there were moments when her fatherlessness made her feel as if she had been cast out of her own life. Memories could not replace what it was to *be* her father's daughter. It was unbearable, an unrecoverable loss, not to have him anymore, not to be the object of that shy but earnest delight in her, his one and only child. Her carefully reconstructed inner balance began to give way, and she felt the miserable shame of tearing up in front of a stranger.

"Your father did not tell me his daughter was such a beauty," Rafael said as though he sensed her need for distraction. "You have a real Jewish face, like in the old days."

From the way he spoke, his eyes alight, his posture bent solicitously toward her, Ellen understood he meant this as a compliment. "Someone at the Old Synagogue in Kraków told me that," she said, remembering how she had thought it bizarre that her looks might once have been so common among Jews that she could be recognized as a type. At home, people usually guessed from the reddish hair and fair skin that she was Irish. No one had ever told her she looked like a Polish Jew.

"Come inside, Ellen Leiber," Rafael said. He directed her to the right, into a long room lined almost entirely with bookcases of tall books, most of them leather-bound. She understood, from the narrow, drooping bed pressed into the corner and piled with rough, torn blankets, that this was the single room in which he lived. At the far end, on a table, was a copper samovar and the remnants of a meal of bread and tea.

She paused in the doorway, taking in the brownish, water-stained wallpaper that was peeling in places. Between the bookshelves, six or seven lacy white paper cutouts of animals, menorahs, and intricate Hebrew lettering had been tacked to the wall. She smiled at these, hoping to lift her own spirits as well as his.

"Mr. Bergson," she said, turning to him, "my grandfather's name was Leiber, but mine is Linden."

"You changed your name," he said tightly.

"No, actually my parents changed it before I was born. Their name is Linden too."

He combed his beard with his fingers.

Ellen thought he was angry, but he began to chuckle. "Call me Rafael, Ellen Linden," he said. "I see you are not entirely your father's daughter. *He* let me go on calling him Leiber, the *mamzer.*"

She wasn't sure she'd understood what he had meant, but she had heard that word, *mamzer,* before. Her grandfather had used it, always in a derogatory way. She was about to defend her father, to try to explain the name change, but she saw a small boy's mischief in Rafael's eyes. She knew then that she liked him, that he was not at all the humorless religious man her father had led her to expect. She let the comment pass.

"Let us sit." He leaned forward and swung his arms as he walked, exerting what, to Ellen, seemed a great deal of energy to propel himself faster toward the other end of the room, like a man impatient with the physical limitations of advanced age. When he reached the covered round table, he pushed the bread and the empty tea glass behind the samovar and held out a chair for her. It was such a gentlemanly gesture that Ellen felt clumsy about pulling off her unwieldy backpack to sit down.

Unbuckling its front flap, she handed Rafael the Plexiglas container of sugar with the meadow painted on it. "I found this among my father's things in his study," she said. "It's for you." She handed him the canister and the note.

Rafael dropped heavily into his chair and turned the painted canister slowly around in his hands until he had made a complete revolution. Then he read the note. "Finding a meadow and planting a seed," he said, repeating Nathan's words.

Ellen had looked down, ashamed not to have admitted that she had found the canister in her father's cabinet, next to the top half of Freidl's gravestone. He had not made much progress with planting it. So, before he had a chance to ask her about the stone, she took out the envelope of traveler's checks and handed them to him. "My father said it's from the Bundists."

Rafael nodded at the checks and accepted them from her. "They have Bundists in America still?"

She realized he had not been deceived by her father's sweet fiction that the monthly checks had come from aging American Bundists. There were tears in his eyes now. Her own followed just as quickly, despite the no-crying grimace she used to hold them back.

Rafael placed both his hands on his knees and patted them simultaneously. The slow, rhythmic motion reminded Ellen of how her grandpa Isaac used to comfort her by patting her back until she fell asleep. "I will make us some tea," he said. He started to rise but lost his grip on the arm of the chair and fell clumsily back to his seat.

Ellen jumped up to steady him.

Embarrassed, he waved her off.

"Let me. I'd love to make the tea," she said, glad for an activity.

He made another attempt to stand, trying to make light of his difficulty. "What does an American girl like you know from samovars?"

She liked the way he was trying to joke with her.

"Over there, in the kitchen, I have a plate of biscuits on the shelf," he said. "Bring it here. They are for you, after such long travels."

She pushed open the narrow door to the kitchen, in the middle of the bookcase-lined wall, and found a chipped china plate, around which he had arranged five sad-looking crackers.

When she returned with it, his stomach growled loudly and long. "The body," he said, pointing to the offending portion, "it wants to remind me I am too old to make talk with a beautiful girl."

"Thank you," she said, finding him utterly endearing.

They smiled at each other.

"Why don't you have a few of these to hold you before lunch?"

He looked uncertain. "Lunch?"

She pulled her plastic sack of provisions from her knapsack. "Guaranteed kosher," she announced triumphantly.

He surveyed with obvious joy the small feast before him of rolls, juice, fruits, vegetables, hard-boiled eggs she'd cooked on the hot plate in her room, and the packaged kosher soup mixes she'd brought from New York. He mumbled a prayer, then his calcified fingers reached for a cracker from the china plate. It disappeared quickly into his mouth, leaving a small scattering of crumbs in his beard. "For such a meal we need to make the table!" he said.

Ellen wondered what else he had to eat in the kitchen. She went to look for plates in the cupboard and found a half loaf of bread and some milk on an oilcloth-covered side table near the stove, but not much else. She made them both a salad and served it with the rolls and eggs. "I've brought you more food in the car," she assured him when he hesitated to eat. "Besides, my grandma Sadie — Grandpa Isaac's wife — would never allow us to leave anything on our plates. It's a family tradition. So you better finish."

Rafael looked at the salad suspiciously and laughed for the first time since they'd met. "Grass," he said.

She noticed that his teeth, though mostly intact, were almost brown. But to her relief, he ate everything she put before him as he talked enthusiastically about herring and onions in cream, poppy-seed rolls, and bowls of fresh berries.

"That's Grandpa food." Ellen laughed.

"That's *our* food," he said.

When they had finished, he seemed invigorated. But leaning toward her, he said, "I am glad you are here, Ellen. The truth is, my time is almost over. Who would have thought I would live to see such an old age, older than Freidl when she went, *aleha ha sholem* — rest her soul in peace."

The mention of Freidl surprised Ellen. She would have expected him to compare his age to her grandfather's when he died.

"You know about Freidl," he said. "And now that you are here, she comes to you herself."

Ellen felt as if she'd been knocked slightly off balance, as if she'd been hit with a wave and couldn't tell which way was up. "How do you know my dreams?"

"She tells me." Rafael leaned back in his chair as if this was explanation enough. "An 'air spirit,' she calls you. Come, Ellen." He pitched himself forward intimately. "You did not know it was her?" His breath smelled like rotted cantaloupe. "Your father did not tell you about her?"

"He did," she said, still reeling, wondering what an *air spirit* was.

"What? What did he tell you?"

She squirmed in her seat, impatient to be the one asking questions. "He told me she was childless. He said she was the daughter of a famous scholar." She looked at him, hoping he would be satisfied.

"And?" He raised his eyebrows.

Ellen raised hers, conscious of mirroring him. "He said Grandpa Isaac broke her gravestone in two when he hid behind it." She hesitated before adding, "On the night when you got into trouble with that man."

Rafael cut her off with a dismissive grunt. "A storyteller should not be afraid of her story. In the details is the juice, you understand?"

Ellen couldn't stand it anymore. "Rafael, how do you know about Freidl coming to me?"

He waved her question away. "I want to hear what your father told you about her."

"He said you stayed for her, that you've made a memorial in the cemetery for her from small stones." She toyed with one of the faded tassels edging the table cover.

"What else? What did he say about her soul?"

His insistence made her feel more uncomfortable. "I don't know what my father thought about souls," she said. "Actually, I doubt he believed in them."

He rapped the table impatiently. "A person should not speak against the dead. But always it was the same with him. Always he was afraid of what others will say." He glared at the canister. "Finding a meadow, planting a seed. No, he did not do for her what he promised."

Shaken by his anger, Ellen looked around, trying to see the room as her father had seen it, trying to imagine what he had promised Rafael here. "You have no idea how much you affected my father," she said. "He never read the Bible in his life, and he actually gave me a *Tanakh* to read before I met you. He respected you, and he worried about you. I almost think he let me come to Poland just so I could make sure you're all right. He just didn't know what to do for Freidl. He didn't know what to do." Ellen watched him nervously, waiting for him to respond.

Rafael rubbed the joints of his fingers. He moved from one to the next, massaging each in a well-practiced manner. "Freidl always said Itzik's soul was like an uncooked potato," he said. "Your father's soul, God forgive me, I think it was only half-cooked." He looked up and suddenly smiled at Ellen. "But you?" He raised his eyebrows with a look of pride. *"Fun a proste bulbe kumt aroys di geshmakste latke."*

"What does that mean?" Ellen said, her own hands now clamped in nervous dampness.

"From a humble potato comes the tastiest pancake."

The two of them looked at each other and laughed.

"There is something I really want to ask you," Ellen said.

Rafael raised an interested brow.

"My father was so afraid of my coming here. He talked about Poland like it was the Land of Evil. He told me you gave him the gravestone not just because of my grandfather but because you said it would be safer in America. Is that true?"

Rafael shrugged. "There is evil here."

His tone was so mild, she didn't believe he meant it. "You wouldn't condemn a whole country because of some peasant a hundred years ago, would you?"

He smiled at her indulgently. "It is written, 'Evil does not grow out of the earth. . . . Men make mischief just as surely as sparks fly upward.' You think a hundred years changed this?"

She still wasn't sure how literally he meant this. "But there are almost no Jews in this country today. You're not saying that's the Poles' mischief, are you?"

He put his forefinger to his lips and shook his head that she should let him speak. "You are a young woman, but old enough to understand these things, maybe more than your father even. So, listen."

She sat very still.

"Today, you have returned to the town of your family. But our Zokofer Jews are now just dry bones, and I am the only one left from the five thousand in your grandfather's time. Whose fault? The Nazis, yes. They organized." He frowned. "A talent for organization the Germans have, not like the Poles. The Poles are full of narrishkeit about freedom! Honor! But what to *do?*" He raised his upturned palms. "Gornish! Nothing. Now, I will tell you something, Ellen Linden. It is not my purpose to lecture you about what was after the war. But I want you should understand something of this. It will help when we talk about Freidl. Because it is Freidl we are here to talk about."

Ellen nodded, although she didn't entirely understand the connection. She noticed that he, like Freidl, used the word *narrishkeit,* which she now took to mean *nonsense.*

Rafael slowly shifted his position in his chair, organizing his presentation, it seemed to her. "When I returned to Zokof after the war," he began, "one of my Polish neighbors came to me. He said, 'We weren't all anti-Semites.' I said to this man, 'Wytold,' I said, 'we knew you couldn't help us. We knew it was too much to ask a person to risk his life, his family, for us. But we did expect that you, our neighbors, would not turn us over to the Nazis for a kilo of sugar.' You know what that man said to me?" He squinted at Ellen.

Everything had become eerily quiet to her. "What?" she said.

"Nothing. He hung down his head, and he walked away. But in all these years since that day, that man, Wytold, the only one in this town who ever said a word to me about the Annihilation, never once did he come again to my door, to talk, to be a neighbor, to bring a piece of cake. Nothing. Are there Nazis here to stop him?" Rafael threw his arms dramatically in the air, as if searching for Nazis. "So, I ask you again, what's different today?"

A tense silence followed. Ellen looked around. The cracked plaster ceiling and the walls now seemed vulnerable to her, as if the weight of the townspeople were pressing against them, as if it were their intention to pummel this last refuge to bits and dust. She got the same shaky feeling she'd had in the Old Synagogue, only this time the threat felt closer.

Rafael coughed and began to work on his fingers again. "Of course, there is another way to look at the situation. Maybe we could say I am the fortunate man."

"You survived," Ellen suggested.

"Yes." He nodded thoughtfully. "After the war, in towns all over Poland, towns like Zokof, the Poles did not make confessions to Jews." He glanced up at her. "They made pogroms." His gruff voice was barely audible. "They don't like that word here, *pogroms.* They say pogroms were only in Russia. But in Kielce — you passed it on your way here — they killed forty-two survivors, wounded hundreds. After. *After!* You understand?"

She did not. Nor did she understand his change of mood.

He narrowed his enormous eyes and appraised her as he raised a cautionary forefinger. "Ellen," he said in a low voice, "about this, your father was not wrong. You are in a land of unrepentant evil."

Ellen felt a twinge at her temples. She realized then why he had sent the stone to America. It had been an act of protection, of unselfish love. How difficult it must have been for him to give it up. "Why don't you come to America?" she said. "We could sponsor you."

He shook his head. "For me, at my age, it hardly matters anymore. The only move I will make now is from here to the grave."

She tried to protest.

He waved her off. "Every life has its end. But it is a mistake to think that if you turn your back to evil it will not follow you."

Ellen thought of Freidl's gravestone, wrapped and hidden in her father's cabinet. She knew Rafael wanted her to do something about it. But she didn't know what.

Rafael sighed. "Could you pour me a glass of tea? I'm a little dry."

Ellen refilled the glass and handed it to him. His fingertips were cold. She placed her hand over his, as if to steady the glass, but really she meant to insulate the warmth that already seemed to be ebbing from his body.

He took several short sips and put down the glass.

"You look like you could use a rest. How do you feel?" she said.

"Feel? I feel like a man old enough to touch a woman not his wife and not fear God for it." He smiled distractedly. "Did your father tell you that when I was a young man, I had a wife and a child?"

Ellen shook her head.

"In sleep they came back to me. For years." He clenched his hands in his lap.

It seemed to Ellen this clenching of his hands caused him additional pain.

"From them, I heard the *mamaloshen* — the mother language. My daughter, my Sonya, when I dreamed, was a young woman already. How could it be, to grow in death? I wondered. But they came to me. They were women together, my wife and my daughter. She would tell her mother, 'I am going to bake a challah for Poppa. A braided challah.'" He gestured an imaginary challah about two feet long. "Eggs and raisins is what they talked about. And how to lay the challah in the oven. But after so many years, my wife, my daughter, they left. Maybe it was because I forgot already how women talk to each other."

"You've been alone a long time," Ellen said understandingly. She got up and went to the front window, to try to absorb this newest layer of loss in his life. A car had pulled up to the house across the narrow lane, and a man and a woman got out, talking as they shut their doors. They saw her. She waved at them tentatively, but they did not wave back. Ellen stared after them as they went into their house, depressed by the sense of isolation their coldness had engendered. "Why did you stay here for Freidl? What good did it do?" she asked Rafael.

He sighed again. "Good. Heh. You are right. That God will not let her rest, this, you think, has something to do with good?" He tilted back his head awkwardly and let out a dry, rasping laugh. "We think maybe God was not satisfied that she did good enough by Itzik, who you call Isaac. He did not believe, maybe, that she could do better in America with him. So He kept her here, with me, to wait. She got the idea that she should do something for me, to make me remember that once I feared God. That this might be good. Who else could she care for? I am the only one left. You see, before the war I was a socialist. After, when I came back to Zokof, I believed in nothing, and I was not afraid of God. God? I said. If He was in the world, what could He do anymore to put fear in me? What He could do was done." Rafael pursed his lips until they disappeared under his mustache. "If God could take my wife and my child, He was a fool, I said. I did not accept this idea that God acts with a greater purpose, not when He allows evil to ruin His creation."

Rafael pressed his hand to his yarmulke. "I thought maybe it was time for God to be afraid now. I thought, He knows that for what he did to my wife and child, I *should* curse Him. I am not Job that He should play tricks on me, to make my life a misery."

Ellen was relieved to at least know who Job was, even if she did not entirely understand the trick to which Rafael referred.

"Freidl came to me," Rafael said. "'Be a mensch,' she said. This made me weep because I saw how much of the mensch in me was gone. That I was a man lost to myself." He shook his head. "Maybe you are too young to understand such things."

"Tell me anyway," Ellen said, wanting very much to understand him.

"When I was at the end of my hope, she said to me, 'Believe in your God. He brought you to me.'" He looked at Ellen. "That God would come back to me and I to God, this was almost too much for me. Should a man be asked to bear such a thing? After what He took? This is what I asked Freidl. But she said, 'Be a mensch.'"

He shrugged. "What was I to say to this? I could say, a dead woman I never met cannot come to me and tell me to be a mensch. I am talking to myself. I am putting words in her mouth I do not want to say myself. But in the end, what does it matter if it is her speaking or me? Maybe it is God telling me, Rafael, be a mensch. In the end, I said, all right, what is, is. I put on the *tallis* and the tefillin, and I prayed as a Jew, every morning, afternoon, and night. It gave me comfort. And in time, with Freidl, I began to study again like I did as a boy in cheder."

He looked at her. She understood cheder. That was the school he was coming from the night he and her grandfather met the peasant with the whip.

"I went from house to house here in Zokof. I asked the Poles here for Hebrew books they found from before the war. They handed them over. What did they want with them? And I think it made them feel better, that they did this, something decent. Some of them told me who gave them this book or that. Some kept them for a memory; some remembered where they were told books were buried." He swept his arm around the room, at the shelves of books. "Behold the Jews of Zokof, *Am Ha Sefer* — the People of the Book." He nodded. "With Freidl I read in Hebrew, the father language, and in time, my faith was returned. My God is not a fool."

He smiled slightly. "I light the candles on Friday night, like a woman, to welcome the Sabbath. I do this because she cannot. I do this for my wife and daughter, because they cannot." He pulled absently at his sleeve. "She stands behind me in this room, at this table. I feel her presence, watching me."

Once again, Ellen noticed how he talked about Freidl in the present tense. "Does that mean that if Freidl returns to her grave, you'll be alone?"

He began to rock back and forth.

"Is that why you waited for my father to find you, instead of you finding him?"

The rocking increased. He closed his eyes.

Ellen couldn't bear to push him any further.

"I didn't want to let her go," he said softly. "I don't want to let her go. But it's a shonda, my shonda, what I did. A sin, you understand?" His eyes remained shut.

"It's not a sin to want to talk to someone. You're all alone."

"She needed me to find Itzik."

Ellen could scarcely believe he could be saying that a dead woman had asked him to find her grandfather. But then she remembered Freidl had told her that Marek, the langer loksh, would return with her to Zokof, and in her dream, Ellen hadn't doubted her at all. Why would Rafael?

"It was after the war. I promised her I would find him. He was in Brooklyn, New York. I wrote. He answered. He said he would never come back to Poland. That's all. He would never come back. And he would not pray." Rafael recited these facts in a mechanical manner, as if he had examined them many times before. His hand dropped to his side. "Ach! Itzik. Itzik the Faithless One!"

Tears fell from his cheeks, like her grandfather's at the Passover Seder. Ellen dug around in her backpack and produced some tissues for him.

Rafael wiped his eyes and tried to smile. "*Mine* mensch. That is what she calls me. But sometimes I don't know. I am confused. What is true, what is my imagination? I see things, not just Freidl. Across the market square, I see the back of my neighbor, Yossl Greenberg, from the old days. I open my mouth to call to him, 'Yossl, it's me. Rafael Bergson!' But always it is the same. The man turns around. It is not Yossl Greenberg. It is some Paweł or Jan or Tomek, not one of us. To them, the Pawełs and the Jans, I am only their Jew, their little Jew."

Ellen must have looked so bewildered by this that he felt the need to explain.

"In the old days, every Pole had a little Jew, someone they thought was a little better than the rest of the Jews, someone they could tolerate. Mostly, that was someone they needed, a doctor, a shoemaker, and now, me, their tailor."

His contempt was so evident, Ellen was glad Marek was not there. He was *not one of us,* and she knew his presence, at this first meeting, would have made Rafael feel intruded upon. She toyed with the notion that his unavailability might have been Freidl's work too.

Rafael sighed yet again, his fingers enmeshed in his beard. "I am an old man. I was given my life to live to an old age. This is a blessing. And to have such a guest as you, this is proof that life can still surprise, and in surprise, there is hope, even now, when death sits on my nose and makes me a fool. When I pray, I hear God laugh. And I thank God for Freidl, that she did not leave me, that she would not leave me, even when I failed her. She wanted a memorial. She wanted me to find the other half of her stone, the bottom half. She told me where it was, in the cemetery, facedown. They made there a path from the stones so no one should know it was a cemetery. Then, after the war, they had a building project. They came for the stones and took them to town. Freidl's was under so many others, I could not get it for her. She begged me. But alone, a man could not lift such weights without being found out. They took her stone and used it to support the pavement. I knew where it was, but I could not get it. Then a farmer goes over there, Wladek Głowacki is his name, and it is gone. Just like that. This is where things stand now. He has the stone. I cannot get it. And Freidl is making me heartbroken from this. What can I do? I put pebbles at her grave, to mark her place. But I cannot do more. I do not have the strength to build her a memorial, and it is not a memorial that will return her to her grave."

Ellen listened to him, realizing he was reciting what went on in his head every day, all day, for years and years. She began to understand his refusal to quit Zokof. If he left, he would be turning his back on his responsibility to Freidl, which he alone had borne all these years. If he did not find a way to let her rest, if he died before achieving this, she would be left to an uncertain fate, for there was no one else to take up her cause.

"What does she need, Rafael?"

"Prayer," he said simply. "And I know it is the Leibers' prayers she needs more than mine. She came from death for Itzik, and no one but him or his descendants can return her there, to show God that she did good by defying the law of death."

32

THEY SAT SILENTLY AT THE TABLE. ELLEN RAN HER FOREFINGER around the rim of her tea glass. "She wants me to pray for her?"

A floorboard creaked. Another car drove by. "Do you pray?" Rafael asked. He didn't wait for her to respond. "You think it is nonsense to pray, yeh? Don't deny it. The face tells the secret."

Ellen opened her mouth, hoping to finesse an answer that would suit them both. "I don't know if it's nonsense. I just have never understood it. If I don't believe in God, how can I pray for Freidl?"

He didn't answer.

She frowned, not knowing how to explain herself adequately to him. How could she possibly impart the level of hostility toward faith with which she had been raised? "My grandfather always said God is for primitives." She looked at him nervously. When he merely nodded, she thought him gracious. "When I first came to Kraków, I went to Wawel Cathedral and watched people pray. The Catholics don't pray like Jews, but I couldn't help wondering how people don't feel idiotic, shutting off their reason and asking God for favors. I don't understand what they're doing."

Rafael stroked his beard. He seemed to be listening very closely to what she had to say.

When she paused, he nodded his head. Encouraged, she wrapped a tendril of her hair around her finger and twisted it slowly, nervous about saying these things out loud for the first time. "You know, when I was little, I used to be very curious about heaven. One of my friends told me prayers went there. But my parents and my grandfather convinced me there is no such place. There is no God, and there's nothing out there at the end of the universe."

Rafael laughed. "What is so interesting to you about heaven? God, you think, lives in a nice house up there? What does it matter? The end of the universe!" He laughed again. But when he saw that she was not laughing with him, he stopped. "When the Baal Shem, of blessed memory, was in the hour of his death, he said, 'Now I understand the reason I was created.'

You see?" He pointed meaningfully to the earth. "We are to rejoice in life here and live mindful of God's judgment of our deeds."

"I wouldn't have a problem with the 'rejoice in life' part," Ellen said. "Though after seeing this town, I don't know how you do it. It's the God part that I get stuck on."

He looked toward the window.

"Don't get me wrong," she said, not wanting to insult him in any way. "A lot of people I respect believe in God. And to me, believing only in science seems just as primitive. One-tracked, you know? Who knows, maybe the universe is expanding because it's reaching for heaven? But why pray? That's what doesn't make sense to me."

Rafael turned back to her and smiled. "And my knowing that you dreamed about Freidl, this makes sense? But you don't deny it's true."

She could not argue.

"And God? God makes no sense to you because you were not trained to recognize Him, to see the hand that moves behind all things in the world. For you, it is easier not to believe. But if we turn our backs to God and not our faces, it does not mean He is not there."

"Like evil," she said.

"Like evil." He nodded. "Into the darkness God brought light, but still, there is darkness."

She felt relieved and a little excited by a certain comfortable solidity to his argument. "You have no idea how ignorant I am," she said, embarrassed somehow that she didn't know more about Judaism. "One year, when I was about thirteen, I decided to observe Yom Kippur. At that age, fasting seemed like an interesting idea. You may think this is funny, but I didn't know anything about Yom Kippur except that religious Jews fast on that day. No one told me that I was supposed to be in a synagogue. My parents took me downtown to the aquarium."

"*Tsk.*" Rafael shook his head.

"It was really crowded and hot inside, and I fainted in the middle of a dark hall lined with these huge gray fish." She sighed. "I can still remember the fish. My parents picked me up off the floor, got me outside, and stuck a sandwich in my mouth. That was the end of my religious experience."

It surprised her that again he laughed.

"Your parents were afraid you would become a *frummeh* — an observant Jew — if you knew what is Yom Kippur?"

"Maybe so," she said, realizing she recognized the word *frum* from her dream of Freidl. She saw herself dressed up in a wig and a long denim skirt with sneakers, like the Orthodox women in New York, and she too had to laugh.

Rafael looked at her. "You knew to fast on Yom Kippur. That is something. A memory that remained, yes? It would have been better if your parents knew what they *didn't* believe in before they taught you not to believe."

She screwed up her face in puzzlement.

"In Jewish we say, *Ersht lern zikh, un dan lernen ondere* — first learn, then teach. That is what I would have told them."

"Yeah," she said, loving that he was speaking to her in her grandpa's language, the *mamaloshen*, even if she hardly understood a word. "So, a question," she said. "How does my being able to pray for Freidl make any difference for her?"

He studied her. "Prayer brought our five souls together." He held up the five fingers of his hand and counted off. "Your grandfather Itzik prayed for Freidl to protect him. Freidl prayed for me that I should survive the Annihilation and help her rest. I prayed for Nathan to find me, and he prayed for the Leibers at Freidl's grave." He looked at her. "We pray to console ourselves, the living and the dead. And you must pray for Freidl's resting place to be cleared of the stones of Lamentations."

"Lamentations!" Ellen cried. "When I left for Poland, my father told me to read that for you. He said it's pure poetry."

"Then read and you will understand about the stones." He seemed satisfied with her. With some difficulty, he stood up and walked, in his labored fashion, to a hulking dark wooden wardrobe along the street side of the room. He opened the doors and slid open a drawer, removing a yellowed envelope. Returning to the table, he handed it to Ellen and sat down.

"When your father was here, I told him this photograph was stolen from my coat on my way home to Zokof. Yesterday, a man came to my door. A Pole. He tells me he broke down a wall in his house a few years ago, to make a new room. In the wall he found this. He asked if I wanted it because his house used to belong to a Jewish family, and he thought maybe I knew the people in the picture. They did that, during the war, you understand? Jewish people hid their photographs in the walls. Or they buried them, like the books, for after. Or they gave them to Polish neighbors, for safety."

"So this is a photograph from before the war?" Her arms tingled as if she had touched electricity.

He nodded. "I asked my neighbor, why is he bringing it to me now? He said his conscience was bothering him. He meant to give it to me years ago, when he found it, but he forgot." Rafael shrugged. "Yesterday, something made him take the envelope and bring it to me. Something, yeh? Freidl came to me last night and told me how she scared this Pole into bringing me the photograph for you. She wants you should have it."

Ellen could barely speak as she began to open the envelope. "Thank you," she whispered.

Rafael shrugged again.

The photograph was mounted on a card, in the old style. It was very much like the framed one her father had in his study. She pulled it out carefully and saw her grandfather seated in a chair, wearing the same clothes as in her dad's photograph. But standing beside him, with a protective arm on her grandfather's shoulder, was a beautiful young man. His long dark hair was combed straight back, startlingly like Marek's. She loved the jaunty yet elegant way he held his body. It perfectly complemented the defiant look on his face.

"That is Hillel," Rafael said, pointing to the young man. "He was a musician, a Jew. He played guitar. Freidl wanted I should tell you that to him she sang a niggun — a tune — in his ear. He was a socialist. Still, she thought he looked like a mensch. She sang to him so he would stay with Itzik and watch out for him, which he did, gave him passage to America. Now I will tell you something. Not so long ago, in Kraków, Freidl sang it again. But the tune, you know which one, it is from her. Her prayer for you."

Ellen felt her face flush. "I know which one," she said, filled with love and awe of this woman.

*T*he afternoon grew late. Ellen asked to use the bathroom.

"The toilet is in the back. This is an old house," Rafael said, as if he felt he needed to apologize. "Use the kitchen door."

It took Ellen a moment to understand that she would have to go outside, to an outhouse that stood at the end of a footpath about thirty feet from the house. The stench of it reached her before she got to the wooden door, and once inside, the fetid smell of urine warned her not to sit. Squatting over the hole, she grabbed a few sheets of the abrasive gray paper he kept there as toilet tissue and peed as quickly as she could. It would soon be dark. She wondered how he managed this at night. Or in the winter snow.

She washed her hands in the kitchen and returned to Rafael in the living room. He had closed his eyes. She would have liked to press him about how Freidl's tune was a prayer, and if he knew that Marek now played it with his musicians in Kraków, but he seemed so tired. Still, when she told him she would have to leave, his chest contracted ever so slightly, as if her departure caused him physical pain.

"I'll be back soon," she said. "Next time, will you show me the cemetery where Freidl is buried?"

He looked up at her with a tenacious tenderness and rose to escort her to the door. "Next time. Yeh."

She squeezed his arm gently. "I'll be back."

"Good-bye, shayna maidel," he said with some difficulty as he watched her tuck the photograph of her grandfather and Hillel into her backpack. "I leave you in Freidl's good hands, *aleha ha sholem* — upon her may there be peace." He walked her to the vestibule and opened the door. "Tell your driver to be careful, yeh?"

She spread her arms to say good-bye, and he did not resist her when she enfolded him. He wore so many layers, the demarcation of body and cloth was indistinct. At close range, his clothes gave off the stale odor of dead skin and dust.

She walked back to the main square. Krzysztof sat smoking on a bench next to the war memorial. He greeted her, and they chatted pleasantly on their way back to the car, making liberal use of hand signals, which they continued to do all through their ride back to Kraków. They spoke about the Polish love of mushroom picking, and how the pollution from Nowa Huta was affecting people's health. At some point, Ellen rearranged her crocheted shawl on her shoulders, and as she did, she caught the distinct smell of Rafael's musty clothes. It made her very happy to have been able to take it with her.

33

*T*HAT EVENING, MAREK CALLED THE PALACE HOTEL. "ELLEN, we are still in Łódź. I'm sorry I could not take you myself to Zokof. Did you find a ride?" He didn't wait for a response. "I did not know about my group's engagement. I came to your hotel to tell you, but you were not there and I had to leave. My group, well, we are not as organized as we should be. I don't see them when we are not working."

"Don't worry about it," Ellen said, enjoying his asking her to forgive him almost as much as the sex in his rolled *r*'s. "It worked out. I spent the day with Rafael. We'll go there together some other time."

"Good, good. Any time you like. But if you are not going tomorrow, will you come out with me for dinner? I will be back in Kraków in the afternoon."

She cupped the phone in her hands, smiling. "Sure. I'd like that a lot. Where do you want to go?"

There was a pause. "Well, you are always in the city. Maybe you would like to see a different kind of place. I know an inn in the forest."

Ellen didn't like the sound of this. Too far for a first date, and in one of their recent conversations, her mother had told her to stay away from Polish inns. "Your father told me they're cement rooms where men go to get drunk," she'd said.

"Why would we go to an inn instead of a restaurant?" she asked.

"You don't like an inn?" He seemed confused.

"Is it one room, where people just drink?"

Marek laughed. "Oh, no. Not that kind. How do you know about that?"

"My father told my mother about them, and she told me."

"Your father went to such places?"

"I think he might have walked into one by mistake." She could easily imagine him doing this, then backing out like a dog from a skunk's burrow.

"Don't worry, you will like this inn," Marek said. "Very beautiful. They serve meals outside in the garden, or inside. It is very nice inside too. People also come to stay the night."

When she still hesitated, he added, "Not us, but people."

Ellen smiled at his nervousness and thought that if Freidl could trust Marek with the "For-a-Girl Tune," she should trust him to take her to dinner. "Okay, tomorrow," she said.

*T*he following evening, Ellen descended the grand staircase of the Palace Hotel. In her right hand, she held her beaded jean jacket and a small embroidered purse with a golden chain. Halfway down the stairs she saw Marek enter the hotel. In chocolate-brown jeans and a close-fitting black shirt, his hair blown back, he looked fantastic.

She slowed her pace, remembering that well-bred women kept their heads lifted when they walked down stairs. Lately, she had developed a desire to attend to notions of nineteenth-century etiquette. The architecture at the Palace seemed to require it. So did the strappy metallic heels she was wearing.

Marek's wide mouth parted into a shy, approving smile when he saw her. "Good evening," he said.

She liked the even shape of his white teeth as he smiled up at her. Only the silly tuft of red hair below his bottom lip upset the look she liked. "Hi!" she called down to him, and abandoning all pretense at old-world manners, leaped down the remaining stairs, her new amber droplet earrings swinging wildly along the sides of her neck. On the second step from the bottom, she stopped to look at him, his gold earring, his oval face, the wavy flow of his long brushed-back hair.

Unconsciously, she raised her free hand slightly above the curved banister. He took it in his and kissed it. She was surprised by the gesture, and wondered if hand-kissing was as customary a Polish greeting among people her age as it apparently still was with older Poles like Konstantin Pronaszko. Or, she wondered, did Marek mean something more by it?

His dark-brown eyes roved merrily from her face to the softly folded neckline of the white chiffon blouse she wore.

She noticed this with pleasure.

He pointed to the door. "My car is down the street," he said, gallant as a knight.

Together, they walked to his miniature muddy white Fiat Polska. Marek opened the door for her. Ellen eyed the lopsided black upholstery and quickly folded her long legs into the passenger seat, glad she had worn her satin-silk slip skirt, cut on the bias to stretch when needed.

They chugged slowly out of Kraków, the Fiat emitting grunts and fumes at every stop. "It can make the trip," Marek assured her. "And I can fix it if anything breaks down."

"With those musician's hands?" she said in mock horror.

He smiled at her.

In the car's tight proximity, she could feel the heat of his forearm as he shifted gears. He was one of those men, she noticed, whose body was always the right temperature. His hands, with their long rectangular fingertips, cupped the steering wheel in a manner suggesting a graceful and certain lover. She leaned back happily in the hard, uneven seat.

Marek slid a cassette of a Chopin mazurka into the portable tape player and informed her, with a certain pride, that they could play music wherever they went.

She opened his cassette case and was surprised to discover tapes by B.B. King, Robert Johnson, and Rickie Lee Jones. "We seem to have the same taste," she said.

He sent her a quick sidelong smile.

She watched how his fingers caressed the wheel and decided this was not the time to tell him about her visit with Rafael.

Twenty minutes later, they turned off the highway onto a narrow road that took them through a birch and pine forest. Shortly after, they reached a clearing. In the waning light, people were still seated at small tables in the patio garden of an intricately crafted wooden chalet.

Marek parked, and Ellen put on her jean jacket in the cool pine-scented air. They followed a flower-lined stone path to the front entrance of the inn.

"It may surprise you, but this building is new," he told her. "This is a replica of a traditional wood architecture that was destroyed during the war." He seemed very proud of the place.

"It's beautiful," she said.

Marek smiled. "I thought you would like it, but you look cold." He examined the thin fabric of her outfit with concern. "We will sit inside."

They were seated at a table for two near the open hearth of a lit brick fireplace. The mantel was crowded with brightly colored carved-wood figurines, each with painted red cheeks. The carved women held fish and ducks. Some of them churned butter. The men carried baskets of birds. "Aren't they wonderful?" she said to Marek.

"Yes, and so is the food."

"What should I order?"

"Try the *bigos,*" he suggested. "Very Polish. This is a cabbage stew, with meats and sausage. At home, my mother serves it after church on Sundays. A good bigos takes most of the week to make."

Ellen could not imagine Marek as a churchgoer, and she didn't particularly want to try. It only served to underline the differences between them. She had not even begun to try to imagine his family. Perhaps his mother was one of those solid Polish women of indeterminate age, like the ones she'd seen in Zokof carrying grocery sacks, wearing scarves tied under their chins and knee-high stockings with their thick, round-toed shoes. "Where do your parents live?" she asked.

"In Kielce."

At once, her ears began to burn. She did not want to ask Marek if he knew about the forty-two Kielce Jews who'd been killed after the war. Instead, she stared at the hearth fire.

"What do you know about this boy?" her mother had asked her. "A good-looking boy, a kind face," Freidl had said. Ellen glanced at Marek and thought it strange to be connected to Polish people, from Kielce, through their son. Those people seemed so much more foreign to her than he did.

The waiter arrived.

"You know, the bigos sounds a little heavy for me," she said. "Do they have salads?"

He rolled his eyes playfully. "I forgot. Americans eat grass."

She thought of Rafael.

He conferred with the waiter. "Maybe you would like to try the wild-mushroom salad or tomatoes with onion?"

"Wild mushrooms," she said, in the interest of avoiding onion breath.

"For the main course, they have fried pork cutlet or a stuffed cabbage. Also duck with apples inside. That is very good."

"I'll have the duck," she said.

"And I'll have bigos and a beetroot soup. You can taste mine." He winked at her.

Ellen smiled again, trying to banish the whole business of Kielce from her mind. It was ridiculous to dwell on it. She didn't know anything about his family. Maybe they didn't even live there after the war. "This inn isn't at all the Poland my father described to me," she said.

"Your father should have seen it with a Pole. And you, you have been almost nowhere. Do you like to go hiking?"

Ellen told him that she did.

"Then you must see Zakopane, in the Tatra Mountains. It's not far from Kraków. I could show it to you. This is the best place in Poland for hiking. There are trails through the valleys and the granite peaks, to the *Jaskinia Mroźna,* the Frosty Cave. My family used to go camping there on holiday in the summer."

The fire lit his smiling face with gold and reddish hues, and she thought him beautiful. A langer loksh, Freidl had called him. She felt at ease with him again.

"Zakopane is the most beautiful place anywhere," he said.

Ellen shook her head, teasing him. "Couldn't be. The Adirondacks, where *we* used to go for the summer, is the most beautiful place. There are mountains and lakes and the most orange salamanders on earth. I ought to know," she whispered conspiratorially. "When I was a little girl, I used to fill paper cups with them and carry them down the mountains. The funny part was, when I fell asleep on my father's shoulders, they were always gone when I woke up."

Marek chuckled. "You dropped them?"

"No, I think my father took pity on them and let them go. Otherwise, I would have tried to make a home for them."

"A house for salamanders?" Marek laughed. "There is a song I knew when I was little, about a boy who catches lizards until one night he wakes up in the house of the king lizard. They serve him for dinner, of course."

She made a face.

"It is not a nice story," he said, laughing. "The melody is not very good either."

"But it kept you from torturing lizards, I bet."

"No, my mother did that. She is like your father."

Ellen tilted her head slightly, relieved at this information about his mother. She smiled at him again. They laughed some more. He slid his hand across the table and took hers. "I'm glad we met," he said.

When they returned to the hotel, Marek turned off the motor. He pulled a cassette tape from his jacket in the backseat and handed it to her. "In Łódź, my group made a special recording for you of that song you liked."

She took the tape from him, overwhelmed that he had done this for her. Yet she was still reluctant to tell him how the tune had come to him.

His smooth fingers closed over hers, warm and insistent. Instinctively the two of them looked down at their hands, locked together over the gearshift. She peeked up at him and found him doing the same. They smiled briefly at each other, lips closed shyly. Then he reached over and opened her door for her.

They walked the short distance to the hotel's entrance. He held her elbow protectively. A current rippled up and down her arm. She turned to say good-bye. His hand slipped comfortably around her back.

"This has been an incredible evening," she said, praying for composure.

He cocked his head and returned her smile. "Do you know your eyes are the same color as your hair? What is that color? The color of the moon in autumn. Not gold."

It occurred to Ellen that had she been in Rome and some guy had said this to her, she would have laughed and put him off. "Copper," she said encouragingly.

"Yes, copper." His eyes didn't leave her face.

The pause grew longer. It was clear he wasn't going to break it. She said, "The copper moon in autumn, we call it a harvest moon."

His eyes didn't waver. "So do we."

She poked him playfully in the chest. "You should see it over the Manhattan skyline."

"I'd like that, someday."

He leaned forward and kissed her softly, just next to her mouth. His skin was smooth as it brushed hers, and she felt the pull of his mouth playing on her cheek, the tickle of the tab of hair beneath his lower lip. Straightening, he ran his other hand over the crown of her hair, his eyes and mouth equal parts smile. "Good night, Harvest Moon Girl," he said. "We will see each other soon, I hope?"

She liked the way he didn't assume anything. "I hope so too," she said, and kissed him lightly on the mouth before she turned and, under the soft lights of the hotel entrance, skipped up the grand staircase, knowing that his eyes were on her still.

Later, she lay on her bed, eyes closed, afloat in a hopeful desire for him. She listened repeatedly to his "For-a-Girl Tune" on her Walkman, reliving every phrase, every glance they'd exchanged all evening, as if watching a fast-action film of a blossoming. She knew she was being stupid and juvenile, but she didn't care.

She rolled over on her side, thinking she had never had a relationship begin so effortlessly, like a clean leap, the secret of whose fluidity is the strength of each partner's body.

The "For-a-Girl Tune" ended. She turned off the tape and fell asleep, content.

I came to her in the night as she slept. I sat by her bed, called her name. But she did not open her eyes as before. She had wrapped herself in her blanket and, even in sleep, had assumed a lover's posture. What new foolishness had I begun with my envy of the living? Carelessly, I had carried Aaron's tune with me into the world so that a Pole, even if a mensch of a Pole, had heard it. And now Ellen, my hope for redemption, was enveloping herself in a distracting passion for this boy. Yes, the heart takes what it wants. I always said it. But a union between these two? God forgive me. What kind of legacy was this from what Aaron gave me?

34

ELLEN WAS AT THE STUDIO THE NEXT MORNING AN HOUR BEFORE the dancers arrived. She rolled down the waistband of her black nylon sweatpants, faced the mirrored wall, and fastened on her Walkman. The "For-a-Girl Tune" began slowly and quietly, like a shy lover entering an unfamiliar bed. Playing it in the studio lent it a forbidden quality. She rolled her shoulder, extended an arm, and followed the tune's slow opening, looking for dance phrases to wrap around its beat. Then she sat down with a bottle of water and listened to the tape again, eyes closed, her head leaning against the mirror. She realized she really wasn't sure what the tune meant, what she might want to say with it. A warm breeze blew the back of her neck, startling her because it felt so like a breath. She shrugged off the sensation, turned off the tape, and began to make choreographic notes. Looking at the movement on paper, she was reminded of Pronaszko's warning not to make movement just for movement's sake.

The birds cooed at the windowsill. Step back, she told herself. Get moving with the company. Maybe they'll have some useful ideas. She didn't usually work this way. Usually, she choreographed a piece with the music and taught it to dancers, or she worked it out directly on their bodies, incorporating their individual styles into the music as they went along.

Pronaszko arrived just as she was returning the tape to her backpack.

"I'd like some time with the dancers today," she said. She was tempted to play the "For-a-Girl Tune" for him, just to see how he would react to it. But she couldn't bring herself to do it. Like new love, it was too delicate to share yet.

With his usual detached good humor, Pronaszko told her, "Whatever you need."

When the dancers were assembled, he took them through a warm-up. Then he straddled a backward-facing chair and fisted his hands under his chin. "Ellen has some work for us," he said in English.

She dumped out her bag of tapes and came to the front of the room.

"Let's do some contact improvisation," she said. "Approach someone. Feel your hips. Get down. Get earthy." She threw a Zap Mama tape in and turned up the volume on the boom box. For forty-five minutes she pushed the dancers hard to move in ways that were clearly uncomfortable for them. She had them try hip-hop and jazz moves, samba, anything she could think of to pull them away from their tendency to move with stiff spines and turned-out walks.

The results were mixed. At best, they took her instruction as sanction for them to dance the way they did in clubs. At worst, they threw away their technique altogether and flopped about looking pained and awkward.

Tomek, Joanna, and Henryk milled shyly against the long dirty windows and nodded to some Ziggy Marley music. Midsong, they stepped forward to the center of the sun-striped floor, looked to one another for support, and began to bounce alternate shoulders with one another as if on a trampoline.

There's a start, Ellen thought. If nothing else, she had the sense that they were finally connecting with what she was asking them to do. When class ended, quite a few of the dancers called to her a good-natured "Get down!" in thick Polish accents as they left the studio.

Pronaszko gave her a short, approving nod and slipped out the door. She was about to ask him to wait for her, when Jacek popped his head from behind the changing screen. "We are going for a coffee and something to eat. Will you come with us?"

"I'd love to," she said, delighted to be asked.

"That was very good music." He smiled. "We will wait for you."

And indeed, when she opened the studio door, she found Jacek, Henryk, and Genia smoking on the landing.

"What about Andrzej?" she asked Jacek. It worried her that she might not be able to communicate without his translations.

Jacek looked at his watch. "Oh, I think now he is with that German boy he met at the Czartoryski Museum. He stands at the paintings of naked men and talks to the foreign visitors. He knows who he is looking for."

Henryk and Genia gave each other knowing looks.

For Ellen, this was the first hint that perhaps Andrzej was not the beloved leader she'd taken him for, that his constant peddling of himself might annoy them as much as it did her. It was a relief. So was hearing these three speak English.

The little group descended the marble stairs single file, past the nearly toothless cleaning woman whose chatter Ellen could not understand at all. They followed Jacek down to the street. The three Poles jostled one another good-naturedly on the narrow sidewalk. Ellen smiled. Henryk whistled.

They stopped at an unmarked door, behind which a steep, uneven stone stairway led them down to a dark, fairly small, but beautiful cellar café with arched brick walls. The place was packed with students and afloat in cigarette smoke. Ellen's group settled at a corner table lit with candles. They ordered coffee.

"You are fortunate we do not speak English like Maria speaks Polish," Henryk said.

"Who's Maria?" Ellen asked.

He puckered his mouth and did a perfect imitation of the cleaning woman.

She wouldn't have guessed that Maria was unintelligible to them too. She laughed, feeling at ease at last. "You all speak English so well," she said. "Why do we need Andrzej as a translator?"

They looked at one another. Genia giggled. "Our English is not so good," she said, drawing in her chin coquettishly.

They all nodded in agreement and drank their gritty, Polish-style coffee.

Ellen turned to Genia. "Are you all from different parts of the country?"

Genia tipped back her head delicately and smiled, close-lipped. "I think so, yes. Jacek is from Lower Silesia, near Wrocław. Henryk is from near Łomża. I am from near Gdańsk."

Ellen remembered that Pronaszko said they were from small towns. "Everyone is from *near* somewhere then?"

"Except Andrzej," Genia said. "Of course, *he* is from Warsaw."

The dancers all laughed at this.

"He seems like a big-city boy," Ellen said gravely, hoping she had gotten the joke.

"Oh, yes," Genia said, opening her eyes wide and nodding agreeably. "He likes boys very much."

They all laughed again, Ellen less comfortably. She was unused to hearing such homophobia among dancers.

"Hey, when did those guys start coming in here?" Jacek said, nodding in the direction of two blue-uniformed men.

"Are those policemen?" Ellen asked him, wondering if she should be concerned.

"I am not sure. There are only two of them."

Ellen didn't understand why the Poles thought this funny.

Henryk glanced at the policemen and leaned toward her, his eyes bright with mischief. "It is an old joke. Why do policemen always go in threes?"

"Why?" Ellen said.

"One reads, one writes, and one guards these two intellectuals."

Ellen laughed, so he followed up with half a dozen more stupid policemen jokes, punctuated by Genia's stilted but helpful explanations. When he paused to light up yet another cigarette, Genia raised herself in her chair, her face fairly aglow. In her little-girl voice, she asked, "How do you take census in Polish village?"

"How?" they said in unison.

"You roll a *zloty* down the street, you count the legs, divide this by two, and subtract one for the dirty little Żyd who steals it."

Ellen felt as if the room had just sunk under water. The ambient sounds became distorted, and everything seemed to float. She stared at the faces of the happy dancers, looking for clues to how they could continue to smile after what they had just heard. *Pan Bergson ten Żyd?* she heard the woman in Zokof ask again.

She pushed back her chair and stood slowly, uncertain of her balance. "I have to go," she said, throwing a handful of zlotys on the table. "I forgot, I have an appointment."

The Poles seemed somewhat taken aback, but they nodded understandingly and said good-bye.

Ellen zigzagged her way between the tables and scrambled up the perilous stairway two steps at a time. Once outside, she took off down the street, her distress increasingly fired by adrenaline. *Idiots.* She began to mutter, not caring about the looks she got from passersby. "Fuck them. I should have told them a Polish joke. I should have said most Americans only know Poles by jokes. Like hey, Jacek, what's a Polish firing squad? A circle. Ha! Oh, not laughing? You don't think Poles are stupid? Does that make you feel like the dirty little Jew?" She was practically running now, enfolded in her manic, but strangely seductive, anger. By the time she arrived at her hotel room, she was out of breath.

The Tanakh still lay on her night table. She ran her hand tentatively down its spine, wondering what part of this book gave the world the idea that a Jew is a cartoon, dirty and little. She pulled the book protectively to her chest, physically pained by Jacek, Henryk, and Genia's betrayal. She'd refused to believe they weren't as modern as they dressed. Who in *her* generation would ever think like that, much less say things like they did?

A couple of curls had come loose from her topknot, and she twirled them around her finger. If only she'd done something, made a point. Now she knew she would never again feel entirely at ease with them.

She pulled the cassette of the "For-a-Girl Tune" from her dance bag and turned it over in her hand. If she played it for them now, it would require explanation. She would have to protect it from their ideas about Jews. How would she tell them why she had chosen it? Because she would *have* to explain it, even if this was an unusual thing for a choreographer to do.

She rose from the bed and made circles on the floor with her toe, remembering her unsatisfying experiments with the music that morning. This could be another Adam Mickiewicz debacle, she realized. If she faked it, playing with material she knew nothing about, they'd know. She felt like an adoptive mother, not quite knowing how, or whether, she had the right to claim a baby she didn't know how to handle. She felt helplessly inadequate.

The wind blew through the open window, flaring one of the long curtain sheers like a woman's skirt. She pressed the cassette tape to her lips and inhaled.

I really love this music, she thought. She exhaled. The curtain fluttered to her face like a veil, and she rubbed it reassuringly against her cheek.

35

THAT NIGHT, ELLEN DREAMED FREIDL WAS STANDING AT THE edge of a forest holding a kerosene lantern from which white sparks burst, then flittered up to the trees. Her proud bearing, the noble beauty of her angular face, the large deep-set eyes, the improbably full lips made so powerful an impression that Ellen remembered it even after she awoke in the morning.

"Freidl?" she had said in the dream.

The woman had blinked slowly. She smiled, examined Ellen carefully. "Such curls," she said. "This color you call *copper?*"

"You heard me and Marek?"

"I heard."

But I had not come to talk of her distraction with this boy. I came about the Polish girl, about the cruelty of words. A Jew should not be afflicted by strangers insulting her bloodline. A Jew should be able just to live, to love if she can. Yet have we not seen it time and again, how our God uses hatred to return our lost ones to us, who have become strangers to their own people? Terrible. Terrible. I was sorry for Ellen. She was not a fool, but poor soul, she did not know how to defend herself from these wolves.

The woman put down her lantern and made a circular, dismissive motion with her hand. A strong breeze swept over Ellen's face, blowing back her hair, reminding her of the breath at her neck that morning. She closed her eyes briefly, and although there was no grass anywhere, she detected its scent. Cut grass, she remembered, piled high behind Freidl in another dream. Cut grass. The scent had wafted in the air around Zokof and had led her to Rafael. "You've been with me, haven't you?" she said.

"We have a saying in Jewish," I told her. "'Man plans and God laughs.'" But tonight it is my time to laugh." I let the shawl fall from my head and reveal the white, luminescent square cloth, tied in knots at its four corners. It floated gently above me. She was shocked, I could see. The handkerchief was her grandfather's, the one she had sent back to Poland with her father.

I laughed, touched the handkerchief. "I watched over him. He told you this, yes?"

She looked at me in a way I knew something was not right, that he had not told her.

"You watched over my father?"

"Your grandfather," I corrected. But her tears were for her father.

"I watched over your father too," I told her. This quieted her.

"My dad showed me your gravestone," she said. "He told me your father was a famous scholar. He said you were a scholar too."

I bowed my head that she should not see my disappointment. She did not know of me from Itzik. He had told her nothing. "I was not famous," I said. "A woman does not get her share from being a scholar. It is said, in the World to Come, her share is to be her husband's footstool."

She made a face. "That's awful," she said. "Things would have been very different if you had been born in our time." She looked so certain of this, as if I should envy her. I was not so sure.

"Things would have been different if my husband had been a shayner Yid *and I had given him his due," I told her. "I did not make for him a peaceful home. My father, may he rest in peace, warned me often. 'Freidl,' he used to say, 'if you swim against the stream with your mouth open, you will also swallow hooks. And who wants to marry a girl with hooks in her mouth?' 'Papa,' I told him, 'if I don't open my mouth, I will starve.'" I laughed. "For this, he called me Freidl the Mouth."*

Now she laughed.

"Shah." I hushed her. "My husband also called me Freidl the Mouth. But he said it like a curse."

In my anger, I stood up, spread open my arms, and showed myself to her, my full breasts, strong limbs, bound in mud-caked white linen. My shadow was immense.

She drew back, frightened.

I had upset her, and this I did not want to do. I hoped to teach her that night, not to frighten her. "We should begin," I said. "There are things you should know. Your father gave you a ribbon, yes? Bring it to me."

She seemed surprised I knew about the ribbon, but she went to the Tanakh her father gave her. Between the pages was the ribbon. The red had faded.

I took it from her and held it above her head. "This belonged to your great-

aunt Hindeleh," I said. "The night your grandfather ran from Zokof, she gave it to him. It was red then. A ribbon from her hair. Four years old she was, with copper curls, like yours, exactly."

I could see her anxiety. She asked what happened to Hindeleh. What could I do but tell her the whole story? "They went east, toward Chelm. The poor child died in an orphanage."

Her chest contracted. "Why an orphanage?" she wanted to know.

"Your great-grandmother Sarah, may her name be inscribed, perished on the road to Chelm."

She took the ribbon from me and placed it on her palm. "My grandfather never told me he had a sister with hair like mine," she said.

My heart broke for her. "He did not know what became of them," I told her, though we both knew this was no excuse. "The Leibers became like scattered birds. One by one, I watched them fall from the sky. God would not let me do more." My grief at this returned to me, sudden and terrible. Worse for seeing it also on her face. "They suffered," I told her. What could I say? It was the truth.

She reached for me, tried to brush back the loose strands of my gray hair under the white handkerchief that was still floating above my head. The ribbon fluttered upward, back into my hand, and turned red again.

I said, "Thanks God for what I see in your heart. But we are not here tonight to recite Lamentations, Elleneh, or to ask how could this have been."

"Then why are we here?" she asked.

"To make a strong Jew from a seed," I told her.

And this girl had the chutzpah to say she did not know if being a strong Jew was what she needed to be. "In my world being Jewish is just not that important," she said.

Such narrishkeit. How she inflamed me with these sentiments. But I spoke calmly to her. "A life in the Golden Land is what I made possible for your grandfather," I said. "Very pleasant. A life of summer. A place to forget that a Jew has to be strong, like a tree. That you should grow roots and branches and have a trunk made tough by the seasons. And why?" I let her wait for the answer, like my father when he wanted me to know he was making an important point. "Why am I here to make a strong Jew from a seed?"

She looked at me.

"So when a Polack makes of you a joke, you do not fall down and begin to die."

Even in her sleep, my words made their mark. The blood rushed to her face.

But I did not give her peace. I came at her, full of force. I said, "You let them make you afraid. What is that, that you don't even know where to turn to answer them? At such times as those, you open your Torah, your Talmud, even your Tsene Urene."

"My what?"

"Gevalt, you never heard of the Yiddish bible for women?"

But she had nerve of her own. She gave me a look. "What good would those books do in my situation today?" she demanded.

I said to her, "Asses bray all the time, Elleneh. So? It is for you to remember the proverb. If you have learning, you will never lose your way."

There was a hint of understanding in her eyes. This pleased me. "Now," I said, "what is that turning and jumping I saw you do today? What is this?"

"I'm a dancer," she said. "The kind of dance I do didn't exist in your day. It's like ballet, but not quite."

"Ballet?" I said. "I never heard such a thing." It came to me that Miriam danced, so I asked her, "Why do you dance?"

This surprised her, but I saw she was glad I thought her dancing was important. "Dance is movement from the soul," she said. "It's like your tunes, in a way, except the dancer sings through her body."

Such an unusual girl. I put my fingers to my lips, as if the tune of a dance might be there. "What does it say, your dance?" I asked her.

She dropped her head. "Nothing, yet."

I was disappointed for us both. I tried to encourage her. I asked, "What is this dance for?"

She liked that. "Sometimes I make dances about the beauty of the movement," she said, "like a beautiful tune. Sometimes I tell a story, like a song, or I try to make a point about something."

She saw I did not understand this entirely. She said I was like her grandma Sadie. "When I tell my grandma Sadie about my work," she said, "she pats me on the head and says, 'That's wonderful, my darling, you should enjoy your life.'"

I did not want to be like her grandma Sadie. I asked, "With what are you making a point?"

This only seemed to upset her. "I don't know yet what I'm trying to say. The director wants me to have a point of view, a cry of passion. I want to use your tune, but I don't know how yet. I don't know enough."

She was getting frantic, this even I could see. I put my arm around her shoulder and tried to draw her close. I had never done such a thing to anyone in life. I knew she could not feel the shape of my hand, or my arm around her back. Still, maybe she could feel something from me, maybe I would send up the smell of pines in the forest, or grass, to reassure her. I told her, "The Hassidim say it is a great blessing to have a soul that dances."

But I felt I should tell her also the truth. "Part of your soul, Elleneh, stays in the ground, away from the light, like Itzik's," I said. "The night he came by me, I knew this was a soul that needed to be cooked into a cholent, to let go of its flavor. But it seems he did not cook."

Fear and hope together gathered on her sweet face. "Listen to me," I said. "You come from a beautiful people. Without your Jewish soul this dance, what you call it, will not have that flavor. From you will only come pareve. *No* tam, *you understand me? No taste."*

She pulled away from me. "I'm not a Jewish dancer," she said. "I don't have to be limited to that. I'm just having a problem with this piece, with the music. I don't know enough about it. But it's not who I am."

I pulled away from her too. I told her, "I would have given so much for a taste of such freedom as you have. The holy books lie open before you, and you say it's not who you are, that you don't want to be limited to have to read them? This is how the daughter of a scholar talks?"

This only made her angry.

"I don't want what my father wants," she said. Then the tears came because she had spoken of him as if he were still alive. "What I want isn't in books," she insisted. "What I want is in the body."

I was gentle with her. I knew what it was to be a father's daughter with her own ideas. "You told me you don't know what you want to say in your dance," I reminded her. I lifted the lantern. Sparks flew out of it into the trees.

She stared in wonder.

"Listen to me," I said. "A little Torah now could help."

"Torah? What would the Torah do for me?"

I thought, did I really have to explain this? "You want something more the Torah should do for you?" I said. "This is the book from God, His prayer to His people! This is His people's prayers to Him, asking, What we should expect from each other?"

I had spoken too harshly. She looked confused, heartbroken. "I'm sorry,

Freidl," *she said to me. "I just don't know the Torah any more than I know
how to pray."*

*I was ashamed for us both. I was not a good teacher. "Shah, shah," I com-
forted. "Listen. Tonight, I want you should read Torah as a Jew reads, as a Jew
prays, with an open heart and a mind full of doubt. Try, Elleneh. For me, try."*

"I didn't mean to offend you," she said to me.

*Such a lovely girl, such a good heart. I could not help wondering, was this
how it was to have the pleasure of your own child? She picked up her father's
Tanakh. We were standing now by a tall lamp, along a forest path. I looked
at her book's blue cover. It said, "Tanakh, The Jewish Bible," for the wholly
uneducated, I supposed. I began to laugh, God knows why. I said, "Come sit
by me, my shayna, and open to the book of Exodus. This is where the story
of Passover is told, what we retell every year at the Seder table, yes?"*

She nodded and gave me a hopeful smile.

*"Turn the pages and I will tell you where to begin, in the 'Song of the Sea,'
as we call it."*

"Song of the Sea. I like that phrase," she said, happy like a child.

*She opened the book to Exodus, pressed down on the stiff new binding,
and turned about twenty pages.*

"Read to me," I said.

"'Thus the Lord delivered Israel that day from the Egyptians.'"

"No, after," I prompted her.

"You know this by heart?" She seemed amazed at such a thing.

"Naturally," I said.

"Then tell me which page it's on."

*"Page?" I pretended to take offense. "Not by us, pages. Such a thing maybe
you find in a goyish book."*

I was making jokes. And now she understood me. We had a laugh.

I waited just until I saw her find it, then I left.

Sometime later, Ellen awoke. She remembered dreaming that the bells of
Saint Mary's had begun to peal unbearably loudly, the notes of the hejnał
encircling her like a hundred taunting Christian bullies. She remembered
putting her hands to her ears to shut out the cacophony.

"A choleria on them," Freidl had said, and in the dream the bells had
gone silent. The rest of her memory of what she and Freidl had said or
done came to her only in disjointed pieces. They had talked, yes, but it all

came apart when she tried to remember the specifics. Something about getting stronger, something about being a strong Jew. What she had managed to retain most were the dream's images. A fish with a hook in its mouth, a little girl, Hindeleh — yes, that was her name — with a red ribbon in her hair, Ellen's hair. It was all upsetting and exhilarating at the same time. The sun had begun to cast a dull light over the room. She closed her eyes and slowly became aware that her hands lay outside the covers, holding an open book. A prickly sensation swept across her back, down her arms to her fingers. She was certain she had not been reading when she had fallen asleep.

Sitting up, she stared at the Tanakh on her lap, amazed at having awoken to a tangible remnant of the dream she had been having. What was she to make of the fact that she knew the book was opened to a passage she had found for Freidl. *Then Miriam the prophetess, Aaron's sister, took a timbrel in her hand, and all the women went out after her in dance with timbrels. And Miriam chanted for them: "Sing to the Lord, for He has triumphed gloriously;— Horse and driver He has hurled into the sea."*

She reread the verse six or seven times, curious at Freidl's choice. She liked the timbrels. But she felt chilled by the phrase *horse and driver.*

36

*F*OR DAYS AFTER HER DREAM OF FREIDL, ELLEN WORKED ON HER dance piece from early morning until late at night. She established that it would begin with the sound of timbrels, a call to the audience. She bought a tambourine and tapped out rhythms in the studio as she tried to develop movement sequences. She reread Freidl's Exodus passage so often, she knew it by heart.

Baruch ata Adonai, she repeated at various intervals, exhausting her vocabulary of Hebrew prayer. Alone in the studio, it sounded to her like a voodoo incantation. She felt slightly embarrassed and fraudulent about making an appeal to a God with whom she had never before conversed. But she was determined to attempt the language of prayer and to overcome that helpless feeling she had retained from the encounter with Genia's Jewish joke.

She began another ritual, humming the "For-a-Girl Tune."

Marek called from the Ariel Café.

"Is this Ellen, from America?" he asked.

"You have an Ellen from somewhere else too?"

He laughed. "I am glad you think I am a Casanova. Are you free tomorrow afternoon? I was thinking we could meet at the Starmach Gallery. It is very near your hotel, on Rynek Główny."

"What's there?" she asked, not really caring. She wanted to see him.

"I have been thinking, this gallery is something you will like to see. You've heard of Andrzej Starmach, the art historian?"

"No," she admitted, wondering if she should have heard of him.

"He shows work by the Kraków Group — Tadeusz Kantor, Jonasz Stern, Maria Jarema. You know these artists?"

She didn't, although she did notice that Kantor and Stern were both Jewish names. This sudden hyper-Jewish consciousness about things annoyed her, and she scolded herself for being provincial. "What kind of art do they do?"

There was a short silence on the line. "I do not really know how to explain," he said. "This is something very important in Poland. The Kraków Group were the great modern Polish artists before the war, and after. They refused to make art in the style of socialist realism. You've heard of this?"

"Of course," she said, hoping to combat the impression that she didn't know anything about art in Eastern Europe.

"And also, Tadeusz Kantor made a special kind of avant-garde theater. Cricot Two, it was called." He added this tentatively, as if he thought he should not impose more information without a further sign of interest from Ellen.

"Sounds great," she said. "If you give me the address, I can meet you at five."

*W*hen Ellen saw the paintings at the Starmach Gallery, she knew she had been invited to another Poland. They were huge, fiercely colorful, and full of ideas. She was especially intrigued with a painting by someone who was not of the Kraków Group, a young artist, Marek said. His canvas was dominated by the black back of an armed policeman facing a blue, decapitated man. The man's head was attached to his lapel with a dragon-shaped pin. His upturned red lips suggested either foolishness or defiance. The painting elicited sympathy for the blue man, and Ellen realized that he probably represented the artists of Poland under communism. She thought of Pronaszko. "I like this one," she told Marek. "It's a very good painting."

He smiled. "Yes. Very good." He put his arm around her and played, tentatively, with the sheer crimson scarf she had draped over her shoulder.

"What does the dragon mean?" she asked, brushing her hand lightly over his.

He tilted his head toward her, caressing her shoulder as he spoke. "To me, it is the mythical dragon of Kraków, who is under us always. He is the symbol of our city."

With a cryptic smile, he took her hand and pulled her out the door, into the thick pedestrian traffic on the square, where they walked, arm in arm, around the Cloth Hall, scattering gatherings of birds.

They headed down Floriańska Street, toward Florian's Gate, stopping at a café for a small dinner of dumplings and salad. Marek charmed Ellen with his talk of Polish art and Polish film and Polish music and festivals, the rich underground life of his country. He mentioned a performance piece he had seen. "It continued for days," he said. "We followed the singers and the actors from one setting to another, from an apartment to Kościuszko's Mound to a jazz club to more apartments, and even to LOT, the Polish airlines office. It was something great. The performers and the audience were one living part of this big experience, together. It was very Polish, something for the soul," he said, drumming his chest. "It reminded me, exactly, of the Passion plays in Kalwaria during Holy Week. I remember this from when I was a child and I went with my family. Kalwaria is close to Kraków, a very holy place in Poland. It is the tradition for the local people there, and the monks, to act out the last days of Christ's life. They go, in a procession, from one chapel to the next; there are more than twenty chapels, I think, and at each one they have a sermon. For these two days, Thursday and Friday, people come from all over Poland. They are part of the play too. Everyone goes together. When you are living the story like that, it is so real. You believe the suffering of Christ. You see it!" He paused, as he seemed to realize that Ellen might not share his sense of wonder and delight about such an event.

As for Ellen, she could not help asking herself the very question her mother had put to her: *What do you know about this boy?* Until that moment she had not feared discovering the distance between them. But now she saw the rootedness of his Catholicism, the superficiality of his connection to Jewishness, saw that he was not nearly as close as she'd chosen to think he was.

He took her hand and squeezed it gently. "Of course, most of the reason my family went to these performances, I think, is because it was during the communist time and we could only show that we were Poles by being Catholic. Today, I think, maybe only the country people or the old go to these plays. Or tourists." He cocked his head and grinned. "But I am talking too much like a crazy Pole. You must tell me about your work. That is what I want to hear."

She smiled weakly, took his hand, and caressed his smooth skin with her thumb, choosing, for this moment, to believe in his basic goodness. "Let's walk through the Planty Gardens," she said. "You can show me your favorite piece of kitschy art at Florian's Gate on the way."

"It's terrible stuff, what they have there, isn't it?"

"It ain't the Starmach Gallery."

Thus, in each other's good graces, they strolled through the neighborhood and around the circular brick battlements of the medieval Barbican. "Let's sit," Ellen suggested, pointing to a bench in the Planty.

Several pigeons waddled by, cooing and pecking sharply at the grass.

"I've been doing a lot of thinking about my dance piece," she said. "The thing is, I'd like you and your group to do the music for me."

Marek's eyebrows rose in surprise. "What music?"

"What else? The 'For-a-Girl Tune.'"

His gave her a reserved smile. "What will be the idea of your dance?"

She opened her purse and took out the oversized envelope Rafael had given her. "I think it will be something about this." She slid out the photograph of her grandfather and Hillel. "This was taken in Warsaw in 1906."

Marek edged closer to look.

She pointed to the seated figure. "That's my grandfather," she said. "He was fourteen. This is just before he left Poland."

Marek nodded.

She pointed at the young man standing with his hand on her grandfather's shoulder. "And this is Hillel. He was a musician, like you." She smiled at him. "Handsome like you too."

Marek screwed up his face. "He is better-looking."

"Actually, he reminds me of you," she said shyly. She had noticed the resemblance the moment Rafael had handed her the photograph. But only now she realized that it was not so much in the similarity of the two men's long hair and thin frames, but in a certain sensual wistfulness they shared. She put her hand on his. "When my grandfather arrived in Warsaw from Zokof, Hillel took him under his wing and arranged his ticket to America."

"Where did you get this photograph?"

"Rafael gave it to me. I thought you'd be interested in it because Hillel learned the 'For-a-Girl Tune' from my grandfather."

Marek took the photograph from her and studied it more carefully. "Where did your grandfather hear the tune?"

Ellen's heart beat rapidly. She wasn't sure how to navigate her answer. "Rafael says it came from a woman in Zokof named Freidl." She averted her eyes, hoping he wouldn't ask for more particulars.

"You found where it came from? And you did not tell me first thing? You are a very bad girl." Marek wagged his finger at her.

She could see he was only partly joking. "When we go to Zokof, you can ask Rafael about it," she said appealingly.

"Yes, that will be good."

They looked at the pigeons.

"You like history," she said. "Do you believe it leaves ghosts?" She half hoped he would take her question in jest so that she would not have to figure out a way to explain Freidl quite yet.

He shrugged. "I like to make fun that now the communists are gone, the churches that were full for Solidarity are almost empty, because now we have our freedom. But you know we Poles are mostly Catholics, ninety percent of us, or more. We come into life hearing of the Holy Ghost. So I suppose, yes, it is understandable if we, if I, believe in ghosts." He glanced nervously at her, as if he wasn't sure how she would take this. "I think our ghosts are everywhere, all the time," he said with more confidence. "The past does not leave us. And we do not leave the past."

"Like the dragon of Kraków," she said.

"Like the dragon." He smiled. "But we cannot worry always about dragons. We must kiss beautiful girls too." And he did. "Invite me to your hotel, Harvest Moon Girl," he said.

She was surprised at his directness, but not offended. "Follow me," she said confidently.

Evening was upon them. They walked back along the Planty to her hotel, holding hands, sharing short kisses, in the way of new lovers.

Side by side, they climbed the grand staircase of the Palace Hotel. At her door, he rubbed the back of her neck as she retrieved the room key from her purse.

When they were inside the vestibule, he took her hand and kissed it. She brushed back the bolt of wavy hair that had fallen over his face and led him into the room. With only a cursory look around, he slid sideways onto her bed, his long legs stretched in front of him, his neck angled against the headboard. They looked at each other. Ellen glanced at the empty place beside him and put down her purse.

"I love your eyes," she said, turning on the bed light in the darkening room. She took off her crimson scarf and draped it over the light, creating a pinkish glow. "You have the warmest eyes in Poland." She was immediately sorry she had said this, as it reminded her of the cold eyes she had seen in Zokof, and of her father's warnings. But she resisted the urge to retreat, and lay down on the bed beside him.

He smiled, leaned forward, and kissed her. When she didn't quite respond, he tried again. "Ellen? Is there something wrong with my eyes now? Or with Poland?"

She knew he was trying to be playful, but she said, "It's Poland."

His excitement seemed to dim. "It is only that you do not know us yet," he said. "We are not what those Americans at the Ariel Café think we are."

She wanted to believe him. With some effort, she allowed herself to again adore the shape of his parted lips.

They kissed again, and their tentative hands began to struggle with his shirt buttons and her fitted skirt. She explored the soft round cushion of brown hair on his chest and the smooth skin of his back. They rolled over each other, testing the sensation of the other's body. When they rolled too far to the edge, they fell, ungracefully and with a solid *thump,* onto the carpeted floor, in the open space between the bed and the wall. "Hey!" he said.

Ellen laughed.

Marek reached up and, with a jerk that would have been the envy of any magician, whisked the white brocade spread off the bed. It settled over them like an elegant arched tent, enveloping them in whiteness. Snapping off her bra, he pulled back to look at her. "You have beautiful breasts," he said, and kissed one.

She wrapped her arms around his back. "Do you know, your body is just the right temperature for me? Just the right warmth."

He kissed her, adoringly digging his fingers into the ringlets of her hair.

Without shyness, they watched each other work their way out of their remaining clothes, then climbed back under the bedspread. The bed light and the setting sun gave their skin a rosy cast.

Ellen traced the line of Marek's hip to his groin. "This is the most beautiful part of a man's body," she said, "and I don't even know what it's called." She ran her fingers up and down the ridge, watching his sharp breaths. Finally, he grabbed her hand and held it still.

"Stop," he said. "Look what you are doing to me." He pressed her hand to his erect penis and pulled her to him.

She too pulled him close, as much for the feel of his warm skin as to lose sight of his fleshy uncircumcised organ, so unlike the mushroom-smooth penis heads with which she was accustomed. She wondered if it would feel different inside her. But Marek was so nimble, and so sweet a lover, it became easy to ignore the foreskin, even after he came and they lay in each other's arms, dreamy and dumb.

The sun had set. They were in shadows. Marek rolled onto his back.

Ellen took his outstretched hand in hers and kissed it. Its coolness felt good on her overheated palm. "You're my first," she said, chuckling.

"What?"

"My first uncircumcised man."

He remained strangely motionless. "Then, you only go with Jewish men?"

"No, but almost all the guys our age in the States are circumcised. They just do it in the hospital when babies are born."

"Sweet Mary, Mother of God! No one is circumcised in Poland."

"Sweet Mary circumcised her boy."

There was a brief silence between them.

"Does this mean you do not want to be with me again, if I'm not circumcised?" Marek asked cautiously.

She stroked his cheek. "Marek Gruberski, I want to be with you. But if you ever want to make love to me again"— she nipped at the tuft of hair below his lip —"this thing has got to go!"

He laughed with obvious relief, and hugged her to him. "Easier to cut the beard than the foreskin," he said. "Tomorrow morning, I promise, the thing is gone!"

They kissed each other good night. Ellen rolled over. Marek curled around her.

God forgive me, but I watched them. In my life, I never dreamed people could have relations like this. For me, intimacy between Jew and Christian was already a scandal, but this unholy nakedness! I could not have imagined passion that would pull a man and a woman to the floor, not even with Aaron. Of course, my knowledge of these things had its limits. I had buried desire so deep in my marriage bed, it got lost with the feathers. And if the women of our town whispered of such matters, I had stood too far apart from them to hear. Such familiarity offended me, as my father taught me it should. Not from timidity then, but from pride I had closed myself off from their community. But this night I knew my father had been wrong to advise isolation. I had remained undeveloped in some important way. When the two lovers quieted, I was like a child, understanding little but that I had witnessed something strange and immodest, but touched with a gentleness that opened my heart.

They lay with their arms around each other. The fire of envy and admira-

tion burned in me. Womanliness, with its tenderness, its compassion and patient wisdom, I had denied myself for a seat in a house of study. And what had come of it? A lonely life, a small life, affecting nothing because I had affected no one. I cursed myself for having lived lazy as a drunk in my indifference to life. I scolded myself for having been so proud that the Angel of Death had come easily by me. Why not? For years I made a home for him among my lifeless daily rituals. As it is said, those who do not grow, grow smaller.

I was nearly exhausted from heaping scorn upon myself like dirt on my grave, each shovelful a memory of another sin. Ellen turned away from her lover. On her face I saw her grandfather's lost expression that had drawn me from my resting place that I might help him find his way. "Be vigilant," my father had said. "Return her timbrel, and she will make an opening for you to return." I looked at this girl from the Golden Land and understood. The choice was mine, to enter her life and teach her in the way she should go or to remain outside observing her. To cross this boundary between us was no small thing.

37

In the middle of the night, Ellen opened her eyes and saw Freidl rocking back and forth in the wingback chair, a half-smile accentuating her high cheekbones.

"Your langer loksh has a light in him," Freidl said.

Ellen stared across the room at the bed where she and Marek slept, her nakedness barely covered by the bedspread, his arm draped over her upper thigh. She did not understand how she could be outside her body, yet, vaguely aware that she was dreaming, she was not alarmed.

"Aaron Birnbaum had a light like that." Freidl nodded approvingly. "And a head for Torah too."

Ellen didn't know who Aaron Birnbaum was. As for having a head for Torah, she thought Freidl was chiding her for sleeping with a non-Jew.

"My Aaron had a talent for *niggunim*, like your langer loksh," Freidl went on. "For him, the tunes came like fruit from a tree. He had only to pick them."

"*Your* Aaron?" Ellen said, intrigued by the woman's excitement about a man.

Freidl pursed her lips slightly. "You think I was always an old yideneh? When I was a girl in my father's house, I knew what was love. My Aaron sang to me every day, from the street. His voice was, for me, like the sound of a shofar. I could hear it over all the others. God forgive me, but when Aaron sang, it was like my own Messiah had come, heh!"

Ellen marveled that a love more than a hundred years old could still look so fresh on a woman's face.

"Sometimes he whistled, like a Pole."

Ellen looked at her uncertainly.

"Does a Jew whistle? If Aaron whistled, my father would not suspect him. He would think it was just someone in the street." Freidl clapped her hands to her mouth and muffled a peculiarly lusty giggle.

Ellen realized Freidl was not like her grandma Sadie, a woman so embarrassed to admit any knowledge of or interest in sex that she insisted her children had been conceived while she was asleep.

"You understand," Freidl said, the buoyant expression fading, "my father, may his name be for a blessing, did not approve of Aaron Birnbaum. Aaron was a Hassid. My father was not. 'Their faith is backwards,' Poppa said. 'The music is for the Jew, not the Jew for the music.'" She lifted her chin proudly. "But, Elleneh, I tell you, as I am here with you tonight, my father was wrong. In Aaron's tunes, every one, there is the essence of a prayer, of what it is to stand before God and dare to show Him that deepest feeling, what it is to be a *ben Adam* — a son of Adam, a human being."

Ellen thought it strange and magnificent that God would have to depend on human beings to tell Him how it feels to be one of His creations.

Freidl's lips tightened again. "My father, of course, forbid a union between Aaron and me." She clenched her hands to her breasts. "But the heart takes what it wants."

The two women looked at the sleeping Marek. "The 'For-a-Girl Tune' was Aaron's, wasn't it?" Ellen said.

Freidl nodded. "His music was all I had of him who should have been my husband."

Ellen shrugged slightly. "It would have been different if you had had him for a husband. With a musician, you'd have probably had to go out and work to make ends meet, feed the kids, pay the rent and all that." To her, this seemed merely obvious.

"But I loved him," Freidl said meekly.

Ellen saw no point in disillusioning her about a life with Aaron.

Marek murmured something in Polish and rolled onto his stomach. The two women waited until he settled back into sleep.

"Your langer loksh, he reminds me of the other one who loved music, the boy in the photograph, with Itzik," Freidl said.

"Hillel. Yes, I think so too. Sexy guys," Ellen said half-jokingly.

Freidl looked away, and Ellen thought the remark's overtness had offended her. "I'm sorry if I upset you," she said.

Freidl shrugged again. "Upset?" She seemed distracted. "What I am today, this shape, is not my body. There are times when the light goes out from me altogether and I am afraid that I will be exiled forever from the world." She sighed. "That is how it has been, from the night your grand-father came by me. But still, these two could be like brothers." She nodded again, as if trying to comfort herself.

Ellen took this as her moment to ask, "Freidl, what happened that night, when my grandfather came to you?"

Freidl stopped nodding and gave Ellen a serious look. "From the grave I followed Itzik," she said. "I sang to him. I sang to him the deepest prayer I knew, Aaron's niggun. He did not hear me. He was that kind of boy. What his eye did not see, his heart did not feel."

Ellen wondered if her grandfather's refusal of God arose from the same stubborn literalism that was evident throughout his life. She had always found it so difficult to understand this about him, how a person could be so progressive in his thinking but so unwilling to explore his own imagina-tion, and so resistant in his personal life. He never went to the theater or even to the movies, steadfastly ignoring the pleas of his wife. She remem-bered once, when at ten or eleven, she had wanted him to join the family for a visit to the Museum of Science. He had dismissed the idea so abruptly it had scared her.

"Still, I prayed," Freidl continued. "I told myself, God doesn't always answer us the first time, or the second." She shrugged. "I prayed when he went by Avrum Kollek's house, when he said good-bye to his family. I prayed for him on the road to Radom, in the station where he bought the ticket, on the train when he fell asleep."

Ellen watched her closely, so fascinated by this succession of events that she was reluctant to interrupt for details.

"I looked for someone who could help him. In the Warsaw train station, when your grandfather arrived, I was so frantic already, I sang the tune to Hillel."

"How did you know Hillel heard you?" she asked.

"He asked Itzik about it. Itzik himself he didn't care about, not in the beginning. It was the tune that kept Hillel. Heh! A socialist begging to hear the tune of a Hassid! He wanted it, in the way a man wants a woman. I made him think it was Itzik humming, when it was me at his ear." She smiled sadly. "I could see, from the way he moved, like a cat, that Hillel was a man always ready to escape. I had to watch him, to make him want to stay, to take care of Itzik."

"And he stayed. Not bad for a socialist." Ellen couldn't help teasing.

Freidl conceded this with a gracious smile. "A mensch is a mensch. He took care of your grandfather to the end."

Ellen tried to imagine Hillel and her grandfather as friends. Their pose in the photograph, with Hillel's hand on her grandfather's shoulder, suggested friendship, but their expressions revealed little else. "Is that how my grandfather became a socialist, when he met Hillel?" she asked, since this was the one thing she knew they had in common.

"Your grandfather was no socialist when he came by me," Freidl said tightly. She leaned forward, as if inviting Ellen to join a closed circle of talkers. "When he came to my grave, he wrapped his arms around my stone, my *matzevah,* and he prayed to *Ha-Shem,* the Almighty."

Ellen had an image of her grandfather on his knees at Freidl's grave, and the muscles tightened around her chest.

"Itzik the Faithless One. *Ptuh!* Like I said, such a joker is God, who would send this angry boy to my stone, as if he were my own child. That He would choose *me* to save him, a fertile woman gone childless to her grave, a woman restless as I was with regret."

She raised her open hands. They were filled with blades of grass. "Two handfuls of grass Itzik dropped on my grave."

Ellen inhaled the unmistakable sweet smell of grass that seemed to accompany Freidl wherever she went.

"That night when Itzik came by me, with grass in his hands, I thought it was a sign," Freidl said, her voice breaking. "For the first time, I knew what it was to pray with a mother's heart. You cannot imagine what this was for me. *Ruler of the Universe,* I said, *it is written, 'Every blade of grass has its own guardian star in the firmament which strikes it and commands it to grow!' Let a spark be lit in him and let him grow!*" Freidl covered her face with her hands, her voice having given out.

Stunned by the depth of Freidl's passion for a child, her grandfather, Ellen tried to approach her. But Freidl had not finished. She shook the fistfuls of grass at the heavens. "'Grass!' he said. I should have known when he kicked it from my grave that he did not mean to pray for me. I should have known that, good as he was, he would not hear me. I was a fool. I thought he meant a prayer for me, that I too should sprout from that place as grass sprouts from the earth. But he meant the grass that made Jan the Peasant fall to his death. I am sorry, but truth is truth."

"It's all right," Ellen said, seeing the pained yet apologetic look on Freidl's face.

Freidl turned away. "I have asked myself, was it for me, or Itzik, that God answered my prayer that night?" Her voice was barely audible. She looked at Ellen. "His power He gave me, to make a mensch of this boy, your grandfather, who had stood between the wicked and the innocent. And what did I do? I failed him and God both." Freidl put her hand to her mouth and held back a cry.

"What can I do for you?" Ellen asked her.

Freidl hesitated, then spread her arms. The walls fell away, and she rose into the enormity of a starry sky. Above her head, a white linen shroud floated like a wedding canopy.

Ellen hovered just below, a child peering up at a mother who was trying to teach her something she could not comprehend.

Freidl looked down at her. Her expression was gentle but distressed. With a whooshing sound, she returned to the wingback chair. The walls rejoined. She regarded Ellen expectantly. "Your prayers for mercy are what you can do for me," she said. "The soul cannot endure forever in such a state as mine. You who hear me must redeem me. Return me to rest with my body in the place Rafael has marked with stones in Zokof cemetery. That is what I ask of you."

"If I knew how to pray for you, Freidl, for it to be real, you know I would do that for you. But I don't know how," Ellen said.

Freidl rocked back and forth, restored to her grandmotherly state. She patted her chest feebly and said, "Make a start, with the open book. You can pretend, as if it is the first day of your school — your cheder. Your teacher gives you a word from Rebbe Nachman of Bratslav." She smiled at the name. "Rebbe Nachman, you should know, was a Hassid whose faith even my father admired. Rebbe Nachman said, 'Pray for an open heart, and in your dance you will attach yourself to God.'" She sat back, apparently satisfied. "Don't be afraid to tell me a little Torah — a *shtickl Torah,* as we say."

Even in her consternation, Ellen smiled at the funny sound of the word *shtickl,* which made her think again of her grandpa Isaac and how he had also made her laugh.

"You have begun already, with Miriam and the timbrel."

Ellen thought there was a hint of playfulness in her smile, and something slightly secretive. She wanted Freidl to stay. She wanted to talk to her, to know her more. But the white linen shroud, now lit from within, floated in through the open window. As it drew close, Ellen recognized the pattern on Grandpa Isaac's handkerchief. She watched, in dumb fascination, as the shroud wound itself around Freidl and swept her into darkness, leaving behind an empty chair.

Ellen suddenly felt the weight of the bedspread on her shoulder and the warmth of Marek's body next to hers. She inhaled deeply, so grateful to have been returned to her body. As she exhaled, she whispered, "Thank you," surprised that it was God to whom she spoke.

❦ 38 ❦

ELLEN AWOKE WITH THE MORNING LIGHT, BENEATH THE WHITE bedspread. The words *a shtickl Torah* rolled around her head. Marek kissed her neck, and she turned to him. He stretched, surveying her through slit eyes as his arm crept under the sheet. He smiled as he found her lower back and pulled her close.

Aroused by his breath on her skin, she ran her fingertips up and down the length of his torso.

He arranged a handful of her curls with his free hand. "Good morning, beautiful Ellen," he said.

She thought his courtliness charming. "How did you sleep?"

"Well enough to perform my morning duties," he said, with lascivious good humor. He tumbled her, punctuating his kisses with playful bites. She wrapped her legs around him, her hands and tongue at his neck and shoulders, then she let him go.

His eyelids opened in surprise. "Don't stop," he said.

"I'm not stopping, just looking," she murmured, and slid from his sight, down the thin, hairy path to his groin.

Afterward, they lay together in the damp sheets, lightly tracing circular shapes on each other's arms.

"I had a strange dream last night," he said, smiling shyly. "I was in Warsaw, at the apartment of my friend, on Nalewki Street. There were several of us there, playing music, singing old Polish songs. The door opened and there was Hillel, from your photograph, with a guitar. He sat down and he played for us. No words, just tunes. Amazing, no?"

Ellen's face and neck became rigid. Rafael had told her Hillel played guitar, but she was sure she had not mentioned this to Marek. There was no guitar in the photograph.

"It was so strange to see him there, alive," Marek said. "My friends did not know he wasn't from our time, and he did not speak. But he looked at me, and his tunes touched my heart. I remember thinking this in the dream. This touches my heart." He put his hand to his chest and looked at Ellen.

Ellen thought of Rebbe Nachman of Bratslav.

"His melodies were like your 'For-a-Girl Tune'" Marek went on. "Only now I cannot remember them." He pulled at his hair in frustration and raised himself on his elbows, staring absently at the light now streaming through the open window.

Ellen said nothing, thinking it too much to invite Freidl into the conversation.

"Now you must let me perform the rest of my duty," he said, turning back to her with a soldier's solemnity. He got up, went into the bathroom, and closed the door. The water ran for several minutes. The toilet flushed. Ellen began to wonder what he was doing, until he emerged, clean-shaven. She leaped from the bed and ran her forefinger over the place below his lip where the little tuft of hair had been. "Wow!" she said, laughing. "You look great!"

He tickled her nose. "Shall we try a kiss without it?"

"Absolutely." She draped her arms over his shoulders and kissed the cleanly shaven place. "'Bye, little beard," she whispered, and kissed his lips. They nuzzled, gawky as teenagers, nose to nose, lips to forehead, cheek to cheek, neither wanting to give up the embrace, until Ellen felt a breeze from the window and saw the curtain flutter slightly. It made her think of the white linen shroud floating there in her dream. She sighed. "I have to go to the studio this morning. I need to work," she said.

He nodded. "I have a rehearsal today also." He winked at her as he began to let her go. "I will see you tonight?"

"You bet." She missed him already.

*A*n hour later, she sat on the studio floor and stared at the question she had written in her spiral notebook. *Who is Miriam?* She took a pen and the Tanakh from her backpack and wrote, *Dancer, leads women, plays timbrel, crosses Red Sea to the Promised Land, a prophet.* Nothing about this attracted her. It was like a description of one of those awful paintings hanging on Floriańska Street.

A knot formed in her stomach and sent up a wave of nausea that tickled the back of her throat. Ellen took a deep breath and stared out the window at the sky, which was very blue that morning, like on the day she had walked into Szeroka Square for the first time and had seen the reflection of clouds in all the windows. She realized that something had begun for her that day, although she couldn't yet say what it was. Her temples pulsed as she began to consider her other worry. She rubbed them with her thumbs. Why would any of this help Freidl rest?

Konstantin Pronaszko opened the door. "Good morning, my innovator from America," he said brightly. "How is the work?"

Ellen felt like a schoolkid caught unprepared for a test and desperate for excuses. The tape player gave her the idea to say, "I have the music." With that, she realized she could probably lay out enough elements of the piece to satisfy him.

He grabbed a folding chair and, turning it backward, seated himself. "Let me hear."

She played the tune, vacillating between feelings of certainty and strength about how right it was for her to use it, and fear that she was exploiting something private and fragile.

When the music ended, Pronaszko, his head cradled in his hands, waited a dramatic minute or so before asking, "And the dance. What is it about?"

"It's a prayer," she said, surprised at her own certainty.

He scratched the back of his neck and stared skeptically at his own image in the mirror behind her. "What is the prayer? This is Jewish music. You are not going to bore us, please, with bad Nazis and suffering Jews?" Without pausing to give her a chance to correct him, he charged on. "This has been done. And done. I do not want my company to revisit Auschwitz with an American. That is a very uninteresting aspect to me."

Ellen was not put off by his unexpected vehemence. After all, she had no intention of doing the kind of piece he was describing. What made her scalp crawl, from the hairline back, was his linking the words *American* and *uninteresting*.

Pronaszko put down his satchel and let his focus drift to the pigeons nestling on the studio's window ledge, as if trying to think of a way to salvage the situation with her.

Strangely, Ellen got the feeling he was trying to be supportive, that he was leaving her room to elaborate. Something disturbed the pigeons. They flew off with a powerful rustling of wings, reminding her how the crow who had fallen into her apartment air shaft in New York had regained its strength to fly.

"The dance is a prayer for grass to sprout from the earth around the gravestones," she said. "It's about Miriam the prophetess — Moses' sister — and her timbrel." A smile came, almost unwittingly, to her lips at having offered Pronaszko a sampling from her list of elements, enough to let him know she was not going to Auschwitz. "I'm thinking it's a dance about Poland, from my eyes."

He looked at her as if he had no idea anymore who this girl was.

Members of the company began to arrive, and Pronaszko was forced to turn his attention to them. Ellen gathered her things. "Let us see something next week," he called to her as she left. She thought she detected excitement in his voice.

She walked downstairs with a sense of confidence, which she hoped would last.

39

WHEN SHE ARRIVED AT HER HOTEL, ELLEN PICKED UP A MES-
sage from Marek asking her to call him at the Ariel Café.

"Forgive me, a hundred times, that I forgot to tell you," he said when
she reached him. "There are so many festivals in Kraków in the summer.
But the Jewish Culture Festival is new this year. My group is on the schedule to play. Today, when we were making arrangements with the organiz-
ers, I realized you would be interested. Not for my group, you can hear us
other times. But they have organized workshops all over Kazimierz, of Jewish cooking and dancing and arts, and things like this."

Ellen thought the idea of a Jewish Culture Festival in a city of almost no
Jews rather strange. "What's the festival *about?*" she asked, hoping this
was not going to be another kitschy Polish interpretation of Jewishness,
the sort of imitation thing his band did, with the black-and-white clothes
and silly hats.

"I have the schedule here. Tonight is a music concert by a Jewish com-
poser that I think we will like. A quartet."

Quartet somehow sounded relatively harmless to her. "Where is it?" she
asked, wondering who but the two of them would be interested in attending.

"It is at the *Stara Synagoga,* the Old Synagogue, near the Ariel Café. You
know it?"

"I know it," she said. Seated on the edge of her bed, she pointed her feet
and watched goose bumps rise on her calves as she pictured the photograph of the girl in the black suede pumps. "I'd like to go."

That night, they met for dinner at a small restaurant near Wawel Hill, a
block from the café where she'd had coffee on her second day in Kraków.
They sat side by side, in the European way, and Ellen realized that even if
the neighborhood, with its imposingly lit cathedral on the hill, had become
familiar to her, it was still not hers in the way New York had become hers.

Marek handed her the schedule for the Jewish Culture Festival. "See
how many workshops there are all week?" He ran his finger down the list.

"Cooking. Hebrew calligraphy. Singing. Klezmer. They also have films and lectures."

She was taken with his almost proprietary pride in the festival.

"Look," he said, pointing to an event scheduled to take place at eleven o'clock the next morning, "even a workshop in Jewish paper-cutting."

She took a look at the schedule. "Rafael has paper cutouts hung on his walls," she said. "If you want to see the real thing, you could drive me to Zokof tomorrow. What do you say, partner?"

Marek leaned toward her. "You are really an American girl, the way you talk." He smiled at her provocatively. "You are just like in the movies. I like it." He touched his newly shaved chin. "And I would like very much to go with you to Zokof tomorrow. It is almost as wonderful as my idea." He pulled his cloth shoulder sack from the floor and discreetly pulled out a plastic shopping bag. "I have brought my change of clothes so I do not have to go back home tonight."

She played with the indigo silk shawl draped over her shoulders and gave him a studied sideward look. "Are all Polish guys this presumptuous?"

The last word threw him off. He seemed uncertain if she was annoyed with him. "The students where I share rooms are having fun guessing where I was last night," he said.

Ellen realized she knew almost nothing about how Marek lived his daily life. He had never mentioned roommates. "Then let's keep them guessing." She winked, preferring for the moment to keep him for herself, without social connections.

Later, when they arrived for the concert, the Old Synagogue was almost filled. The audience was mostly Polish. Ellen expressed her surprise at the large turnout, but Marek explained how Poles love music concerts. "We like to get dressed up and tell everyone *shhh,*" he said. Ellen laughed, and on cue, the people in front of them turned around. When the quartet began, she and Marek held hands. The white-vaulted sanctuary glowed brightly, even without sunlight. The music was intricate, modern, and otherworldly, like a conversation of distant voices. Marek clasped his other hand over hers and held it tight. At intermission, she took him by the arm and explained, with some satisfaction, this was the bimah, and that was the Aron Kodesh, where the Torah scrolls were kept. He nodded appreciatively. "I have seen this building only from the outside. I did not ever go in because I was afraid it was a dark place, like a prison, you know? I did not imagine it would be so beautiful."

Ellen was startled and touched that he had had the same reticence about entering the building as she'd had. "It is beautiful," she said, admiring the interior space anew. She was glad they had come.

They took the tram back to Old Town, content with their evening's success. Fog had lifted from the Vistula. It snaked through the streets in long puffs that made Ellen think of Kraków's dragon. Arriving at the Palace Hotel, they went up to her room. Their heads brushed together slightly as Ellen searched her purse for the key. She smiled at him, opened the wing of her shawl, and led him into the room. Marek slipped his satchel off his shoulder and followed her onto the bed, where he unfastened the long line of crocheted buttons that held together the front of her dress. She cupped his head in her hands, ran her fingers through the length of his hair, and kissed him. He laid her back against the pillows and slid his hand between her legs. "Now we make our concert," he said.

*I*n the morning, they awoke to the street sounds of a working weekday. A truck gate opened with a loud squeal, and Ellen sat straight up in bed. "We better get going," she said.

Marek rolled over to see the clock. "No problem. It is only seven thirty. We have time." He pulled her back into his arms.

She patted his chest impatiently. "Time to go," she said.

He pretended to be injured. "You are tired of me already?"

She jumped out of bed, grabbed his hand, and pulled him after her. "How could I possibly get tired of a langer loksh? Take a shower with me?"

"What are you calling me?" he said, following her into the bathroom, all smiles again.

After breakfast, they shopped for fruits and vegetables at an outdoor market. Marek bought a bouquet. "We cannot visit your friend in Zokof without flowers," he said. "It is the Polish custom."

"It's a very nice custom," Ellen said, pleased by the respect implicit in the gesture. But she stopped him from buying chocolates. "They're probably not kosher."

"But he can say a blessing on them and make them kosher," Marek protested.

"It doesn't work that way," she told him. But she was mildly puzzled herself at how it did work. In her room, she had another package of kosher goods ready for Rafael. She'd asked her mother to send it. All the items were marked with a kosher symbol, but she had no idea what requirements they'd had to meet.

They left Kraków in the Fiat in the muggy July heat and headed north into the rolling yellow hills. They passed corrugated-roofed barns, grazing black-and-white cows, fenced gardens surrounding tiny wooden houses, slanted sheds, and farmers in horse-drawn wagons, all of which now looked somewhat less novel to Ellen. She rested her head against the window frame and closed her eyes.

"I am looking forward to meeting your friend," Marek said.

She glanced at him, aware of potential trouble ahead. There was a real possibility that despite Freidl's blessing, Rafael might not trust Marek because he was a Pole. "I'm sure he'll enjoy meeting you too. But he can be gruff," she warned. "Be patient."

Marek reached across the gearshift and touched her knee. "He is old. I know about old people. My grandfather is eighty-six."

"That's not what makes him gruff," she said uncomfortably.

"I understand. It is the war that changed them, that generation." He glanced at her. "They are different from us, because of what they lived."

Ellen did not want to argue the point. She had no idea what had happened to Poles like Marek's grandfather, and she didn't feel like discussing Rafael's past before the two men had met. "I'm sure that's true," she said, looking away.

"The old people teach us to keep Poland's freedom in our hearts." He touched his chest demonstratively, as if he didn't think she would understand. "We have a holiday in November, All Saints' Day. This is a holy day everywhere, but in Poland it is when we mourn for our heroes, and our past. We take flowers and wreaths and light candles at the graves and the monuments from the Nazi time. The air on that day is thick with smoke from millions of those candles, like a blanket over us."

Ellen nodded, thinking of the *Yahrzeit* candles she'd seen at Jewish memorials in the past. It struck her how closely Polish and Jewish symbols and sensibilities dovetailed without touching. "I think your grandfather and Rafael might remember the war very differently," she said.

"I do not think so," he replied. "The war came to everyone in Poland. When they tell their stories from that time, we know that history does not happen to strangers. It happened to them."

Ellen regretted their having once again stumbled onto the detritus of the Holocaust, which always seemed to create conflict between them. She shrugged slightly. "You know what I'm starting to think? I think it matters less what you believe, what faith you follow, than what kind of a person you make yourself because of that faith. The world is full of monstrously religious people."

Marek patted her knee again. "Good, because now we are in the beautiful Małopolska Uplands, where a person should love nature and not worry about monstrously religious people."

She grinned, knowing he was trying to bring them back to common ground. "Okay, Mr. Tourist Guide, tell me all about the beautiful Małopolska Uplands."

"First, some Bruce Springsteen," he said, pulling out a cassette tape.

Ellen loved the sheer absurdity of hearing "Born in the USA" burst from the clanky little Fiat's speakers in the middle of Poland. They sang along, laughing that neither could make out the words for half the stanzas.

Not long after, they crossed the plain of fallow summer fields and arrived in Zokof. Seeing it again, Ellen was almost sorry at having brought Marek to this shoddy little place.

It was nearly noon, and people were out shopping. On the street that led to the main square, Marek braked for a group of boys kicking around a soccer ball. The bell tower chimed from the onion-domed church. The air was filled with the sweet smell of cut grass. Ellen breathed it in and realized she would have been disappointed if it hadn't been there to greet her return.

At the now-familiar curved narrow lane that led to Rafael's house, the breeze blew gently through the open car windows and mussed their hair. That Freidl was somehow with them at that moment comforted Ellen and even made her smile. "Marek, turn here," she said.

They approached Rafael's house. "There he is!" she shouted.

Rafael, in his broad-brimmed black hat and his gabardine, emerged from the door and stood waiting for them.

"How did he know we were here?" Marek asked.

Ellen flicked a lock of Marek's hair into place and prepared herself to make the introductions. "I don't know," she said. They parked in front of the house.

Rafael stepped down to the street as Ellen jumped out to greet him. Without thinking, she hooked her arm in his.

"She came to me last night!" he said, looking down at his arm.

"She came to me the night before." Suddenly realizing his embarrassment at her touch, she turned hastily to Marek, who was standing by the driver's side of the car, looking quizzically at the two of them. "Rafael Bergson," Ellen said, dropping her hands to her sides, "this is my friend Marek Gruberski."

Marek offered a friendly wave.

Rafael acknowledged him with a nod. "So this is the one she talks about."

Marek smiled hopefully. "I hope she speaks well of me."

It was clear to Ellen that Rafael had referred to Freidl, not to her, but she said nothing, hoping to forestall further mention of Freidl until the two men had gotten to know each other better.

Fortunately, they were all distracted by the arrival of a man walking a dog with a rope for a leash. The man stopped a few yards from the car and stared at the three of them. He seemed particularly interested in the bouquet of flowers Marek had taken from the car. When it became apparent that Rafael did not intend to introduce the young strangers, the man pulled at the tip of his cap, offered a muffled greeting to Rafael, and moved on.

"Now the whole town will be talking," Rafael muttered. "Come inside."

They unloaded the food from the car and carried it into the house. "It's all kosher," Ellen assured Rafael. The house was hot, and the smell of dirt and sweat hung in the humid air. She took the flowers from Marek, glad for their fresh fragrance.

Rafael glanced at the grocery bags. "So much kosher food I did not know we had in all of Poland," he said. "Am I such a *fresser?*"

Marek smiled, but Ellen could see he didn't understand.

"A fresser's someone who eats a lot," she explained on her way to the kitchen for a flower vase. "I learned that from my grandmother. To her, it was a compliment. But trust me, Rafael's no fresser." She gave him a look of mock disapproval.

Marek laughed. "My grandmother is the same! Always trying to feed."

Rafael showed them how to stock the kitchen shelves. It seemed to Ellen that Marek knew his way around this kind of rough kitchen, with its porcelain-tiled stove, its dented enamel pans, the coal bucket, and worn linoleum floor. It occurred to her that the two men knew a daily way of life that was completely foreign to her.

They all sat down at the round table at the end of the main room. Ellen pointed out the Jewish paper cutouts, and Marek admired them. He mentioned the paper-cutting workshop being held at the Jewish Culture Festival in Kraków. Rafael acknowledged that he had heard of the festival. But beneath this politeness Ellen sensed some tension.

"I'm very honored to meet you Pan Bergson. Perhaps Ellen has told you I play Jewish music," Marek said, as if he felt obligated to justify his presence. "I'm especially interested in the music from this region. I wonder if you could tell me why there is more Jewish music from here than from most other regions of Poland."

Ellen almost did not recognize this earnest musicological researcher. She had expected Marek to simply ask if Rafael knew the "For-a-Girl Tune" or to question him about the tunes he'd heard in his dream.

Rafael gave Marek an indulgent look. "The reason for the music, Gruberski, is God. This is music from God, music to God." He was frowning, but his tone was like a teacher's. "You young people like the tunes because they are lively. But for us, these are prayers. They free the human soul from bondage." He stroked his beard, assessing Marek's reaction.

Marek nodded but remained respectfully silent. Ellen wondered if he would have the nerve to say to Rafael that he, a Pole, also heard prayers in Jewish music. She wondered how Rafael knew that young people liked the tunes and which young people he meant. Most of all, she hoped Rafael would not dismiss Marek as someone whose interest did not matter, like the Jewish boy Kopelman who had not mattered at Marek's school.

Rafael squinted. "You ask, why so many tunes from this area? I'll tell you, Gruberski, how it was. Before the war, the streets in our town were twisted as a *yeshiva bucher*'s argument." He raised his crooked, arthritic fingers. "You know what a yeshiva bucher is?" he asked testily.

"A student?"

Ellen wondered how Marek knew.

"In such streets as ours, melodies made echoes." Rafael cupped his hands and held them out for Marek to see. "We lived and prayed like in a musical nest." Almost imperceptibly, he pushed out his chin, suggesting a challenge.

"Are you saying the reason for the music is architectural?" Marek asked tentatively.

"The reason for the music, Gruberski, is God."

There was silence in the room. It occurred to Ellen that a non-Jew's interest in Jewish culture was so inconceivable to Rafael that he regarded it merely as Marek's attempt to ingratiate himself.

Marek wiped his perspiring forehead and looked at a loss as to how to proceed. Ellen was about to come to his rescue when Rafael added, "You have heard of Rebbe Israel, son of Rebbe Samuel-Elie, *alev ha sholem?*"

"I have heard of Rebbe Israel," Marek said.

Ellen hadn't counted on Marek really having that much expertise, and she was pleased.

"They said Rebbe Israel wrote more melodies than King David." He bent toward Marek. "You know also of Aaron Birnbaum? Less famous, but maybe more talented."

The hair stood up on the back of Ellen's damp neck, sending charges up and down her back.

Marek looked dejected, as if he sensed things were not going well between him and Rafael. "I do not know him."

"Aaron Birnbaum wrote the 'For-a-Girl Tune'" Ellen said quietly. "And probably the others you heard."

Marek turned to her in surprise. "How do you know this?"

"There was a woman named Freidl. She was from this town. He sang those tunes to her." The explanation seemed so inadequate, she added, "Because he loved her."

Marek smiled, apparently mistaking this for flirtation. "If I could hear some of Aaron Birnbaum's tunes, I would be very grateful," he told Rafael. "My group would be very interested to learn them, even if only for their liveliness."

Ellen realized he was delicately trying to make the point that he was interested in the music in a serious way, but Rafael would not go along. He seemed suddenly annoyed. "If you want to learn, then listen for them," he said flatly. "They are still here, underneath."

Marek looked at Ellen uneasily, but she didn't know what, or how much more, she should say about the music, or Freidl, or why Rafael had reacted as he had. "Why don't we eat lunch?" she suggested. "Then, Rafael, could we go to the cemetery?"

"Of course we will go to the cemetery," Rafael said evenly.

"Maybe you'd like to rest first?" Ellen asked him.

Rafael rose and began to set out the dishes for lunch. "Rest? Rest is for the dead." He winked at her.

40

*I*T WAS EARLY AFTERNOON WHEN THEY LEFT THE HOUSE AND drove through town to the cemetery. Ellen had climbed into the Fiat's backseat. Rafael sat up front. "Slow. Slow," he scolded Marek.

Through the streets and narrow lanes, people watched them with the studied, impassive expressions that Ellen had at first excused as curiosity, but now regarded as hostility. They recognized her Jewish face, she thought, and she blushed. What bothered her was not only that people chose to look at her as a Jew, but that it mattered to them. She wanted to know what satisfaction they got from playing this game of *Us versus You*. She looked at Marek. She wanted to ask him what the Zokofers might be thinking, but she didn't want to embarrass him in front of Rafael.

"I will show you first where was Avrum Kollek's mill," Rafael said. "Your grandfather told you about Avrum Kollek?"

Marek glanced at her expectantly.

"No," she said. "Who was he?"

Rafael dismissed her question with a grunt. "Your grandfather worked in Avrum Kollek's mill. On the night the peasant Jan Nowak died, he went from the cemetery to Avrum Kollek. He had a daughter, Shuli. A gorgeous girl, everyone said. And she had eyes for Itzik. She heard everything Itzik told her father. She was there when Avrum left to ask the Russian magistrate to protect the people." He shook his head. "Ach! A waste of breath."

Marek seemed about to ask him a question, but Rafael went on. "After, Shuli ran to Itzik's mother's house, to Sarah, to tell him to leave Zokof. A brave girl to do that, with what was going on in the town that night."

Ellen listened to this, completely captivated by the thought of a gorgeous girl named Shuli having a crush on her grandfather. Perhaps, she imagined, at fourteen her grandpa Isaac had that shy, reluctant quality that girls, herself included, found so attractive. Perhaps this was what had hardened, in adulthood, into his well-known stubbornness.

"Later, a year after Avrum went to his death, alev ha sholem, she married a *gozlin* named Pinchas — a swindler, you understand? He married her for the mill, a business he didn't know from."

"What happened to Shuli?"

Rafael shrugged. "What happened? Your grandfather she must have taken for dead. When Pinchas blessed her with a son, she named him Itzik." He smiled slightly at Shuli's mischief.

"Is she still alive?"

"*Ptuh!* She went to Treblinka, with a transport of Jews from Garbatka. Stop here," he directed Marek. Ellen and Marek exchanged uncomfortable looks. Rafael pointed to an opening between two small shacks set at odd angles to the street. "These were part of Avrum Kollek's mill that used to be here."

Across the street, a squat elderly couple stared suspiciously at them. Ellen thought that the woman, in her kerchief, and the man, in his tie and white shirt, looked much like the Polish couple she'd met on the Warsaw–Kraków train. But now the sight of them made her angry, and she began a manic tirade in her head. She glared at them. *Where were you during the war? What did you do when they pulled the Jews out of their houses here? Did you take the food from your neighbors' tables? Did you steal the clothes they left drying on the lines?* Yet she knew that if she crossed the street, if she pressed them, with Marek translating, the old couple would talk about how it was for them during the war. It would all be very civil and genial. They would tell her how terribly they'd suffered. This would complicate her understanding of what did happen. This dual possibility so annoyed and frustrated her, she swung her attention back to Avrum Kollek's shacks.

"Now go to that street, by the tree," Rafael said impatiently. "I will show you where was the market square, before the war."

Marek took these directions from Rafael without comment. Ellen wondered if he was intimidated or if he was hard at work listening for tunes.

They approached a large concrete apartment block.

"Stop in front," Rafael said.

Marek shifted into park.

"Tuesday mornings, this place here was full of wagons." Rafael made a wide arc with his arm, indicating the area before them. "Over there," he said, pointing to the left, "the women sold fruits, vegetables, baked things, from *stalls,* you say?"

"Yes," Ellen told him, although she hardly knew what he meant.

"The cripples and beggars went from one to the other. Such a *tummel!* All over the town you could hear the chickens and the children. And peddlers — Shmuel the Bookseller." Rafael smiled. "Moishe the Shoemaker's fingernails I remember. Half smashed, the other half gone."

Marek looked out the window. Ellen thought he looked bored, and feeling responsible somehow for sustaining his interest in the tour, she quashed her desire to question Rafael further.

Rafael scanned the area, as if he could see the people he had described. "I must tell you about Velvl the Water Carrier. He came every Tuesday, with the buckets swinging from the yoke on his shoulders. The Iron Yoke, he called it, like in the days of Babylon under Nebuchadnezzar. Velvl, may his name be for a blessing. He lived, as we say, on air. A *luftmensh,* you understand?" He opened his mouth, took in a deep breath, as if to fill his lungs with Velvl. "On Shabbos, such a man was for us a king, a *tzaddik* of the sweet mysteries of the Zohar."

Ellen watched Rafael's shoulders rise and fall until, unconsciously, her own breaths began to synchronize with his.

"In summer, there was dust everywhere," he continued. "In spring, we were up to our ankles, or more, in mud. Now, let's go." He rocked forward and back, as if paying private homage to the site.

Marek shifted into first gear and, at Rafael's direction, drove to the birch-lined, two-lane blacktop that led out of town. About a quarter of a mile farther, they turned left onto a dirt road.

Rafael turned around to Ellen. "I took your father here. He wasn't so willing to come as you, but I insisted."

Ellen nodded, easily imagining her father's resistance, given his discomfort at all things emotional and all things religious, not to mention his hatred of cemeteries.

The dirt road curved to the left, back toward town. On their right lay a striped, planted field. On their left, the forest. About two hundred yards farther, Rafael announced, "We are here. Park the car."

They got out and crossed the road to the forest. A path of stone pavers, littered with broken glass bottles, led inside. A crow cawed from the treetops. Several more joined in, and the harsh chorus quickly grew.

Looking up at the birds, Marek broke his silence. "When I was a small boy," he said, "my uncle Leszek would sometimes put me to bed. I remember he told me, 'Our angels watch over us.'" Marek stroked his bare chin and glanced at Ellen.

She wasn't sure what it was about the crows that had prompted him to say this.

"Uncle Leszek told me he talked to the Jewish ghosts. He said, 'They are in the trees; they are with the birds; they are in the sky before a storm.'" He glanced up again at the birds. "Maybe they watch over this place."

Ellen looked from him to Rafael, hardly knowing how he would react to this.

Rafael turned toward the path into the forest. "The wall is almost gone. No one can be buried here now."

"Why not?" Marek asked.

"A Jewish cemetery needs a wall so no *Kohane* will enter without knowing he has crossed the boundary." Rafael turned and led them forward, as if no further explanation was warranted.

Ellen shrugged at Marek's quizzical look and followed Rafael into the forest. The crows made a frightening racket in the trees.

"Your father made a *tsimmes* about the birds," Rafael said, without turning.

"He told me about them," Ellen said, remembering their conversation in his study.

"I told him he should pray, and he prayed. For your grandfather, alev ha sholem, he prayed. And for Freidl, he prayed also."

Marek looked startled. "Freidl? The woman with the musician, Birnbaum? Why would he pray for her?"

Rafael halted his march and turned to them. "He prayed because a Jew must pray for the souls of his dead."

"But how was she *his* dead?" Marek asked.

Rafael looked from him to Ellen. "For almost a hundred years she has wandered Poland, our Freidl, without children to pray for her, without Itzik, your grandfather. When your father came, we thanked God and hoped for rest, but he did not finish what he promised. He wrote me letters like a schoolchild. Excuses is all he made from it. It was not enough."

Ellen reddened. "You're not being fair," she said. "How could you expect him to become someone he wasn't, just because you wanted him to?"

"I asked him for no more than what he knew he could do. He knew what was expected. This is why his daughter is standing here with me today."

Ellen's hearing dulled, as if she were underwater. "But he didn't know I would be invited to Poland."

"He knew the Leibers have responsibilities here. The rest was a gift, a coincidence, you could say." He smiled that slight smile of his.

A rushing noise, like water, again filled Ellen's blocked ears, and she remembered her father using that word, *coincidence.*

"Beshert?" she said. "You're telling me it's beshert that I'm standing here?"

Rafael gave a short affirmative nod. "Your father had responsibilities."

The image of Freidl's stone, buried in her father's cabinet, now made Ellen feel nauseous. "Can you show me the pile of stones where Freidl is buried? My father told me about it."

Rafael glanced from her to Marek, who seemed confused by this talk. "Come, I will take you to her grave," he said, and he led them farther down the stone path.

They reached a tall wrought-iron gaslight, the only one. Rafael gave its trunk a few friendly pats, as if in greeting. "It is written in the book of Zechariah that in his dream the prophet saw a lamp stand of gold." He gripped the gaslight. "Zechariah asked God what it meant. God said, not by might nor by power but by His Spirit alone could the Holy Temple, which was in ruins, be rebuilt. God asked, 'Does anyone scorn a day of small beginnings?'" He cleared his throat. "And so it is with us today, in this place." He looked up at the lamp stand.

Marek looked up at the crows.

The rushing sound continued to course through Ellen's ears.

They reached the center of the cemetery, where all paths met. To their right, under a tree, was a pile of small stones. They tramped through the thick underbrush and stood before it.

Ellen didn't know how they would proceed, if she was expected to know a prayer, or if Rafael would consider it some sort of sacrilege for Marek to participate. She waited for his cue.

He merely stared at the stones.

She thought she should step away from the religious and ease the tension she felt between all of them. "Rafael, how exactly did you find the top of her gravestone, the part you gave my father?" she asked.

He picked up a small stone, which he placed on top of the others. "I found it after the war, when I came back to Zokof. The town was a shambles. Blown up. My house was gone. This I told you when you were here last time." His voice was low and rough. He paused, as if checking to see if she remembered.

Ellen nodded slightly.

"I had nowhere to go, so I went to the cemetery, the only Jewish place left." He pursed his lips. "The crows were here already. The gravestones . . ." He made a dismissive cut with his hand. "Gone." He frowned. "I was standing here, alone. But inside me was a sound, a note, and it felt, this sound, like such a power, like what could reach the heavens. I stood here in this place, and I prayed in that note, that sound. '*Ribbono shel Oylom* — Master of the Universe,' I said. 'What have you done here? What have you done here?' I was frightened of myself, of the anger in that note. But I could not stop it. *Be ashamed,* I told God in that note. *Be ashamed.*"

He paused before continuing.

Ellen thought of her altered voice, manic with anger at the Poles, and she wondered, fleetingly, if this was the feeling of prayer. Not the anger, but the heightened sense of listening to one's own voice, speaking words, but not aloud. A madness, but temporary. Not a descent into schizophrenia, but an opening up, a lightening.

Rafael looked at her. "For centuries we have called our cemeteries the Houses of the Living because here the dead return to their ancestors and to God, who is always the God of life. But I cursed Him that day. 'You are the God of the dead,' I said.

"Then, one day, after I was already living in the town, I was walking home. I took the short way, over there." He pointed at the area that bounded the western side of the cemetery. "There were a lot of stones there, that used to be the wall of the cemetery, and I stumbled. Before I knew what was what, I fell on my face in a ditch. A stream had been there once, but it was dried up for years. That is where I found the top of Freidl's gravestone, covered with fifty years of dirt and leaves. I pulled it from the earth and held it in my arms. I remember sitting in that ditch, holding it to my chest, rocking it like a child, asking, Is this God's answer to me? I could not grasp it. My heart was below my feet. I sat in the dirt, holding the stone. It was terrible, how completely alone I felt. I wanted my wife."

Rafael began to weep, cupping his hand to his forehead so that Ellen and Marek could not look at him.

Ellen glanced over his shoulder at Marek, who politely averted his eyes. She patted Rafael's arm reassuringly, but he shook himself resolutely and continued. "You understand? During the war I did not think, I *survived*. For this woman, Freidl, to come to me in this way, it reminded me that I am a man who could have that kind of freedom again — to think, to feel something in my heart, to know that I could reach God with a single note, uttered in despair and anger and fear. This was a gift for which I can never thank her enough."

Ellen handed him a tissue, resisting the impulse to ask him how he could thank God for what he or Freidl had been through, but understanding now why he listened to Freidl's request that he be a mensch and read Torah again.

"El Molei Rachamim," Rafael prayed.

Ellen reached into her purse and took out the blue booklet of memorial prayers her father had given her in his study. Laid across a page was her great-aunt Hindeleh's faded red ribbon. She wound it around her finger protectively and searched for the prayer. "Is it all right if I say it too?" she asked, when Rafael had finished. "The transliteration is right here."

He leaned over her shoulder at the words to which she pointed and shook his head. "Read the English, so you should understand."

Ellen turned the page and read the translation, filling the blank space with Freidl's name, when it was called for. *Compassionate God, eternal Spirit of the universe, grant perfect rest in Your sheltering presence to Freidl Alterman who has entered eternity.* Her hands began to shake with the enormity of standing at the grave of the woman who had come to her in dreams, in her linen shroud, with her regal face, her open heart.

From deep in the blue, Freidl prayed, *"Compassionate God, hear this heartfelt voice. Let me return to the place where Itzik's granddaughter stands."*

Ellen clutched Hindeleh's ribbon and prayed, *"O God of mercy, let her find refuge in the shadow of Your wings, and let her soul be bound up in the bond of everlasting life."* Crows rustled their wings in the branches of the trees. *"May she rest in peace."*

"*Yes. Let it be so,*" said Rafael.

"*And let us say. . . .*"

Marek stepped forward and put his arm around Ellen. "*Amen,*" he said.

"*Amen,*" Rafael echoed. He looked up at the birds. "With them, we always have a minyan."

41

*T*HEY RETURNED TO THE HOUSE IN MIDAFTERNOON. RAFAEL EX-
cused himself and went to the outhouse in the backyard. Marek stood before one of the white paper cutouts Rafael had tacked to the living room
wall. "We call this *wycinanki,* in Polish," he told Ellen. "We make them
for holiday decorations." He examined the paper's semicircle of Hebrew
lettering. Beneath it, Rafael had cut a seven-branched menorah and surrounded it with lions, birds, and deer perched in small, neat squares. Marek
studied the workmanship closely. "Very beautiful," he murmured.

"Rafael calls them *oissherenishen.*" The funny-sounding Yiddish word,
so evocative of her grandpa Isaac, made Ellen smile. "He says they give
him something to do, but I think he does them for Freidl. He said she used
to make them too."

Marek shook his head. "Everything is Freidl to you and him."

Was he mocking her, she wondered, or was she just misreading him
again? She turned to the window, observing Rafael's slow progress up the
dirt path to his outhouse. "How does he manage in the middle of winter?"
she said.

Marek also glanced out the window at Rafael. "It is sometimes very difficult for the old people in our country, especially the ones like him, who are
alone in the small towns. But he is fortunate to be a Jew. He can go to the synagogue in Warsaw, and they will give him money from Americans. The Jews
send it to them." Marek brushed some remnant of the forest from his sleeve.

Ellen felt, once again, as if she was sliding into the perilous gap that lay
between them. She turned to him. "You think Polish Jews are *fortunate?*
Didn't you notice your uncle Leszek's Jews are ghosts?"

Marek shook his head impatiently. "Not those. The ones who survived.
People say there are many more Jews in Poland now than they tell us. Jews
have more money, and in the communist times, many of them had a lot
of influence. I am sorry. This is true." He began to examine the Hebrew
books on the shelves.

Ellen stared at him. "I'm sorry too," she said softly. "I'm sorry you think you know so much and you understand so little. You're standing in the house of the last Jew of Zokof. There used to be five thousand Jews living here. I don't think the rest of them are under the bed."

Marek's eyes did not waver from the books. "Maybe they moved somewhere else. Many people moved after the war," he said evenly.

"Marek, that doesn't make any sense. If they just left, why doesn't anyone know where they are?"

"The government census knows where they are, and this information they keep secret."

"So what are you saying? The country's full of secret Jews?"

"We do not know."

Ellen thought of her father. Proving a negative, he used to say, is a losing strategy. "Then who's living in their houses — free, I should point out?" she asked.

Marek's mouth tightened into a flat line. "We did not take from the Jews. Those are stories told by outsiders, people who do not like Poles. They are not true. Look around you. Do you think it's possible for him to live in this town for forty-five years after the war without Poles taking care of him? You think it is Freidl who carries his firewood?" He waved at the stove in the kitchen. "I promise you, without his neighbors, he would not be alive today."

Ellen flicked at her hair. "Marek, his neighbors desecrated the cemetery. You were just there."

"It was the Nazis that did that, not the Poles," he said. "If you do not believe that, Ellen, you go too far."

"Too far? They stole the bottom half of Freidl's stone."

"You do not know this is true." He shrugged. "We always come back to this. I promise you, Ellen, the Poles are not *all* anti-Semites."

"Would you help me get her stone back?"

Rafael returned to the house. Marek watched him wash his hands in the basin and drop exhaustedly into a chair. "Where is the bottom half of Freidl's stone?" he asked.

Rafael looked up at Marek, clearly surprised. "At Władek Głowacki's farm."

Marek glanced at Ellen. "We are thinking we would like to get it."

Ellen was shocked.

"The Messiah himself could come before Głowacki would give me her stone," Rafael said. "I have tried. It was in a shed behind the town hall. People came and took those stones for building and for making streets, the *gonifs*. Then Głowacki, that *cham*, took Freidl's for himself. I have heard people say he uses it to support the foundation of his barn." Rafael turned to Ellen. "You will go with him?"

Ellen's heart did a little jump. She nodded, thinking he looked slightly disoriented, as if he needed time to appreciate that it might actually be returned to him. Finally, he rubbed his hands together in a measured way. "Good," he said. "But first, you must have something to eat."

Ellen smiled at him. "Marek, help me light the stove," she said. She made the three of them a meal of eggs and onions with bread and butter, the kind of meal her grandpa Isaac used to love, and tried not to think about what she and Marek had just said to each other.

Rafael was delighted with the food. He adjusted his yarmulke, barely able, it seemed, to contain his happiness as he said a prayer and spooned up the eggs. "I will tell you how to go," he said. "At the main square, on the street next to the church, you will see a metal fence at the corner of the second street. There is an apple tree, an old one, very twisted. Take that street out from the town, until you see some houses with fences. You pass these and take the road to the right. Głowacki's place is the next one. A house and a barn you will see. After him, it is only forest."

"How long a drive is it?" Ellen asked him.

"You could be back in an hour, if you don't have trouble with him. He is a *shikker,* a drunk, you understand? So be careful. And watch the dogs." He was like an officer sending his troops on a mission.

When they were ready to leave, he spoke to Marek. "It is written, 'As the musician played, the hand of God came upon him.' May God inspire you and bring you success. I wish you *mazel tov* — good luck."

For a moment, Marek stood wordlessly in the doorway, seemingly dazed. "Thank you," he said quietly.

Ellen sensed that Rafael wanted to speak with her alone. "Marek, can you wait for me in the car? I want to talk to Rafael for a minute."

"Of course," he said, and closed the door after himself.

A fly buzzed at the windowpane. The sky had begun to gray, and the impending rain intensified the room's odor of dust and old leather bookbindings.

Rafael chuckled. "Who but Freidl would find such a man?"

Ellen fingered the curtain sheers and looked out at Marek, seated in the Fiat, his long neck thrust forward with a kind of grim determination at the task ahead. "Do you think Marek's a mensch?"

"I think he doesn't know what's what from a Jew, but he has a curiosity, an interest, yes? Our music makes a spark in him. He wants to give it life. That is good. In this instance, God takes with one hand and gives with another." He shrugged. "What more can you ask?"

Ellen could not entirely agree. "Something bothers me about him, Rafael," she said. "At home, I have so many non-Jewish friends. They don't have this attitude. He has it less than some other Poles, but it's there. It's as if we're some kind of problem for them. And they don't let facts get in their way. He just said that Poland's full of Jews. Why would they even want to believe that? It's as if everything has another meaning to them, like there's some big conspiracy to get them. There's no logic to it. They could just as easily say the Jews are this or that because the moon is made of blue cheese. It's craziness." It was the first time she had articulated what she had been feeling, and it sounded so prejudiced, she scared herself.

Rafael closed his eyes and clasped his hands tightly together. "But now, you must put this from your mind," he said. "You cannot change them. You can only do what you must do. For me, I am responsible for my Jews in this town, even if they are dead." He began to rock back and forth, as if he was praying. His lips moved, but he barely made a sound. "There is no one else to pray for them," he said gruffly, "to say their memory should be for a blessing. And Freidl. You must understand this, Ellen. She must rest."

Ellen sat down on the chair opposite Rafael, feeling eerily disoriented. The sound of the ticking clock seemed to warble. Her fingers swayed slowly, as if underwater. Large raindrops began to tap insistently against the windows, and the room became dark with the sudden change of weather. Rafael rose and lit the lamp on the table.

"Listen to me," he said. His voice sounded muffled to her. "Freidl does not let you see her in the empty eternity where her soul is bound up in suffering. Her freedom to move about, to speak, to sing, everything you imagine of her, this is an illusion."

"But she comes to me. She talks to me. I know her face. She wears a plaid shawl. Who is that, if not her?" Ellen argued.

Rafael carefully placed his hand on the table. "We say, 'Trust that the seed you have planted will bloom in someone's heart.'" He raised his finger instructively. "Her planting a seed is what you see of her. That is all I could ever understand about it." He shrugged in his usual way.

Ellen could hear her heart's beat. She felt dizzy as the air slowly began to circle around her. Panicked, she focused on a tall book that stood on the shelf behind Rafael and forced herself to concentrate on it, as if she were spotting turns. The circling sensation slowed, then stopped. Ellen took a long breath. "What was that?" she said, deeply shaken.

Rafael rapped several times on the table. "Listen to me. Ellen, you are the last generation to whom I can speak for her sake, to tell you to listen to the still, quiet voice, to hear God's echoes in the world. Already I feel the cold touch of the *Malach Ha-Moves* — the Angel of Death." He brought his hand to his chest in a loose fist and beat it against his heart. "Do what you need to do."

She was trembling. "All right," she said. "But for now, you should rest."

He agreed to lie down until they returned. "When I wake up," he said, "may God grant that I see either the Messiah or her stone." His laugh, rumbly and deep, made him cough as he shuffled to his bed on the other side of the room.

She left soon after he had lain down and closed his eyes, distressed at having seen how death would look on him.

42

*T*WENTY MINUTES LATER, MAREK AND ELLEN BUMPED ALONG A country road lined with poplars. The rain had passed like a mood, and the sun shone over the yellowing fields of fallow July grass. They drove past plum orchards, stands of birch, and farms where small, mixed-breed dogs lay chained to trees or posts. The Fiat's wheels spun back pebbles and mud.

At last they came upon the cluster of fenced cinder-block-and-brick houses Rafael had described, their front casement windows all shuttered closed. Ellen pointed excitedly at the fork in the road ahead. "That's where we turn right." Soon after, they arrived at Władek Głowacki's house and barn at the edge of a forest. The house was an architectural confusion of stone, brick, and wood. About a hundred feet to its left, the ash-gray wooden barn listed precariously.

Marek parked by the side of the road, and together he and Ellen negotiated the muddied ruts of the farmer's driveway. Several dogs barked. Ellen slipped her arm through Marek's. He called out, "Pan Głowacki," just as one of the dogs burst from the barn and tore toward them through the scattered farm equipment and the rubbish that littered the property. The dog's speed so alarmed Marek, he pulled Ellen behind him and called Głowacki's name again.

A small, bony-cheeked old man in a frayed cap appeared from behind the house. "Ee-yah." He shooed the animal away. When he was within feet of them, Ellen saw that his face was deeply lined and bearded with white stubble. He was missing the third and fourth fingers on his left hand. Marek took her firmly by the arm and led her forward, greeting Głowacki brightly in Polish.

The farmer squinted and glanced rapidly back and forth between his two visitors. "Good day. Good day." His voice was hoarse, and the words, in Polish, whistled between his missing teeth.

"Good day," they said.

Marek began to speak. Ellen understood only a word or two of what he was saying and nothing of what Głowacki said in response. Without a translator, she began to feel frustrated as a deaf person. But she was afraid to interrupt, lest her English compromise the goodwill Marek was clearly trying to establish. She wondered if he had yet asked about Freidl's stone.

Marek pointed at the barn and seemed to ask a question as he took a few tentative steps toward it. Głowacki's dogs began barking again. Ellen held his arm like a child, her fingers stiff with anxiety.

"Tak. Tak." Głowacki nodded warily.

Marek advanced slowly toward the barn. Głowacki walked with him, apparently reassured by the younger man's steady manner and his easygoing voice. At last they reached the structure's open wooden door, where they stopped. A breeze blew the fetid smell of unmucked stalls toward them.

Ellen, with only her sense of sight and smell to guide her, began to search for some sign of Freidl's gravestone. Along the right side of the barn, a rough sty of stones and wooden posts had been built. Four pigs snuffled in the muddy enclosure.

Głowacki now seemed to be talking about the barn. Marek kept repeating "I understand" in Polish. This was all she could make out. She noticed that Marek seemed to be using the pauses in his conversation with Głowacki to look around. Then she spotted a rectangular stone that had been partially lodged under the right corner footing of the barn. The rest of the stone jutted into the pig's sty and was coated with slop.

Marek saw it too. "What's this?" he asked. The three of them stared at the stone, as if they expected it to speak.

With the toe of his shoe, Marek gently knocked some of the dirt off the exposed part of the stone.

Głowacki let loose a flurry of words.

It seemed to Ellen that he was trying to explain something about the stone's purpose as he pointed to various parts of the barn. She stared at the stone, obviously a gravestone, and felt sick.

"I understand," Marek said.

The sun slipped behind clouds, throwing them into shadow. Głowacki looked down at the stone and seemed to smile. "*Czy wy jesteście Żydami?*" he asked.

Marek didn't respond.

Głowacki repeated the question.

Marek looked at Ellen. "We must offer him money," he said in a measured voice. "Do you have fifty dollars?"

"Yes. What did he just say?"

"He wants to know if we are Jews. Do not say anything to him."

Ellen felt as if someone had just grabbed her by the hair. The sting ran from her scalp down her back like an electric current.

Marek spoke quietly to Głowacki, apparently trying to force the man's attention away from Ellen, who now seemed to interest him.

She evaded his inquisitive looks by peering into the barn. The slats of the outer walls were set so widely apart that long shafts of the now-gray daylight exposed the interior space, including a treacherous-looking hayloft.

Marek turned to her. "He says the stone is valuable to him because it is the right size to hold up the footings. I think the writing is on the other side, facing down. We must offer him more money. Do you have one hundred?"

She nodded, knowing the insult wasn't Marek's. The whole situation had become absurd to her, with Głowacki standing there, thinking he was entitled to restitution for a stolen gravestone. "Can't you threaten to report him?"

"*Americańska?*" Głowacki indicated Ellen.

Marek nodded perfunctorily. He turned to her and, without expression, told her, "I cannot threaten him. We are strangers here. He says it was here, on his property, so he used it. If we return the stone to the cemetery and he steals it back, who will stop him? You must think of Rafael."

Her dilemma made Ellen feel light-headed. Justice, the kind her father had taught her to believe in, required that this matter be heard in court. It demanded that she refuse to pay. But such justice would not serve Rafael or Freidl with either the necessary immediacy or in the long term. She smiled at Głowacki. "If a troll has to be paid so we can cross this bridge, I'm going to pay him. May he rot in hell," she said sweetly.

Głowacki said a few more words to Marek but agreed to take the hundred dollars.

Ellen continued to smile, in the hope that denying the existence of any ill will between them would continue to move the transaction along more quickly.

Głowacki offered Marek a spade and dragged out a weathered piece of floorboard from the barn. With the spade, Marek began to slowly dig around the adjoining stones and dirt so that he could maneuver the gravestone free of the barn's weight.

Ellen noticed Marek tense at what Głowacki said to him next. She grabbed the stone at its mucky end and steadied it while Marek did his work.

Głowacki picked up a broken ax handle near his feet and gave it to Marek, apparently with the suggestion that it be used to keep the space wedged open after the gravestone was removed.

Once the handle was in place, Ellen began to ease the stone out by rocking it from side to side. But the weight of the barn exacted a toll, and with each scraping sound, she imagined the letters and images on the other side were being defaced. That she would be responsible for ruining Freidl's stone brought tears to her eyes. She brushed them away with the back of her hand, not wanting Głowacki to see her cry. It would not have mattered. He was standing a few feet away, in the reemerged sunlight, wholly immersed in cutting down the floorboard he meant to use in the stone's place.

It took at least ten minutes before they had the stone dislodged. It came free with a heavy *thump,* revealing that straw and a piece of wood, not stone, had lain directly beneath it, insulating the face from the violence Ellen had thought she had done to it. "All right!" she shouted.

Marek picked it up and brushed off the bits of rotted wood that clung to both sides. The stone was a few inches in depth and about two and a half feet high. Their rescue almost complete, Ellen peeked nervously at the underside to see if this was indeed Freidl's stone. But the stone was so encrusted with dirt, the engravings could not be seen. Perhaps Głowacki had stolen more than one gravestone, she worried. Yet this ragged, broken-off end was so similar in size and shape to the one she had seen in her father's study, she felt almost sure it was Freidl's.

With Marek's help, Głowacki shoved the replacement board into place. He had become rather talkative. The pulsing of Marek's jaw indicated to Ellen that he was not pleased with what the old man was saying, although he offered noncommittal interjections and nodded agreeably. She almost panicked when Głowacki grabbed a dry rag from the barn floor and took the sty-soggy end of the stone from Marek. When he merely wrapped it in the rag and handed it back, she exhaled sharply with relief.

Marek pulled the package to his chest and told Ellen that she should pay Głowacki. Without wiping her hands, she counted out the hundred dollars. "Money touched with shit," she said pleasantly, and handed him the cash, which he pocketed efficiently.

"Good day," they each said politely. Ellen eyed the distance to the Fiat, planning a clean extrication from the situation.

Głowacki tipped his cap; his odd smile returned.

All the way to the Fiat, Ellen's heart beat violently.

Marek opened the trunk and laid the stone in a nest he fashioned from sheets of newspapers and scraps of cloth.

Głowacki stood at the door of his barn and watched them drive away.

When they were out of sight of the farm, Ellen turned to Marek. "What was he saying?"

Marek shifted his hands on the wheel and tightened his grip. Like hers, they were unnaturally red and covered with cuts from the digging and scraping.

"He said he had people coming around before, asking for Jewish grave-stones. Some of them offered him money. Not enough money, he said. Some wanted just to take pictures. I knew he was saying this because he wanted me to make him an offer. He had his price. He wanted one hundred American dollars. He knew you are a Jewish girl. He knew you had this money. He said I bargain like a Jew."

"How did you explain why you wanted the stone?"

"I said I was a student of local history and I heard he had one of the gravestones from the old Jewish cemetery. I said I like to collect these things." Marek shrugged. "That must have been why Głowacki decided to tell me a story about the war. The Jews had all the gold, he said. The Poles had only dirt. Two Jews came and offered him their gold. He said he didn't take it. It was too dangerous to hide Jews. He had a wife and children. But they hid in his barn anyway, and he let them stay above, in the hayloft. It was winter and very cold."

Ellen thought of the widely set slats and how the snow must have blown in.

"He was saying this as if it was shameful to him, to hide Jews. Then four days later, the Nazis came. He had to give them up. He had no choice. He said, 'A Jew wasn't worth a fly on a pig's ass.'"

Ellen blanched.

"He said their names, the two Jews. He knew them from town." Marek bit his lip. "I think there was more he did not tell me. He talks in a circle. He makes excuses, even though I did not accuse him." He wiped his cheek with his sleeve and glanced nervously at Ellen. "He said he found the stone on his property. This must be a lie. How could it come here? Rafael said he took it from the town, remember?"

"Yes."

"He said it keeps away the ghosts. The two Jews, I suppose. I asked him, then why sell now? I didn't understand his answer. Something like if the stone goes to Jews, he has protection anyway, I think." He shrugged. "But it is more possible he only wanted more money, that he was looking for the highest price, for his hundred dollars American."

Marek glanced furtively at Ellen, as if he was afraid she thought he had betrayed her by letting Głowacki get his price.

Sensing this, she said, "Don't worry about Głowacki. We got the stone. That's all that matters."

He nodded, but he still looked upset. "We must stop and clean the stone. We cannot bring it to Rafael so dirty," he said.

Ellen agreed. "And we better get the pig stuff off our own hands too."

They stopped beside a well. A breeze blew back Marek's long hair as he got out of the Fiat. Ellen met him at the back of the car. They stood beside each other, looking at their reflections in the rear window. "I'm sorry about what I said before, at Rafael's house," she said.

"Yes. I am sorry also," he whispered.

"This was so incredibly generous of you."

He looked at the ground, embarrassed. "*Generous* is not a good word for any of this," he said. "This taking of a person's memory and throwing it in pig's dirt. I think the whole town must know he has this gravestone." He seemed so shaken that she put her arms around him.

He opened the trunk and took out the stone, cradling it until he could remove the rag Głowacki had given him. He threw it on the ground like a soiled diaper.

She touched the stone, trying to conceive that her grandpa Isaac had broken it in two, that this was indeed the lower half of Freidl's stone.

They scrubbed it with well water until every lettered indentation was clear of dirt and they could see that on its face, its borders were carved with what appeared to be the bases of two candlesticks. Between them were several lines of large Hebrew letters.

"You should bring back the other part, so they can be read together," he said.

She passed her hand over the Hebrew inscription at the center of the stone. "I wish I could read the words."

Marek held her. Her whole body began to shake from the tension of the afternoon. He soothed her, told her she had been very patient with Głowacki and even with him. She smiled at him. He told her that Rafael would be so happy to see them, that they should go to him now. And she agreed. All during their drive back to Rafael's house, he caressed her wrist with his thumb.

*W*hen Rafael saw them park in front of his house, he opened the door and raised his hands above his head, shaking them, as if he didn't know what else to do with them.

Marek took the stone, now wrapped in clean cloths, from the trunk of the Fiat and held it up like an offering.

Rafael began to weep.

Ellen ran to him. Marek followed, and together they went inside in a triumphant procession. Marek laid the still-covered stone on the table. Rafael stood before it, rocking back and forth, stroking his beard, unable to take his eyes away but not touching the stone, as if it was too much for him to unveil it yet. "Głowacki gave it to you, or you had to pay?" he finally asked.

"We paid," Ellen said.

"We would have taken it if we had to," Marek added indignantly.

Rafael said nothing.

"I'm sorry we were away so long. It was very dirty; we stopped to make it clean," Marek said.

Rafael turned to him. "This was a great mitzvah you did. A blessing. I did not think he would give it back. Never." He frowned. "For Głowacki, this means he has lost his fear. They say Lipman and Kravitz used to cover his dreams with their ashes, aleichem-sholem."

Marek bit his upper lip. "Those are the names he said to me. He said the Nazis got them, the two Jews that hid in his barn. He said he did not take their gold."

Rafael rubbed his eyes tiredly. "He took their gold. He took what they had. And after, he went looking for Nazis that he could denounce them to get them out of his barn."

Marek looked at Ellen, who had turned pale realizing that Głowacki, the man she had just met, had done this. She remembered his smile.

Yet she thought it strange that Rafael was taking the time to talk about

Lipman and Kravitz when, after almost a century, Freidl's stone had just been returned. Perhaps it was his way of coping with the enormity of a moment he had spent so much of his life anticipating. She uncovered the stone so he could finally see it.

He began to rock from the waist up. *Boruch atah Adonoi, Eloheinu melech ha-oylom ha-Tov v'ha-Mayteev.* He rocked. He threw his whole body into his prayer, overtaken by his lament.

Ellen shivered, anxious that he was preparing himself, bolstering his will to let Freidl go. She realized too that he now probably saw the Angel of Death as close as the end of his nose, as he had said. "Rafael, what do the words on the stone mean?"

Rafael, oblivious to her, continued to rock and pray.

"Rafael!"

Startled, he opened his eyes.

"I can't read the Hebrew," she pleaded with him.

He became still and pointed to the words on the stone. "*'She died on the fourteenth day of the month of Nisan in the year 665.'* This would be for the Jewish calendar year 5665, 1905 to you. He continued his translation, pointing to where the corresponding Hebrew words appeared. *'May her soul be bound up in the knot of life.'*" One of his hands began to tremble, then the other.

Ellen was afraid he might be having a stroke. "Rafael, what's the matter?" she said. "Marek, help me get him to his chair."

With one sweep of his arm, Marek grabbed the chair and steadied Rafael so that he could sit down. "I will get you a glass of water," he said, and went to the kitchen.

Ellen kneeled before Rafael, and he leaned toward her, his torso almost collapsed over the arm of the chair.

"Her way back to the grave, to rest with her body, God has blocked with cut stones, as it is written in *Eicha* — Lamentations."

He raised his right hand and dropped it, dejected. "Another year has come. We are nearing the ninth day of the month of *Av,* Tisha Bov, when a Jew reads Eicha."

Ellen swallowed hard. Was she not a Jew because she did not know, had never heard of Tisha Bov? She promised herself to read Eicha, Lamentations, when she returned to Kraków. She looked at Rafael and imagined death itself was on his breath. It had deepened his voice so much that it was difficult for her to understand him.

"Please, don't go," she begged.

Marek stood still in the kitchen doorway, as if he knew he should not intrude upon them.

Ellen reached for the glass of water he held in his hand. He gave it to her and retreated to the kitchen.

Rafael took a sip. It seemed to revive him slightly. "Do not forget what you owe to Freidl," he said.

"What should I do for her then?"

He closed his eyes. "Once, she told me, her father came to her, on the echo of a ram's horn. It passed her so fast, like a comet. He said, *Be vigilant and await the coming of Aaron's sister, Miriam. Return her timbrel, and she will make an opening for you to return.*" He cleared his throat several times. Then he opened his eyes and gazed at Ellen.

"Freidl showed me something in the Torah about Miriam," she said, hoping to engage him, to bring him back. "I've been reciting it to myself so often, I've memorized it. It goes, *Then Miriam the prophetess, Aaron's sister, took a timbrel in her hand, and all the women went out after her in dance with timbrels. And Miriam chanted for them: Sing to the Lord, for He has triumphed gloriously. / Horse and driver He has hurled into the sea.*" She looked at him hopefully.

Rafael made an effort to smile. "Years ago," he said quietly, "Freidl asked me, Why Miriam? I had no answers for her. For years, I studied the holy books. I asked, Why was Miriam so important for her in the eyes of God? I thought maybe it had to do with your grandfather hurling Jan Nowak, the horse and driver, yeh, into the sea of death." He shrugged. "But then you, Ellen Leiber, granddaughter of Itzik the Faithless, arrived in Poland to dance." He cast his hands upward weakly, in what seemed sheer amazement. "Who can understand God's plan? To dance!"

Rafael put his hands on the table and spread his arthritic fingers. "You are her Miriam." He managed to give her a wink.

But Ellen was skeptical. "Do you really think Freidl will be returned to her grave with a dance and a timbrel?"

"I do not *think* it. I can only *believe* it," he said. "What else can I believe, with what I have seen in my life?"

Ellen looked at the stone, frustrated to tearfulness at not knowing what to do. From the corner of her eye she could see Marek's shocked expression.

"I think you must join the stones again," Marek said. "I think you must bring back the top half from America."

Rafael sniffed. "Advice from the *shaygets?*" he said. "In America the stone is safe."

But Marek insisted. "It does not belong in America. It belongs in Poland, where she belonged."

"And what will protect it from the vandals? The bones and remnants of Zokof's Jews?"

"We will protect it. It will be safe," Marek assured Rafael. "We will talk to the city fathers. They should know about it. They should make this their memorial too, like the one in the town square."

"But who's going to make a memorial of Freidl's stone?" Ellen asked.

"I know the man who can do this," Marek said. "My family knows him. He is a stonemason, and he worked on the Jewish memorial at Kazimierz Dolny a few years ago. People say he is a Jew because he does not go to Mass. Like a Jew he goes on Fridays, they say." He paused, looked away.

"What's the matter?" Ellen asked.

"I remember my father defended him. He said, 'We all know Łukasz Rakowski is a Catholic. People should not blacken his name.'" He glanced quickly at Rafael, and away again. "I never thought about it, that what my father said is an insult to someone who is not Catholic, maybe even to Łukasz. Because Łukasz never said yes or no. He just rubbed his hands, the way he does." Marek shook his head. "I do not know if Łukasz is a Jew or a Pole, but I think if I ask him, he will make a monument for Freidl that will show people she is someone important."

Rafael looked appalled at the idea. "You want to invite people to come here, to stand on the graves like a park?"

"Like a sacred, remembered place," Marek said. "Have you been to Kazimierz Dolny?"

"I do not go to those places."

"They made a memorial wall with hundreds of broken Jewish gravestones climbing the hill. In one place it is split up and down with a crack — for the sudden destruction of the Jewish community. When you step through the crack, behind the wall, you are in a deep forest where there are the old graves, normal graves." He suddenly seemed aware of his animation and of Ellen and Rafael looking at him. "Anyway, Łukasz Rakowski will know how to make something special for you."

But Rafael was not convinced. "First, if the stone from America is brought here, you will have two stones for Głowacki to steal. I think it is safer in America." He stroked his beard worriedly; then he seemed to give up. "I do not know what the right place is. Even Freidl herself does not know."

"It would make Freidl's memorial whole again," Ellen ventured. "My grandfather broke it. I should fix it. For you, Rafael, it would be like repairing a torn oissherenishen."

Rafael glanced at the cutouts on his wall and seemed to consider this. "I do not know," he said. "Maybe you are right that we should make a repair. This is the Jewish way, yes? But I must tell you that first the cemetery must have a wall."

"Why?" Marek asked. "There aren't any of those people you called *Kohanes* here anymore."

Ellen was relieved he wasn't arguing that there were still Jews around.

"Without a wall, it is not a Jewish cemetery," Rafael responded. "Without a wall, no one can be buried there."

"But all the people are already buried there," Marek said.

Rafael sighed. "All but one."

No one moved. Each of them looked at the stone.

"Then *I* will build a wall. You will tell me how," Marek said.

"You will?" Ellen could hardly believe he was willing to put in that kind of effort.

"It is better that I make the wall. For Głowacki and the people here, it is better." Marek looked at Rafael. Then he crossed the room and sat down with his clasped hands bridging his knees. He bent his head, as if in supplication. "Before, when we were in the cemetery and I talked about my uncle Leszek, who said our angels watch over us. I did not say that when he told me the Jewish ghosts are in the trees, with the birds, and in the sky before a storm, I said, 'Uncle Leszek that is because God does not let Jews into heaven. They killed our Lord.' I remember how sure I was of this. I was so sure, that I was not sympathetic when he said to me, 'All the dead are sacred.' I would like to make this wall, Mr. Bergson, to my uncle Leszek's memory."

The two men exchanged discreet, respectful looks. Large raindrops again began to tap against the windowpanes, and the room became dappled with sudden changes of light.

Ellen looked at Rafael. "It's time for us to go," she said. "I'll be back soon. I'll write you to tell you when."

Marek rose, still obviously upset.

They said their good-byes with restraint. "Do not forget Freidl," Rafael said. "And take the gravestone with you today. It is right that you should make a repair."

43

ELLEN AND MAREK HEADED WEST OUT OF ZOKOF, THROUGH streets of houses fenced with chain link, each with their lacy curtain sheers hanging like a national flag across the front windows. Ellen wondered what remained of the town her grandfather had known. The blotches of grass riddled with footpaths? The slammed-on room additions of brick, stucco, wood, and stone? Her ancestral home depressed her. Her only real regret about leaving was Rafael.

When they'd parted, he'd walked them to the threshold of his house and had stood anxiously, clasping and unclasping his knotted hands. "Elleneh," he'd said. "Write and tell me what's what."

She'd kept herself from offering him the impropriety of an embrace. "I'll write you," she promised again. "Don't worry."

He'd shrugged and turned to Marek. "Don't worry. What does this mean?" Then, with all the awkwardness of a man long out of the habit of hand-shaking, he stuck out his hand. "Marek, it was a blessing, what you did today," he said earnestly. "Our rabbis taught that by their deeds all men are equal in the eyes of God, and by their good deeds they bring God's presence into the world." He nodded, his eyes full of feeling. "Today, you brought God's presence into the world. You are a good boy, a mensch."

Marek had taken Rafael's hand in his own, then clasped his other hand on top, pumping it warmly. "Thank you, Mr. Bergson," he said quietly.

To Ellen, the moment had felt suspended and holy.

"Come back when you can," Rafael had said to them both. "My house has an open door." He'd seemed almost cheery then, but the mention of his door had only heightened Ellen's sense of his vulnerability.

Twenty minutes later, they were on the two-lane highway approaching Radom. The rain had stopped. The sun needled its way through the clouds. Zokof had disappeared behind them, its western border marked only by a line of trees at the end of the plain. Ellen slid the "For-a-Girl Tune" cassette off the dashboard and held it protectively between her palms.

"I see you are thinking," Marek said carefully.

She tilted the tip of the cassette to her chin. "There were holes in the blanket on his bed," she said, more to herself than to him. "And those sheets. I have to get him new bedding."

"He does not need a new blanket in July," Marek said. "In the winter, he has an eiderdown cover. Everyone has such a cover." He glanced at her and, perhaps, seeing her consternation, softened his tone. "This is how people in the countryside live. It is a difficult life. You are looking with American eyes. To them, it is no problem."

Ellen didn't feel like arguing. She had only mentioned the bedding as a passing thought. "I guess I just can't help being an American." She sighed.

Playfully, he chucked her under the chin. "I like that," he said.

The day had begun to take its toll on her. She closed her eyes to rest, but the more she thought about it, the more it bothered her that Rafael should not even hope for a new blanket, that he should be content, in this day and age, to ruin his eyes reading Talmud by kerosene lamp, that he should have to put up with the difficulties of his kitchen stove, even if other people brought him wood and coal. She pushed the cassette into the recorder.

At the first rhythmic notes of the tune, Marek began to tap his fingers on the wheel. Ellen opened her eyes and found him looking at her, as if trying to gauge her mood. She tickled his ear.

For the next few miles, they talked about Kraków's summer concerts, using any excuse to brush against each other's skin, to stroke each other's knees and arms and shoulders. Soon they drifted into a comfortable silence. Ellen played with a lock of hair at the back of Marek's neck. The tune was still playing. She listened to it more closely, certain that Marek's arrangement would play well to a young audience. The tense rhythm was modern, edgy. It provoked a certain anxiety she liked. She admired how he'd arranged the original tune to appear high above the musical landscape, like the comet on which Freidl's father's voice rode. How had he caught that sense of something bright sinking into the fray until it disappeared? She stopped the tape. "When we were at the Ariel Café, you said you heard prayers in the notes. What made you think of that?"

He seemed surprised by the question. "I listened to the music."

"But what makes it a prayer?" she insisted. "What takes it to that next step, beyond something merely beautiful?"

He laughed nervously, as if he was afraid she might mock him. "It is like complete pouring out." He squinted and shook his head.

Ellen sensed, once again, that there was something impoverished about the atheist worldview with which she'd been raised. She turned the tape player back on and realized, not without shame, that she envied what he knew about faith, and that she was jealous of the authenticity he'd accomplished with music she had more right to own than he did. She looked out the window, realizing that her dance would have to be poured out of her, and that the pouring would require resistance to her natural urge to think.

They passed a roadside shrine of a blue-robed Virgin Mary decorated with flowers and long ribbons. *Primitive,* her mother would have called it, meaning *colorful, delightful to us,* but ultimately *childish.* Her father would have agreed. Now Ellen saw instead an adornment that marked the transformation of an earthly place into a doorway to God, and she understood it. She thought of the other ribbon, the one that had once tied back the copper hair of her great-aunt Hindeleh. It now lay between the pages of her little blue prayer book, hidden as her grandpa Isaac had kept it. She dug her nails into a seam on the armrest, angered by her grandfather's secrecy, by his refusal to listen to anyone but himself. But for this, he would have heard the tune and Freidl's prayer — *Every blade of grass has its own guardian star in the firmament which strikes it and commands it to grow! Let a spark be lit in him and let him grow!*

He had an *uncooked* soul, Freidl had said. Ellen refused to allow this as an excuse. He could have listened. He could have grown. He could have spared Freidl the pain of waiting through two generations to return to her grave in peace. She was sickened by the thought that her own inability to hear the prayers in the tune suggested she was just as uncooked as her grandfather and father. "Before I leave Poland, I'm going to finish Freidl's memorial," she said.

Marek's eyes didn't waver from the road. "When are you leaving?"

"I can't stay too long after the performance. I have a grant to do a new piece this fall." The words slid out so quickly. Not until she glanced at him, saw his pursed lips, did she regret having spoken so casually. "Sorry," she said. "I'm not looking forward to going."

He looked at her. "Yes, well, I never thought you are the kind of American who would like to live here in Poland. The Americans I see who stay in Kraków are mostly confused. They think being here, behind the old Iron Curtain, is enough to make them interesting to people back home. But what is that, Ellen, to be someplace without a purpose, only because it might be more unusual than Paris?" He shrugged dismissively, in a manner that reminded her of Rafael.

"Maybe you'll come visit me in New York," she suggested, hoping he would promise her right then that he would.

He twisted a piece of loose thread off his shirt cuff and nodded. "Maybe. I would like that."

She wasn't sure if this was just talk or if they were making a plan. She looked at his musician's hands, so delicate on the wheel. It would be no different for him in New York than it would be for her in Kraków. If he came to stay he'd be just another foreigner, driving a cab, with an occasional music gig. And even that was doubtful. What did a Polish klezmer player have to offer in a city of real Jewish musicians? And how would she see him in America, where his Polishness would be highlighted? Did it really not matter to her now that he wasn't Jewish, as good as he was, and as committed to her? Her enthusiasm for his visit became confused, and she sank into sadness. She stared at his hands, remembering how good they'd felt when he'd spread them over her naked back and down her sides, how well those fingers knew her. She would miss the way he handled her, his confidence in bed, his smell, his lips at her neck.

They arrived at the hotel. Marek parked the Fiat. "I hate that I have to work tonight," he said.

Ellen held his head between her hands. "Come upstairs."

They walked hand in hand down the street and up to her room, where he closed the curtains on the side that faced the apartment across the narrow street.

Ellen went to him, put her arms around his neck, and kissed him. They made love until evening.

"What will you do tonight, after I am gone?" he asked.

Ellen sighed. "I'll work. I have to. There's so much to put together. I have all these elements, but they're like body parts. They're not connected. They're not alive. You know what I mean?"

He smiled and brushed a stray curl from her forehead. "What are your elements?"

"I have the tune, of course, and Freidl, Miriam's timbrel from the Bible, and proverbs." She sighed again, this time to allay her growing anxiety, and rolled over on her back. "There's a line that keeps floating into my head. I don't know where it comes from, if I read it or whatever. It goes, '*They have hardened their hearts to each other, like Pharaoh in Egypt, each seeing and feeling only their own martyrdom.*'"

Marek turned on his side to her. "There is only one way for martyred peoples to care about each other."

"How?"

He smiled and placed his hand on her left breast. They both felt her heartbeat. He took her hand and placed it on his chest. "Here, in the spaces between words, where there is God."

She slapped him gently. "You're a hopeless romantic."

He laughed. "Of course. I am Polish. We are romantics."

When the hejnał struck eight, Marek said he had to leave. "I will call you," he promised.

They got out of bed, and she held him close.

After he'd left, she dozed off again. She had an image of Marek, his eyes closed, performing the tune on the violin, praying. It woke her up. She threw on a robe, took out her notebook, and wrote down one word. *Pour.* Then she opened her nightstand drawer, took out the Tanakh, and turned to the book of Zechariah. She took out her great-aunt Hindeleh's ribbon and ran it through her fingers, scanning the page until she came to a passage where God said, "Does anyone scorn a day of small beginnings?" She remembered how Rafael had recited this question at the lamppost in the cemetery.

She fingered the page, knowing she had found the title of her piece.

*T*he next day, before she went to the studio, Ellen called her mother in Cambridge.

"Mom, I need you to send me the broken gravestone Dad kept in his study," she said.

"Why, dear? I thought we would display it in the living room, in honor of Dad's trip to Poland."

Ellen wasn't sure how much to explain. She knew she had to be cautious when speaking to her mother about her relationship with everything to do with Zokof, and that to mention religion would only lead to argument. She didn't want to have to defend opinions she wasn't sure she was committed to. But she was certain about the gravestone. "It doesn't belong in our living room, Mom," she said. "It's disrespectful."

"Then why was it given to Dad?"

"Rafael thought it was safer in America, but he and I have talked about it now and I think Dad would agree it belongs here."

There was a short pause on the other end of the line. "Well, all right, if that's what you've decided. What would you like me to do?"

Ellen appreciated her mother's respect in not arguing any further. "Can you FedEx it so it gets here ASAP? And be sure it's shipped at their highest level of care, whatever it costs."

"Okay," her mother promised.

When she got off the phone, Ellen pulled out her book on Jewish gravestones and began to consider symbols she wanted to add to the gravestone's new center. The text, she hoped, would come to her when she began to work with the stonemason.

All through the week Ellen worked on her dance. She found that the more she put her notebook aside and let the images she had written there flow through her head and into her body, the more the piece seemed to organize itself. When she had a fair number of choreographed sections in place, she set up a meeting with Pronaszko. The piece wasn't finished. She just hoped that what she had assembled would hold.

"The dance is called *A Day of Small Beginnings*," she said. "I took the title from the Book of Zechariah. God asks, 'Does anyone scorn a day of small beginnings?'" She glanced at him quickly and decided against elaborating further.

He listened, head bowed thoughtfully, as she told him she'd be using Polish and Yiddish proverbs along with ambient sounds, also Polish folk and jazz music in addition to the klezmer tune he'd heard at the studio. "The piece is in four parts," she said. "It juxtaposes Polish and Jewish images and evokes the difficulties of the relationship between the two peoples."

He nodded in his measured way, seemingly undisturbed by the subject, as he had been when she'd introduced it to him weeks before.

She was nervous. "I have musicians," she said. "They're the only ones who can do the klezmer tune."

"That is fine, if their price is reasonable. I like what I am hearing. You have something nicely elusive here," he said, fluttering his fingers. "But with substance."

She tried to suppress her almost giddy relief that he was pleased.

Straightening his back, Pronaszko raised his head imperiously. "You have read the Book of Zechariah," he said. "You must remember the rest."

Ellen had not expected him to be familiar with the Bible.

"In Zechariah," he said, "God promises there will be other people, citizens of great cities, who will come to seek Him in Jerusalem. 'Ten men of nations of every language, He says, will take Jews by the sleeve and say, we want to go with you, since God is with you.'"

He eyed her like a prankster and said, "When I was a young man, I studied for the priesthood. But . . . Terpsichore seduced me instead." He sat back and laughed, enjoying her surprise. "I was always taken by those words from Zechariah. They made for much discussion among the seminarians after the war, when the Jews were almost gone. Now tell me, what will we need for sets?" He lifted his chin expectantly.

She was tempted to ask what the seminarians had said, tempted to tell him why the phrase appealed to her, but she did not want her creative confidence rocked by the notion that he knew more than she did about the very phrase that would ignite her work. She told him she wanted to perform the piece in Szeroka Square, and he suggested they make a date with his set designer.

He pushed back his chair. "I think this is a day of *good beginnings.*" He smiled. "The rest I will see with the company. In these next weeks, as we begin to work, I promise you I will be very hard on you and the company. But now, when we are still on speaking terms, I think it is a good time for me to say I believe I made a good choice in you." He rose.

"Thanks," she said, hoping she did not appear as overwhelmed as she felt. "We can begin next Monday."

"Monday is good." He shook her hand as they parted this time, like colleagues.

I watch and am astonished. Is this a midrash in dance she wants to make of our story, a teasing out of meaning from Torah? I do not understand. But in my blue emptiness I feel a change, movement like the rise of a wave.

44

THE GRAVESTONE, WRAPPED PRECIOUSLY WELL, ARRIVED UN-
harmed from Cambridge. For a long time, Ellen held it in her lap, tracing
the Hebrew letters she could not read, wondering if the words inscribed
on its rough gray surface did justice to the woman it memorialized. The
stone was heavy, roughly two inches thick and about two and a half feet
high. She leaned it against the wall on top of her bureau and studied it for
a long time, regretting that she had not paid it more attention after her father's death.

That evening, she called Marek at the Ariel Café to tell him the news.
"We need to meet with your stonemason," she said.

"I have already spoken to him. He was very interested to do this work.
You must show him what it is you want him to do."

"I'm working on the design, and I'll have the text ready soon too. But,
Marek, what about the cemetery wall? When will you be able to build it?"

"After your performance, I will have more time." There was a pause on
the line. "You understand, I must work. I cannot be there every day." He
spoke haltingly, as if he would have preferred to promise her it could be
done in a week or two, as she might have wanted to hear.

Ellen had a bad feeling that rebuilding a stone wall around a cemetery
could take months. "What if we get people to help? What about Stefan or
Pawel?"

"Maybe. But I do not think they can come often. And they may not want
to. It is difficult to ask musicians to do work that is not good for the hands.
That is their living."

"I understand," she said, appreciating that it was his living too. "You
know, maybe I should call the Lauder Foundation in Warsaw about it.
They might have volunteers for this kind of thing." She felt better for having thought of it, especially since her father had been the one who had suggested the foundation to her. "It's worth a shot."

"No, no. I promised Rafael I will build the wall, and I will build it."

"But it could take a long time, Marek. I have to get back to New York for the fall."

"It will be done. I promise."

It was clear he did not want her to question him any further about how he was going to accomplish this. She decided it was best to trust him. Before going to sleep, she sat at the end of her bed and stared again at the gravestone. That night, it appeared in her dreams, but when she awoke, it was the space between the two pieces that she thought about. She imagined the upper piece suspended in a frame over the lower one, with some kind of mortar filling the gap between them.

The following night she dreamed she was standing under a dome formed by huge gravestones. She could see the blue sky through the cracks, and Freidl, alone, outside. Ellen ran to her and reached to her through the cracks. But the stones were thicker than her arms were long. She awoke, distraught.

*O*ver the weekend, she met Marek and the stonemason Łukasz Rakowski at a milk bar on Grodzka Street in the Central District. He was a heavyset man, short, with a head of thick hair that rose at an angle to his head. His palms and fingers were callused but warm, and reassuring to Ellen when they shook hands.

She laid out the sketch she had made of the top and bottom halves of the gravestone, separated by a cut-out area in which, she explained to him, a new stone should *float*. "I'll need you to engrave the new stone with text and to carve these symbols," she said, pointing to her drawings. "Can you do that?"

Łukasz studied the drawing and rubbed his hands together. Then he touched the page and traced rough shapes with his thick fingers, as if trying to get the feel of what she wanted.

"Her name is Miriam?" he asked Marek in Polish.

Ellen understood the question. Stunned, she asked him how he had guessed the name.

"Usually, the musical instruments are for Miriam," he said, pointing to the timbrel Ellen had drawn.

Ellen didn't need to ask him if he was Jewish. She looked at him. He met her gaze briefly and looked back at the drawing.

"Tell him I would be honored if he would do the work on this gravestone for us," she said to Marek. "Tell him I'll send him the text in the mail next week. Then if he'll send me back a draft of what the whole thing will look like, we'll be on our way. But tell him I need it to be finished by the first week of September. I'm leaving on the fifth."

Marek glanced at her before translating.

Łukasz agreed to her requirements. They came to terms about the price, and he rolled up her drawing to take with him.

"I'm going to miss the gravestone," she told Marek.

"This gives you reason to return to Poland." He smiled.

"Oh, I'll be back to Poland."

"It is a difficult place to leave," he said.

She realized there were several conflicting ways to interpret this remark. Such were the delicacies of the nation, she thought.

When Łukasz had left them, Marek seemed at a loss. He asked her how *the dancing,* as he put it, was going.

Ellen, not wishing to revisit the subject of her leaving, rubbed her forehead with the palm of her hand. "I made the mistake of asking the company what they thought of the tune when I played it for them. You know what they said? 'We're doing a Jew's dance?' It seems they don't like the subject. 'This is not what we're thinking about in Poland today,' they said." Her eyes hurt from having stayed up three nights, working and reworking the piece, sliding in and out of the feeling that it was losing its flow, its balance, maybe its whole point.

"Maybe you could have them for a coffee," Marek suggested. "Maybe talk could help out the situation."

She shook her head. "I don't have time for group therapy here. I'm up to my neck working with the sets and lighting and everything. You have no idea how much time all this takes. They're just jerks." Her voice cracked. She hadn't realized she was this upset. She put her head down on the table so no one could see the tears that had sprung from her eyes faster than she could stop them.

Marek reached over and stroked her hair.

Ellen balanced her chin on the backs of her hands and looked up at him. "The truth is I don't know what's upsetting me more, them or me. I am making them do this Jewish dance, and what do I know about it? I feel like a fake, like I'm using other people's information, pasting it all together. I have scraps of paper all over my bed with elements I need to get into the dance, but I can't choreograph what's in my heart, because my heart isn't organized and it doesn't know where it's going." She exhaled against the tightness that was corseting her torso. "I don't know how to tie it all together. It's scaring me. Every night I think of Freidl and how I can't let her down, and I can't sleep. My heart pounds like I'm going to have an attack. It's crazy. That's how my father died." She looked up. Her tears puddled and overflowed over the lower rims of her eyes.

Marek wiped them away with his thumbs so that anyone looking at them would have thought he was merely caressing her cheeks. "Maybe you should talk to God," he said.

She looked at him as if he were mad.

"Just talk, like to a friend. Tell Him everything, even the things you are afraid to say out loud, especially those. And do not stop talking, even when you do not think there is anything left to say. Because then you will begin to say it again, and it will be more clear. God can help you, if you let Him."

She wasn't ready to accept this, even from him. It sounded like something a missionary would say. She stuck with the problem at hand. "If I give them exact instructions, they're fine," she said, sniffing. "You know, like *lean out, keep your shoulders down,* that sort of thing. But that's not enough. They're supposed to be setting a mood. They give me blank faces."

He nodded understandingly.

"So finally, I lost it with them. I said, it doesn't matter if this isn't your subject, you make it yours."

He got up, came around behind her, and massaged her neck and shoulders.

"Thanks," she said, even though a stinging shiver had just run from a vertebra in her neck to her tailbone. The day was coming when they would part. Her mouth tasted like chalk.

"Then we rehearsed and I got so impatient with them, I think I just made them feel ashamed that they were terrible dancers." She took a sip of water.

Marek returned to his seat. "If you know how you want them to dance, then you must insist they follow you. That is all." He looked serious now. "Polish people are different from Americans. There is nothing we will not argue about all night, all day, from every side. But when it comes to doing something, making something, yes? Well, then we have trouble. Then you see, we are all argument, no action, no discipline, no organization. Any Pole will tell you that, all night, all day, from every side."

His grin surprised her.

"So when an American says to us, make this yours, be brave, just do it, we come full stop. We want to do our best. But most of the time, we do not know what to do, how to begin. So we do nothing. And then we may discuss how we are doing nothing. We make promises we do not keep. Then we make like we are heroes, defending our doing nothing. After this, we tell you, poor American, you cannot possibly understand us, because the problem is so Polish." He was laughing now.

How could she be upset when he had such beautiful white teeth?

"Come, we must have a drink," he said. "That is so Polish too."

They left the milk bar and went back to her room, where Marek produced from his shoulder bag a bottle of vodka, with a long blade of grass in it. She took out two glasses, and they drank to dancers and musicians and Poles and Americans. He drank much more than she did, much more than anyone she knew would drink. And somewhere between his becoming slightly high and too close to drunk, she again began to doubt how well she really knew him, even if he could step out of his Polishness enough to see it from her side.

They spent the night together, but he fell asleep soon after they got into bed. She lay awake in the dark, turned her back to him, and buried her disappointment in him by visualizing the dance from beginning to end. She kept rearranging elements, adding and deleting parts, but it was the content that bothered her. There was a lack of focus she did not know how to fix.

That night she dreamed of her grandfather. He was a figure in a painting, posed in his upholstered armchair, his face turned toward the outline of a window in the Brownsville apartment. The rest of the canvas was unfilled. She awoke, disturbed at having seen him so flat and unfinished. A question came to her, as if someone had given it to her for dictation, and she wrote it down in her notebook: *What did we lose, what was left behind, once Miriam's timbrel stopped shaking and we found ourselves alone in the land of milk and honey?*

In the morning, Marek awoke full of apologies for having abandoned her the night before. "We Poles drink too much. It is our curse."

She was beginning to find the Polish drinking excuse tiresome. But he was so sweet, finding her robe for her and putting it on with many kisses along her arms and back and neck. The way he looked directly at her, smiling as he brushed back her loose curls, made her want to play. When he turned to get his shirt, she edged herself up on the bed and jumped on his back, laughing as he grabbed her calves and trotted her around the room. "Hey, don't even think about dropping me!"

He did drop her. Right on the bed, where she lay on her back, legs askew, robe open, with the belt still tied, rather uselessly, around her waist, looking up at a man who so clearly desired her. "Come here," she said. He climbed on top of her and pressed himself to her, and into her.

Later they had breakfast at a café down the street and parted soon after. He told her that he didn't know when he would be finished working that day. "I'm painting someone's apartment," he said. She had had no idea this was how he supported himself. There were so many things about his life she realized she didn't know. She gathered her dance bag and walked to the studio through Rynek Główny. It was already crowded with tourists.

All that day she was alternately enticed by the thought of Marek, roller in hand, reaching upward, exposing the smooth white flesh of his side, and by the image of her grandfather in her dream. She took out her notebook and reread the sentence she'd written down. It seemed obscure and strange. Yet the phrase *alone in the land of milk and honey* so perfectly described her grandfather. It evoked all the loneliness she'd always known had resided in him, permanent as his chair by the window. She spent the morning trying to work it into the dance and became irritable when she couldn't find a place for it. The more she tried to force it, the less it worked and the more aware she became that she was running out of time to keep reimagining the piece.

That afternoon, the company seemed fairly pleased when she announced they would be dancing to Górecki's Third Symphony. She told them they would be carrying long dowels hung with traditional Polish religious banners. She asked for suggestions on how the banners and the costumes should look and how they could move with them.

"We could make them with white cloth and very tall, like we do at home," Ewa suggested.

Ellen tried to feed this spark of interest. "Do you know any traditional Polish dances?" she asked Piotr. "Come on," she urged. "Show me something."

Reluctantly, Piotr unfolded his long, slight frame and shuffled to the middle of the studio floor. He splayed his fingers over his hips and took several defiant sidesteps to the right. With his left hand raised above his head, he began a series of turns, knees bent, his neck tipped back at a proud angle. Picking up speed, he circled the room and added a low, controlled kick, which reminded Ellen of the Russian Moiseyev dancers she'd seen as a child. The dancers began to clap out the beat.

Ellen joined them with enthusiasm. "We have to use this," she said. Her notes for this section of the dance were pages long, crammed with unconnected ideas and tangential references. Now she saw how much better it would be to simply present a Polish dance, done in unison.

Piotr finished with a triumphant, short bow, and a small, self-satisfied smile.

*B*y the end of rehearsal that day, Ellen had begun to feel more hopeful.

Andrzej remained behind in the studio. "Where is this from, what you are choreographing here?" he asked her.

Ellen wasn't sure she really wanted to get into a whole discussion about it.

He pursed his lips, perhaps sensing her impatience. "I want to know how you make your choices for the dance. This is what I want to learn." With unexpected hesitancy, he added, "If you will tell me."

Ellen wasn't sure if he was trying to understand choreography in general or her method in particular. "Don't you ask Pronaszko questions like these?"

He clucked his tongue. "Kostek does not encourage me in choreography. He wants me more for himself." He looked off long enough for Ellen to figure out that Kostek was a diminutive for Konstantin, Pronaszko's first name. "It is more difficult for us in Kraków than in Warsaw, where I am from," Andrzej said.

She understood that by *difficult* he meant being homosexual, but he shrugged off her question about how awkward his involvement with Pronaszko must be.

"He is not interested in training someone who might try to take his place someday," he said.

She was surprised at how openly he expressed his bitterness. "Maybe you'll have to go somewhere else to do choreography then."

He did not respond.

"You could go back to Warsaw."

"Yes, but I want to learn about modern dance, and Pronaszko is the best. This is not America. We do not have so many choices here for companies."

"I have to tell you," she said sympathetically, "you're the last person in this company I ever thought I would get to like."

His expression softened. "I know I am a pain in the ass. The company thinks so too. But with my English, I am a useful pain in the ass."

Ellen raised a skeptical eyebrow. "You know, it wasn't so long ago that I didn't think you were such a useful pain in the ass either."

He looked down, like a boy expecting a scolding.

She saw he didn't realize she was joking and felt sorry for him. "Andrzej," she said cautiously, "what do *you* think of my using this subject for the dance?"

"You should not pay attention to what they say," he answered quickly. "They are thinking about the new Poland, yes, but they must know that the old Poland will always be with us too." He shook his head. "Actually, you are lucky, because now it is the fashion to like Jewish things. People our age are becoming curious about them. They think of them more as part of the past. You are the first Jew some of the people in this company have met. They do not know what to say to you."

Ellen was completely taken aback. "You mean I'm a novelty?"

He nodded. "You must understand, it is difficult for us to appreciate who are the Jews. In Warsaw, I grew up in an apartment that was built on a mound. My mother told me this was once the Ghetto. When the war was over, it was less expensive to build over the rubble and the remains of the Jews. So that is what they did."

Ellen was appalled. "I have to tell you, this isn't a normal way to behave toward people who used to live among you."

He nodded. "You are right, of course. What can I say? But that is the way it was. All of Warsaw was a ruin. Rubble everywhere. They had too much to rebuild. It is different with us now, truly. In Warsaw, we have a Yiddish Theater, and almost everyone acting in this theater is Polish. People ask, Who comes here? Who understands this language anymore? But it is not just tourists in the audience, or even the old Jews who know this language. Polish people come. They want to hear these plays and this language. It is part of our history, you see? You cannot separate it."

"But where do you go with that? There are no more Jews here."

He shook his finger at her. "That is not true. I meet Jews here today. When I was a child I had a half-Jewish friend. His parents were very unusual because they raised him Jewish. His mother is the Jew, and he said that makes him Jewish. But he was unhappy because it is very difficult not to be Catholic in our country. He is very beautiful, and the girls always liked him, except there were no Jewish girls. His parents were going to move to Israel so he could marry. But then he met people at a place in Grzybowski Square, most of them half-Jewish also, or with a grandparent who is Jewish. They have a rabbi who comes and talks to them and helps them. So it is better for him now, and I think he is much happier. He has a girlfriend, a half-Jew, but the right half, he says." Andrzej shrugged, with a kind of resigned sadness.

Ellen put her hand on his shoulder. "Thank you for telling me all this. You know, you could choreograph a hell of a dance about you and your friend," she said.

He smiled at her, in his old flirtatious way. "Then I think today you should accept my offer to have coffee."

"I accept," she said, and they went down the stairs of the old building together.

45

*I*N THE DAYS THAT FOLLOWED, SUMMER HEAT AND A GRIMY HU-
midity enveloped Kraków, enervating even the tourists, who could be seen
dragging themselves through Old Town from site to requisite site.

In the studio, Ellen ran on adrenaline and nerves, impervious to the
weather, instructing the company with such determination the dancers
seemed disinclined, or simply too overheated, to challenge her. Most after-
noons, the air was thick with the smell of sweat, which made large spreading stains on their leotards and tights. But she drove them on, demanding
precision and energy in their every movement.

Pronaszko came by every day to watch them work, but he refused
Ellen's invitations to stay for an entire rehearsal. "When you have something substantial to show me, you will let me know," he told her.

With the performance date approaching, she thought such patience
risky and out of character for a man who had insisted on a tight schedule
for finishing the sets, props, costumes, and all her lighting designs. Con-
struction had already begun on the simple, stable tree structure the two of
them had drafted with the set designer. On edge from keeping track of
these details and from the constant adjustments she was making in her choreography, Ellen only hoped Pronaszko's relaxed attitude indicated confidence in her abilities. She gave herself a week's deadline to finalize the
piece, then took Pronaszko aside. "I'm going to have the musicians here
for rehearsal next Tuesday. With the live sound, I think you'll get a feel of
the piece. We'll do a run-through of Part Two."

Pronaszko ran his hands through his hair. "Done," he said happily.

Ellen felt as if she'd just thrown herself out the window.

That night, she took the tram to the Ariel Café and met with the musicians. Paweł and Stefan were both wildly excited about performing for a
dance company. "We will bring our performance clothes with us," they
promised eagerly.

"No. No," Ellen said, hoping not to sound so alarmed by the suggestion that they would take offense. "Wear your regular clothes."

"But what will we wear at the performance?"

"We're going to get you black jeans, white T-shirts, and black baseball caps." She didn't have the heart to tell them their sentimental Polish ideas of Jewish dress were *uncool,* and that she wasn't interested in reinforcing their notions of mythological Jews in her piece. She assumed they would figure out for themselves that the caps looked like modern yarmulkes. Marek had put his arm around her and said, "You are the director. We'll wear what you think is best." She'd laughed, he had kissed her cheerfully, and they'd all had a shot of kosher vodka.

*T*he following Tuesday, Marek, Pawel, and Stefan appeared at the studio door with a bass, a clarinet, and the electric violin Marek had suggested they use because he thought the sound would carry better outside. The whole company was there, rehearsing. Ellen was nervous, for herself and for the musicians. "Come in," she said, hoping to sound welcoming. She introduced the musicians to the company and asked Marek to explain to them why he was interested in Jewish music.

She watched him speak to them in Polish, and noticed that with him, they asked questions. She didn't know if this was because they were now more absorbed in the dance piece or if his commitment to it, as a Pole, held more weight with them. Henryk spoke up fervently. Marek responded, and the discussion took on a heated quality. She saw that he was already at home among them, while she, in her folding chair, felt awkward in her inability to participate. They all had so many opinions, she thought, none of which they ever expressed to her. Their distrust, or whatever it was, pained her, and her inability to follow what they were saying made her feel, once again, the frustrations of the deaf.

When the dancers and musicians had finished talking, she took Marek aside. The dancers began warming up. Stefan and Pawel were getting out their instruments. "What did you say?" she asked him.

"I said I was trained in classical music, but I discovered Jewish music quite by accident and now it is the music I love most. I said I think of it as Polish music and that the more I play it, the more it is evolving into something not really all Jewish anymore, and not really Polish, but something between." He winked at her. "I said that to me, this music is a sacred king-dom. Henryk did not understand this." He shrugged. "But I told them that the story of the tune we're playing is very special to you."

"What did you tell them?" Ellen asked anxiously.

Marek picked up the electric violin and began to tune it. "I told them it is the story of how a man named Aaron Birnbaum, who wrote some of the best Jewish music of his generation, loved a woman named Freidl, and how he made his love live for generations with this tune, even if he and Freidl had no future."

Ellen got a knot in her throat. Marek must have seen her distress because he laid down his violin and tenderly began to stroke her back. She saw An-drzej glance up at them and knew that he had guessed their relationship.

Marek whispered, "You know, they told me they like this dance. They are discovering things in it. They think it is very spiritual. The Jewish part, for them, is exotic. That is all it is. But they like it. It is not what they thought it would be." He smiled at her. "I thought maybe I should tell you now because probably they will not. They don't know how to talk about this with you."

"But I need them to talk about it so they understand it."

"No. You need to teach them the feelings you want them to dance. It is not their job to have to know what everything means."

She wasn't sure if he was right about this, but still, it came as a tremen-dous relief to hear him say it.

*T*hat evening, Ellen returned to her room completely exhausted from the rehearsal. It had gone more smoothly than she had expected, and Pro-naszko had seemed genuinely pleased. But now she lay on her bed staring at the wingback chair, overwhelmed by the enormity of what she did not know about Torah, Talmud, Jewish history and lore. Such ignorance could cost her, she told herself. She could be making gross historical and theological mistakes in her choreography and not know it. That would bring dishonor to the memory of her father and grandfather, to Freidl, to the Jews of Zokof, to Polish Jews, to Jews everywhere. She would be ridiculed. Pronaszko would turn his back on her. Her work would never be commissioned again. Her head chattered on and on. She felt as if she were falling. Instinctively, she curled into a fetal position. Her breathing became shallow and quick.

Minutes passed. She clutched two fistfuls of her hair and finally forced herself to say aloud, "That's enough, for God's sake. Breathe." She sat up and leafed through her notebook, looking for something to distract her from her anxiety.

Halfway through, she stopped at the question she had written at the studio. *Who is Miriam?* It seemed to her that if she could find Miriam's place in the dance, the prayer would truly pour out of her heart, as Marek had suggested it could. At the very least, it calmed her to search the Tanakh for references to Miriam.

What she found was that after Miriam's Song of the Sea, much is made in the Torah of her two younger brothers, Moses and Aaron, but other than one strange scene where God struck Miriam with leprous white scales for disapproving of Moses' marriage to a Cushite woman, the only other time she is mentioned is at her death. *The Israelites arrived in a body at the wilderness of Zin on the first new moon, and the people stayed at Kadesh. Miriam died there and was buried there. The community was without water, and they joined against Moses and Aaron.*

Ellen thought it odd that the death of Miriam was followed not with descriptions of her burial or how people mourned her, but by the absence of water. She recalled a Passover Seder a few years back, when her cousin Laura, who had taken on the peculiar job of being the "Jewish one" in her family, had placed a glass of water on the table. "It's a symbol of Miriam's Well," she had said. "We need to bring the women back into our story." But Ellen didn't remember her explanation of what exactly Miriam's Well was, and she couldn't find any mention of it in the Tanakh. Eventually, she closed the book and fell asleep.

*F*reidl stared intently at Ellen from the wingback chair. The white handkerchief floated above her head, filled with light. But under the great plaid blanket her bearing suggested a profound sadness.

Ellen sat up in bed. It had been many nights since Freidl had come to her. "Where are you when you aren't with me or Rafael?" she asked.

Freidl shrugged weakly. "A place like that you shouldn't know from."

It occurred to Ellen this was the expression her grandfather used about Poland. "What happened to you after you left your resting place?"

Freidl fingered the fringes of the great plaid blanket for some time before answering. "It is written in the Book of Lamentations what happened to me," she said. "*He has walled me in; I cannot escape; He has blocked my ways with cut stones. He has made my paths a maze.*"

"But where are you?"

"I am in the blue. That is all. I do not know where this is or even what it is, only that there is nothing there but blue and silence. Without the walls of our House of the Living around me, Elleneh, I have no way to mark my way back to Him. I am floating there alone."

"Floating?" Ellen was taken aback by the image. "You're in water?"

Freidl shrugged.

"How do you escape it to come to me?"

She shrugged again. "God has His ways. I do not understand them. What it is He wants of me now, I do not know. Only that at certain times, He allows that I should leave." She looked at the Tanakh at Ellen's side. "So tell me a shtickl Torah."

"I want to know why it says that when Miriam died there was no water."

Freidl's face lit up with pleasure and pride. "Such a Jewish head you have!"

Confused by the compliment, Ellen blushed.

"You should know that centuries ago the great sage Rashi asked that same question in the Talmud. His midrash was that for the forty years the Israelites were in the desert, they drank from Miriam's Well."

"I've heard of Miriam's Well," Ellen said excitedly. "But what is it?"

"It is said that on the second day of creation, God hid living waters in the earth. Those who drank of them were reminded that His Torah is the source of restoration and redemption. Their location was revealed only to a few. Abraham knew, and Miriam, whose intimate knowledge of the waters led us out of slavery in Egypt and redeemed us in the desert. But when Miriam died, the well ran dry and disappeared. There are those who believe that her well is still in the world and that those who study Torah cause new wells to spring forth. Even here in Poland, the Hassidim say that the well reappears whenever Jews sing to it with the proper kavonah, the right heart."

Ellen looked at Freidl. "Are you in those waters?"

At first, Freidl seemed taken with the idea, but then she said, "It cannot be. A well is a circle, an enclosed place. I am without boundaries, in a great blue emptiness." She seemed to collapse inward when she spoke of it. "There is no opening above."

But Ellen could not let go of the idea of Miriam's Well as somehow connected to Freidl's redemption. She felt a sense of urgency. "Is there another midrash about the meaning of Miriam's Well's disappearance?"

A puzzled smile appeared on Freidl's face. "How is it you knew to ask this question?" She shook her head. "My father used to teach his students a certain midrash about Miriam's Well. He told the story that when the great Rabbi Bunam was on his deathbed, may his name be for a blessing, he asked his wife, 'Why do you weep? My life was given me just so I might learn to die.' But that is not why his wife wept, my father said. She was about to lose the one who had sustained her for a lifetime. When we lose such a person, the well dries up."

Neither of them spoke. Ellen's eyes were awash with tears for her father. So were Freidl's.

Freidl looked off. "There is another reason I know. We cry for the dying because we ourselves are afraid. In the hour of his death, my father's face shone with love for all of us gathered around him and with love for his God. That is the share of one who is able to look with satisfaction at having filled his life with what is important and passed that on to others. To die with the taste of such knowledge as that on our lips is to die well. For me, there was no such death. All my life I beat against the walls. I injured my love for my father with anger when he denied me Aaron Birnbaum. I destroyed what peace I could have made with my husband, Berel, by seeing only what he lacked. I cursed him that he did not give me children, that I could not nurture a new generation.

"But when Berel went to his grave four years before me, I discovered that the source of my misery was even deeper than what I thought. I was alone for the first time. And for the first time it became clear to me that life was not forever. This fury at being denied Aaron Birnbaum, this anger at my husband, I saw they were only distractions, my excuses not to love life itself, as God commands us.

"In the end, when I faced the Angel of Death, I knew my real sin. I had refused to love. I had made nothing worthy of my father's name. I left nothing. And still I thought of myself as someone specially set apart by God, so chosen that Death would not touch me. When my time came, I met it with my old friend Anger that I should not have to go that way alone. I breathed my last reciting the spiteful Psalm of David. '*What do You gain by my blood if I go down to the Pit? Can the dust praise You or proclaim Your faithfulness?*' And for such chutzpah, I have been banished to a blue eternity to contemplate these sins and to despair of hope for redemption from a God who no longer listens to my prayers."

Ellen was shocked by the vehemence of Freidl's confession. But there was really only one thing she now wanted to know. "What was it that you *really* wanted from life?" she asked. She could see Freidl's confusion, how she was struggling to compose herself.

"I wanted that I should be first in my father's eyes, as his student. I wanted the love of Aaron Birnbaum. I wanted a child," she whispered.

"You did all that," Ellen said.

Freidl looked mystified.

"You were first in your father's eyes. You were the one he called on when no one else knew the answer. He taught you in the way you should go, and when you grew old, you did not depart from it. Proverbs 22?"

Freidl smiled at Ellen's recall.

"As for Aaron, you took what you loved best about him with you, your passion for him. It went into the tune you've been singing for three generations. What greater act of love is there?"

Freidl's expression hardened. "But what you had with your langer loksh, I never had," she said bitterly.

Ellen laughed. "Okay, you missed good sex. But remember that night Marek and I were together? Remember when I asked you how long it would have lasted between you and Aaron when he brought no money home and you had to go out and make the living? No more studying, Freidl. It would have been up to you to feed the endless children all your sex would have produced."

Freidl rose swiftly. A dark shadow swirled around her. "What does it matter anymore what I wanted? My life is done. I wasted everything, and I am cut off, blocked out, suffocated in blue waters with no way to redeem myself. Don't deny it."

The words poured forth, wild and hysterical. "*'Return her timbrel, and she will make an opening for you to return.'* My father promised me!" She raised her arms until they stretched like wings under the blanket. "Do you see me? I have no timbrel. I sing and they do not hear. I call out and there is no sound. You cannot make an opening for me because I did not teach your grandfather how to be a Jew. I did not teach your father either. And I have not taught you anything but what I know, the head, not the heart. It is not enough. Your Jewish soul is too small, too unnourished."

Ellen moved toward Freidl with open arms, offering her an embrace.

"Do not dare to come to me now," Freidl screamed. "I do not know how to nourish you. I am unfit for such motherhood. I am lost."

Before the frightened and deeply hurt Ellen could argue with her, Freidl was gone, swirled away and swallowed by the shadows in the room.

When Ellen awoke the next morning, her Tanakh lay on the floor, its pages ripped from the bindings and scattered about the room like the white scales of Miriam's leprosy. She had no idea whose anger had done this, hers or Freidl's. A wail tore from her throat at the destruction of the book her father had entrusted to her with so much hope. It filled the room with an awful sound and broke into waves of sobs.

But when her tears subsided, it was with a sense of rebellion that Ellen spoke, in a still, quiet voice to the woman who had entered her dreams and her memory. "My heart and my head hear you when you talk to me," she said. "And however you manage to do that, you have taught me something. You may not think it is enough, but I know better than you how you have touched my heart."

46

In the last days before the performance, Ellen awoke with burning eyes that cold washcloths barely soothed. Her headaches often lingered until she fell asleep late at night. At rehearsals, under the intense pressure of time running out, she exhorted the dancers to *do it bigger, deepen the movement, listen to what the music is saying! Go! Go! Go!*

They had begun to show greater interest and engagement with the work. Individually or in groups, they would shyly tell her they thought the dance was *spiritual,* although they never seemed to be able to elaborate. Ellen didn't know how to interpret such praise. They did not try to explore the Jewishness of it with her, but one afternoon, as she watched them, she was stunned to see tears in Monica's eyes. Taking her aside, she asked why.

"You cannot know what it is for us, to be able to show our faith in God's power to make us grow," Monica told her. "Thank you."

"Thank *you,*" Ellen said, struck by how like Freidl this Polish girl sounded, with her insistent hopefulness about God's presence in the world. Later that day, she stared at the dust motes floating aimlessly in the stray sunbeams shining through her hotel window and thought, a God who commands that His creation grow, free of Him, might not be so stupid or naive an idea as her grandfather and father had led her to believe. He starts us, we finish ourselves. There was a certain logical dignity in it. What seemed wrong to her now was her grandfather's rocket, stuck in an infinite universe that never grew, but merely *was. The universe, even if made of only inanimate objects, is expanding, always growing. That's science, not stupidstition, Grandpa,* she chided him. She wrote down what Monica had said about having faith in God's power to make us grow and made a ritual of rereading it every day, trying to cleave a God frame of mind to herself.

Marek began to bring dinner for the two of them to her room, leaving bags of fruit for her to eat the next day. In bed one night, he ran his fingers over her ribs, telling her, "You are becoming too thin."

She pulled away from him, not because she was ungrateful for his concern, but because combining love and worry had been her father's specialty. Tears formed. She brushed them off with the back of her hand.

"What is wrong?" Marek asked.

She didn't want to talk about missing her father. "It's just that staging a dance is always so intense at the end," she said. "I see what it should look like as a whole now, but if I don't pull it together just right, it'll fall apart." They lay together in silence for a while. "I'm just scared," she said quietly, frightening herself even more by admitting it. "I could be building this entire thing and it could be completely off and it's too late to change it. There's my nightmare."

"Well, not tonight." He cupped the back of her neck and gently massaged it with the tips of his fingers. "I will pray for you to sleep without dreams."

She wrapped her arms around his back and kissed him. "I'm sure God has better things to worry about than how I sleep."

He pulled the covers over them both. "I think how you sleep is exactly what God worries about," he said. Then he surprised Ellen by singing her a melodic, slow song in Polish.

"What does it mean?" she asked him when he had finished.

"It says, 'Let us remember the old carp in the river, the dun horse in the mist, and how when we who were in love, never slept.'" He looked away with an expression that made Ellen uneasy.

"What's the matter?"

He shrugged slightly. "My parents and their friends used to sing this song with us sometimes, when I was a boy. It was something we would sing when we were all together, at home or in the forest, around an open fire." He rubbed his cheek pensively. "Before my father began to leave us."

"Where did he go?" Ellen asked, not recalling him ever mentioning that his father and mother weren't together anymore.

"My father? He did not go anywhere," Marek said. "He lost his job. So he sits by the river fishing every day, with his bait and his bottle. To me and my mother, that is how he has left us."

"I'm so sorry," she said, as heartbroken to hear this as she was stunned.

Marek shrugged. "It is the Polish sickness, the drinking. We hope he will get better someday, when he has work."

"It will get better. You're just at the beginning of a long change," she said, hoping he'd be reassured by her confident tone. She stroked his hair until he fell asleep, disturbed at remembering him drunk in her bed not so long ago, and the frustration and anger she had felt toward him then. She drifted into her own sleep that night wondering how deep a mark his defeated father had left on him. At six thirty the next morning, she awoke, still uneasy, and left him sleeping.

*O*n the evening of August 20 the audience gathered in the center of Szeroka Square, swelling well beyond the rows of folding chairs set out for the performance. Except for peripheral street lighting, it was almost dark. From behind the scaffolding erected on the broad expanse of pavement in front of the Old Synagogue, Ellen paled as she watched how many people were arriving. Most of them were young, although she could spot older people in the crowd by their neckties and jackets. She wondered how they would see this *thing* she was presenting, or what they would see that she hadn't intended. This thought sent her into something of a panic. Her ears became blocked. She could hear the muffled sounds of the musicians tuning up backstage. Then she lost her hearing altogether and could only feel her heart pounding. *Breathe. Just breathe,* she told herself, afraid to move, forcing each inhalation, praying for the stage manager to signal the beginning so that she would have something to do, anything to stop this terrible feeling.

To distract herself, she checked the set, beginning with the central tree trunk, which formed the back wall of the stage. The four vertical railroad ties, cut to ten-foot lengths, had been expertly lashed together in a crisscrossed pattern to allow for climbing. From the bottom of the trunk, a single, powerful spotlight shone a white beam into the sky. She liked the wooden branches the set designer had arranged at angles to each side of the trunk. It had been her idea to wrap them with strings of tiny blue-and-white lights, like an Orthodox Jew's tefillin.

She had begun to regain her equilibrium, but when she glanced back at the audience she got shaky again. Strangers were reading the program notes she had written. A friend of Pronaszko's, a professor of English at Jagiellonian University in the city, had written the Polish translation. They were reading her title, *A Day of Small Beginnings,* and her dedication to Freidl:

> *Strength and dignity are her clothing,*
> *And she laughs at the time to come.*

She opens her mouth with wisdom,
And the law of kindness is on her tongue.

Proverbs 31:25-26

Spotlights came up on the transparent gauze veil that stretched from above the tree structure and slanted down over the entire stage. The dreamlike boundary it created with the audience did not make Ellen feel any more secure. On a scrim above the stage appeared, in English and in Polish, the words:

PART ONE: GENESIS
Listen to my heart, calling in the wilderness,
shaking like Miriam's timbrel.

And then, her piece began. A timbrel, held to a microphone, was struck and shaken. Ellen nervously clicked her fingernails as Marek, Paweł, and Stefan, in black jeans, white T-shirts, and baseball caps, emerged from the wings and climbed the tree trunk, their bodies silhouetted by the spotlight. Each settled himself in the branches, among his instruments and musical paraphernalia. The sight of Marek and the confidence with which he and the other musicians moved calmed her. The timbrel faded under a rising recorded caw of crows.

The Sparks — Henryk, Genia, Ewa, and Tomasz, dressed in mustard tank tops and loose-fitting trousers, appeared at the top of the tree branches holding lit cigarette lighters, leaping from branch to branch.

"My real name is Leiber," Ellen's voice said. "My grandfather, Itzik Leiber, a Jew, came from the town of Zokof, near Radom, where my family lived for many generations. In 1906, my grandfather left Poland for America. He never returned. He never told us why he left his home in Zokof or who he had left behind." The dancers stopped and faced the audience. Offstage, Monica translated Ellen's monologue into Polish. After a pause, she added, *Bist a Yid? Are you a Jew?* she repeated, in Polish.

There were sounds of alarm from the audience as the dancers jumped five and six feet to the floor. Ellen, unable to determine if it was the acrobatics or the words they were reacting to, grabbed the pair of compact binoculars she had brought with her and aimed them at the crowd. Among those seated in the first few rows, she saw surprise, perhaps confusion, and she wished more than anything that they would understand this was not fiction. Maybe she should have been braver, less obscure. She turned to watch her Spark dancers perform their flamelike elevations. They burst and floated, exactly as she had envisioned, better than she had even hoped.

But before that moment of small satisfaction had passed, she felt a wave of fear, that what she had created was not enough, that art alone could never be sufficiently powerful to change Freidl's fate.

From stage right, the *Grass* — Jacek, Monica, Piotr, and Magdalena, dressed in green, rolled onto the stage area in earthtone blankets. Over the loudspeaker, a recording of blowing winds layered itself neatly over the recorded crow caws, and Konstantin Pronaszko said in Polish, "May you sprout from this place as grass sprouts from the earth."

The timbrel shook again. A white screen with a cutout of a horse, a wagon, and a driver appeared. Ellen swallowed hard. "Horse and driver He has hurled into the sea," she recited to herself from Exodus.

Andrzej, in his oversized cap and ragged clothes, burst from stage left and tore through his angry solo. It ended with him falling onto the screen, crushing the image of the horse, wagon, and driver. Dark figures wrapped the screen over him like a shroud and dragged him offstage. Ellen wondered nervously if the paper horse, driver, and wagon had reminded anyone, especially any of the older people in the audience, of the Jewish boy accused so long ago of killing the son of the famous peasant who had seen the Virgin Mary over the Tatra Mountains, not so very far away from Kraków.

The wind, crows, and timbrel built in volume. The Grass dancers fell and rose in circles around the stage. They rolled over the Sparks, extinguishing them with their blankets until the two groups lay still, piled grotesquely atop one another. Before the blackout, Ellen wondered if this sight made anyone in the audience think of Auschwitz, an hour away. Many faces did, in fact, seem stunned.

On the scrim above, the following words appeared:

PART TWO: NATIONALITIES AND BOUNDARIES

Górecki's Third Symphony began and was greeted with prolonged, effusive applause. Ellen could almost feel the audience's relief at hearing familiar music.

Now spotlights illuminated dancers wearing contemporary clothes, carrying six shiny white satin banners mounted on tall wooden dowels shaped like crucifixes across the stage. Each banner bore the image of an eagle and a cross. Wide, colorful ribbons streamed from the three points on top. Piotr, in traditional Polish dress, performed his solo. The audience clapped enthusiastically, until the Górecki symphony died into the sound of the wind, and the stage darkened, leaving them alone with their applause. Ellen sensed their discomfort at having been cut off. They coughed and talked and moved in their seats as if anxious about what would happen next.

She could see Marek sitting in the shadows. She knew he could see her too, in the pale backstage light where she was standing. He held the ram's horn she'd had sent from America. Before he put it to his lips, she held up her fist, thumb concealed. "It is the Polish way of saying good luck. I am holding thumbs for you," he'd explained to her at a rehearsal a few days earlier. In the darkness of the stage, she couldn't see his face. But she could see him returning the gesture, and it gave her the courage to believe that God would not take offense at a Gentile blowing a shofar, or at her for using it in a secular forum. She even found herself addressing Him directly, saying that Marek had been vigilant in learning how to play the ram's horn correctly, that he had gone to the Remuh Synagogue across the square and pestered one of the elderly regulars to teach him how to make the strident blasts.

Now Marek began to blow the unbroken note of the *Tekiah,* one of the calls of the shofar. She'd found an explanation of it by Maimonides in a book she'd bought at the Jewish bookstore. "Awake all you who sleep, and you that are in slumber, rouse yourselves. Consider your deeds, remember God, turn unto Him." Standing there in the darkness, listening to Marek, she repeated the words.

The lights came up on four rectangular gray boards, laid like pavers across the stage. Genia, dressed in white, stood to one side. Facedown, beneath each board lay a dancer. Genia began a precarious walk across their backs. As she had stepped off the last board, the dancers stood, revealing that they were gravestones inscribed with Hebrew letters and designs. The audience reacted with cries of recognition.

Marek lay down the shofar and played a disjointed, slow version of the "For-a-Girl Tune" on his electric violin. Ellen got chills hearing it fill the square, over pavement once touched by the soles of a certain pair of black suede pumps.

At center stage, in a square of white light, the gravestones rocked forward and back, one foot in front of the other. The Polish banner dancers, emerging in a procession with Piotr swinging an incense burner, swayed from side to side. For the audience, the two groups were set apart from each other by these two contrasting directions.

Still moving, the dancers began to recite.

"A proverb is a true word," the gravestones said in Yiddish. Pronaszko's voice recited an English translation.

"A proverb tells the truth," the banners responded in Polish.

"A man comes from the dust and in the dust he will end — and in the meantime it is good to drink a sip of vodka," the gravestones said in Yiddish.

Ellen was relieved to hear a few laughs from the audience.

"You are dust and dust you will become," the banners said in Polish.

Stefan struck a triangle. The gravestones raised their hands above their heads, as if beckoning to God. Slowly, they began to list and lean against one another, evoking, Ellen hoped, a look of abandonment and indignity.

Andrzej, in his cap and tattered clothes, wove his way between the stones, tentatively touching their inscriptions. The stones rose hopefully toward him. He pushed against one, folded himself over another, tore around the stage, using the gravestones as launching points. His movements were alternately fluid and frenetic, excited and distraught. He clutched a gravestone to his chest, ducking when the clarinet shrieked like a human voice, and the "For-a-Girl Tune" built tension and speed. The lights dimmed, and the long gauze curtain covering the front of the stage was pulled violently away before the light faded to black and the music came to a stop.

The scrim read:

PART THREE: PRAYERS AND DREAMS

The stage was bathed in blue light. Paweł shook the timbrel. Andrzej lay in a heap on the floor. A pile of small stones had been set at the base of the tree.

From a distance voices recited, in Polish, the prayer for the dead on All Saints' Day.

A huge, shadowy female figure draped in a plaid shawl appeared in the tree.

Marek blew the shofar. *Shevarim!* The pensive, sad wail was Monica's cue to lead the line of women forward in circles around the stage, arms raised above their heads, palms forward, fingers shimmying with ancient cries to God. The movements had come to Ellen late one night as she lay in bed, repeating the words Freidl had shown her about Miriam the prophetess, Moses' sister.

Now they came to the section Ellen found difficult to watch, where the Spark dancers entered, holding their lit cigarette lighters above their heads like Statues of Liberty, and the Grass dancers lifted the crumpled Andrzej, supporting his crippled body as he slowly contracted and refused further contact with the world. Ellen began to cry, almost believing she was seeing the embodiment of her grandpa Isaac's potato soul, even while being amazed it could be so well understood by a gay Polish dancer.

With the flick of their thumbs, the Spark dancers extinguished their flames.

In the darkness, Ellen found herself being carried aloft, to Zokof's cemetery, where she was immersed in the silence of those who had lain buried there in peace for generations. A long, raw exhalation poured out of her. She was filled with its power, with awe, and with an ineffable gratitude at having been given the ability, even if fleeting, to sense it.

The scattered applause for the end of Part Three tapered off as new words appeared on the scrim:

PART FOUR: RETURN AND REMEMBRANCE

Ellen was drawn back to the performance by the sound of the gravestone dancers, standing in their square of white light. They were chanting the prayer El Molei Rachamim. The dancers themselves did not know that Ellen had taught it to them with the name Freidl Alterman inserted in its proper place, beseeching God to grant her perfect rest in the shadow of His wings, to let her soul be bound up in the bond of everlasting life.

Genia appeared at the trunk of the tree holding a white handkerchief. A spotlight illuminated the female figure in the tree, who turned her back to the audience, extended her arms, and dipped, as if performing an American Indian eagle dance. But with the "For-a-Girl Tune" playing again, and a certain uplift in the woman's arms, the dance took on a slightly Hassidic quality. Genia climbed the trunk. The two women met, danced briefly side by side, the handkerchief held between them, until the draped figure climbed to the top of the trunk. Directly lit by the white spotlight, she balanced so high up, and so precariously, Ellen was afraid she might fall. Stretching open her arms, she revealed that the inner side of her plaid blanket was lined with tiny golden mirrors. Each of them, illuminated by the spotlight, shone like sparks.

Marek blew the shofar. *Teruah!* The ram's horn's staccato screams sounded its battle charge, saying, *Transform the world to one of justice and compassion! Speak up! Say, Here I am! Bringing light where there is darkness, understanding where there is ignorance, healing where there is illness, and hope where there is despair.*

The Polish banner dancers entered in a line from stage right, each with a hand on the shoulder of the person in front. The Jewish gravestones entered from stage left, each with a hand on the shoulder of the person in front. As Poles and Jews they formed two lines, facing the audience, one behind the other.

A wild, laughing refrain of the "For-a-Girl Tune" took over from the shofar, and magically, the mirrored blanket, tied with ribbons at its four corners, rose from the female figure's shoulders and swooped forward toward the banners and gravestones. Tied to the dowels, it became a wedding canopy over their heads.

The music stopped. The figure, illuminated by the tree-trunk spotlight, shook a timbrel. The sound of approaching wind grew louder.

In unison, the dancers pivoted a quarter turn and faced each other in two lines, as modern Poles and Jews, under the wedding canopy. Ellen was startled at how fraught the moment was with tension and love, confusion and hope — a holy moment, she thought, separate from the world and at the same time brutally of it.

Suspended in that uncertainty of which way they would go, the dance ended in a blackout.

*T*here was a slight pause before the applause began, as if the audience needed a moment to collect itself. The dancers came forward and took their bows. The applause built. They turned and clapped for the musicians, who stood and took their bows from their places in the tree. The dancers took more bows and applauded their audience.

By the time Ellen came onstage there was a standing ovation and what she understood as Polish *bravos*. She beckoned Pronaszko to come from the wings. Ever the gentleman, he presented her with a large bouquet of flowers and kissed her hand before taking his bow. "Perhaps we should think of an American tour," he said, smiling, not taking his eyes off the audience. "God be praised."

Backstage, Ellen was overwhelmed with almost uncontainable glee at having brought about the din of rejoicing that had broken out among the cast. She startled Andrzej with a hug, telling him how great he'd been, and laughed at Piotr, who was swinging Ewa around, screaming. But her joy began to dissipate as she posed for photographs with Pronaszko, traded compliments with the set designers, and smiled at the dancers until she could feel the muscles of her face.

Sadness, like an enveloping silence, began to separate her from everyone. Claiming to have a bad headache, she declined their invitations to celebrate, sincerely promising a rain check.

Leaving the dark streets of Kazimierz in Marek's car, she wrapped her weary arms around his neck and kissed him. "You were so beautiful," she told him. "So amazing." He stopped the car, took her head in his hands, and looked at her. "What is troubling you?" he said.

She was glad he had not been fooled by her smiles. "Marek, I don't know if we did anything for Freidl."

He didn't offer his opinion, and she was grateful he didn't argue. "We will go to Zokof," he said.

47

THE COMPANY PERFORMED *A DAY OF SMALL BEGINNINGS* FOUR times that week, although for Ellen, never so powerfully as on that first night. The morning the set was struck, she walked the length of Szeroka Square, from the Old Synagogue to the grassy memorial for Kraków's Jews, and stood for a long while surveying the Remuh Synagogue and the surrounding buildings, with their windows reflecting a clouded sky.

She had hoped for a glimpse of Freidl, but there had been no sign of her. No dreams. No images. No tune. Through the days and nights following the last performance, Ellen had found herself whispering, "Where are you?" Before she went to sleep she would plead to her, "Don't be angry with me. I need you. Come back." It horrified her to imagine she had sent Freidl back to the blue emptiness, to eternal conscious suffocation and silence. "Teach me in the way I should go," she said. But still Freidl did not return.

She sent Rafael a note asking him, in the gentlest way she knew, if anything had *changed,* but she hadn't yet heard back from him. If she could, she would have driven directly to Zokof, as Marek had offered. But Pronaszko had insisted on setting up meetings with her to discuss future projects. She could not just abandon him, or the company.

On her last day at the studio, it seemed to her the dancers sensed her distance. In a new, halting, and embarrassed English, they tried to entice her back into their circle with amusing stories of things that had gone wrong backstage and how they had worked them out without help from her or from Pronaszko. She appreciated this, and she told them so. She told them she hoped they would do other pieces together. Privately, she encouraged Andrzej to start working on his choreography, promising to send him dance tapes she thought might inspire him. But even as the company lingered, offering their reticent good-byes, she was content to let Pronaszko reclaim his flock.

By the end of the week, her clothes lay strewn over the lumpy bed and the wingback chair, ready for packing. She knew that when she returned to

New York, she would remember that chair like a floating object in a Chagall painting. In its arms she would always find either the naked Marek or the proud Freidl. She snapped a Polaroid of it and held it, side by side, with the studio picture of her grandpa Isaac and Hillel.

Now all that remained was the trip back to Zokof. She had not seen much of Marek after the last performance. He'd had several engagements with his group, but he'd made a short detour to Kielce to check Łukasz Rakowski's masonry work on the new gravestone. Late that night, he had left with the desk clerk at her hotel a batch of Polaroids he'd taken with her camera. "Almost finished," he'd written on the outside. The photos showed the new inscription that she had written. Ellen had been thrilled at the meticulousness and creativity of Łukasz Rakowski's work.

A few days later, Marek picked her up at the hotel.

"It seems like forever since I saw you," she said.

He smiled, brushing his hand along the soft folds of her blouse. "I have the stone in the trunk. It is wrapped many times around, to make it safe."

Ellen had thought they would be picking it up along the way in Kielce. Excited that the finished gravestone was in her reach, she asked to see it.

"We should wait," Marek said. "It will be better to see it again when it is where it belongs. That will be more respectful, I think, than to open it here in the street."

He looked so earnest, and he had put so much time and effort into getting the stone made, she couldn't refuse him. "Okay. I can wait." She kissed him and got into the Fiat.

Inside, he reached into the backseat and grabbed some newspaper clippings and a magazine.

Ellen saw a challah, loosely wrapped in paper, lying there. "Did you get that at the Ariel Café?" The little restaurant where they met was already evoking nostalgia.

He handed her the reviews. "Look at these first. Then I will tell you about the bread." He put the car in gear and negotiated the narrow streets of Old Town toward the Planty.

Ellen slid her seat as far back as it would go and put her feet up on the dashboard. She scanned the reviews even though they were in Polish. "Pronaszko told me we got a good review in the Catholic weekly paper." She fanned herself importantly with the reviews. "I've become his new personal saint."

Marek pointed to the illustrated magazine in her lap. "Then let him pray that you will accept his commission for a new piece. Look at the article they wrote in *Przekrój*. This is a very popular weekly magazine here. And did you see that one from the *Gazeta Wyborcza*? That is a major national paper."

"I know. Pronaszko went completely berserk when he brought it in. Their reporter came to the dress rehearsal and asked me a couple of questions about modern dance and our staging. But I didn't think he was particularly interested in what we were doing."

"Well, he *was* interested. He calls it 'a passionate prayer for Polish-Jewish relations.'"

Ellen held up the *Gazeta Wyborcza* article. Its accompanying photograph showed her dancers facing each other under the wedding canopy, the Freidl figure overhead in the tree. She examined it for some sign of Freidl's departing soul and, despite her better judgment, felt disappointed when she couldn't see it. "You'll have to translate these for me later," she said. "Tonight?"

"Of course, tonight." He grinned at her.

They were almost on the Radom road when she asked him about the challah in the backseat.

"About three or four days ago, I received a letter from Rafael," he said.

Ellen was surprised, and slightly hurt, that Rafael would write to Marek and not to her.

"He gave me the name of a woman in Puławy, not far from Zokof, who knows old Jewish tunes from that area, including, he said, tunes by Aaron Birnbaum."

She put her hand to her mouth at hearing Aaron Birnbaum's name.

"Rafael said he and this woman in Puławy have not been in contact since the old days. She was living in Israel, but someone told him that recently she returned to Poland with her brother."

"Someone?" Ellen asked, immediately suspecting Freidl.

Marek pulled the car to the side of the road. Producing Rafael's letter from his pocket, he translated it for her. She could see the handwriting was askew, as if penned with great difficulty. The letter read, "I have again been reminded by one whose wisdom I cannot question that our faith teaches, according to his deeds does God's presence rest on a man. And so I send you the address of Sarah Gutman, who, God willing, will help you in your research."

Marek read silently down the page and reported to a perplexed Ellen, "He says Sarah Gutman came back here against her children's wishes. She said she wants to die at home." He looked at Ellen, clearly pleased that Sarah Gutman called Poland *home.*

"Yesterday, I went to Puławy to see her, and she sang me tunes I never heard before. They gave me, I think, a special inspiration. What I heard are those voices we are missing in Poland. I tried to tell her this. It was very surprising to her. When I asked if I could make a recording, she was very happy. She said she thought she would never live to see such a thing as someone like me. So she fed me poppy-seed cake, and all afternoon she sang to me and I recorded everything. She baked that challah for me to take to Rafael, to thank him for sending me to her."

Ellen bit her lip, knowing how filled with memories challahs were for Rafael. "And you let me go on about my reviews instead of telling me about this first?"

He laughed. "What does it matter, when?"

She smacked him playfully on the arm. "You're unbelievable." Opening the window, she remembered their first dinner at the Ariel Café, how he'd told her his grandmother thought the *spice* was gone in Poland. She believed now what she could not believe then, that this feeling of loss was genuine, and as complicated as the Jewish roots of Christianity itself. "Let's have dinner at the Ariel Café tonight," she said. They hadn't eaten a meal together there since that evening.

"That will be perfect, yes."

A humid wind blew back her hair, sprinkling her with the first drops of the morning rain.

*B*y the time they arrived at Rafael's doorstep, the rain had slowed to a drizzle. Ellen remembered how nervous she had been the day she first stood at that peeling painted door trying to imagine what sort of a man she was about to meet. She was no less nervous now.

When Rafael opened the door, her throat tightened at the sight of him. He seemed much frailer, even smaller somehow. His rich brown eyes were watery and dull. They became teary when Marek presented Sarah Gutman's challah. "From Sarah Gutman, I know it is kosher," he said, trying to make light of his emotion. "But now I want we should go to Freidl's grave." He did not refuse Ellen's arm down the steps.

They drove through town, where many bright flower bouquets had recently been laid before the war memorial. At the corner of the main square, a man holding a plastic bag of groceries gave Ellen the by now familiar Zokof stare.

Marek shifted gears, braked for pedestrians, and appeared utterly absorbed in the business of driving.

Rafael looked off and said nothing.

Ellen guessed he was probably thinking of Freidl.

Just shy of the entrance to the cemetery, Marek parked the car. "What do you think?" he asked brightly.

Ellen and Rafael looked out the window at the rising piles of stones that had begun to define the entryway of the cemetery. "You've been building the wall!" Ellen cried.

Rafael stared with obvious surprise.

"I have been coming here on those days we did not have rehearsals," Marek told them. "I always begin my time here by gathering more stones. So, I will meet you inside at Freidl's grave." He got out of the car and hurried across the rutted dirt road into the forest. Ellen did not protest his leaving, knowing they would soon be unveiling the gravestone together.

When he was gone, she leaned forward apprehensively. "Rafael, where is Freidl?"

His body slumped, and it seemed an effort for him to turn even slightly in his seat to look at her. She saw a tremor in his fingers, fatigue and melancholy on his face. He looked down at his hands and covered one with the other.

"Are you feeling all right?" she asked.

His sour breath hung in the close air of the car. The heat was becoming oppressive. Ellen was worried. "Let's go over to the trees."

Without answering, he opened the door and slowly got out, leaning on the doorjamb as he straightened. Together, they made their way across the road into the shade of the forest, where he sat down heavily on the fallen trunk of a large tree. The air was still. Ellen sat on the ground next to him. Flies buzzed along the top of the lichen-patched stone that lay half buried between them.

Ellen tried again. "Rafael, where is Freidl?"

To her amazement, he produced her grandpa Isaac's handkerchief from his pocket. "She is gone. Even I do not know where. In my last dream there was only the tune." He dried his eyes carefully, the way her grandfather used to at the Seder table on Passover.

It struck Ellen that grief was what had so diminished him. Here was a man who had sacrificed almost fifty years of his life to tend a grave and the soul of the woman whose body lay there. For such vigilance, he had lived as a stranger in his own town, where his intellect was untapped and unappreciated. He had become an old man, and now, suddenly, he was truly alone. Watching the difficulty with which he moved, Ellen could not help thinking of how it would be for him in the hours of his death, helpless and alone, peered at as a curiosity by his neighbors. That she would not be in Poland when that time came filled her with sorrow and shame. "I know you'll miss her. I'm so sorry," she consoled him. It was a pitifully inadequate thing to say.

He sniffed. "For what should you be sorry? The stones are gone. You made an opening for her to return."

She hardly knew what to say. "I-I did?" she stammered.

Rafael planted his heel in the moist earth. Its scent blossomed upward. "Elleneh, you knew her. She was a woman of valor, but stiff-necked about her troubles. I have learned in my life that despair is its own kind of solace. It becomes a home that is not so easy to leave. You asked her what she wanted in the world. A simple question. A child's wisdom is also wisdom." He bent toward her and gave her a paternal pat on the shoulder. "But for a woman who stood apart from her community, who would not do what she said she came to do, such a question made her soul wither. You made her afraid. For love of you, she wanted to answer your question. But for this, she had to leave that terrible blue home, the despair. Understand?"

He rubbed his hands together. Ellen could see they were still trembling.

"She was angry at me."

"Of course she was angry. You had made for her an opening but a difficult one. We do not want to close our eyes and slip into eternity if we have not done what we said we came to do. You made her see."

"She said I couldn't make an opening for her. She said my soul was too small and unnourished." Even repeating the words hurt Ellen.

Rafael shook his head. "Not so small that you did not fulfill your promise to her."

"What did I do?" she said in bewilderment.

"You know what. This dance you made. This mishegoss, some would say, beating a timbrel in front of the goyim, giving a Polack a shofar to sound the awakening Tekiah! But all of it you made with the right heart, what we call kavonah! Listen, my shayneh, you made a prayer for her that redeemed her in the eyes of God. As the Baal Shem Tov said, the dance of the Jew is a prayer."

He reached out and patted her again. "Thanks God it's finished here. I am the last."

"But you're not the last," Ellen said mischievously. "And it's not finished here, or you wouldn't have written to Marek about Sarah Gutman. You meant for him to come and hear her songs and taste that challah he brought you. It seems to me you're planting seeds to make something grow here."

Rafael regarded her with a mixture of amusement and skepticism. "Maybe you know more than me. It is a wise woman who hears one word and understands two."

"Thanks," she said. "But before we move on, I want to say good-bye to her."

Rafael wagged a scolding finger. "Say your good-bye at the grave. Say El Molei Rachamim. But the rest, that *is* finished. She will not come to you again in dreams. Remember her, but do not call for her."

His vehemence unnerved her. "Why not?"

"Because it is written, 'Do not turn your face to ghosts, even of favorable spirits do not inquire. They will defile you. Turn only to your God.'" His face had a tense, hard look. "'Turn to your compassionate God.'" The anger and sarcasm in his voice were undeniable.

"How can you tell me not to turn to ghosts when it was you who brought her to me?"

Rafael looked down at his dusty, worn shoes. "Because I am not a good Jew. Even your grandfather knew not to turn to her. It was to God he prayed for mercy, not to a woman one year in her grave. A Jew's duty is to life."

Ellen's face flushed. "You are a shayner Yid. There is no more beautiful Jew, no one like you, and there will never be anyone like you."

"Do not praise me as the people praised Moses," said Rafael, scowling. "What kind of Moses am I who has no one to lead?"

"No one? You led four. My grandfather, my father, me, and Marek. It's enough for us."

Rafael looked utterly shocked.

Somewhere in the forest Marek let out a whoop of joy.

"He's going to ruin his musician's hands building that wall for you," Ellen said.

Rafael nodded helplessly. With Ellen's help, he hoisted himself up. "Well, let us go see your langer loksh then," he managed to say.

Together they walked toward the entrance of the cemetery. When they reached it, Ellen saw that the path had been swept of all liquor bottles and trash. To the right of the entryway, a wooden structure, like a birdhouse with the front side open, had been planted. Inside, a typed piece of paper had been sealed to the back wall behind a sheet of glass. She stepped closer and was astonished at what it said, in Polish and in English: IN MEMORY OF THE JEWS OF ZOKOF, WHO HAVE RESIDED HERE SINCE 1554.

As they entered the cemetery, Rafael said nothing about the memorial, but Ellen could see that he was moved. They reached the lamppost and found Marek climbing a shallow embankment on the western side of the cemetery. He looked gleeful as a child, clutching a large, muddy, flat stone.

"This is from the old wall! I found it in the riverbed," he called. The knees of his pants were muddied and torn. "It is wet down there," he said, wiping himself off.

Ellen smiled at the thought of water running in the riverbed again. It seemed a good sign. "Your memorial out there is beautiful. Thank you," she said, pointing toward the entrance to the cemetery.

"I did it in memory of my Uncle Leszek," he said shyly.

The three of them tramped the short distance to the place where Freidl's little pile of stones lay.

Marek smiled secretively at Ellen. "I have to get something from the car," he said, and bounded off again.

The songs of sparrows and starlings drifted into the cemetery from outside. Rafael looked at the pile of stones and, almost imperceptibly, began to rock forward and back. "I want you should know something," he said. "Years ago, Freidl told me that if the day should come that her soul rests again with her body, she wanted I should be buried next to her when my time came. I protested. I told her a man and a woman do not lie side by side in the grave. How would it look? I was a stranger to her in life. I was a small child when she went to her death."

Despite the solemnity of the subject, Ellen was amused by his sense of propriety. "What did Freidl say?" she asked.

"She said better she should lie with a wise man in hell than at her fool husband's feet in paradise."

Now Ellen grinned.

Slowly, so did Rafael.

They were laughing when Marek reappeared, struggling with the long cloth-covered object in his arms, looking at them quizzically.

"We have something we want to show you," Ellen said as Marek set the heavy object down against the tree and pulled the cloth from its surface.

Rafael's face went pale, and Ellen thought for a moment that this might have been too much for him. "You brought it back," he said. His voice was gruff with emotion as he pointed to the top of the gravestone that he had given to her father to take to America.

"It belongs here."

"You put it with the part from Głowacki." He could barely get the words out. It seemed difficult for him to focus on anything but the re-united gravestone, now contained within a stone frame. Between its two original parts was a newly engraved section. Łukasz Rakowski had deco-rated Ellen's inscription with a carved bookcase, a fish swimming against an oncoming stream, and a timbrel. Small metal swirls, resembling sparks, were embedded in the background.

Rafael squinted at the new section. "What did you write there? It is dif-ficult for me to see it," he said.

"It's in English, but I also had the rabbi at the Lauder Foundation in Warsaw translate it into Hebrew. See?" She pointed nervously at the writ-ing. "I'll read it to you."

> *Precious guardian, now among the great line of women after Miriam*
> *Who awakened a family with your Tune*
> *And with an open heart and a deep well of knowledge taught your children to love God*
> *We have returned, and will return.*

Rafael nodded decisively. The image of his face as he stood in the forest was so inextricably bound to her memory of Freidl, it made Ellen cry.

They dug a hole and set the stone in place. Marek stood to the side as a witness, his hands clasped before him. Ellen lit a Yahrzeit candle, Rafael placed a pebble on top, and together they recited El Molei Rachamim.

Not long after, as they left the gravesite, Ellen grabbed a handful of grass and opened her palm. The wind blew the blades around the trees and sent up a warm summer smell of earth and living things.

A C K N O W L E D G M E N T S

This book could not have been written without the counsel of my husband's family, the Lipsmans, and their extended family, the Goldfarbs, the Bulkas, and the Strums, Polish Jews who, unlike my family, did not come to America in time to escape the calamity that befell their world in the 1930s and 40s. Their generosity in sharing an intimate knowledge of Polish-Jewish relations and the flavor of their childhoods, their explanations of Polish and Yiddish linguistic subtleties, their assistance in explaining how life was in a town like Zokof, whose fictional name was their creation, all inform this story. So, too, did a trip to Poland I made with several of them and their grown children, in the 1990s, when we visited their hometown of Zwolen, whose cemetery, forested and bereft of gravestones, was haunted by the cacophony of the crows nesting above.

For years of devoted, ruthlessly honest editing, I thank the angels of my writing group, Carol Abrams, Ann Bronston, Carrie Hauman, Truusje Kushner, Jeanne McCafferty, Sandi Tarling Powazek, and Linda Temkin. Their spirited engagement with the book's characters convinced me that this is a more universal story than I had originally thought.

I thank my agent, Jennifer Rudolph Walsh, for staying up all night reading my manuscript the day she received it and for her passionate work ever since on its behalf.

For her early enthusiasm and for her insightful suggestions about the manuscript, I can forgive my editor, Judy Clain, her lack of interest in dance. Thanks, too, to all the dedicated people at Little, Brown who have put so much effort into giving this book its final form and delivering it to the public.

I want to express my special appreciation to my rabbi, Jeffrey Marx, of the Santa Monica Synagogue. His weekly Torah study classes and far-ranging knowledge of all things biblical, historical, and obscure, secular and religious, have been invaluable resources for me both as a writer and as a person.

No acknowledgments could be complete without recognizing the role family has played in bringing this novel to life. Special thanks to my mother, who brought dance, music, art, and adventure into our family life, and to my father, whose lifelong social and political activism has been an inspiration to me and to my sister, Amy. No less important, I thank my husband, Walter Lipsman, who among other acts of kindness, if not bravery, sent me off to Poland, leaving him with our five-year-old and eight-month-old daughters, Ariana and Maya, in tow. If this story contributes to their understanding of the world, it will have more than met its intended purpose.

LISA PEARL ROSENBAUM has worked as both a choreographer and a lawyer. She studied religion and philosophy at New York University and completed postgraduate work in international relations at the Hebrew University in Jerusalem. She lives in Los Angeles with her husband, Walter Lipsman, and their daughters, Ariana and Maya. This is her first novel.